Fell For You

Sunny Brook Farms, Book Two

USA TODAY bestselling author

RENEE HARLESS

For a list of content warnings in Fell For You, please check the book's page at www.reneeharless.com/fellforyou

All rights reserved.

ISBN: 978-1-962459-00-6

Copyright ©2023 Renee Harless

This work is one of fiction. Any resemblance of characters to persons, living or deceased, is purely coincidental. Names, places, and characters are figments of the author's imagination. All trademarked items included in this novel have been recognized as so by the author. The author holds exclusive rights to this work. Unauthorized duplication is prohibited and this includes the use of artificial programs to mimic and reproduce like works.

All rights reserved

Cover design by Porcelain Paper Designs

Editor: Kayla Robichaux

Proofreader: Crystal Clear Author Services

Paperback Edition

Fell For You

Sunny Brook Farms, Book Two

USA TODAY bestselling author
RENEE HARLESS

Running my sister's bed-and-breakfast in our small town should have been a piece of cake. Until I opened the door to our new guest and came face to face with the man I had a one-night stand with a year ago. And he was looking at me like I was a total stranger.

Nate Sullivan was fourteen years older than me and was my brother's best friend. Not to mention a billionaire CEO that looked just as good in well-worn jeans and a T-shirt as he did in a suit. And when he was with his girls? There was no way I couldn't fall for him.

We both had tarnished pasts that kept our hearts out of the mix. But being with him now gave me a confidence I didn't know was missing.

It wasn't until his girls forced us to dance that we acted on our chemistry. And though it was explosive, our time together was limited. As the nights ticked away, we learned time wasn't the only thing that worked against us.

Dedicated to the girls that are forced to smile through the pain in order to take their next step.

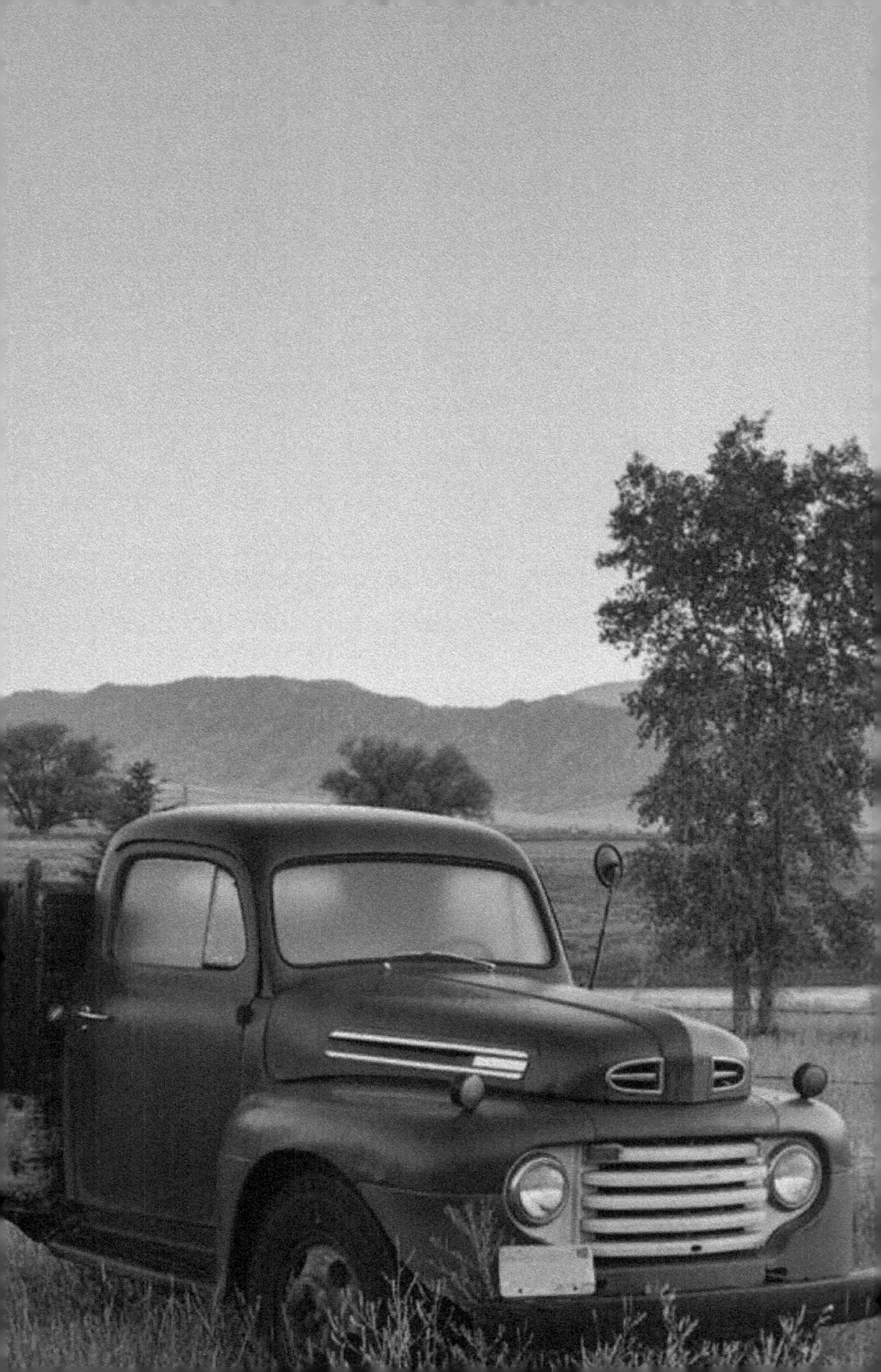

Chapter One

Alexandra

"I see you took my advice and grew your cucumbers bigger," old Mrs. Hensen said as she stroked one of the green vegetables in front of our family's stand at the town's farmer's market. The lady seemed to have some erotic fascination with the small number of vegetables harvested from our garden that we brought to the weekend market. Last year, she requested we grow the cucumbers larger while simultaneously making eyes at our local hockey coach. It was just a fluke that this harvest, the cucumbers included, grew double in size.

But I wasn't about to tell her it hadn't been at her request. We needed her sale, after all.

"They are about four inches longer this year, Mrs. Hensen. And a bit wider too, I might add."

"Hm… that's good," she said as she continued to stroke the vegetable. I tried not to make eye contact with her as she inspected the display, but that left me looking at the townspeople passing by the booth, who also seemed curious about what Mrs. Hensen was up to. She had a knack for causing secondhand embarrassment. Usually, my best friend Tami tried to join me when I covered the market stand. She absolutely lived for Mrs. Hensen's shenanigans.

I waved at Lily and Brett Chisolm as they walked by, an all-knowing smirk growing on Lily's lips as she took in who was standing at my booth.

"Well, I'll take all you have of these, dear," Mrs. Hensen said as she set down what I assumed was going to be her new best friend.

"What?" I said, in shock. I'd come to expect her shenanigans, but she rarely ever made a purchase. And if she did, it was only a vegetable or two.

"Yes. These will do quite nicely for pickling. My dear Roy, bless his soul, loved when my homemade pickles had lots of nubs like these. The stores just don't sell them that way anymore. And don't even get me started on the jars of pickles." She followed that up with a disgusted sneer.

While I bagged up the cucumbers, I tried to ignore the watery look in her eyes as she spoke of her late husband. Mrs. Hensen had been widowed as long as I knew her, and she'd always spoken of a love so true that she never needed to find a replacement when he passed away.

I always wondered if a love like that only existed for a select few. People like Mrs. Hensen and my parents. I knew in my case I'd only be reading about epic love stories in the books I devour late at night. A romance like that wasn't in the cards for me. Nor did I want to seek it out. I learned a long time ago that the only people I could rely on were myself and my family. There was no need to put my trust and heart in the hands of another.

"Here you go, Mrs. Hensen. Thirty of our finest Sunny Brook Farms cucumbers."

Her strong but wrinkled hand reached out and grabbed the bag from my fingers. "Thank you, Alexandra. I'll come back next week to see if you have any more."

"Yes, we should have a new batch ready just for you."

I turned my back to her and unloaded a crate of summer squash from the back of my vintage truck, placing them in the spot the cucumbers vacated. When I turned back around, I noticed Mrs. Hensen hadn't moved away from the stand.

"Is everything all right?" I asked her.

I'm not sure what I expected her to say. Really, she was notorious for having no filter. But asking me if I was single was not at the top of my list.

"Um... yes, I am."

"I should introduce you to my neighbor's grandson. He's just around your age."

Wincing, I wrapped my arms around my waist, a mostly unconscious way of protecting myself. I'd been doing it since....

Shaking my head, I did my best to rid myself of the dark thoughts that tried to seep their way into my mind. It took years to learn how to keep the memories from taking over.

"What do you think, Alexandra?" Mrs. Hensen prompted, and I forced my arms away from my body to hang limply at my sides while I forced a pleasant smile.

I must have failed, because the woman's eyebrows furrowed in confusion and concern.

"I appreciate it, Mrs. Hensen, but I'm just fine. Thank you, though."

"Well, maybe I'll just put a bug in his ear to come visit the market then," she said with a chuckle.

"You do that. Have a great day." I did my best to dismiss her kindly, and luckily, she took my cue and waved before heading over to the jam and jelly stand a few spots down the line.

Exhausted from the conversation, I took a few steps back and leaned against the bed of my truck. I felt stuck, out of place. Not as in here, in my hometown, but in my life in general. Unlike my sister, Autumn, I loved everything about our tiny town of Ashfield. I loved the people just as much as I loved the gossip. But sometimes, it all felt like it wrapped itself around my neck and continued to tighten until I suffocated.

People smiled and waved as they passed by the booth—the one I used to share with my mom and sisters every Saturday, but now we just took turns. We'd been growing small vegetables at our ranch since we were little, and the town did their best to support us. The main business for Sunny Brook Farms was corn, and there was never any shortage of need for that. My parents did very well with their ranch.

But sometimes, I felt like that was all people saw when they looked at me and my sisters. We were the Easterly girls. The pretty blondes who obeyed their parents and rarely ruffled any feathers. That was all until my eldest sister broke everyone's hearts and left as quickly as she could.

I idolized my older sister and wanted to spread my wings just as she had, but after watching how heartbroken my mother became in her absence, I continued being the obedient daughter and stayed, leaving my own dreams on the back burner. Ashfield had a lot to offer, and I knew whatever I decided to accomplish, I could do it right here.

But Autumn was back now, with a new husband to boot, and I couldn't help thinking that maybe now was my time to see the world a bit.

Just as that idea began to take root, I quickly dismissed it. I was being ridiculous. That time for me passed by long ago. I wasn't a naïve teen anymore. And now that I started to spread my wings here with a job and a place to call home, I was content. I had responsibilities and people that depended on me. Plus, I was part of a business venture with my family—an event venue on the ranch. Each of us had a part in it, but really it was Autumn's baby, and she asked me to help with the catering. It was something I took seriously, and I couldn't flake out on it, even though I mostly delegated my part to others. I wanted to help as many other businesses around Ashfield succeed as I could. I was going to have to be content with my job at the bar and the side project I wanted to get up and running.

Glancing beyond the gravel lot, I took in the scenic view. If there was one thing I'd miss if I ever left town, it would be the mountains. Their green, lush beauty in the spring was unmatched. At least in my eyes.

Our little town was nestled between the mounds of the Smoky Mountains. Generations of my family gazed up at these same peaks from the valley where Ashfield, Tennessee rested.

Closing my eyes, I let the smell of the freshly cut grass and a hint of honeysuckle cascade over my senses. To me, it was the quintessential smell of spring transitioning into summer. Tilting my head back, the warmth of the afternoon sun caressed my skin like a gentle kiss. The kind that left your body heated in its wake.

"Wow," a tiny voice said from close by.

I pried open one eye, and I was shocked to find a little brown-haired girl staring at me in awe.

Quickly, my eyes darted around the market, looking for a frantic parent trying to find their missing child, but my search came up empty.

"Uh, hi!" I said warmly as I approached her, moving around to the other side of the booth and squatting down to her level.

Thinking back to my sister Rory's first-grade class, I assumed this little girl was no older than four or five. She was a tiny one though.

Her dark hair was up in two lopsided pigtails, each tied with a different-color ribbon. The silky strip was tied in knots instead of bows, and the little girl kept flicking the ends as they tickled her ears. That's when I noticed the flesh-colored hearing aid tucked behind her left ear.

"Hi!" the little girl responded enthusiastically. The curls of her pigtails bounced in unison. "You look like a Barbie doll," she added with wide eyes, as if seeing something miraculous. I imagined that if she thought her favorite doll were real, then she'd be in shock.

"Thank you. You're very sweet."

"Is that your truck? It's pretty. My favorite color is red."

"Oh. Well, thank you… again." Reaching out, I grasped her hand and noticed the dirt stuck underneath the trimmed nails. "Sweetie, where is your mom or dad?"

Her wide smile quickly crumbled into a sorrowful frown. "My mommy is gone." In a typical young-girl fashion, her smile readily grew at her change of thought. "But my daddy is around here with my sister, Eloise. They were looking at some books, and I got bored. I saw your vegetables, and I wanted a carrot."

"Oh. Well, carrots are my favorite too."

Standing, I leaned over the display and found the best carrot in the stand.

"You know, normally, we charge money for our veggies, but this carrot is the prettiest in the stand. And you're just the prettiest little girl. So, I figure the prettiest carrot should go to you."

I didn't think the girl's eyes could widen more, but she surprised me when they shifted to the size of saucers.

"Really?" she asked in a breathy, surprised voice.

"Yeah, of course. I'm getting ready to pack them all up and take them to some people who need them more than I do."

"Wow. Can I take one to my sister?"

Well, damn if that wasn't the sweetest thing.

"Of course. I'll even let you pick it out."

The girl gleefully clapped her hands as she moved to the other end of the display and grabbed an almost-identical carrot to the one I had given her.

"Eloise will love this."

"Okay, sweetie. Now, do you see your dad anywhere?"

She spun around and pointed to the far end of the market toward two figures standing at the local library's stand. It didn't even look like her father noticed she was missing.

"Okay. Well, maybe you should head back so he doesn't worry."

"Yeah. You're right. My dad worries *a lot*. Like... all the time."

"Hurry, then. I'll watch and make sure you get over there all right." The farmer's market was going to be closing up soon, and I needed to pack the crates in my truck to get them across town before I was due to help my sister.

"Thanks, Miss Barbie, for the carrots."

"How about you call me Alex?"

"Okay, Miss Alex. I'm Molly," she said as she held out her tiny hand again. I shook it and copied her smile.

"Nice to meet you, Molly."

The girl quickly hurried across the lot to her dad, who appeared shocked she had left his side. I couldn't see them well across the expansive lot, but the man turned and waved in my direction. From what I could tell, Molly handed her sister the carrot, and all was well and forgiven.

Even from this distance, something about the man seemed familiar, but I couldn't pinpoint it. I had a type, after all. My sisters always went for the tall, dark, and handsome ones. Me? I preferred men with blonde hair and a surfer aesthetic. A little rough around the edges with a warm, quick smile. Long and lean muscles and defined, broad shoulders.

But this guy across the lot screamed he was a three-piece-suit-wearing, order-giving alpha of a man. His hair was clipped short, and there wasn't a five o'clock shadow in sight. He did have the tall, muscular thing going for him though.

The man turned back toward me again and caught me staring in his direction, cocking his head as if trying to figure out if I was a weirdo or not.

"Shit," I murmured as I turned around and hefted one of the display crates into the bed of my truck. I hoped he would see I was busy and not come over to confront me for my staring.

After I stacked a few more crates into the back, my phone vibrated in my pocket.

Autumn

Don't forget to stop by the house, so I can give you the run-through.

I'll be there in an hour. I just need to drop off the food.

See you then.

With the warmth of the sun bearing down on my back, I continued to load the truck until the stand was empty. Luck must have been on my side, because the mystery man never resurfaced, but neither did his adorable daughter. I wondered if her sister was just as cute.

Officially closing down the stand a bit earlier than normal for a Saturday in peak season, I hopped into my truck and turned on the ignition. I loved how the entire seat rumbled under my legs as she purred to life.

After my grandfather died, my dad and I worked together to fix up the 1950s Chevy to pristine condition. Some of my favorite memories were working with him late at night, far past my bedtime, restoring what we could. I worked hard to keep her in the best shape I could.

Shifting the gears, I pulled out of the lot and headed down Main Street toward the opposite end of our tiny town. It was only a few blocks before I turned into the local church's parking lot. They took the produce that didn't sell and delivered it to families in need. It was an agreement my family made with them generations ago, long before my parents were born. My father's ancestors were one of the founding families of our town, and we were proud of that heritage. We did our best to uphold the things they'd done to carry on our small-town living.

The staff were waiting for me when I arrived, and we quickly unloaded the goods before I made my way toward Colton and Autumn's house.

The drive took about thirty minutes, and I couldn't fight back my smile as I approached the renovated farmhouse high on the hill that bordered Sunny Brook Farms. Despite Colton and my sister's rocky start—he outbid her for the house at auction and convinced her to help him renovate the property she always dreamed of turning into a bed-and-breakfast—they were blissfully in love. Just last weekend, we celebrated their wedding at the Easterly Venue, and now they were about to head off on their honeymoon. I was here to man the fort, so to speak.

Parking the truck, I hopped out and dashed up the stairs, admiring the newly laid flower bed on my way. My fists banged against the wooden door as I waited for my sister to answer.

As the door whooshed open, Autumn said, "Hey. You know you don't have to knock."

Laughing, I followed her outstretched arm into the house as she closed the door behind me. "Yes, I do," I explained. "After the incident last year, when I saw way more of you and Colton than I ever needed, I will forever knock first."

My sister's cheeks flushed a deep-red in embarrassment as we made our way to the kitchen area at the back of the house—the area I was most familiar with.

"Where's Colton?" I asked as I stole a cookie from the tray resting in the middle of the island.

"He's finishing up packing his bag. I've been packing all week. He decided to wait until the last minute." Her eyes rolled as she snagged a cookie as well.

"Better late than never though, right?"

"Right."

"Okay, so tell me about the family staying here for the summer."

With a mouthful of crumbled cookie, Autumn replied, "It's Andrew's best friend, remember? The one from college who came around during the summers when we were little."

With another cookie in my possession, I pointed it in her direction before taking a hearty bite. "Nope. I was always away at dance camp when he came by, remember? And then he moved to California or something like that. It's why Andrew travels out there so much."

"Ah, yes, that's right. I always forget you never actually met him, but you've seen pictures of him at college with Andrew. And when he had his kids."

"Autumn, any pictures I remember seeing of Andrew's friends in college were not stored in my long-term memory. And if I saw any pictures of this guy with his wife and kids, I really don't recall. Hate to disappoint you. I've been so busy trying to finish this degree that I've mentally been in my own world the last five years."

Autumn narrowed her eyes at me as if trying to determine whether I was lying or not and then shrugged.

"Anyway, he's super nice and very, very private. He paid for the entire B & B while he's here with his family."

"Oh, why so secret?" I asked, mimicking Heath Ledger's Joker.

"He, uh, came into a lot of money recently and doesn't like others snooping around."

"Oh, rich daddy. What does he do?" Swiveling away from the counter, I made my way over to the cabinet beside the fridge, grabbed a glass, then poured myself a glass of milk from the jug in the refrigerator.

"Robots or something. I have no idea. Andrew could go on about it for hours. I usually get bored after the first sentence. But anyway, all you have to do is clean the rooms he's using, make sure there's some sort of food available during the day, and cook the nightly meals as they need. Pretty much, just be at his beck and call."

"What about the wife?" I asked, curious. Autumn had yet to mention any of the other family members.

"No wife. Andrew said she was a witch, if you know what I mean. It's just him and a couple of kids." As I sneered, Autumn added, "Everything will be fine. Andrew has assured me the kids are well-behaved. If you have trouble, you know you can call Rory. She's out of school for the summer, and she's great with kids."

Since Rory was a first-grade teacher, she was the most patient of all us sisters when dealing with children.

"I'll keep that in mind."

"Andrew texted they were finishing up lunch, so they should be here in about an hour. Thank you again, Alex. I know Randy wasn't too thrilled when you requested three weeks off of work."

"It's no problem. I had the time. Enjoy your honeymoon. I can't believe you guys decided to go to Iceland instead of some idealistic beach."

"No better way to spend a honeymoon than keeping each other warm," Autumn replied with a cheeky grin.

We chatted for a little while longer before Mom arrived to take Autumn and Colton to the airport.

The house was pretty tidy from the cleaner Autumn hired to come in once a week to get in all the nooks and crannies. I opted to grab my bag from my truck and claim the bedroom on the second floor, the farthest away from the rest of the guestrooms. Autumn designed this for those who wanted more privacy from other guests.

I unpacked what I brought, knowing I could head back to my apartment in town whenever I needed to restock. With time to kill, I laid back on the white down comforter and scrolled through my phone, searching for my favorite video clips—military family reunions. They always left me a teary mess, but I couldn't stop watching them.

I was thankfully saved from my sobfest when the doorbell rang.

Jumping from the bed, I dashed down the hall just as my feet planted on the floor.

"Showtime."

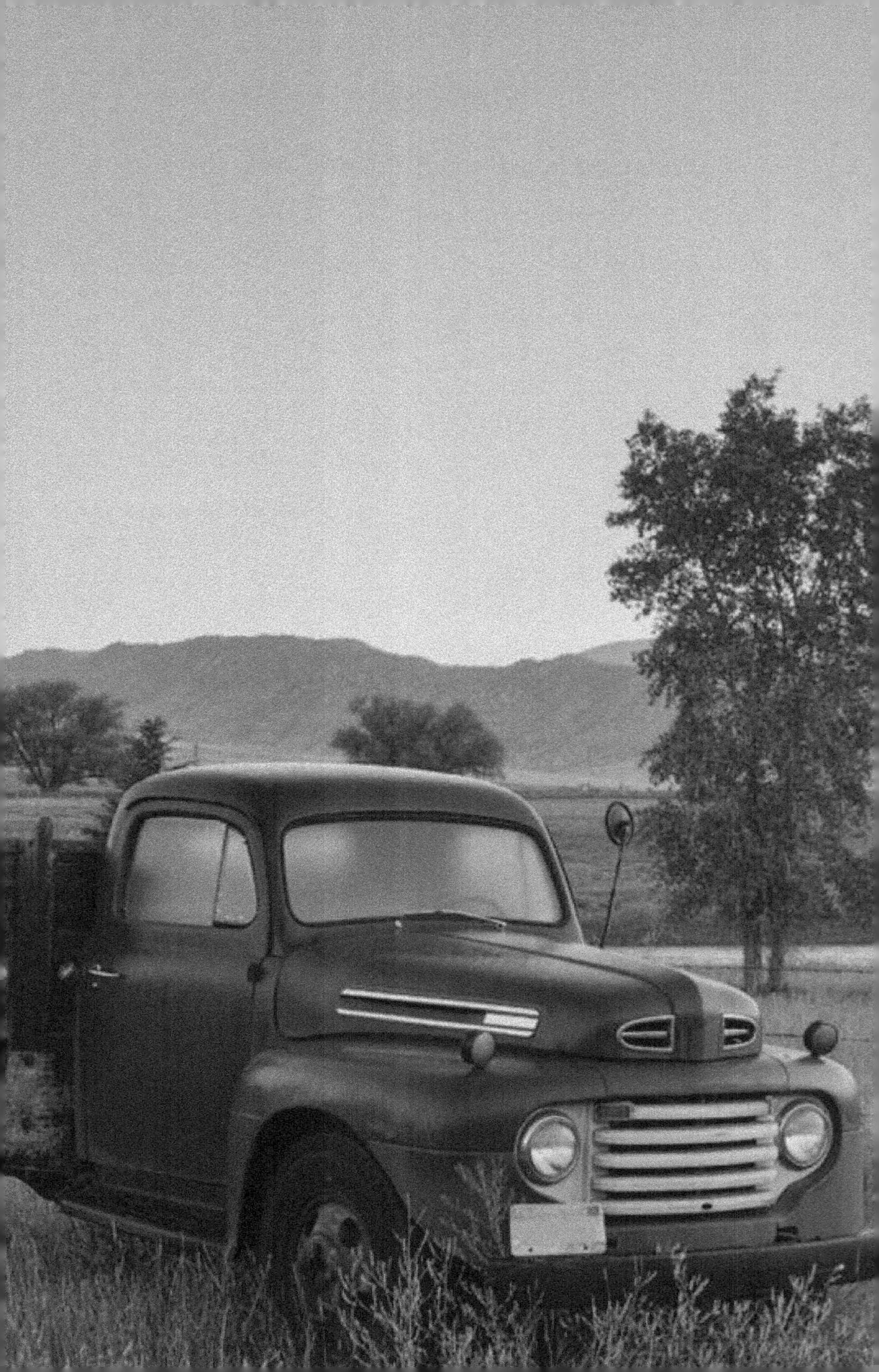

Chapter Two

Nathaniel

"**D**addy, that was so much fun!" Molly shouted from her car seat behind me as I pulled our SUV out of the parking spot I managed to snag on the street earlier. Eloise continued to sit quietly next to her sister, letting her twin carry the conversation.

"I'm glad you enjoyed the market, Molly. We can try to do that again while we're here."

"Yes!" she cried out enthusiastically.

I glanced in the rearview mirror and found her with her fist jutted up in the air like the ending of *The Breakfast Club*.

"Eloise, did you have a good time?" I prompted.

In her soft-spoken voice, she replied, "Yes, Daddy. Thank you for my book."

Glancing at her using the mirror, I watched as her tiny fingers gripped the edges of the hardback princess book she clutched to her chest. "You're welcome. Now, is everyone excited about lunch with Uncle Andrew?"

Both girls shouted their excitement at getting to eat pizza with my best friend.

Driving down an alleyway two blocks from where we previously parked, I found another spot in front of Angelo's and maneuvered the oversized SUV with ease. I came here a few times in the past when I visited Andrew over our summer breaks during college.

Growing up, my parents spent most of their time in their lab, experimenting with chemicals and test tubes, instead of trying to create a home and memories with me. You'd think having a son graduate as his high school valedictorian and win a full scholarship to Wellington University, a top-notch Ivy League school, would have been enough for them.

Not to my parents. They couldn't even muster up an appearance at either graduation.

But there had been two weeks every summer Andrew's family flew me out to Sunny Brook Farms. I lived for those weeks. The early-morning wake-ups and manual labor that Andrew and I had to "suffer through" during my stay didn't even bother me. I actually looked forward to it all.

His parents treated me like I was one of their own. And in those two weeks, I felt more loved and cared for than I had in the years growing up in California with my parents. Too bad those summers ended when we graduated—though Andrew and I stayed in touch as much as two friends living across the country could.

I hadn't been back in Ashfield in about a year, which had been a fluke to begin with. I was looking for land in Eastern Tennessee for my robotics project, when my mom called to say my twin girls unexpectedly arrived at their home. Most grandparents would have been frantic, but I was met with indifference.

"It is a huge inconvenience," my mother had scolded. And when I couldn't get a hold of my ex-wife, I agreed.

I planned on driving to Nashville to catch the next flight to California, but Mother Nature had other plans and grounded everything for the following twelve hours because of a severe lightning storm. I'd pulled off the highway when I could no longer read any of the green signs due to wind and rain, and as luck would have it, I ended up at a bar in Ashfield and prepared to drown my sorrows.

"Daddy!" Molly squealed, and I shook my head to clear away the fuzzy memory.

"I'm coming. You can both unhook yourself."

Exiting the vehicle, I moved to the passenger side and opened the back door. The two most important people in the world—and it seemed the only things I ever got right—stared at me with matching grins.

"All right, let's go see your favorite person," I told them as I lifted Molly from the car and placed her safely beside me, then did the same with Eloise.

"Can I bring my book, Daddy?" Hopefulness swirled in her eyes.

"We don't want to get pizza fingers all over the pages. And I know Uncle Andrew is excited to see you. It's been a long time since he came out to California. Maybe we can read it when we get to the house?"

"Okay, Daddy," she said sweetly and handed me the book to place back inside the car. Eloise was the one who never argued with me or threw a tantrum when she didn't get her way. She left all of that up to

Molly. But I worried that meekness had something to do with her holding onto the grief of her mother leaving after having primary custody for the first three years of their life. I'd only had them over the last year, and they spent a lot of that with their nanny and tutor. I worried she was afraid I'd leave if she wasn't the perfect child.

Both girls clutched my hands as we crossed the street, and as we entered the lively restaurant, they tucked their small faces against my pant legs. With wide eyes, I glanced around until I found a booth in the back corner, where my best friend sat with a lazy smile.

In a hushed voice, I told the girls I spied Andrew, and they looked up in unison. Before their next breath, both of them released their hold on me and dashed between the tables. Andrew kneeled with his arms open wide, waiting for the twins as they rushed toward him.

Eyes followed me as I strolled through the restaurant, and I did my best to ignore them. But the gangly teen from my past felt self-conscious, and I wanted to force my chin to my chest to avoid the stares.

"You look different from the last time they saw you," I mumbled to myself, trying to rid the fear of embarrassment.

I traded the skinny limbs for twenty pounds of muscle, and my jeans and T-shirts for structured suits. After my last robotics patent sold for two-point-five billion dollars to an international investor, I restructured my business and gave myself a makeover of sorts. My new public relations team said I needed to dress like the billionaire I now was.

Finally, I reached the table, and my friend greeted me warmly. Andrew clasped my hand, then wrapped his free arm around my shoulders, and I did the same.

"It's good to see you, man."

Stepping back, I smiled at the man who felt like a brother to me.

"You too," he said as he squeezed my bicep. "That's a lot of muscle you've put on there in the last few months."

"Well, some people stress-eat. Apparently, I stress-exercise."

We both chuckled as we took our seats in the booth.

"Well, it looks good on you. The hair too. I haven't seen you with short hair since freshman year at Wellington."

Instinctively, I run my hand across my head, wishing it was my longer, wavy locks but coming up short.

"It was time for a change, I guess." Nervously, I adjusted my larger frame in the seat. I still didn't feel comfortable with the changes I'd undergone, but the PR team was firm with their branding decision. They insisted I needed to look more like a hot-shot engineer and less like a farmer.

I got the girls settled with a coloring placemat and some crayons just as the server came by with some water and menus for the four of us.

"So…," Andrew began, and I darted my eyes toward him in warning.

"Don't."

"Come on, Nate. Nothing?"

"We will not talk about Sasha," I commanded in a hushed tone as I nodded toward my daughters.

With his hands up in surrender, Andrew apologized. I went back to looking at the menu, but the silence that stretched made me anxious.

"Look, even if I wanted to, I couldn't say anything, because she dropped off the face of the earth about as quickly as she dropped them off at my mom's.

She calls every once in a while to talk to the girls, but that's about it."

"Thank God you got out of that marriage before it was too late."

"We never should have gotten married to begin with, which is why it lasted all of six months. Anyway, enough about me. Tell me what's been going on with you. I haven't heard from you in a while."

Andrew went on to tell me about his mother and stepfather's farm and how they opened an event venue on the property a few months back. So far, it was booked solid for the next couple of years, which was a relief to the entire family, as the ranch struggled with finances in recent years.

"Sunny Brook Farm still does well, much better than most in the area, but the recent harvests weren't as plentiful, and costs for supplies continue to go up. It's just how things are right now. Autumn worked really hard to make the venue a success. And it definitely didn't hurt that Colton name-dropped it in interviews a few times. You can't imagine how many people come by just to get a glimpse of him."

"Autumn married a hockey player. I never would have guessed. Of course, in my mind, she's still the little girl in pigtails with her sisters chasing after us in the summer. Man, I think it's been almost twenty years since I've seen any of your family."

"Well, Mom is definitely excited to see you. And they understood why you haven't been around. Work and life get busy, then you blink, and a decade has passed."

"They on you to get tied down?" I asked as the pizza arrived at the table. Without missing a beat, I grabbed a plate and cut up a piece of the pizza for Molly, then repeated the same steps for Eloise. Both girls delightfully dove into their lunch.

Just as I looked back at Andrew, I noticed his gaze trained on the door of the restaurant. Turning around, I spotted a woman about his sister's age hugging a man around the same. When I twisted back, I noted the narrowed gaze Andrew sent toward the couple.

"Um, something going on there?" I asked.

"What?" He shook his head slightly, and his eyes reluctantly tugged away from the couple. "No, that's Sadie, Colton's half-sister." He was absolutely looking at her with something more than familial relations, but I wasn't about to mention that to him. He already looked riled up after mentioning my ex.

"Oh, how old is she?" I questioned lightheartedly as I took an oversized bite of the doughy pizza.

"I think... twenty-one or so. She and Aspen are around the same age."

Aspen was Andrew's youngest half-sister. She was just starting kindergarten when I saw her last, when she was just a bit older than my own girls now.

Changing the conversation, I asked my twins to tell Andrew all the things they had done in the last year. Molly went on about her dance classes, and Eloise chimed in now and then to talk about her gymnastics class. The girls took part in various activities but had their preferred ones. I hoped they wouldn't be too heartbroken when I told them that Ashfield probably wouldn't offer the same things. They liked to be active, but I wasn't sure working on a farm was something on their checklist.

Hell, I planned my entire summer here looking for land to put down roots for me and the twins. Ever since my ex, Sasha, signed away her parental rights, I knew I was going to move them as close to the Easterlys as I could. My parents didn't even bat an eye when I told them I was packing up my small bungalow in the California foothills and moving across the country with their grandchildren. The only people who cared were those working for me, and even they knew I could work from wherever I wanted. I had never spent most of my days in the office but rather clocked my hours in my workshop.

Which was my entire goal here. I wanted land to build a larger and more technological studio for my projects, along with enough space to build my future home for me and my girls. And I knew Ashfield was that place. I just needed to convince someone to sell me some land, and I knew that would be the hard part.

But I had a backup plan just in case things didn't go my way. I couldn't rent the bed-and-breakfast forever, but I could rent another place in town until I found something. I had time, and luckily, the girls wouldn't start kindergarten until the fall.

"Daddy took us to a place that had lots of people. That was sooo fun!" Molly exclaimed as she moved up onto her knees in the booth. Her waving hands knocked into her plate, and the few bits of pizza left went soaring across the table and landed on my lap.

"Shoot," I mumbled as I snagged the individual pieces from the leg of my suit pants and placed them back on the table. I glanced up at my daughter and found her lower lip trembling as she scooted to the far corner of the booth's bench in fear.

"Molly, sweetie, it's okay. It was just an accident."

"But your pants," she whispered, moving her legs and tucking her knees against her chest. "I got pizza on them."

"Naw, they're black. You can't even tell." I watched in horror as my little one continued to sink into herself just as Eloise spoke in her calm and soothing voice.

"Momma woulda got really mad, and she'd yell."

Thanking her for letting me know, I pressed my lips to the top of Eloise's head and then turned back to Molly. "Hey, have I ever raised my voice to you?"

"Yeah," she replied, readjusting the hold of her hands around her legs.

Shocked, I asked, "When?"

Molly sprang up in her seat and straightened her back. "In my room, when I can't find my shoes to put on."

"Well, yeah," I said with a laugh. "I'm at the front door, and if I don't yell, you can't hear me, silly.

But have I ever yelled at you when you've done something wrong or you had an accident?"

"No," she replies with a sigh.

"Right. You don't ever need to be scared of me, girls," I assured, looking between my two daughters. A year later and they still had moments like this. It was getting better, but it always left me wondering how bad Sasha's temper had been and how much she neglected them. "I don't know what happened when you lived with your mom. I only got to see you when she allowed, but things are different now. I promise."

"Okay, Daddy," they said in unison, their sweet, innocent voices sounding like little bells in my ears.

I cut a fresh slice of pizza for Molly as Eloise finished her first one, then grabbed myself another before turning back to Andrew. His eyelids were closed into tiny slits, and his fingers gripped the edge of the table so hard his knuckles turned the same color as the parmesan cheese in the glass shaker at the end of the table.

"What's the matter?" I asked him, setting down my slice and taking a sip of water.

"That… woman. What the hell did she do to your kids?" he murmured angrily, the vein over his eye pulsing with each word.

"I don't know. From what I can gather, she and the live-in nanny ran a tight ship. But I don't have any reason to believe she did anything more than raise her voice at them." The courts didn't either, which was why they stayed with her.

"She better hope not." Andrew mumbled something about hunting her down, but I couldn't quite make it out over the chatter between my daughters, who were talking about the bed-and-breakfast.

Andrew calmed down and chimed in to the twins' conversation, explaining that the house had been in his family for centuries and was one of the first homes in the town before it was Ashfield. Molly and Eloise were riveted as he told them how the house was nothing more than decrepit wood and bricks until Colton bought it and renovated it with Autumn.

"Is that why it's called Craw… Crawford?" Eloise asked as she set down her fork and took a sip of her water.

"Crawford Bed and Breakfast. Yes, it is. My sister made the place incredible. It's almost like a museum in there."

In horror, Molly asked, "We can still play, right?"

"Of course, you can," Andrew responded, but I wasn't so sure about that. My girls weren't known for being careful. I had a painting that hung in my previous home that now bore a nasty slash through the middle due to a rogue doll that thought she could fly.

We finished up with lunch, and I asked Andrew a few more questions about our stay. He assured me that, although Autumn wouldn't be there, his sister Alex would make sure we were taken care of. She was going to stay on the property for the few weeks Autumn and Colton were on their honeymoon.

"You'll have full access to the kitchen, but she'll be making your dinners unless you have other plans."

"Can she cook?" I asked as we stepped out of the restaurant. Unless it was spaghetti or mac and cheese, I was hopeless in the kitchen. A chef delivered our meals for the last year since the girls came to live with me. Before that, I relied on takeout.

"Better than my mom, but don't tell her I said that," Andrew joked as he helped Eloise into her car seat as I did the same for Molly. "You sure you're okay to get there? Sorry I can't follow. I have a Farmer's Association meeting in about an hour."

"On a Saturday?" I asked.

"You're one to talk," Andrew jested. He wasn't wrong. There was no weekend for me, not until recently when I sold my most recent patent.

"Yeah, yeah. Think your dad would be up for a visit tonight or tomorrow?"

"I bet my parents will be at your door long before you get yourself settled."

Laughing, I said goodbye to my friend and started the SUV.

In the back seat, the girls sat quietly looking out their windows, taking in all the beauty we passed. The fields and mountains off in the distance never ceased to amaze me. The last time I drove through here, I was headed toward the airport with the sun moving over the horizon, ready to start the day. I'd left an unfamiliar apartment without a backward glance or a chance to consider whatever I'd gotten into the night before. Ignoring my cottonmouth, I had my sights set on the first flight back to California to get my girls.

The road began twisting around the hills, and I knew we were getting closer to our destination. Before I knew it, we crested the ninety-degree turn, and the majestic house perched on the hill came into view.

"There it is, girls."

I took in the glory of the massive brick farmhouse with its two-story porch. As we got closer, I noticed a porch swing gently rocking with the breeze, and the fields of wheat mimicked the movement.

"Wow," Eloise said, and I peered over my shoulder to find her leaning as far as her car seat allowed her to get a better view past her sister. "It's so pretty."

"I think so too," I replied, turning into the gravel driveway that led to the property.

We passed under a large metal sign that read **Crawford Bed and Breakfast**, leaving a cloud of dust behind us.

The girls were bouncing in their seats as I came to a stop, and they didn't hesitate to free themselves from their confines when I gave the okay.

"Wait for me!" I hollered as they ran as fast as they could with their little legs toward the porch. They were already standing at the top of the steps when I turned off the vehicle, their lopsided pigtails rocking with each bounce of their impatient bodies.

"Can I press the button? Please, Daddy, please?" Molly pleaded as she tugged my pant leg when I joined them.

I glanced over at Eloise and noticed she had the same eagerness in her eyes, but I knew she'd never speak up over her enthusiastic sister. "How about we let Eloise press it this time?"

Molly released my pant leg and stepped back as she gently nodded.

"Thanks, Molly," Eloise said as she took a step toward the doorbell. Her slender finger reached for the button and hovered, then pushed it. The sound of an antique chime wailed around us, and the three of us jumped in alarm before laughing.

It didn't take long to hear the telltale signs of feet stomping on the other side of the door before they froze. A few metallic noises of gears moving and sliding occurred, then the door opened wide to a woman wearing an easy grin.

"Daddy, look! It's the Miss Barbie from this morning. I told you she was pretty," Molly, my daughter who's never met a stranger, immediately exclaimed as the door's opening widened, but the woman's eyes never left mine as her smile melted into a frown.

When our host remained silent, I ran my hand over Molly's head, wordlessly telling her everything was okay, and then held my hand out in greeting.

"Hi, I'm Kate Sullivan, and these are my daughters, Eloise and Molly. It's nice to meet you."

I had a chance to take in the woman's face, and she was stunning. There was something familiar about her, but I chalked it up to her being related to Andrew. I also saw her at a distance this morning at the market. She'd been the one to give Molly the carrots.

"Nathaniel?" she asked as she slowly brought her hand up to mine. Our palms touched, and I swore the earth stopped spinning. I'd felt this hand before. Experienced its soft skin against my own. There was an intimacy in the way our fingers brushed against each other.

But I knew that wasn't possible. I'd never met this woman before in my life. There would be no way I could forget her.

"Um, most people call me Nate," I replied, thinking that perhaps Autumn listed the name on my credit card as the reservation guest's name. "And you are?"

Her hand slipped free of my grasp, and she took a step back, her eyes steeling at the same time as her spine. She looked at me in a way that made my skin crawl, as if I was missing something pivotal. "My name is Alex. Let me show you to your rooms."

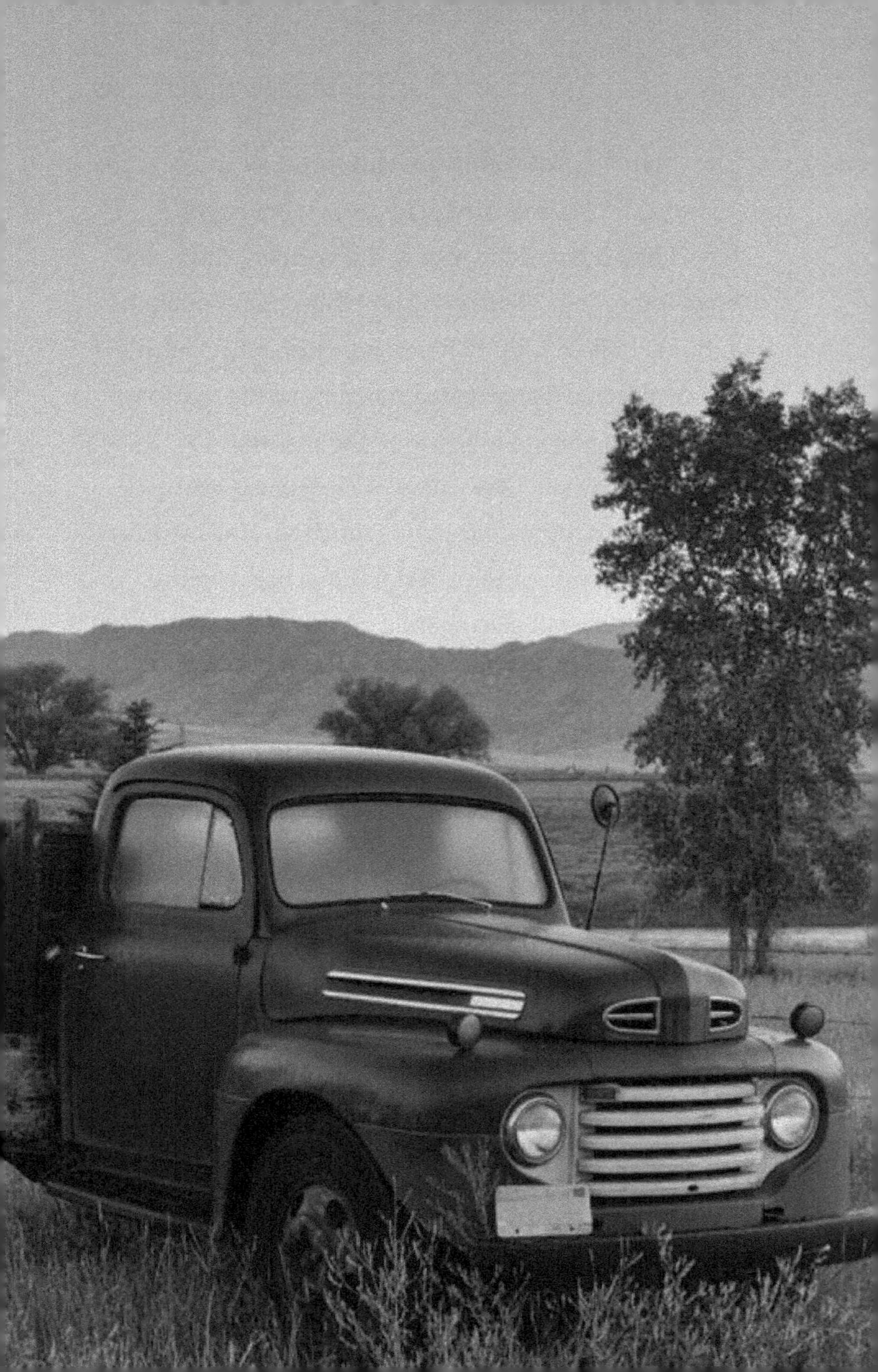

Chapter Three

Alex

I could feel his stare on my back as I guided them through the first floor where they'd find the kitchen, living room, library, and game room. The way he looked at me made me want to huddle away in a cocoon high in a tree somewhere.

He didn't remember me, and I felt like an idiot. He'd been at the bar for a few hours when I met him. I flirted with him a little when I went behind the counter and the bartender on duty assured me Nathaniel, as he asked everyone around him to call him that night, was still in his right mind, just angry and depressed.

Well, seemed we were both wrong.

When I opened the door to find Nate standing there, I thought he had to be a mirage. I had recurring dreams of this man for the last year, and now he was standing on the porch, waiting for me to let him in.

I was Cinderella, right? And my fairy godmother was granting my ultimate wish?

No. Nothing in my life ever went the way it was supposed to. My plans were always foiled, and it left me lurking in the shadows of someone else's successes.

"And this is the library," I said with the most enthusiastic voice I could muster. And by the way Molly's face squished together, I was certainly failing.

Then, by surprise, I felt the softest little hand wrap around my own. The other child, Eloise I thought Nate said, squeezed my hand as she took in the view. Then I recalled she had been perusing the library stand at the market today.

Crouching down to her level, I asked Eloise if she liked to read.

"Yes." She nodded. "It's my favorite."

I knew little about children, but from what I could gather, most kids her age couldn't spell, let alone read. I took a chance and glanced up at Nate, who was gazing lovingly at his daughter. If I weren't so pissed that he had zero clue who I was, then I'd probably find it endearing. Instead, it only added fuel to my fire.

"Eloise can read at a second-grade level. She took to books the minute she came to live with me."

I noticed his eyes lost their sparkle at the mention of the girls moving in with him. It made me wonder if there was more to the situation than he disclosed to me at the bar that night so long ago. All I knew was he and his wife divorced. She had primary custody of the girls, then one day dropped off their kids with his parents without a second's notice.

Turning back to the little girl, I did my best to smile again. "Well, we have an entire section of children's books I'm sure you'll love. My sister, Rory, picked them out."

"Rory? That name is silly," Molly chimed in from behind me.

I twisted my body so I could face both girls. "Yes, we call her Rory, but her name is Aurora, like the princess. She's a first-grade teacher at our school here." Winking at Eloise, I added, "And I know she put a lot of thought into picking out these books. I'm sure you'll find something you'll love."

"Wow. Daddy, can I stay here?"

I could see he was thinking it over, but then he gingerly shook his head and told her she could come back later.

"Why don't you girls go find your bedrooms upstairs?" It was only a split second before they were darting away from the library and toward the stairs. I didn't get the chance to tell them there was a back staircase they could've used because they moved so fast. Like little tumbleweeds caught in a breeze.

"Just not the blue door! That's mine!" I shouted as I followed after them.

"Wait, you're the one staying here?" Nate asked abruptly.

"That's the plan, Stan. My sister and her husband live on the third floor, and... well, I don't want to go anywhere near their love nest. So, it's the second floor for me. But don't worry, you won't even know I'm here."

I planned to stay as far away from the house as I could. There was no reason to make everything worse for myself. It was bad enough this man didn't remember me, but it was even worse knowing how unattainable he was.

Autumn said the guy had money, and judging by the suit he wore, there were a lot of dollars to spare.

Of course, who wore a suit to a farming town? He stuck out like a sore thumb, just like he had a year ago.

He'd filled out since then. The suit that hung so loosely on him at the bar was now snug in all the right places. The long hair I stroked my fingers through as he got well acquainted with the sensitive spot between my legs was now long gone. If I'd seen him walking down the street, I probably wouldn't have given him a second glance, but his eyes drew me in. When I opened the door and they latched onto me, I felt them the same way I had when he slid his cock inside me over and over again.

"Did you just moan?" he asked from behind me as I started climbing the stairs.

"No," I answered quickly. "I just... have a sore muscle in my leg. That's all."

I went back to ignoring him and finished the climb, then took a left down the hall, where I found Eloise and Molly in adjoining rooms. One was covered in pale-pink lace for Molly, and one was in matching lace but pastel-yellow for Eloise. Autumn decorated them specifically for the two girls visiting this summer. Normally, crisp-white duvets adorned the queen-sized beds, but she figured the girls would want something a little more colorful. She also added a dollhouse and a few kid toys off a list from Rory.

"So, what do you girls think?" Nate asked as he stepped inside the room Eloise snagged. She sat delicately in a rocking chair overlooking the backyard.

"I like it."

Like a hurricane-force wind, Molly came running into the bedroom, tossed her body on the newly made bed, and sighed in contentment. Eloise's small face cringed as she looked at her now crumpled bedding.

"Daddy, I love it. It's like being a pwincess in an old castle. Did your home look like this when you were four?" She held up four fingers.

I tried to hold back my laugh. I really did. But the giggle won over and spewed from between my closed lips as I looked at Nate's exasperated face.

I may not know much about kids, but damn, his were freaking hilarious.

"Yeah, Daddy. Did the houses look like this when you were young?" I asked in jest, but I didn't miss the way his eyes glazed over when I called him Daddy. Instead of considering all the possibilities of being in the same home with this devilishly handsome man, I hardened my face and turned back to the girls.

"No, Molly. When I was little, the homes looked just like they do now. I'm only thirty-eight."

Well, at least now I knew how old my mystery man was. Fourteen years older than me, which was more up Autumn's alley than mine. Colton was eleven years her senior.

"Thirty-eight is old," Molly said through a know-it-all exhale.

"No, it's not, Molly," Eloise replied quietly from her corner. "Can we go outside? There's a swing set."

"There's also an ice rink and pool, but you need an adult with you to go to those, okay?" I tried to say sternly, but I'm pretty certain I failed. "House rules."

Nate took the moment to explain to the girls that they needed to unpack their things from the car before getting to explore anything more on the property. Quietly, I slipped out of the room and made my way to the front door. I wasn't a part of their family and didn't want to encroach on any conversation that didn't directly involve me.

Outside, I took a chance and pressed the button that would open the rear hatch of the SUV and was surprised he left it unlocked. Most people who never lived in a small town, especially Ashfield, always locked their doors out of habit. Something I learned when I worked at the bar and through the gossip grapevine.

Reaching into the trunk, I hefted the first suitcase out of the vehicle, only to have it swiped from my hands.

"I've got it," Nate said as he set the luggage on the ground. Rolling my eyes, I went for another. "I said I've got this," he repeated as he grabbed the second suitcase from me.

"I heard you the first time. I'm just choosing to ignore you."

"Are you always this argumentative?" he asked as he stole a third suitcase from my grasp.

"Yes. Now let me do my job."

"I can get our luggage. It's fine," the infuriating man said as he tried to tug the handle from my hand. I held firm.

"No."

"Yes." He yanked at the handle again, and our eyes met and held as something more than our petty argument passed between us. I wondered if his body responded to me the same way mine was responding to him. I tingled all over, and the area between my legs he so thoroughly explored during our time together awakened in reverence.

But as quickly as my body roused, he shut down.

"No," Nate said sternly, jerking the handle once more with a force that drove me to let go.

"Fine." Spinning around, I didn't wait to see him stumble with the weight of the bag now in his grasp or try to figure out how he was going to get all the suitcases into the house. The stubborn man could figure it out himself.

Instead, I planned to go to the place that kept me calm and gave me a sense of peace—the kitchen.

It was nowhere close to dinnertime, but when I was frustrated or stressed out, I baked. It was something my mother taught me when she noticed I was growing anxious. Something about kneading dough and plucking fresh fruit from our garden took my mind off whatever was bothering me. In the last five years, I baked a lot.

Grabbing the flour, sugar, baking powder, and other ingredients from the oversized butler's pantry, I laid everything out on the butcher block countertop and got to work. I no longer needed the crumpled piece of paper containing the recipe for my pie dough; it was something I could make in my sleep.

I closed my eyes and went to work, sifting the ingredients into the mixer and then mixing them to perfection. From the fridge, I pulled out some blueberries from our garden that I'd given to Autumn yesterday. A few minutes on the stove and the berries were ready to go on top of the crust in the pie tin and bake.

Within a few minutes, the sweet smell of blueberry pie enveloped the kitchen and filtered through the house. For me, it was the smell of summer. Mom always made a blueberry pie the day school let out. It would be waiting for us the second we got off the school bus, and my sisters and I couldn't wait to dive in.

On a working farm, we usually had to wait for all the ranch hands to join us before eating anything in the house. It was something my parents stood by. Those workers were just as much a part of the family as me and my siblings were.

But on the last day of school, that blueberry pie was something special. It was just for us.

It didn't surprise me to hear the pitter-patter of footsteps as I pulled the pie from the oven. The grin that grew on my face just as those two little girls rounded the corner was automatic. I wondered if my mom felt the same way when she saw the group of us clamoring for her desserts.

The girls climbed up on the barstools in front of the kitchen island, where I set the pie and stared adoringly at the crumbled goodness on top.

"Wow," a deep voice stated, pulling my eyes away from the twins. I hated and loved that he changed out of his suit and now had on a pair of well-worn jeans and a snug T-shirt that stretched against the muscles of his chest. He'd filled out since I last saw him, and as someone who usually went for a leaner build, even I was impressed.

"Glad to see you lost the suit," I told him as he joined his girls at the island.

Bashfully, he ran his hand across the back of his neck and turned his eyes downward. "Habit, I guess." It was clear he wanted to say more, but Molly saved him as she asked when she could have a piece of the pie.

"Not until after dinner. It needs to cool down," I explained to the trio's growing frowns.

Something about the disappointment on all three of their faces had me caving instantly. I turned toward the cabinet and drawer closest to the sink to fetch some plates and utensils.

"Don't ruin your appetite," I scolded them lightheartedly as I set down the plates and forks in front of Nate and reached into the drawer of the island, grabbing a pie server. "We're having scampi for dinner."

"What's scampi?" Eloise asked as her sister drooled over the slice of pie Nate set in front of her.

"It's a noodle dish with a light buttery sauce. Do you like shrimp?"

She looked to her father for an answer as he handed her a slice of the blueberry goodness.

"I'm not sure they've had it before," he answered before divvying out his own piece.

"Well, it's a great time to try something new then, since you've moved to a new town and all."

The little girl looked skeptical as she squished up her face, distorting her features.

"Why don't you eat your pie? If I can make something this good, imagine what I can do for dinner."

It didn't take long for them to fall into a sweet pie haze. Wordlessly, I cleaned up the mess I made while baking and slipped out of the kitchen through the mudroom. I'd kill for a chance to head to my parents' house and work in the garden, but I needed to stay here and make sure the guests didn't need anything.

I found my way over to the large oak tree. Autumn insisted the construction crew kept it in place during the restoration of the farmhouse. Amongst the fields, the tree offered a cool respite from the heat of Tennessee summers.

A small wooden swing dangled from one massive branch, and I settled myself onto it. It was just low enough that I could rock myself with the toe of my shoe. I rested my head on one of the ropes that held the swing up and closed my eyes. The only sound was the leaves rustling above me, and it transported me to heaven. It wasn't often you could escape the noise and chatter of Ashfield, despite what people thought of small towns. Whether it was gossip or farming equipment, there was always some sort of racket, but here in this space, there was nothing but tranquility.

I could see why Autumn savored it so. After living in New York City for the previous five years, her mind must have been overloaded with noise.

After a while, I expected to hear the girls, but Nate must have put them to work unpacking.

Nate—or as I knew him, Nathaniel. That's what he told me to call him at the bar, and though I thought it fit the well-suited man I met today, he seemed more like a Nate once he dressed down.

The man rocked my world that night and did things I'd only read about in the romance novels we chose for our town's book club. But just as quickly as he followed me up to my apartment above the bar, he dashed away. I left to go close up the bar around 4:00 a.m., when I knew the staff was finishing their cleaning routine. When I returned, my bed was bare.

Normally, I was the one to kick them out before the sun rose, and maybe that was why his disappearance bothered me so much. It was just as well though. I only ever had one-night stands. The one and only time I committed myself to someone, it changed my entire life.

Subconsciously, I straightened my spine and tightened my core at the thought of Stephen. Someone who crossed my mind one time too many today. He was the end of all my dreams, all my happily ever afters. The man was a walking villain with the smile of a saint.

More minutes passed, hours, before I realized my bottom and shoulders ached. After a quick glance at my watch, I saw it was close enough to dinnertime to get it ready for the guests. At least it was something to keep my mind off Stephen, Nate, and all the ways I was lost in the world. My problem was that I knew exactly what I wanted. I just didn't know quite how to get there, or if it was even possible.

It felt like I was walking in a haze as I approached the back of the house. Stepping through the mudroom, I saw there was no trace of the pie I made earlier on the kitchen counter, nor were there any dishes to be put away. It seemed Nate cleaned up after himself and his girls.

As I gathered the ingredients for dinner—nothing fresh, but I planned to change that in the future—my phone buzzed in my pocket.

Andrew
> Everyone settled in okay?

It wasn't until I read the message for the third time that I realized something catastrophic.

I slept with Andrew's best friend, and I hadn't even known it.

"Oh, shit," I mumbled as my fingers shook over the keyboard.

> Can't you ask him?

> He didn't reply. He never has his phone. The girls usually steal it.

> He's all settled. I made them Mom's blueberry pie.

> No way! Any left?

> Doubtful.

> Mom and Dad want him to come over for family dinner tomorrow.

> I'll relay the message.

The bubbles on the screen appeared, then disappeared, then appeared again.

> **Keep an eye on him for me, all right? He's been through a lot.**

If only Andrew knew the way I wanted to keep my eyes on Nate, specifically his tight backside.

> Aye, aye, Captain.

Setting the phone down, I went to work making dinner. The shrimp scampi was an easy fix, and I made a batch of plain noodles just in case the girls didn't have an adventurous palate.

In the dining room, I set the table and called up to the twins, who hurried to claim a spot at the table. I scooped a small amount of the meal onto their plates, along with a piece of garlic bread I toasted in the oven.

"Where's your dad?" I asked, as he still hadn't shown up.

"He was on his phone."

"Okay, let me see if I can get him to hurry down."

With quick strides, I made it up the stairs and down the hall, where I gently knocked on his door, calling his name. "Nate, your dinner is ready."

When he didn't respond, I twisted the knob and cracked the door.

"Nate?"

There was no response, and something in me feared the worst. Swinging the door wide, I called out his name one more time, only to find the missing man standing beside his bed, completely nude.

"Oh my gosh, I'm so sorry!" I cried out as I turned on my heels and slammed the door shut behind me. It wasn't like I hadn't seen him naked before, but my memories didn't do the guy any justice. He was a freaking work of art, a masterpiece I needed to scrub clean of my mind, because there was no way I was going to sleep with my brother's best friend again.

Chapter Four

Nate

Usually when I'm standing naked in front of a woman, she looks me over with hungry eyes or, at a minimum, makes it clear she likes what she sees. It took years for me to be comfortable in my skin with no complaints. So, watching Alex dash out of the room like she'd seen a ghost instead of my one-eyed monster left me in shock.

I'd been on the phone with Sasha again, trying to figure out what she was planning. Her calls were suddenly coming more and more frequently, despite what I told Andrew, and I feared she was having regrets about leaving our girls. Those repentances must've been eating away at her, but I had very little sympathy for her decision. Our marriage was a rash decision made when she'd seen those two pink lines on the pregnancy test. We learned quickly that the only place we were compatible was in bed and were divorced before the girls were born. The only reason I stayed in California was to see the twins when Sasha would allow.

"Shit," I mumbled as I tossed my phone onto the bed. This was definitely some first impression I was making on our host. From the moment I stood at the front door, the woman gave off the vibe that I'd done something wrong. And I had no clue what that might've been. Outside of being friends with her brother, she knew very little about me. Yet I still couldn't shake this sense of familiarity about her.

Tugging on a pair of shorts, since Molly spilled some of her pie filling on my jeans earlier, I left my room, yanking on a gray T-shirt along the way. The strong scent of garlic assaulted me as I stepped into the hall, and I realized Alex must've been at my door to alert me about dinner.

I hurried down the stairs toward the dining room, where I heard the girls chatting away as they slurped noodles. Stepping up to the table, I found a vacant seat, then looked around the room as I sat down, searching for Alex. She stood in the corner, refusing to make eye contact. She reminded me of a scared animal. Her limbs twitched like she was ready to bolt at a second's notice.

"Are you going to join us?" I asked her as I shoveled some of the main dish onto my plate.

Before Alex could answer, Molly began begging for her to eat with us, "Please, Miss Barbie? Pretty please?"

"It's Alex, remember? And I don't usually eat with the guests."

Both girls turned on their greatest attempt at puppy-dog eyes, and I'm not too ashamed to admit I even tried my best at them as well. Something about Alex called to me, and there was no reason for her not to sit at the table with us.

Alex's eyes narrowed and fists clenched at her sides, but then she surprised me as her shoulders hitched up toward her ears and her hands relaxed. I could sense a war waged inside her.

"All right, you convinced me."

Her eyes never met mine as she sat down at the table beside Molly. There was no dull moment or awkward silence during the rest of the meal, as my daughter knew how to keep a conversation flowing, and I suspected Alex chose that spot on purpose—the farthest one away from me. The beautiful woman was an enigma for sure, and she drew me to her in a way I never experienced before. It was clear she drew my daughters to her the same way, as they hung on her every word. Molly was about to slip off the side of her chair with how close she continued to scoot toward our host.

As I glanced around the table, I couldn't help but ponder if this was how most families came together in the evenings. I did my best to eat with the twins every night, but most of the time, I was stuck in my workshop or in a meeting, and their nanny served them dinner.

That was all going to change. Starting today.

"How often do you think you can join us for dinner?"

Alex seemed to choke on the food she just forked into her mouth when I spoke to her directly. As if any communication from me was uncalled for.

"Um… I mean… I rarely eat with any of the guests. Neither does my sister. Today is a special occasion, I suppose."

"Could you do it again? Every day, maybe?"

Her big blue eyes narrowed into slits, and wrinkles formed between her brows at my question. "Why?"

Why, indeed. I didn't dare disclose it was so I could figure her out like the Rubik's Cube I kept on my desk for when I needed something to challenge my mind. Or that being in her presence simply made me feel lighter, despite her grumpy first impression. And I'd only known her for a couple of hours.

Instead, I went with the next best answer. "Well, the girls enjoy your company."

"Oh, the girls." Her blue eyes twinkled as she smiled adoringly at Molly and Eloise. "I guess I could join more frequently. I usually make extra anyway. Except, you should know I usually only bring food by once a week and store it for my sister to heat or cook later."

"Really?"

"Yep. Depending on guest requests, it's either breakfast or dinner. Sometimes both, for an added fee. Clearly, you're a special guest."

Her nose scrunched when she said I was special, and it was one of the cutest things I'd ever seen. I almost told her so but stopped myself.

"Well, I appreciate it."

Silence creeped agonizingly slowly around the table until Molly filled the space again with her chatter. Thank goodness for little miracles.

I swirled the remainder of the buttery noodles around my fork and glanced up quickly to find Alex's eyes on me. As I lifted my fork toward my mouth, I shot a wink in her direction, solidifying that the pink tinge deepening on her cheeks was now my favorite color.

When the girls announced they were finished with their meal, I quickly gathered their plates and utensils from the table along with my own and headed toward the kitchen. Alex was quick on my heels.

"You don't have to do that."

"I insist," I stated as she approached the sink.

My hands grasped the edges of the dishes, my fingers brushing against hers as she reached for them. Electricity sizzled up my arm as if I held a Fourth of July sparkler too close to my skin. I trained my eyes on Alex to see if she felt the same sizzle, but her face remained impassive, unchanged.

"Please," I reiterated, and Alex finally relented her hold on the plates.

"Just so you know, this won't be happening again," she said as I got started rinsing off the plates and pots that were sitting in the large farmhouse sink.

Alex propped her backside against the counter beside me. It felt... comfortable.

"And why is that?"

"Because you're a guest here. You already cleaned up after the pie earlier. Autumn, Colton, and Andrew would be appalled to learn you're putting away your own dishes. Imagine what your business investors would think."

Dropping the plate back into the sink, I turned toward Alex, ready to clear the air of whatever I'd done to offend her, and it was obvious from her crossed arms and stiff back she was ready to spar.

Just as I was about to open my mouth, Eloise came trotting into the room with her cup, followed by Molly.

"Daddy, can we go for a walk outside?" Eloise asked, her doe eyes blinking up at me. There was no way I could deny her request, despite my desire to squash the tension between Alex and me. I also wanted some time to explore the yard.

"Sure." I grabbed the girls' cups and gently placed them in the sink and then turned back to Alex. "Guess you got your wish. We'll stay out of your hair for a while."

I snaked around the kitchen island, guiding my daughters toward the mudroom I'd seen earlier, leaving Alex to do the dishes she so adamantly pursued.

Outside, the girls frolicked in the lush grass, giggling with each step as they approached the swing set. Even at my now-sold California home, the girls didn't have a yard like this when they visited me. And their mother lived in a high-rise condo. Besides some trips to the park, this was most likely their first venture in an expansive backyard. Watching them push with their legs while on the swings, the blue-hued mountains in the background, I wished I brought them here sooner.

I had to bide my time though. Finalize the decisions that would change the courses of all three of our lives. And this place was the last piece of that puzzle.

As they continued to swing, I let them know I was going to wander farther to see the ice rink and pool Colton installed. Along the way, I peered into an old shed that was filled with workbenches and equipment.

Elation filled me as all the pieces fell into place for my plan.

Inside my pocket, I felt my phone buzz, and I brought it out to see my ex's name flash on the screen.

I'd already spoken to her today and had zero desire to do so again. But this was her MO to drive me crazy lately. She'd call repeatedly until I caved and let her speak to the girls. She did this before, but then she'd disappear for weeks at a time. Sasha was notorious for getting their hopes up and then quelling them just as quickly. I should know. She'd done the same to me.

Heaving a deep breath, I answered the call and told her to hold on before she could get out a single word. Approaching the swing set, I told the twins their mother was on the phone. While Molly enthusiastically snatched the phone from my hand, I sensed the hesitation from Eloise, with her downcast eyes and deepening frown. But despite her sister's reluctance, Molly turned on the speakerphone and persuaded Eloise to join their conversation.

One I had zero desire to listen to, as Sasha reminded them over and over how much she loved and missed them.

But I stuck around, because I knew my ex, and the minute Sasha would surely ask when she could visit, I'd need to end the call.

After she abandoned the girls and signed away her rights, amongst other lifestyle factors, the courts decided her involvement in their childhood would be emotionally damaging. My ex was lucky I allowed the calls at all.

It was also the reason I didn't disclose where we moved to, though I was certain Sasha had a good idea based on my friendship with Andrew.

"Okay, girls, time for your bath," I reminded them as I looked down at my wristwatch. "You can talk to Mommy later."

Molly complained, as did Sasha, but Eloise nodded and came to stand by my leg. I was going to have to keep my eye on her. She seemed more and more withdrawn with every call.

After I pried the phone out of Molly's hand and pressed End Call, I lugged a tantrum-throwing four-year-old back to the house while her sister walked quietly beside me.

"Cheer up, buttercups. I packed your favorite bubble bath, and I know you'll love the big tub in my bathroom." Thankfully, that calmed down the wiggling package I carried up the porch steps.

The house seemed empty when I walked inside, so the girls and I quickly made it up the staircase and got their bath started.

Thank goodness it was less eventful than the walk back to the house, and I allowed the twins a few extra minutes in the tub to play with their Barbies and bubbles. Molly even pointed out one particular doll that reminded her of Alex.

I didn't see the resemblance other than both were blonde and blue-eyed, but Eloise agreed with her twin.

By the time they resembled their favorite snack—raisins—in the tub, the sun was finally setting behind the mountain.

Their nighttime routine went quickly, and we chose Eloise's room for story time. I kicked off my shoes and leaned back against the antique wooden headboard while my girls nestled up against me. Normally, I read two books, one of each girl's choice, but tonight we barely made it through half of the first before the excitement of the day caught up to both of them.

Their gentle breaths brushed against my chest where their matching heads rested. Their still-damp hair would leave marks on my shirt, but I didn't care. Staring down at these little miracles, I had a hard time believing they were mine. I always wanted to have a big family, someone to love and care for in all the ways my own parents lacked. Outside of television shows, I'd never met anyone with multiple siblings or one who ate with their parents every evening. I relied on shows like

Step-by-Step, Full House, and Family Matters to fill that void for me. That was, until I met Andrew in college and learned those families really existed.

There were times I wished things worked out with Sasha so the girls would have two parents who loved each other. Maybe I could've put in more effort when Sasha complained. Or maybe I should've taken the time to get to know her better, instead of jumping the gun and heading down the wedding aisle. Hindsight was a bitch, though. I couldn't change the past, but I was more than capable of giving the girls the amount of love of two parents. That was the reason we were here in Ashfield and why I sold the patent to my first robot. I wanted more time with them and to give them the childhood I wished I had.

Wiggling my hips, I slid down the bed and out from under their heads. Normally, I'd carry Molly to her own bed, but the girls were in a new place, and I felt it was better to let them have this one night together.

Carefully, I adjusted their bodies so they each occupied a pillow, and I checked the nightstand closest to Molly, seeing her hearing aid was clearly visible so she could wear it in the morning if she chose to. There were days when it bothered her, and she preferred to go without the device. Her doctor said her impairment was minimal, but the hearing aid would help her as she learned to speak and read.

I kissed the top of each chestnut head and turned off the lamp glowing dimly on Eloise's nightstand.

"Goodnight, girls. I love you," I whispered before slowly closing the door to the room, thankful the hinges didn't squeak.

Alone in the hallway, I contemplated my next move. Thoughts of Alex assaulted me, and I wondered where she disappeared to after the dishes debacle.

The blue door at the end of the hallway drew my attention, and I was halfway to her room before I even realized I'd taken a step. With each stride that took me closer to her room, my palms grew clammy and beads of sweat pooled along the base of the back of my neck. I wasn't sure why I was so nervous about approaching Alex; she was my best friend's little sister, after all. I'd never been nervous around his other siblings, but Alex was a whole different ball game. There was just something about her, and I couldn't pinpoint what that might be.

When the rug gave way to the hardwood, there were only about twelve inches before I came face-to-face with the cornflower-blue door. Raising my hand, I intended to knock, but it hovered instead.

Did I want to disturb her?

Would she even have answers to my questions?

I expelled a heavy breath and gave myself a mental pep talk, then rapped my knuckles against the door three times. I secretly prayed she wouldn't answer, but my hopes were squashed when I saw the brass doorknob turn.

Then suddenly her beautiful face came into view, and I forgot how to breathe.

"Can I help you?" she asked with furrowed brows.

My entire being reverted to my timid teenage self at the sound of her naturally husky voice.

"Glasses," I blurted out, then shook my head at my lame attempt to say anything.

"What?" Her voice was pitched in confusion.

"Uh… you um… I didn't know you wore glasses."

Delicately, she slid them up her face until they rested in her hair like a headband. The soft waves of her blonde hair caressed her shoulders, which were left bare by her olive-green tank. Defiantly, she rested a fist on her hip clad in loose black running shorts. The stiffness in her body contradicted the comfortable-looking loungewear she wore.

"You've known me for all of a couple of hours. How could you know if I wear glasses?" Alex's eyes focused on my mouth as she spoke instead of my eyes, which led me to believe there was something not truthful about her claim. "They're bluelight glasses to keep me from getting a headache while I work."

"What kind of work are you doing in there?"

"Is that really what you came to ask me?" she questioned, her knuckles turning white as she fisted the doorknob.

"No, but I thought we could chat for a bit. I spend most of my time around business partners, employees, and two four-year-olds. It would be nice to have a conversation about something other than work or Barbies."

"Hmm."

"Come on," I pleaded. Once the idea took root, I was gung-ho to hang out with Alex as much as I could. I knew from Andrew, and from my own experiences today, that she enjoyed cooking and baking yet worked as a bar inventory manager. But I wanted to know more. She... intrigued me.

"Fine," she relented as she pushed her door open wider and stepped into the room, wordlessly allowing me to follow her inside. I shut the door behind me.

"Wow," I murmured as I took in the space. The room spanned the entire width of the house. They set it up studio style, with both the living room and bedroom occupying the same area. "This is bigger than most studio apartments in New York."

Alex stepped over to a hunter-green velvet lounge chair and closed a laptop. "Yes. That was Autumn's goal when she designed this room. It's specifically for people opting to stay longer than a couple of days."

"Well, it's a beautiful space."

Turning back to face me, Alex cocked one eyebrow and asked, "Why are you really here?"

Chapter Five

Alex

I was trying extremely hard to seem more put together than I felt. Just having Nate show up at my door was enough to knock me for a loop. The man made me so nervous that it felt like pterodactyls were flying around in my stomach.

He was different from that night at the bar when I took him up to my little apartment. I'd been so confident and sure of myself, because Nate—or Nathaniel as I knew him—flirted shamelessly with me. There was no way I was going to deny his invitation for more. That was even before he beefed up.

Nate had gone from Henry Cavill in The Tudors to Henry Cavill as Superman. It left me wondering if that change in him was what set me on edge.

Bravely, I turned to face him, hating that my nipples puckered underneath my bra as his steely blue gaze trailed over my body like a panther assessing its prey. A minute longer and I'd allow him to take me any way he wanted.

"Why are you really here?" I asked, my voice catching midway through.

Nate stepped farther into the room, and I noticed just beyond him that he shut the bedroom door. He trailed a finger across an antique console table Autumn refurbished for the room as he continued to walk closer to me. I wanted to step back, increase the space between us, but the chair blocked my retreat.

"There's a shed out back. I don't recall Andrew or Autumn mentioning it, but I wondered if I could use it to work on my project."

His response surprised me. I expected him to ask why I came off so brash toward him, not about the old shed on the property.

"Um... I don't think it'd be a problem. Autumn is going to call me when she lands in Iceland, but I'm sure it will be fine."

"Thanks. It'll be temporary until I can find a plot of land here to build on."

That caught my attention. I knew his stay in Ashfield wasn't temporary, but I didn't expect him to buy land and build his own home.

Cocking my head, I crossed my arms, which lifted my breasts and brought his attention to my pebbled nipples. I was trying my damnedest not to let it bother me, because clearly he had seen them before and paid extra close attention to them, even if he didn't remember. But I still wasn't an exhibitionist.

"What do you plan to build here, Mr. Sullivan?"

I'd swear I heard a groan echo in the room as Nate's eyes darkened, then closed. "I like the way you said that."

"Said what?" I asked, and he opened his eyes again, pinning me with their stare.

"My name."

It took everything in me not to moan and dissolve into a puddle of goo at his feet. The change in his voice reminded me of the soft feel of leather. There was a darkness and heaviness to the tone, but it washed over me like a caress. It was the most erotic thing I ever experienced, and all he did was say two words.

"Are you okay?" he questioned, his voice returning to its normal tone.

Had I imagined it all? Was a memory of our one-night stand messing with the present?

"Yes," I croaked. "I'm fine." Needing to distract myself, I yanked my glasses off my head and tossed them on top of the laptop, then moved toward the small settee underneath the large picture window overlooking the backyard. It was my favorite place to sit and watch the sun setting behind the Smoky Mountains.

"So, Mr. Sullivan," I began, tossing an arm over the back of the sofa and crossing my legs, "I'll ask again. What do you plan to build here?"

"Well, a home, for starters. I want the perfect place to raise my girls, and I always felt Ashfield would be the perfect place."

"That sounds nice."

"I also need to build a workshop of sorts to work on a project for Sullivan, Inc."

Now this is what I wanted to know. His real reason for coming here. The perfect little family bit didn't fool me. Developers were trying left and right to snatch up a piece of land to develop their businesses here. First, it would be this workshop, and then, before we knew it, some big-box manufacturing plant would stroll in and buy up all the farmland. It happened to towns all around Ashfield and rural Tennessee.

"Tell me more," I said sternly, uncrossing my legs and resting both elbows on my knees.

Nate took it upon himself to sit in the armchair across from me and mimic my stance, except he seemed far more confident than I felt.

"I'm a robotic engineer, specifically focusing on agriculture. I'm working to develop an AI-based device that can read soil, pH, ground temperature, and other variables to determine and assist in increasing crop growth. I have the technology in place, though my team is still working on the coding. Which is why I need the land for testing."

Damn, his idea was intriguing, and I could clearly see the use of such a device.

"Interesting."

"It is. I believe this is the next step in farming without removing the farmer all together. They know their land the best, but this will be a way to help them make the most of it."

The way he spoke, I could feel his passion for this project coming off him in waves. His whole body grew more animated as he indulged me.

"You're really passionate about this, aren't you?"

"I am. Ever since I came to work on your father's farm with Andrew all those years ago, I knew this was something I wanted to do. Creating the robot took years, and now the technology has caught up for the rest."

"Explain to me the AI part."

"It's not sentient like you're probably thinking. It's more able to compile a bunch of data on various items, whichever the farmer deems necessary, and provide the proper feedback. It's a tool that will still require human input to start."

"What makes it different from some others that are popping up? I'm pretty sure Andrew was telling my dad about a few companies launching AI robotics."

"You know the self-propelled vacuums and lawn tractors? It will work like that, able to scope a piece of land completely unassisted."

"Hmm," I replied.

Nate lifted one hand and rubbed his index finger across his bottom lip as he sat back in the chair. "I was hoping your dad might have some land I could purchase. I know he has the largest property in Ashfield."

That comment had my spine straightening. It was common knowledge my parents owned the largest farm in town, but it wasn't well-known that they owned the majority of the open land from the edge of town toward our home. It was their way of preserving the town that once belonged to my ancestors. There were plots my dad set aside for each of us in our names to claim when we were ready.

"You seem angry about that." Nate's too-good-looking face pinched.

"I just don't like strangers trying to buy our land. My dad works hard to maintain all of it."

"I know, but I'm also not a stranger. And I'd pay far more than what it's worth."

"What is it with you billionaires tossing around your stacks of money like it's nothing more than pocket change? First, Colton, and now you," I said, my voice rising with each syllable. "You all want to come in here and change everything. Did you think that maybe we like things the way they are?"

I stood and began pacing in front of the sofa, wearing a line in the soft rug beneath my feet.

"Woah, woah, woah," Nate responded, standing and gripping my shoulders to halt my marching. "You've got this all wrong. I want to live here, Alex. I want my girls to grow up the same way you did. And if your father isn't able to sell me any land, then I'll look elsewhere. It's not a big deal."

I shrugged out of his hold and wrapped my arms around my waist.

"And to your other comment, I'm not throwing around money. I'm investing in my daughters' future. Think of it that way."

Damn, why'd he have to be gorgeous and intelligent?

Nate stared at me, his arms hanging limply at his sides as his eyes held mine. "You don't like me very much, do you?"

Swallowing against the lump in my throat, I replied, "I like you just fine."

"Could have fooled me."

Like a petulant teen, I rolled my eyes and moved back toward the door of the bedroom, then opened it wide, silently gesturing for him to leave. "If you want to use the shed out back, it should be fine."

"Alex," he said, pleading with me.

"I'll make sure breakfast is served by nine tomorrow morning."

Nate licked his full lips and then blew out a deep breath, then left the room wordlessly and without a backward glance. I watched as he bypassed the door to his room and made a left toward the stairs, descending to the first floor. It was still too early in the evening for either of us to go to sleep, but I was going to have to steer clear of the kitchen tonight.

The moment the stairs creaked beneath his feet, I closed my bedroom door and dove for my phone. At first, I thought about calling Tami, but I never knew when she was sleeping or up in the air. As a flight attendant, her schedule was always changing. I only had one sister who knew about my one-night stand a year ago, so I pulled up Autumn's name. I wasn't sure if she arrived in Iceland yet, but I was praying to every god imaginable that her plane landed.

"Pick up. Pick up. Pick up," I mumbled as I sat on the edge of the bed and listened to the phone ring.

"Alex?"

"Oh, thank God!" I cried out as Autumn's familiar voice answered on the other end.

"Is everything all right? We just landed."

"Everything is fine, sort of. I mean, yes, nothing has gone wrong, but I really need to talk to you."

"Sure. Colton and I are heading toward the luggage carousel, so I have a few minutes."

"It's him, Autumn."

"Who is him?"

"Nate! Well, Nathaniel. Do you remember last year, when you came by the bar while I was doing inventory, and I told you about the guy I had over the night before? He was divorced with kids?"

"Vaguely." Of course, Autumn was in the midst of her own turmoil with Colton when she stopped by to see me that day. I wasn't surprised she didn't recall the conversation.

"Well, that's him, Autumn. The guy staying here is the same guy from that night."

"Oh. Ohhh! So, Andrew's best friend is the same guy you slept with?"

"Yes. Of course, I didn't know that at the time."

"Maybe we keep that to ourselves."

Considering Andrew's temper, I agreed with my sister. "That's not even the worst part."

"There's something worse than sleeping with Andrew's best friend, who our parents consider like another child?"

"Yes! Autumn, he doesn't even remember."

"What? How can that be?"

"Apparently, he was more drunk than he let on. When I answered the door today, I knew immediately who he was, but he had no clue who I was. What the hell am I going to do, Autumn?"

"How do you know he doesn't remember?"

"With the things that man and I did in my apartment that night, there'd be no way he could keep up a façade of not remembering me for a whole day, much less not even let a glimmer of recollection show through on his face. Trust me, it would've been impossible for him to forget… if he were sober."

My sister giggled into her phone.

"Autumn, be serious. What am I going to do? I'm here with him for three weeks until you get back."

"You could just talk to him and tell him."

"Ha! That would be one of the most awkward conversations I've ever had."

"I mean, he deserves to know, but if you're uncomfortable staying there, I can ask Rory to do it instead. She only has a few more days before school lets out."

I blew out a puff of air, then explained I couldn't ask my younger sister to do that.

"Hey, my luggage is here, so I need to go. But you need to tell him before it's too late, Alex. You're going to regret it if you don't."

"Yeah, I know. Ugh, I hate when you're right."

"Well, I am older and wiser."

"Whatever. Enjoy your honeymoon."

I hung up with Autumn and fell back on the bed, my gaze trained on the ceiling. How would he react when I told him? Would he believe me or question my motives?

"Shit," I mumbled as I threw my arms out on either side of my body. I gave myself a few minutes to contemplate my next move but came up empty. I knew I needed to tell Nate we had indeed met before, but I was terrified of his reaction. Seeing a look of disappointment in his eyes wasn't something I thought I could handle.

Rejection was something I was all too familiar with. The pit of my stomach grew sour. It seemed no matter how many years passed, the damage my ex had done to my psyche lingered, holding me hostage in my mind.

It wasn't anywhere near a decent time to go to sleep, not that I would've been able to anyway, so I opted to heft myself back over to the chair I'd been lounging in before Nate stopped by. Flipping open my laptop, I continued reading over the business proposal information I'd been exploring.

With only one more class to finish to earn my business degree, I was one step closer to opening the cake shop I always dreamed of. I'd worry about how that would affect my sister's endeavor with the bed-and-breakfast at a later time.

There was a piece of real estate on the edge of town that would be perfect for the cake shop I wanted to open, but it would require a top-notch business proposal to get a loan. I knew that if I divulged my plan to my parents, they would happily assist me in getting the money I'd need, but I didn't want to do that. My dad was already looking toward retirement. Hell, he was well past that time. My lofty goals wouldn't derail him from that.

Collectively, we all monetarily assisted my sister to start up the Easterly Event Venue on my parents' property. We were lucky the project was already flourishing, and our investments were returned three-fold. I wasn't as ambitious as Autumn, who had a career in event planning and whose talents were well-sought by clients. I was just someone with a knack for culinary delights, and I felt they were being wasted by focusing on meal prep.

Moving away from the proposal drivel, I began working on one of my finance assignments. The darkness grew in the room, and by the time I pulled my eye away from the online lecture, the clock was nearing 10:00 p.m. I was going to have to get up early to prepare breakfast, since I was aware Nate and his daughters were going to join my family for dinner. It was not something I was looking forward to.

Deciding it was probably a good time to catch some rest, I set my work on the small coffee table and changed from my loungewear into my favorite oversized T-shirt I typically wore to bed. It was a man's shirt, and it hung mid thigh. I had it since high school, and the fabric had worn away in some spots, but now it was so soft I couldn't bear parting with it. Slipping my bra off my shoulders, I tugged the shirt over my head and walked toward the mini fridge in the corner to grab a bottle of water. Except the shelves inside were empty.

"Dang it." I was going to have to slip downstairs and restock the fridge with water.

I slowly twisted the knob for my door, doing my best to hide the clunky sound of the metal moving. A breath whooshed out when I saw the coast was clear. Creeping down the hall and then the stairs, I made my way toward the kitchen, thankful all the rooms were dark.

I went ahead and filled up a glass of water from the tap while I was by the sink, gently placing the glass in the dishwasher when I was finished chugging. Continuing to the butler's pantry, I grabbed several bottles of water—six to be exact—and juggled them in my arms as I turned to leave the confined space. With my elbow, I clicked off the kitchen light, thankful for the small lamp that illuminated the hallway. Despite the renovations being new, the house was more than a century old and freaked me out in the dark.

Turning the corner to head toward the front of the house, I smacked into a hard, solid body that caused all the plastic bottles in my hold to crash at my feet.

"Oomph!" I cried out as one landed on top of my foot, cutting off the scream that was about to rip from me instead.

"Shit. Are you all right?" the masculine voice asked from the shadows, and I realized it was Nate.

"Yeah, I'm fine," I mumbled as I kneeled to gather the bottles again.

He must've had the same idea, because our heads knocked together as he bent over to grab the few at his feet.

"Fuck!" we cried out in unison. The bottles in my hands fell to the floor again as I stayed kneeling and rubbed my forehead, which now ached from the collision.

"Sorry about that."

I glanced up to find Nate running his fingers back and forth over the spot on his forehead mine struck.

He was shirtless, with dark hair smattered across his chest.

God, his chest. I had visions of it dancing behind my eyes for months. During the night we spent together, I became very well acquainted with the ridges of his body.

As Nate stood, I came face-to-face with my favorite part of him. Clad in a pair of gray basketball shorts, his impressive cock was hugged by the jersey material. While his chest was a memory I couldn't shake free, his cock was something I added to my female spank bank.

"Can I hand these to you?" he asked as I continued to kneel in front of him.

"Uh, yes," I replied, fumbling with both my words and the three bottles of water in my hands. I gripped them against my body, and Nate stacked the bottles he retrieved on top of them. I hoped the dim light of the hallway didn't illuminate the fact that my nipples were standing at attention. One of his fingers brushed against me through the soft fabric of my shirt as he slipped his hand away from the plastic.

There was nothing I could do to stop the gasp that escaped my lips or the sudden pool of moisture between my legs. Avoiding his eyes, I thanked him for the help.

"I didn't mean to startle you. When I heard the door shut, I wanted to make sure it wasn't one of my girls."

"It's all right. Clearly, I wasn't paying attention, and juggling has never been my strong suit." I giggled, and Nate joined me.

"Do you, uh… want me to help you carry those to your room?"

Hurriedly, I said, "No. No, I can do it."

"Are you sure?"

"Yeah," I replied with a sassy roll of my eyes. If he had any idea how many bottles I usually carried from storage to the bar area on the weekends, he'd laugh at his own question.

"All right, well, I'll leave you to it."

I step around him and make my way toward the stairs, only to peer at him over my shoulder. He turned his body to watch me go, and his eyes were trained on my ass.

Smirking, I asked if he needed anything while I was "downstairs." My lady bits thought I was referring to a repeat performance from last year and practically purred in anticipation. Unfortunately, I simply meant if he needed any food.

"No, thanks. I'm okay."

Nodding, I began to ascend the stairs, then stopped once again and stared at him from over the railing. I felt a little bad for how I'd spoken to him earlier this evening when he visited my room. I'd still been miffed he didn't remember our time together. But I knew, for the next three weeks, I needed to do my best to let it all go and act like the polite host Autumn would be. And maybe when I decided to tell him about our hookup, he'd take it better than if I was being a complete bitch to him.

"Goodnight, Nathaniel."

"Goodnight, Alexandra."

Chapter Six

Nate

Sleep was elusive most of the night. Every time I shut my eyes, flashes of images that made absolutely no sense bombarded me. People I didn't recognize, because their faces were nothing more than a blur, and places that continued to glitch. I chalked it up to the fact that I called Alex "Alexandra." I knew based on staying with her family for so long that it was her full first name, but I never called her that, nor had she asked me to use that version. But in the visions that haunted me, the name Alexandra kept echoing in my head.

    I'd almost given up on catching some shut-eye by the time my bedroom illuminated with the morning sun, but somehow the images stopped around that time, and I was able to fall asleep. I was hopeful for a few hours, because my daughters woke up notoriously early.

The sound of clanging startled me, and I woke with a jolt, tossing the pillow off my face. Groaning, I thought back to the amazing dream I'd been having, centered on Alex's nipples that peeked through her shirt last night. The thing had been so threadbare I could make out the puckered tips and outline of her areola. It was one of the sexiest things I'd ever seen, especially because it hadn't been on purpose.

Glancing down, I noticed my cock tented the sheets, painfully erect from imagining all the things I wanted to do to her nipples.

"Fuck, get your head on straight," I uttered to myself as I pushed away the covers and sat up in bed.

After a horrific cold shower, I tugged on a pair of shorts and a T-shirt before leaving my room. My daughters weren't in their rooms, so I went to investigate the rest of the place. Fear was in the forefront of my mind, but I tried my best to push it aside. The girls were smart enough to know better than to leave the house without me. I never had to worry about them in the past.

The last stair creaked as I stepped on the board, and that was when I noticed the soft hum of music off in the distance. Following the noise, I made my way toward the kitchen, not expecting what greeted my eyes. Alex stood at the range wearing a pair of jean shorts that frayed just beneath the curves of her ass. She tied a loose-fitting black tank top at the back and tucked into itself.

It mesmerized me as she swung her hips from side to side with the beat of the music, plating whatever it was she'd been cooking.

"All right, Molly. It's your turn. Load me up."

Fascinated, I watched as Molly held a large measuring cup with a ladle, then proceeded to pour and swirl whatever the mixture was into a pan.

"Great job!" Alex enthusiastically encouraged her. "Before long, you and Eloise will be breakfast connoisseurs."

From Alex's other side, Eloise tugged gently on the hem of her black tank. "What is a conn... connconsewer?"

Deciding now was a good time to make my presence known, I chimed in, "Connoisseur. I believe it's someone who is an expert."

"Daddy!" both girls shouted as they rushed toward me. Eloise reached me first while Molly carefully stepped down from the small stool and set the measuring cup aside. Collectively, they gripped my legs in their tiny arms to greet me.

"Morning, girls," I said as I ran my hands over their soft hair. With a quick glance up, I caught Alex's eyes, but she quickly diverted them back to the stove. Yet not before I caught the rosy blush of her cheeks. "How did you both sleep?"

"Good," Eloise said. "I had no bad dreams."

"Like I was on a cloud," Molly added for good measure.

"Wow. Well, we'll have to find out where to buy the same mattress, so we can have them for you at our new house."

The girls squealed and jumped around me the same way they did when the ice cream truck was coming down the street in our old neighborhood. As they moved around like little bunnies, I slowly approached Alex, then rested my hip on the counter beside her.

"Morning," I said cautiously.

"Good morning." Without the assistance of one of my daughters, Alex plated something that resembled an extra-flat pancake, then poured and spooned out the batter for another batch.

"What are you making?"

"Crepes, Daddy!" Molly shouted, pulling my eyes away from Alex. I could hear the softest of chuckles from her direction.

"Wow. I bet they're the best crepes if you helped make them."

"Girls, I'm almost done, so if you want to grab all the extras we put in the fridge, we can set the table."

With no pushback, both girls opened the fridge and collected multiple bowls before carrying them to the small breakfast table in the kitchen. This was far less formal than the dining room, but more intimate as well.

As I took my seat, designated by Eloise, I tried to focus on the array of fruits and proteins filling the tabletop.

"I told the girls they could eat these sort of like breakfast tacos." As Alex carried the heaping stack of crepes, I noticed the only available seat at the table was beside me. By the side-eye Molly and Eloise were giving each other, it seemed they planned it that way. Schemed by four-year-olds.

Ignoring their matching smirks, I took everything in as our host scooted her chair under the table.

"This looks amazing, Alex. You didn't have to go through all this trouble."

"It was no trouble at all. The girls woke up right after me, and they were hungry. I already needed to make y'all something to eat, so I asked if they wanted to help me."

"Daddy, it was so much fun. We got to do the indgr... ingra—"

Chiming in when it seemed Molly was struggling to remember the correct word, I said, "Ingredients?"

"Yes. Ingredimients. And Eloise got to use the spinny thing."

The thought of my youngest handling a type of power tool was enough to send my body into shock. Air caught in my lungs, and I subconsciously gripped the fork beneath my hand. My vision blurred as immediate thoughts of my daughter injuring herself assaulted me.

"The hand mixer. She did so great with it. A complete natural." Alex's delicate hand rested on top of mine. Like a gentle ripple in a pond, her touch pushed away all the uneasiness and fear I felt. "I watched them the entire time. I was just a bit younger than them when I started helping my mom in the kitchen."

"It was really fun, Daddy," Eloise added as she reached across the table to begin filling her crepe with hazelnut spread and fruit.

"That's... um... great," I replied as Alex pulled her hand away. I immediately missed her touch.

Leaning closer to her, I tried to not let the intoxicating smell of flowers that seemed to permeate the air around her distract me. "Next time, can you please let me know ahead of time if they're going to be around a hot stove or using electric tools?"

Alex's eyes grew as wide as saucers, and she leaned about an inch or two away from me at the notion that I didn't approve of them helping her cook.

"I'm sorry," she said, her hand pressed to her chest. "I had no idea it was going to be a problem. They asked me if I could help them make you breakfast."

"I know, but I just.... I need to wrap my head around them doing that sort of stuff. I can't let them get hurt." I didn't want to explain to Alex that I had a hard time trusting anyone with my girls. It was why I went through nannies like yesterday's newspaper. Either someone didn't follow my rules, or they did something careless, and one of the girls got hurt. The latter only happened once at a trampoline park, which resulted in a sprained ankle for Molly the year before she came to live with me.

Alex nodded but seemed to retreat into herself. She was quiet the rest of the meal and only ate two of the crepes she spent so much time making with my girls. Maybe I'd been a little too hard on her. The twins were growing up, and they needed to learn new things. Plus, I knew Alex had years of culinary experience. So, if anyone should teach them to cook, it should be her. I just wasn't ready to let her into their lives when it was only temporary. After three weeks, Autumn would be back to run the B&B, and the girls would only see Alex on occasion.

My hand immediately rose to my chest as an ache spread within the cavity.

Alex peered over in my direction, her brows rising in concern as Eloise asked if I was okay.

"I'm fine. Just swallowed a bite that was too big."

Alex rolled her eyes as she went back to eating her crepe. It was clear she didn't believe a word I said, but she wasn't going to press for more.

Beneath the table, I extended my legs, brushing against hers in the process. My cock instantly thickened at the touch, and Alex's breath hitched, letting me know she wasn't unaffected either. There was definitely some chemistry between us, elemental, but she was the type I needed to stay away from. I experimented with enough periodic elements in my time to know that some were safe and controlled, and some explode with contact. I wasn't a chemist by any means, but I knew Alex was my antimony. She was my best friend's younger sister, after all.

She jumped from her chair as if it were on fire, grabbing her plate in the process as she stood. "Can I take anyone else's plate?"

"Nuh uh, I'm going to eat so much my belly explodes," Molly claimed as she filled another crepe with bacon and eggs. Eloise usually picked at her food, so I was happy to see her going after her third.

"We're okay," I said to Alex as I reached forward to make myself another helping. I didn't want her to know it disappointed me she was leaving the table. But I think the three of us instantly felt the difference. Conversation halted, and the only sounds were the girls chewing and the sink running in the kitchen.

When we all filled ourselves on the breakfast that tasted far more like a dessert, I asked the girls to carry the leftover fruit back to the fridge while I piled up the empty bowls that held the eggs and bacon.

By the time I made my way over to the sink, I overheard the twins telling Alex they had to finish unpacking their things and that they were excited to go to dinner at Grandma Marisol's house. Something the girls always called her on the phone with Andrew.

"Will you be there tonight?" I asked Alex, startling her.

"Um, yes."

"Cool, maybe we can all ride together?" I tried to keep the conversation light, but my heart pounded as I thought about her sitting next to me on the short drive over to her parents' house. The girls begged and pleaded until Alex caved.

"I have a few things I need to do around here, and I usually get there early to help Mom cook."

"That's fine."

Bored, the girls scurried away to play with the dollhouse in Eloise's room while I helped Alex load the dishes into the dishwasher. This time, she took my help without argument.

"You're worked up today," I said as she rinsed the mixing bowl.

"No, I'm not."

"I can hear your heart thumping over here."

Not so gently, she dropped the bowl onto the rack and then turned to face me. Her brows were pinched, and she chewed on that plump lower lip that I desperately wanted to taste. I really needed to get my attraction to her handled before I did something I'd regret, ruining a friendship along the way.

"Look, I need to talk to you about something."

Ah, it seemed we were on the same page.

My hand rubbed the damp skin at the back of my neck. "Okay," I replied, hoping she'd take the leap and confess we couldn't act on our magnetism.

"So, like a year ago…," she began, only for screams to echo through the house, interrupting her.

"Shit. We'll talk later, okay?"

Rushing away from a confused Alex, I ran upstairs to find the girls fighting over a bed in the dollhouse. It took a while to remedy the situation, and by the time I made it back down to the kitchen, Alex was long gone. So gone, in fact, she was nowhere in the house. I knocked on her bedroom door, but there was no answer, so either she was avoiding me, or she left the property.

I was hopeful she'd be back soon so we could nip this lustful bud before it was too late.

Hours passed while I helped the girls empty their suitcases into the dressers. The travel storage unit arrived, and I helped them navigate it behind the home and into the spot Autumn designated for me. She'd used orange spray paint to mark the area.

I wanted to spend more time in the workshop, but with no one to monitor the girls, I only got a couple of minutes in there as the girls touched every power tool in sight. I could only overpower my fear for so long before it crashed over me, and I took them back to the house.

Luckily, they were more than content to lose themselves in an ice princess movie, so I could catch a quick shower before dinner.

I wasn't sure what time the Easterlys expected our arrival, especially if we were accompanying Alex. So, I sent a message to Andrew to find out. By the time I stepped out of the bathroom, the message remained unread. If there was one thing I despised about my friend, it was that he was terrible about checking his messages unless he sent the initial one. Like when to meet at a bar or to pick him up from the airport. If it didn't serve a purpose for him, he never checked the messaging app.

Just as I tugged on a pair of khaki shorts, the sound of the front door closing reverberated. I realized it was most likely Alex arriving back at the B&B, but the irrational side of me feared it was one of my daughters leaving through the front door.

Shorts still unbuttoned, I rushed barefoot out of the room and down the stairs, only to collide with Alex as I reached the bottom. My arms reached out to steady her as her hand pressed against my chest.

"Shit," I said as I spun past her to open the front door, looking around anxiously for signs of one of my daughters. Molly would be the one most likely to escape, as she enjoyed testing her boundaries with me.

"Are you okay?" Alex asked from behind me as I worked to steady my breath.

"Yes. Er… was that you coming in the door?"

"Yeah, I…. Do you need to sit down?"

I suddenly felt lightheaded and took her advice to sit down on the steps of the front porch. Then she guided me through some deep breaths.

"I thought it was one of the girls. I mean, I knew it wasn't. They're probably still upstairs watching the movie, but my mind immediately went to the worst-case scenario."

"I'm sorry. I should have called out a greeting or something when I came in. I'm not used to living with other people." Her apology was heartfelt, and when I turned my eyes to her, I could make out the remorse in her gaze.

"It's not your fault. This parenting thing isn't for the weary, that's for sure."

I took her in as we sat next to each other. She wore a pale-yellow sundress with straps that tied at the top of her shoulders. Every ounce of me wanted to untie those strings and uncover the prize beneath. But I knew better.

"Do you ever wear a shirt?" she asked, and it took me a moment to remember I'd only pulled on a pair of shorts before stumbling my way downstairs.

Smirking at the way she stared at my chest with longing, I replied, "Only when it's required."

"Hmm...."

"Earlier today, you wanted to talk to me about something. What's on your mind?"

Alarm registered as her eyes grew, back growing stiff, until she launched up from the stairs. I did my best not to notice the soft-looking white panties she wore beneath her dress as I reached for her arm, but I was too weak and failed.

"Alex," I implored as I tugged at her wrist to sit back down beside me.

It was a warm day in the valley, but nothing compared to the heat that sparked between the two of us. As she sat, I rubbed small circles on her wrist with my thumb, feeling the increase of her pulse with every stroke.

Her eyes were trained to where I held her, and she licked her lips before asking me to refrain from touching her. "I can't think when you're doing that."

"I'm sorry. I didn't mean to make you uncomfortable."

"It's not that. I just… ugh. I'm just going to come out and say it."

"Okay," I replied as I reluctantly pulled my hand away.

"We met about a year ago."

Huh. Well, that could explain why she seemed so familiar, but…

"I don't remember meeting you before."

"I'm not surprised. Apparently, you were quite drunk."

"The last time I was drunk was when I learned about—"

"Your daughters. Yes, I know. You stayed the night with me."

The way sparks flew between us, I already knew there was more than she was letting on, but my curiosity got the better of me anyway. "And we…?"

"Multiple times."

Fuck. I had sex with this gorgeous woman and remembered none of it. After that night in Ashfield, I swore I'd never let myself get as wasted as I had that night ever again. I was embarrassed enough that I'd woken up in a strange place, but I saw no evidence of sex. I rushed out of the place so fast I didn't even look around for pictures or a number.

"Alex, I don't remember anything. What…? How…?"

"It's fine. We flirted. You propositioned, and I accepted. Simple as that. Early in the morning, I went down to the bar to make sure everything was closed up. When I came back, you were gone."

I propped my arms on my knees and tilted my head down. There were a lot of things in my life I'd rather forget. The wrath of my parents when I performed poorly on an exam. The years the jocks fucked with me in high school, because I was a skinny nerd. My marriage to Sasha.

But a night of passionate sex with Alex was not one of them.

And by the way her entire body flushed at her confession, I could sense that our night had been one for the record books.

An apology hovered at my lips, but I couldn't force it free. What exactly could I say? Sorry that I don't remember? Sorry that we had a one-night stand? Sorry that I was an asshole and left in the middle of the night when I had some sort of bearing about me?

Then the fear of all fears came to me and trumped them all. This beautiful woman beside me was my best friend's little sister. She was as off-limits as any girl came.

A few expletives burst from my mouth as I jolted off the stairs and began pacing in front of the porch. My heart was pounding in my chest.

Is this what a heart attack feels like? I asked myself when I leaned over and pressed my palm against my sternum as I tried to free myself from the stifling grip of the enclosing darkness.

"Oh my God. Shit. Fuck," I continued to mumble as I made every attempt to catch my breath.

Hunching over was doing no good, and I found myself falling farther over the edge as I contemplated what Andrew would say if he found out. With zero finesse, I straightened up and tilted my face toward the punishing sun, hoping it would melt me into oblivion.

No such luck.

Instead, my eyes and skin burned beneath the afternoon rays.

"Nate?" a soft voice called out from around me, and I latched onto it like a lifeline. Blindly, I sought out my salvation until I came in contact with a smooth yet firm arm.

"Nate, are you okay?" Alex asked again, her concern wrapping itself around me like a life vest, saving me from myself.

"He's going to fucking kill me." I didn't need to look at her to realize the implications of our actions would be catastrophic. The arm in my grasp flexed, and Alex's entire body jerked in alarm as my words sank in. And, of course, my body betrayed me when it realized she was so close. Those traitorous fingers of mine inched off her bicep to rub against the side of her breast beneath the sundress she'd teased me with earlier.

Suddenly, all my anger and frustration dissipated as I felt her body hitch at my sensual contact. She turned to face me with those captivating blue eyes that held more questions than I had answers.

"We can't tell him," I explained. My voice sounded foreign to my ears. It was replaced with a gravelly dominance that was usually reserved for the bedroom. Leave it to this beautiful mistake to have me worked up after a complete meltdown a few minutes before.

With the subtlest tilt of the corner of her mouth, Alex replied, "My lips are sealed."

And hell if I didn't imagine those lips sealed around a certain snake between my legs.

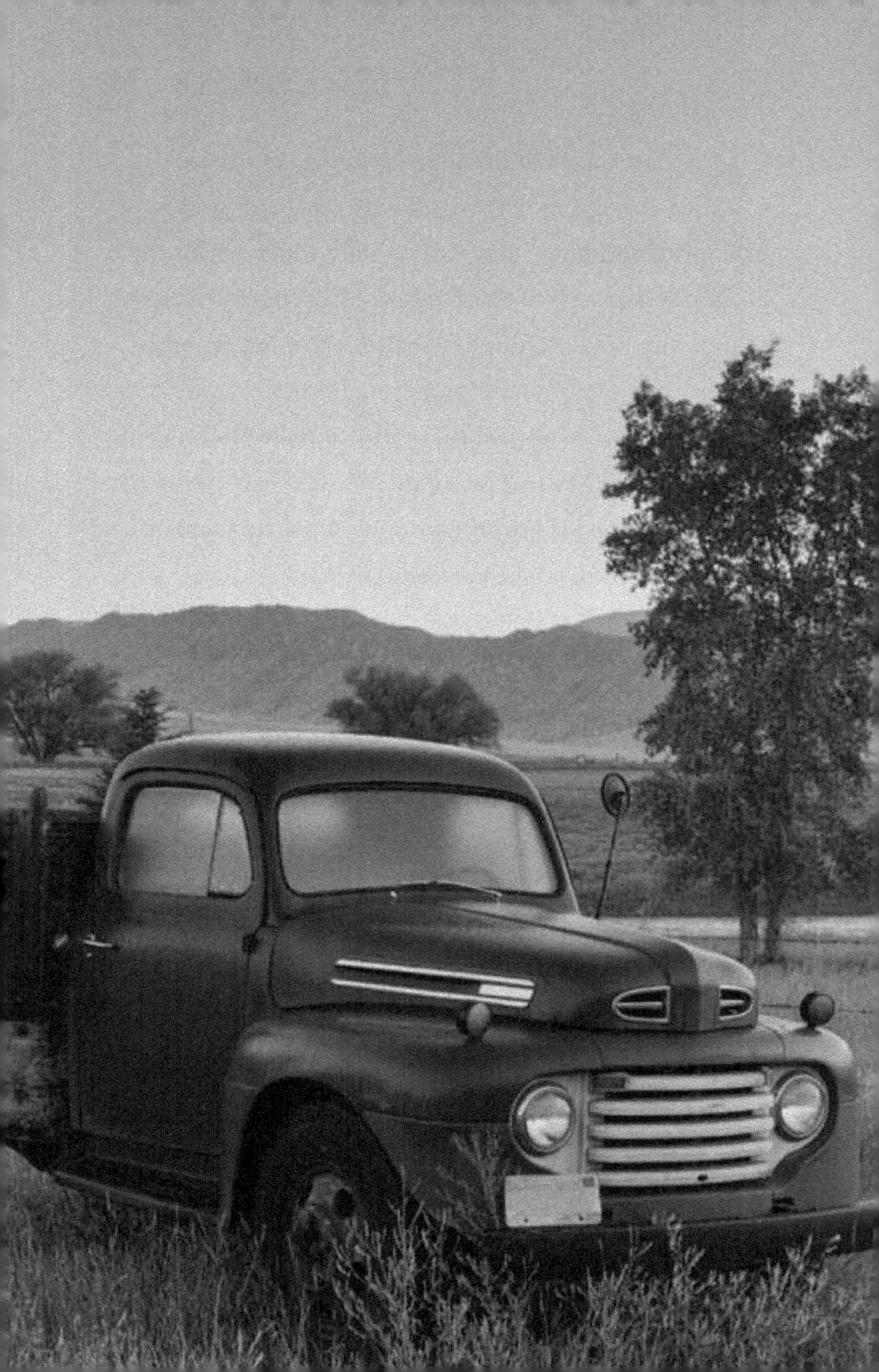

Chapter Seven

Alex

Dinner at my parents' house was… something. It was a mix of awkwardness, excitement, and lust. A whole lot of lust, and not just on my end.

When we arrived, my parents, as expected, engulfed Nate and his girls in hugs that I was honestly a bit jealous of. There were tears from my mother as she took in the sweet faces of Eloise and Molly, two little girls she had never met in person but had instantly fallen in love with. Seemed the apple didn't fall too far from the tree, because I was falling just as fast for those girls in the course of two days as my mother did in two minutes.

It was hard not to when they looked up with those big brown eyes and begged to sit next to me at Mom's table. This offered me the chance to steal the seat Autumn usually occupied, and Colton's was obviously empty next to it. My other sisters shifted down one place to give the twins a seat on either side of me. I was thrilled I wouldn't find myself nestled next to Nate, but my joy was short-lived. As Andrew shifted closer to my dad, that opened the chair directly across from me.

I spent the remainder of the meal trying my hardest to keep my attention centered on my newly acquired guests seated at my hips or on my mother, who was chatting with my sister Rory who was talking about her first full year as a teacher. But no matter how hard I tried, my eyes always flickered to the man across from me, who seemed to struggle equally to keep his gaze trained on his plate. By the time the dessert was brought out—an apple pie I later had no recollection of eating—I'd given up, and my stare had solidly landed on the gorgeous man across from me.

It reminded me of the staring contests we'd have in elementary school, where there never really seemed to be a winner. Instead of my eyes burning, it was my skin. I felt every inch of the way his eyes roamed over me, and my body was on fire. Ugh, why did he have to be so damned good-looking that I couldn't turn away? Luckily, no one else at the table seemed to notice the unannounced game we were playing.

Or so I thought.

The way I constantly wiggled in my chair under his gaze left the twins beside me giggling that I had to use the restroom. Nate chuckled every time, and I hated that I loved his laugh. His deep timbre had my cotton panties soaked by the time the guys collected our plates.

As Mom and Dad collected the twins to take them around the farm after everything had been cleared, I dashed toward the bathroom and did the best I could to clean myself up. I'd consider getting myself off, because something had to be done, but that plan was diminished the moment I heard Andrew knocking on the door.

He asked if I was okay, since I ran to the bathroom so fast. I fibbed and told him that I was having stomach issues. Cringing at my lie, I opened the door, surprised to find not only Andrew but Nate as well. My brother's face was pinched, as if he expected something gross to follow his little sister out of the enclosed space. Fortunately for him, the bathroom still smelled of the floral pot-pourri my mom kept in a basket on the vanity. I was pretty sure it was the same kind of pot-pourri she'd been stocking in that room for decades, just newly refreshed.

While Andrew continued to look like he landed in a pile of manure, Nate smiled, clearly aware of my lie. I was so embarrassed to see him standing there that I immediately ducked past them, my cheeks burning as I went. They were so blistered that it felt like I sat in front of a fire for too long.

Wordlessly, I ducked out of the house and snagged the closest UTV that would carry me back to the bed-and-breakfast. Key dangling in the ignition, I tossed my leg over the seat and tucked my dress under my thighs. Not that it mattered, because no one would be along the back pathway, but I had some deeply ingrained modesty taught by my mother.

Faster than a downed tequila shot by a college student, I darted across the east field toward the well-worn path usually covered under the shade of corn stalks. This year, Dad was allowing the soil to settle by planting soybeans. He rotated the fields every few years so the earth wouldn't tire.

Twenty minutes later, I was back in my room at the B&B, freshly showered, with my favorite remote-controlled boyfriend in my hand, knowing it was going to be a poor substitute for what my girlie bits really wanted. Closing my eyes, I transported myself back to my apartment, where Nathaniel laid me across my kitchen table and had his own personal feast. The man said he was hungry, after all. And I'd let him eat as much as he wanted, because who was I to deny a starving man?

I came crying out his name and praying he was still hanging around my parents' house to catch up, because I was pretty certain anyone in a couple mile radius could've heard Nate's name from my lips.

***

Three nights later

Even though it was Wednesday night, all the adults in town seemed to pour through the doors of Ole Days. I sat in the far corner of the bar, hidden in the shadows, watching them all.

Most people assumed I'd never want to drink at the place I worked, but I secretly loved it. The dark-stained wooden walls, the overly epoxied bar top, the sticky floor. Even the faint stale smell of cigarettes and beer were a comfort to me. Smoking in the bar was banned at least two decades prior, but the scent continued to linger.

Were there better places in town to go for a drink? Sure. But none of them had this old saloon atmosphere you'd find in a movie from the 1970s.

Off in the back room, I watched a few guys play darts and pool. I recognized a few of them, but the others definitely weren't locals. It wasn't just their polo shirts, pressed shorts, and slip-on boat shoes that gave it away. It was the fact that Larry, Mo, and Curly didn't offer them a greeting. Those weren't their names, of course. I just bestowed them on our regulars when I first started working here. The trio loved a good joke and constantly made me laugh whenever I needed to fill in behind the bar. They frequented the establishment so often they had their own seats, and everyone in town knew it.

Giggling to myself, I realized maybe we should change the name of the bar to Cheers, remembering how the show had a steady set of bar patrons with their own seats. I might've only been twenty-four, but I loved 1990s sitcoms and kid's shows for as long as I could remember. My friends were watching shows like Victorious and Hannah Montana while I was at home watching Full House and Family Matters. I would've loved growing up during the TGIF days. Alas, I was born a decade late for that.

Sighing, I tilted my empty glass toward Rachel, the bartender working tonight, silently requesting a refill. After her quick nod, I turned my attention back to one of the televisions across the way. The bar didn't play sports or news; they focused on classic movies. Something to have playing in the background but didn't pull the full attention from the patrons. Currently, an old western flashed on the screen. I inwardly sighed as the lead appeared. I always did love Clint Eastwood.

With a new mojito in hand, I lost myself in the movie of a man seeking revenge, ignoring the people milling around me. It wasn't until I was sipping the remains of my second drink that I felt the air around me shift. My heart began pounding, and the hair on my arms stood on end the way it did when you touched one of those small tesla coils. My body instantly went into flight-or-fight mode, yet my brain wasn't prepared for either.

As if conjured from the depths of hell, my ex, Stephen, strolled through the doors of the bar, looking like the pompous jackass he was. I quickly tucked my body against the wall, my hair a thin veil covering most of my face as I watched him stroll through the room like he owned the place.

The instant fear I felt at his appearance gave way to a new emotion. My fingers gripped around the base of my glass, and I knew the vein that ran down the center of my forehead was pulsating.

How dare he come back to this town, to this place I worked, and act like he hadn't upended my life?

Unsurprisingly, he joined the group of guys in the back room as they continued to hoot and holler obnoxiously. The Stooge trio at the other end of the bar glanced over their shoulders at the newcomer and then immediately looked in my direction. I guess I wasn't being so inconspicuous in my hiding space as I wanted to believe.

My anger popped in brief spurts like an active volcano as I watched Stephen flirt with the lone waitress working their area, but when he smacked her ass as she walked away, I nearly jumped off my stool to put him in his place. He was saved from the embarrassment of me kicking his ass as my brother got up in his face instead.

If my brother was here, that meant….

A hand landed on my shoulder, and out of habit, I swung my arm out, ready to knock back my intruder. The years of self-defense classes always seemed to kick in.

"Woah! It's just me, Ali," Nate exclaimed, hands raised in surrender as he called me by the legendary boxer's last name.

"Sorry, reflex." I pulled my fist back and rested it on the bar while Nate's hand continued to rest on my shoulder. The heat sizzled through my sleeveless shirt, and I was certain I would be left with a handprint on my skin.

Shifting on my stool, I watched in sadness as his hand slipped away and back to his side. It was better this way, simply to face him. If we were in contact, I knew I couldn't trust myself. Nate was a temptation I had a hard time fighting against.

His jaw flexed, and I never realized how much that tiny tic could turn me on. Shifting my legs, I crossed the left over the right, exposing more of my bare thigh. The shorts I had on were already cinched high on my legs. Nate's eyes followed the movement until they found their way back to mine.

"What... er... are you doing here?" I asked, faking a casualness I didn't feel.

Ignoring me, Nate reached out and slipped his hand beneath my veil of hair, tucking it back behind my shoulder. My body quivered as his fingers gently caressed the exposed skin along the back of my arm.

"Cold?" the asshole asked, knowing full well it was stifling in this bar with the crowd. It's why I chose to wear barely anything.

Squaring my shoulders, I told him that I wasn't and waited for him to reply with something snarky as a response.

He didn't.

Nate nodded toward Rachel, who all too gleefully bounced over to take his order. She was a new employee I recently helped hire, but I immediately hated her and her perfect smile and perfectly bouncy red hair.

"Stop… doing that." My hand flailed wildly in Rachel's retreating direction.

"Doing what?" Nate asked, leaning his arms on the bar, glancing at me over his shoulder.

"Flirting with my employee."

"Is that what I was doing?" he asked as Rachel set his freshly and perfectly poured draft beer in front of him.

"Yes," I hissed, eyeing the way the veins in his forearm flexed as he nestled the glass in his grasp. God, I really did love forearms.

A low chortle sounded from his chest just as he took a sip of his beer, ignoring my jab. Half of his beer remained as he set down his glass and turned his full body in my direction. His new position blocked me from the remainder of the bar. It was as if he caged us in our own little bubble.

"Want to tell me why you had that reaction when douchebag over there walked in?"

"No... um... I mean, what reaction? What guy?" I tried to backpedal, but it was clear Nate had been paying attention to me without me knowing. Which had me wondering how long he and my brother had been in the bar. It was a bit unnerving to not have a handle on my surroundings.

"The guy who looks like he fell out of a Preps-R-Us magazine and how, when he walked in, your entire body changed." He'd been watching Stephen when he started speaking, but now Nate's narrowed eyes were trained back on me. It was hard to skirt around the truth when he looked at me like he could read my deepest and darkest secrets.

There was a sudden uneasiness that welled up inside me. A fear of disappointing Nate, and myself, if I told him about my nasty history with the preppy newcomer.

"It's nothing," I projected with a wave, hoping Nate would brush it all aside.

He leaned closer, his breath a mix of mint and beer. The combo shouldn't have worked, but everything about Nate seemed to find a way to mesh.

"I don't believe you for a second, but I'll let it slide for now. But if he causes any more trouble, I can't guarantee your brother will let him out of this bar scot-free."

In unison, we both forced our gazes apart and focused on the increasing commotion in the back room. Not only were the boys harassing each other, but they were doing it to the server and a few of the bar's patrons. If things continued, security was going to have to step in, hopefully before Andrew did. My brother was usually the quiet and brooding type, but he didn't tolerate when people acted out.

"What are you guys doing here anyway?" I asked, begging silently that Nate would allow me to change the subject as I trained my eyes on Andrew, who moved toward a booth with a couple of women I'd seen in here a few times over the years. Not local to Ashfield, but probably from a town across the county.

I felt Nate's stare return to me. It had this penetrating quality I could feel down to the tips of toes.

"When you look at me like that, I feel... unsettled," I confessed while I attempted to fan my hair forward again as a shield from his stare.

"Why is that?" Nate's fingers brushed my hair behind my ear, the tips lingering along the top just a second longer than necessary.

Words I didn't comprehend slipped from my lips in a whisper, but they made him move on regardless of what I actually said.

"Your brother wanted a beer, and your mother graciously offered to watch the girls for me. So, I joined him."

"What?" I asked, my mind reeling from the conversation whiplash.

"You asked why we were here, and it's nothing nefarious. We just wanted to grab a drink."

"Oh."

"Afraid I may be stalking you?"

Tucking my chin to my chest, I didn't want to confess that I, indeed, imagined he followed me here. More in a romantic, possessive lover way, and not that of a serial killer.

I'd been ignoring him over the last three days, since I told him about our one night together. I was afraid if we were alone, he'd ask questions I simply couldn't or didn't want to answer.

"No," I mumbled.

Nate was impossibly close as his arm brushed against mine. I no longer felt like the confident twenty-four-year-old I worked so hard at becoming. I felt more like the naïve teenager in my ballet class, listening to my teacher tear me down bit by agonizing bit.

"Alexandra." My name was a loving stroke from his lips, and it felt as carnal as his hands.

Just as I looked up at Nate, a rowdy man with a beard as long as he was tall jostled into us, spilling his beer across both our shirts. I cried out in alarm at the same time Nate tried to steady the man.

"Sssorry," the man slurred, and it was clear he'd had more than necessary for the night. Even with Nate's assistance, the offender could barely stand on his own two feet. While he and Nate danced around the bar, I eyed Rachel, and she nodded, confirming she called a cab for the man and had our security guy heading our way.

It took a few minutes for Raymond to get the man under control and in the cab, then the shock of the incident took over. My clothes reeked of cheap, warm beer, and I was pretty sure my hair did as well—one of the downfalls of keeping it long.

As Nate returned to my side, his T-shirt clung to him on one side, and though it was appealing to see the distinct line of his taut muscles, I knew it was anything but comfortable. He'd taken the brunt of the spillage.

"Come with me," I beckoned, leaving a twenty on the table. My drinks were on the house, but I wanted to make sure Rachel was taken care of.

The farther we moved toward the back of the dimly lit bar, the more nervous I became. The sole reason I avoided Nate the last few days was to keep us from being caught alone, and here I was, dragging him to my personal haven. Could I have offered to bring him down a shirt? Sure, but I'd never been one to do the smartest thing.

"Where are we going?" Nate asked as he flexed his fingers within my grasp.

"Up to my apartment."

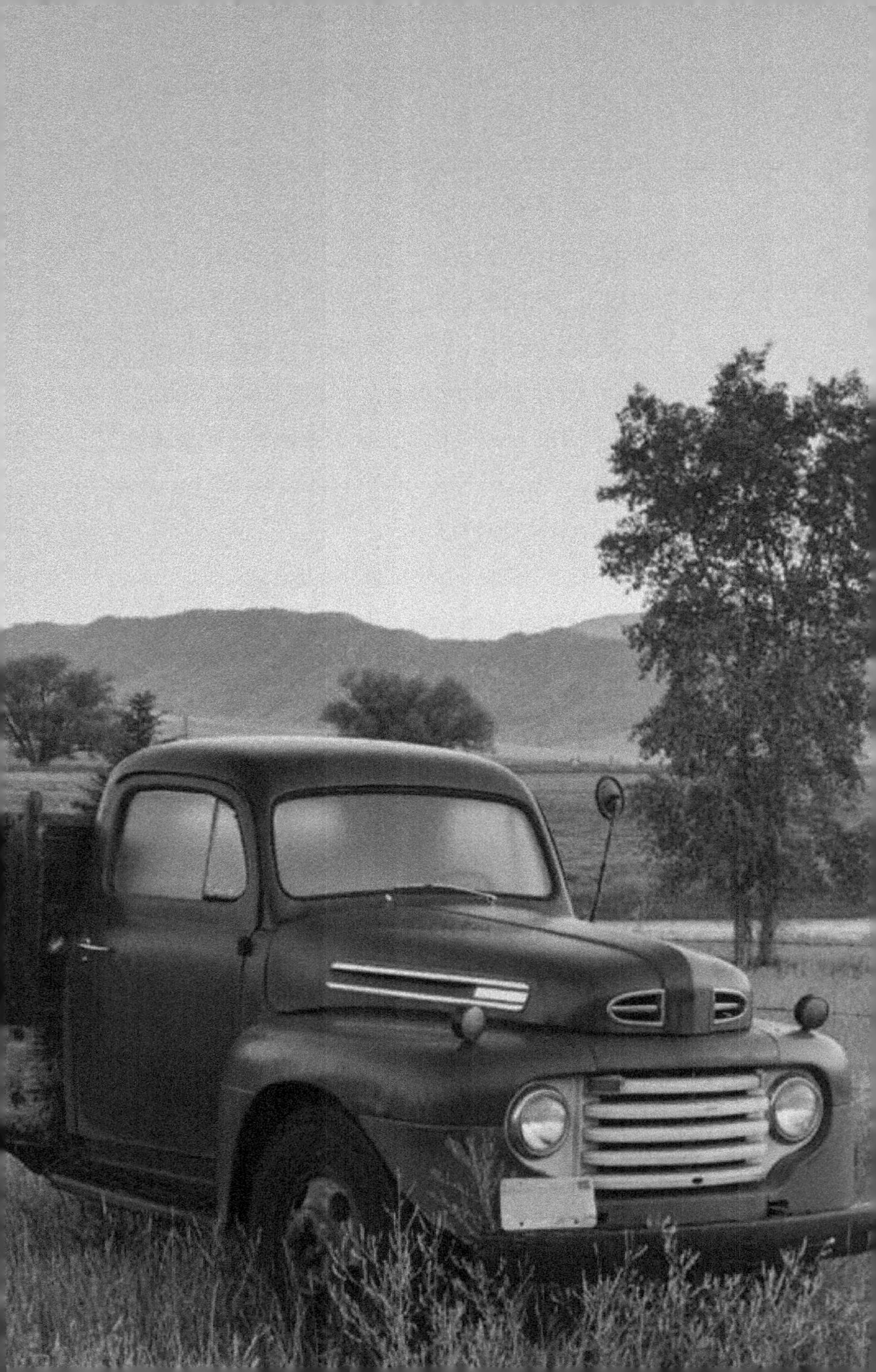

Chapter Eight

Nate

I'd been enjoying my back-and-forth banter with Alex at the bar. Her face was like an emotional picture show. Everything she was feeling was written so clearly across her features. It was fascinating to me. I'd never met someone who could go from angry to bashful in such a short timeframe. And when she blushed, I felt the head of my cock jump. Something about the pink in her cheeks turned me on more than any dirty magazine I ever flipped through as a teen.

The guy who spilled his beer all over us had been the best kind of incident. Were we bothered being covered in the stench of stale beer? Of course. But as she led me toward the back of the bar, I was savoring every second of being in the darkness with her.

I expected her to take me back to an office or storage room to get an employee shirt or something, maybe even ask me to wait while she found one. With the way she avoided me the past few days, I was sure she planned on maintaining that distance. But when she said we were going up to her apartment, I was taken aback. I found myself clutching her hand like she was going to slip away at any moment.

A pair of rickety metal steps barely hung on the exterior brick wall of the bar. I recalled hobbling down them when I retreated from the apartment a year ago, but now imagining Alex climbing them on a daily basis left me sick to my stomach.

Flexing my fingers, I tugged at her hand, silently requesting she hold back. Even in the dim illumination from a nearby outside light, her blue eyes twinkled as she peered at me over her shoulder.

"Is this the only way inside?" I asked, praying there was an alternative. As she nodded, I began seriously calculating what it would cost to replace the steps and wondered why Andrew hadn't done it himself.

"Scared?" she teased as she took the first step, releasing my hand.

"Just assessing the risk of these stairs."

"Come on. It's fine. I've been using them for years."

"That's what I'm worried about."

Alex was already halfway up the staircase as I took the first step, surprised the creaking metal held my weight. I wasn't a small guy by any means. I tested my weight on each step before progressing to the next, missing the opportunity to watch Alex's perfectly shaped ass sway as she made her way to the top.

Swiftly opening the door using a biometric scanner—which surprised the hell out of me, considering the state of the stairs—Alex held it open as I proceeded inside, flicking on the light when she followed.

On one side of the room sat two olive-green reading chairs. A small end table was nestled between them, holding a stack of books. Across from them, an oversized beige couch looked well used with a quilt draped along the back. A clean open kitchen occupied the left corner, and a door led to what I assumed was the bathroom. Turning around, I saw her bed was against the wall, the sheets and comforter pulled up toward the pillows.

I wasn't sure what I expected when I came up to the apartment. A trigger? A memory? A sudden onslaught of visions from that night? But I hadn't expected to sense nothing.

"Are you okay?" Alex asked as she began scurrying around the apartment, picking up little items I hadn't noticed before. It was clear she felt uncomfortable with me being in her space as she darted across the room. "Can I get you a water or something?"

"Just a shirt, thanks," my voice croaked, adding to my discomfort in the situation.

"Shirt?" Alex turned toward me, her head cocked to one side with a pile of small items in her arms. "Oh! Yes. A shirt." She dropped all the items on her bed and stepped over to a dresser, and after a few seconds, she grabbed something black and brought it toward me. I watched her small feet prance toward me as if she was dancing to a melody only she could hear.

"This is one of Andrew's. It should fit."

I was a bit larger than her brother now, so it would be a tight fit, but it was better than what I currently wore. Reaching behind my neck, I gathered the material of my shirt and began tugging it over my head. It was impossible to hide my smirk as Alex's hitched gasp echoed in the room.

I tossed the material in my hand toward the back of the couch and waited patiently for Alex to hand me the shirt she retrieved, but her stare was transfixed on my stomach. Instinctively, I flexed, because it's what anyone would have done in a situation where a beautiful woman was staring at you like her favorite dessert. Hell, I'd even let her lick me like an ice cream cone if she asked.

Just as that thought popped into my head, my cock responded in kind, growing behind the zipper of my pressed shorts. If she didn't hand that shirt over soon, Alex was going to get an eyeful of me that I wasn't sure she was prepared for... again.

"Eyes up here, sweetheart."

Her eyes darted up toward mine, widening at an alarming rate. She reminded me of my daughters when I caught them stealing cookies from the pantry.

"What? I wasn't...." The lie fell on deaf ears, because through her blouse, the distinct outline of her hardened nipples peeked through.

The room felt like it was growing in temperature with every second that passed. There was no way out of the inferno that swirled around us. Reaching out, I ran my hand over her shoulder, down her upper arm. Beneath my touch, her heart rate skyrocketed as I felt it when I reached her wrist.

"Alex."

"Does it help?"

"No, touching you only makes the ache in my dick worse."

She shook her head, the corners of her mouth tilting upward slightly, appearing as if she was fighting a grin. "No. I meant being here. Does it help you remember anything?"

A short laugh bubbled from my chest. "I knew what you meant. I just enjoy watching you blush. I thought it may trigger something, but unfortunately nothing comes to mind... though I do remember the stairs."

She hummed in response, and I wasn't sure if she was as disappointed as I was.

"My therapist..." I paused, but Alex jumped in.

"Therapist?"

"Yeah, the girls and I have visited one weekly for almost a year. Mostly to make sure the transition to living with me, and now the move, isn't upsetting. I called her Sunday after your... revelation. She believes the trauma from learning my ex abandoned our daughters and the fact that I was across the country with no way to get to them caused my mind to shut down. She said it's not uncommon to have memory loss from a traumatic experience like that. Luckily, the girls were young enough that most of it has already been forgotten."

The way Alex's eyes flicked back and forth across mine, I could tell she was processing everything I just revealed. In California, it wasn't unheard of for someone to see a therapist. It was more uncommon not to have the number to one in your back pocket. But I knew there was a chance it was a new concept for Alex.

"I... I feel like... I took advantage of you or something," she whispered, her lips puckering at the sour words she confessed.

"You didn't, Alex. Believe me. The more I thought about it, it's clear I wasn't so inebriated that I blacked out from the alcohol. It was just the combination of everything. I can guarantee I was a willing participant in whatever we did. I'm just sorry I can't remember.

"Being here in this room with you makes me wish I could recall it all. I get small spurts of images in my head, but they flutter away just as quickly. It's nothing compared to knowing the way you taste would, the sound of my name on your lips, the feel of your pussy clamping down around me. I want to remember it all."

My name was nothing more than a whimper from her then. I took a step closer, then another, until my body was up against hers.

Quietly, as if the walls would hear, she asked, "What are you doing?" as my hand slid up to her neck.

"Starting over."

With my thumb under her chin, I tilted her face up toward mine. I brushed my mouth against hers, unable to hold myself back any longer. This woman was my magnetic half, and I had no hope of staying away.

"Nate." Her yearning plea was music to my ears.

The softest of touches trembled across my skin as she tentatively lifted her hands to my waist. As timid as it was, her palms felt like scorching irons against my body.

"Ah, fuck," I growled, sealing my mouth to hers. My tongue begged for entrance, and Alex quickly complied as her own tongue slid across mine.

I may not have a single memory from our one-night stand, but my mouth suddenly remembered her taste, remembered her eagerness. She met me stroke for stroke. I'd never been so turned on in my life by a kiss, and my cock ached in my boxers, craving release.

Deftly, I grasped the back of Alex's thighs and hoisted her up. Her center aligned with my erection as she wrapped her legs around my waist. Fuck, I loved her legs. They were lean and muscular. Alex needed no help holding herself up on my body, so my hands were free to roam.

Blindly, I slid my hands to the hem of her shirt and slipped underneath. Her skin was as blazing as mine felt. I spun us around until I met the arm of the couch, then dropped us onto the overstuffed cushions. My hips rocked against her apex at the movement, earning me a shameless moan from Alex.

"Let me take this off you," I said as I hovered my lips above her mouth, using my fistful of her shirt to tug at the material.

A dinging noise sounded in the background, but I ignored it. Unfortunately, Alex stiffened in my arms.

"Oh my God." Her face turned an unhealthy shade of white as she pushed at my body to get free.

I sat up as she slipped off the couch.

"Someone's coming. Put that shirt on." She pointed to the black material as I stared at her, dumbfounded. Then I quickly remembered her brother came with me to the bar.

"Shit," I uttered, reaching for the mass on the back of the couch next to my soiled shirt.

A knock on the door sounded before Andrew's gruff voice called out Alex's name. The door creaked open without her response just as my head poked through the opening of the shirt. I glanced up at the apartment entrance in alarm, hoping like hell my best friend didn't suspect what I'd been doing with his little sister.

His gaze dashed between me and Alex before landing on me with a sneer I'd never experience from him before. I'd seen it given to others, but I'd never been on the receiving end. It was pretty damn terrifying, and I feared for my balls, to be honest.

"What the fuck is going on here?" Andrew asked, fury swirling about him as his hands planted on his hips, eyes narrowing into slits.

"Calm down, Andrew," Alex said as I yanked down the rest of the T-shirt as it clung to my sweat-soaked skin. She strolled out of the kitchen holding three bottles of water like we hadn't been hip-to-hip minutes prior. "Some drunk spilled his beer on us at the bar. I offered to let Nate borrow one of your shirts. Water?"

"Sorry, man. I tried to let you know, but I couldn't find you," I said, chiming in as I took a bottle of water from Alex. She wasn't making eye contact with me, and that was definitely a good thing, because my cock was ready to continue where we were earlier. Too bad our hindrance was the sole reason we couldn't do anything more than what we had.

"Well, while you two chitchat, I'm going to change my shirt." Alex shoved a bottle of water into her brother's chest. He juggled the bottle, struggling to hold it, before she headed toward her dresser, leaving us in her dust.

"She... uh... was pretty demanding about getting me a new shirt," I tried to explain but stammered through the entire thing.

"Yeah, Alex has always been assertive when she has her mind set on something."

For the first time in our friendship, I felt awkward around Andrew. The look on his face when he walked over the threshold into the apartment would have been priceless if I hadn't been on the receiving end. Knowing I needed to steer his anger and suspicion toward someone that wasn't myself or Alex, I asked Andrew what happened with the guy downstairs.

Twisting the lid off the bottle, he chugged the cool liquid before divulging about the guy. In three minutes, I learned all I needed to know about him. His name was Stephen St. James, heir to a mining business in Tennessee, with a trust fund to boot. He was a grade-A douchebag, which I already ascertained by his appearance, but I learned he was also Alex's ex and the reason she hadn't been in a steady relationship since high school.

"He deserves more than the broken nose I want to give him for the way he broke my sister."

I wanted to ask more, beg for any tidbit of information about Alex and why she would ever date such an awful-sounding guy, but I knew it wasn't my place. If I wanted to keep Andrew in the dark about anything she and I had done in the past, or frankly the last five minutes, then I needed to act casual. Inside, though, my heart was jackhammering in my chest.

Fuck, this was why I told Alex we needed to stay away from each other the other day when she told me everything that happened. I was digging myself an early grave at the rate I was going, because I knew, without a doubt, I wasn't going to be able to stay away from her—no matter how many times I told myself that Andrew's friendship and his family meant more than any attraction I had toward his sister.

Get yourself together, man. You cannot pursue anything with Alex, or you risk ruining any relationship with the only real family you've ever had.

I repeated the mantra in my head over and over until I felt like I hammered it home, while Andrew went on and on about how he wanted to tear Stephen limb from limb, then tow the parts behind one of the farm's harvesting combines. But that all flew out the window when Alex stepped out of the bathroom.

"Alexandra." Her whispered name fell from my lips as I took her in.

I tried to take her in little by little, but I didn't know where to focus first. She wore soft white shorts that pleated down the front of the legs, reminding me of the khakis my parents used to make me wear to school growing up. They were a baggy mess on a gangly schoolboy, but on Alex, they made her appear classy. A black shirt made of some sort of see-through material covered her upper body, revealing a black bra underneath, hiding two of my favorite assets. She must've added the bra, because I knew for a fact she hadn't been wearing one earlier. The sheer fabric Alex considered a shirt twisted in a knot just above her navel, revealing her tan, toned stomach. Her hair was now pulled back with damp ends that brushed against the middle of her back.

Suddenly, an image of my tongue gliding across her waist, dipping into the small crevice as her long hair tickled my cheek, came to mind. I closed my eyes to try to hold onto it, just for a moment, but it slipped away just as quickly.

"You can't wear that," Andrew stated authoritatively. From the short few days I'd been around my temptress, I knew she wasn't one to be told what to do unless she wanted to be. Instead, she was more likely to do the opposite.

"I can wear whatever I like, thank you very much."

The two argued back and forth as I downed the contents of my water bottle, hoping neither noticed my reaction a few seconds prior.

When it seemed like neither party was ready to cave, I chimed in and let them know I needed to relieve their mother of the twins in about an hour. The girls were hesitant to spend the night with Andrew's mom, Marisol. In truth, I wasn't quite ready for that either, but we were slowly working our way up to it.

Agreeing to head back to the bar, I hung back with Alex for a moment while Andrew ventured down the stairs first. I stretched the truth and explained I wasn't certain the rusty metal would hold us all at once, but I really just wanted one more moment alone with Alex.

Grasping her hand in mine as we stood at the door, I squeezed her fingers to get her attention. "You look beautiful, just as you had earlier."

The smile she graced me with was enough to energize me for the rest of the night. I could live off it alone and never tire of seeing it.

"Thank you," she responded in a way I knew I'd do whatever I could to make her smile again.

I wanted to say something more, explain that even though it was wrong, I wanted more time with her. But that all fell away as Andrew called up to us. Alex descended the stairs first, then I slowly followed.

As a trio, we entered the bar, where there was no sign of the guys or Stephen. Either Andrew handled it while I was upstairs handling his sister, or they left on their own. I was convinced it was the former.

"Oh, look! Sadie's here!" Alex bellowed as she focused on the tall brunette I recognized as Colton's younger half-sister.

Alex skirted away once Andrew and I secured a booth. We ordered some beers from the server, but I couldn't taste the hoppy liquid. My eyes too focused on Alex and the way her hand rested on the arm of the man she was speaking with. They were familiar with each other, and I hated it.

Doesn't he know she's mine?

I shook my head, knowing I had no claim on Alex, and I hoped my friend hadn't caught me staring at his sister. When I looked over at him, he was too busy staring at Sadie and the other guy who had his arm wrapped around her waist. The vein above his right temple pulsated as he watched the flirtatious display.

Thankfully, neither woman took the bait those guys were tossing. A few minutes later, they both skipped toward our booth. Alex settled in next to me, stole my bottle of beer, and took a hearty sip. I rested my arm along the upper portion of the booth, twisting my body slightly to face her.

Around me, the bar patrons continued to mill about, but for me, everything froze in place as I waited for Andrew's reaction. The move wasn't something people who barely knew each other would have made. It was intimate, familiar.

I expected Andrew to lash out, to condemn both me and Alex for the display. And I knew without a second thought that I'd do my best to protect her from that onslaught. But just as surprising as her sipping my beer until the server returned, Andrew's face relaxed, and he began chatting with Sadie about her recent job interview.

The coast seemed to be clear for now, but Alex and I were standing on the edge of rocky terrain. The waves were going to reach us soon, and I wasn't sure if either of us would be able to withstand the impact. Whatever we had was going to have to stay in the history books for now. We both had other things we needed to focus on.

But as her thigh innocently brushed against mine, I knew it was going to be hell to stay away from her.

I could do it though.

Right?

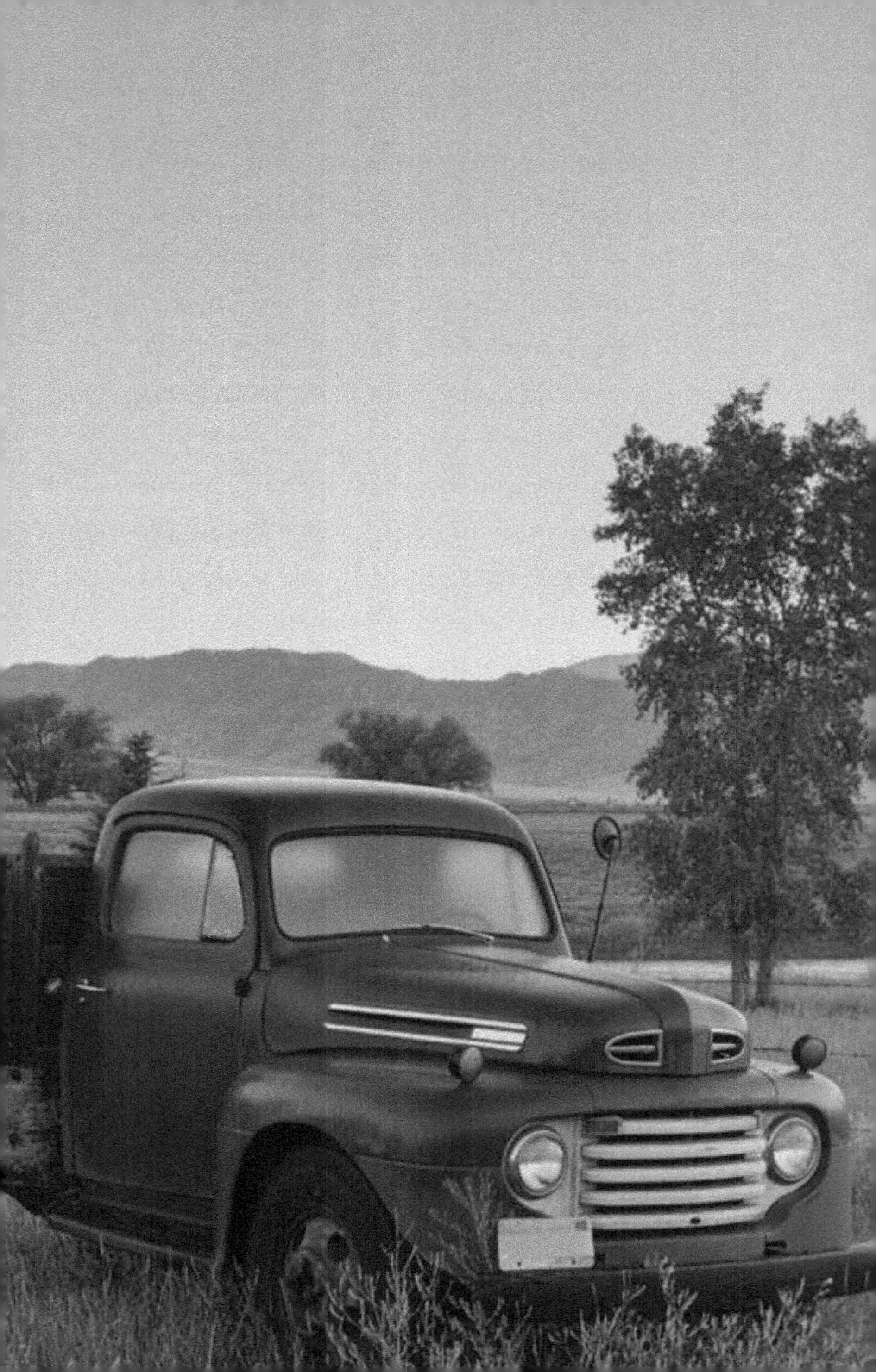

Chapter Nine

Alex

I threw my headphones toward the foot of the bed as I toed off my sneakers. The run had been just what I needed this morning to let off some steam. Earlier this week, I had done the best I could at ignoring Nate. But ever since the bar incident Wednesday, it seemed we switched places. I feared he'd grown tired of me already, even though nothing could come of our attraction. It was silly, but I couldn't control how I processed his actions, regardless of me doing the same to him.

He was gone early in the morning before I even woke up. Which really wasn't all that early, since I tended to go to bed late and sleep in, but it was still well before 8:00 a.m. Then Nate would come in for lunch and dinner and return for good just as night fell across the Ashfield sky. The girls were spending their days with my mom, which she absolutely loved. But I was getting worried about their dad.

For two days in a row, he came to dinner looking more and more harried. The man who wore a suit to the farmer's market when he arrived now donned dirty white shirts covered in grease stains and shorts that had more tears and rips in them than they did belt loops. He looked more like the mechanic in town than the billionaire who graced the pages of magazines.

I didn't mind the dirt and grime. It gave him a blue-collar appeal I found enticing. What I found myself agonizing over were the growing bags under his eyes. It was clear whatever he was doing in the workshop behind the bed-and-breakfast was adding a layer of stress the man didn't need.

I had many ideas on how to help him relieve that stress—only a few of them sexual in nature. Those were things I wasn't sure he would bite at. But I'd have to see him first.

Which was why I was standing outside the workshop in the midst of an East Coast heatwave.

There wasn't much shade in this part of the yard. If it weren't for the subtle breeze that rustled the tips of my hair, I'd be concerned about Nate overheating in the shed. But I had nothing to worry about. He ran a few extension cords into the space and set up a couple of oversized fans.

Hunched over a workbench, Nate's back glistened beneath a large flood lamp. Droplets of sweat raced downward from his neck to the two dimples just above the shorts resting low on his hips. His body was a masterpiece.

I watched in silence as his arms flexed while adjusting something with the tool. I'd been worried about Nate overheating, but as my mouth grew drier with each passing second, maybe I should've been more worried for myself.

Is it hot out here, or is it just Nate fucking Sullivan?

Whatever racket Nate had been making suddenly stopped as his back stiffened.

"Nate?"

Turning toward me, he held a circular device in his hand that reminded me of the robotic vacuum I kept in my apartment.

"Shit. I didn't know anyone was here."

"Clearly. Of course, you've been ignoring me all week, so how would you know if I were around?"

His gaze lowered as he set the device back on the workbench. "I haven't been ignoring you, Alex."

Releasing a puff of air, I told him he could have fooled me. "Besides dinner, you've been holed up in this shed, working. And not to mention, it looks like you haven't slept at all. It's not healthy."

"I'm fine. Come here. Let me show you what I've been working on."

Unable to help myself, I sauntered over to him, curious to see what occupied so much of his time lately. He began speaking, describing the device, its parts and capabilities, and explaining how it was a smaller prototype that would be developed on a larger scale. It was like Pig Latin to my ears, but I fed off his enthusiasm. It was plain as day that Nate was passionate about whatever he was working on.

"Want to head over to your parents' house with me? I want to show this to your dad and go over a few things I discussed with him last weekend."

I had no plans, which was why I was left wandering around the grounds of the bed-and-breakfast. Especially with the twins spending a lot of time with my mom, I was feeling… lonely. Normally, that didn't bother me. I flourished in my alone time, never finding myself bored, but knowing one of my greatest temptations was so close gave me a creative block.

It didn't matter whether it was a good decision or not. If riding over to my parents' house offered me a chance to be alone with Nate, I was going to take it. Frankly, I missed him the last couple of days.

Like a lovesick puppy, I followed him back to the large farmhouse and waited for him to shower. He returned donning a pair of pressed pants, a white dress shirt with the sleeves rolled to his elbows, and a blue tie. Though I loved when he was casually dressed, I was growing really fond of the suit version of Nathaniel. His presence in the foyer called for attention, and he certainly had mine.

He turned down my offer to drive to Sunny Brook Farms, claiming he'd probably bring the twins back with him and needed the booster seats. I completely understood, but at the same time, I was a bit disappointed. I loved my vintage truck and always jumped at the chance to show it off.

With Nate's project tucked securely in the back of the SUV, we traveled the ten minutes down the road toward my family's farm. The fields of delicate wheat swaying in the breeze met us first, followed by a lengthy portion of white picket fencing. We approached the stone and metal signage for the farm, and my stomach did a little flip-flop as Nate's gaze turned toward me for a second.

"We're here," he said.

I wondered if his ex knew what she'd had with him. Did her stomach flutter like an angry nest of hornets when he gave her even the slightest attention? Did his sexy smirk leave her panties soaked as it did mine? God, she was a lucky bitch to have him for the time she did. I was a jealous fool over nothing, because she gave him up, and now he was here with me, traveling down the gravel path that led to my family's property. Even if he wasn't truly mine, I had his time right now. And as he put the SUV in park, smiling at me in that way that left me reeling, I was going to enjoy every little bit of him I had.

Molly and Eloise found us around the kitchen island, sipping on some homemade sweet tea. They both hugged their father quickly, then wrapped themselves around my legs as if they hadn't just seen me that morning.

Molly was still as energetic and outgoing as she had been, but it was nice to see Eloise coming out of her shell a bit. During meals, she spoke up more, not allowing Molly to dominate the conversation, and I even caught her dancing with her twin in the kitchen, something she hadn't done when she first arrived.

I knew my mom was the reason. Marisol Easterly had a way of bringing out the best in people, and I loved her dearly for it.

Mom followed the girls into the house with an exhausted smile on her lips. My mom may have raised five kids, but I knew firsthand that handling the twins was something else entirely. Somehow, I was going to have to convince Nate to let us keep the girls at the house the next couple of days to give my mom a break.

Quickly, I grabbed my phone from my back pocket and shot a text out to Rory, asking if she wanted to come by the B&B's pool this evening. I knew it was her last day of school, and the students let out around lunchtime.

I didn't linger for her message. Instead, I rallied the girls, and we snuck into the pantry to find something delicious to make. By the time we came out with the fixings for a chocolate silk pie, Nate and my dad were nowhere in sight.

Mom helped us in the kitchen, instructing the girls which ingredients needed to be added first. I was in charge of helping them measure correctly. It was a recipe Mom and I mastered when I was in middle school. We no longer needed to read things out, since we knew the measurements by heart, but we made sure to find the old recipe book for Molly and Eloise.

I disappointed them when I said the dessert wouldn't be ready for a couple of hours, but I mixed them up a small fruit salad from our garden.

"Want to help me pick the vegetables for tomorrow's market?" I asked the twins, who jumped at the chance to get dirty.

I didn't have my truck to gather the crates, so I'd have to stop by early in the morning, but it was no hardship. This weekend should have been Autumn's turn at the stand, but I promised to fill in for her. I had nothing else to do except make a quick breakfast for the Sullivans.

The girls dashed in and out of the rows of late spring vegetables, admiring the tomatoes and cucumbers as they went. After I set out baskets for them to pluck the red and green goods, I went to work gathering a variety of peppers and squash.

Every week, we had a new bounty to bring to the market, and I adored that we got to keep up the family tradition. The small garden was started by my great-great grandmother, and my sisters and I worked to expand it, as farm-fresh produce became a hot commodity in our town. Corn was my family farm's bread and butter, but the vegetable garden was something my sisters and I were proud to uphold.

"That was so fun. Can we do it again?" Eloise asked, covered from head to toe in dirt. Little smudges dotted her face, arms, and legs. Her clothes were completely soiled, and Molly matched her smear for smear. I couldn't understand how they got so dirty plucking the vegetables, but I knew children were far messier than anyone realized. I even witnessed Rory covered top to bottom in dirt before, and she was the teacher.

"Sure. We're at the market every Saturday. As long as it's okay with your dad, you can join me Friday afternoons to get the crates ready. You both were a big help today."

"Thank you," they chimed simultaneously with matching grins.

"And you know what? I bet when we go inside, the pie will be ready."

"Yes!" they screamed as they dashed out of the fenced-in garden and up to the back entrance of the house. Both girls stumbled a few times but righted themselves without falling. I couldn't blame them. I was equally as excited about the chocolate pie.

After dumping the baskets into the larger crates, I carried them one by one up to the mudroom so I could clean everything off. By the time I was done, Mom was cleaning the girls up from their finished treat. I thanked her, and she smiled at me in that way that made me feel like I hung the moon.

"Dad and Nate still in the library?" I asked as I opened the refrigerator and gathered my own heaping piece of pie.

"I believe so, yes. I may have dozed off for a few minutes." Mom chuckled as she began washing the plates in the sink. "Those sweethearts make me realize I am no longer in my twenties."

"Well," I said around a mouthful as I came to stand beside her, "you don't look a day over forty." I grinned, showcasing my teeth covered in chocolate.

Just as quickly as I made the joke, Mom swatted me with the dishtowel she'd draped over her shoulder.

"Don't sass your momma."

"Yes, ma'am."

"Anyway, I like you with them. You take to kids naturally."

"Uh, I think you have me confused with Rory. She's the child whisperer."

"Not at all. I stand by what I said." She paused while continuing to wash another plate, then placed it on the drying rack. "I like you with Nathaniel, too."

With my fork halfway to my mouth, it froze midair. There was no way she could tell we had a steamy-hot fuckfest together, could she?

Coughing, I set the fork back on the plate and told her that she was crazy and seeing things. I also reminded her that Nate was my brother's age.

"Maybe so, but age is just a number. Look at your sister and her husband. Besides, you would add a little spice and stability to his life."

"I don't think so, Mom. Anyway, you know my track record hasn't been the best."

"He was one boy, Alexandra."

Reflexively, I nodded, refraining from continuing the argument we had numerous times over the years. The other day, Nate mentioned seeking therapy for himself and his daughters. I could tell it was something big for him to share, but I wondered if he would be surprised to learn I spoke with a therapist regularly as well. Mine was certain I solely chose one-night stands to keep from forming attachments. I had trust issues, and it was easier to keep men at arm's length than to let them close.

"One was enough for me." I gently set my plate in the sink, knowing Mom wouldn't let me clean it if she was already there. "I'm going to go check on Dad and Nate."

When I took one step away from the sink, Mom gripped my wrist in that way that meant business. The kind that said "listen to what I'm about to tell you."

"I love you, Alexandra. It's okay to let others love you, too."

"I love you too, Mom." I smiled sincerely. My mother was one of my best friends, as she was for my sisters as well. Before retreating, I pressed my lips to her cheek, then made my way toward Dad's office down the hall.

Just beyond the door, I peered down the hall to see Eloise and Molly watching a children's cartoon about a mouse on the television. The door to the office was open just a smidge. I didn't want to eavesdrop, but they made it so easy.

"I like what you've done here, Nathaniel. We're all very proud of you."

"Thank you, sir."

I shivered as Nate's velvety smooth voice washed over me.

"If you want to sign this document, I will agree to lease you the farthest two plots of land, as well as the 100 acres on the other side of Ashfield. I can also have Marisol email you a copy of the land's property markers."

I hadn't viewed our property maps in a long time. The grainy images in my head began filtering through, and it alarmed me what I recalled.

"That would be great. Thank you, Nash. This means a lot to me. I'm hoping—"

I burst through the door, interrupting Nate. "What are you doing? Those are our family plots!" I argued, my fists curling at my sides.

The chair Dad was perched on squealed as he pushed it back while standing. I was too angry to take in Nate's face. How could my father consider selling the acres of land he set aside for me and my siblings? I knew they thought of Nate like another son, but this was overstepping.

"Alex, it's not what you think it is."

My steps pounded against the hardwood floor as I approached my father. "I believe it's exactly what I think it is. You're selling Nate our family land. What if one of us wants to build a house on it one day?"

"Alex," my mother cajoled from behind me. "I'm going to say this in the nicest way possible, but you're acting like a spoiled brat right now."

"Mom!" I took on a horrific shrill at the accusation.

"If you would have listened closer, or perhaps asked questions instead of jumping to conclusions, you would have heard we are leasing Nate the land, specifically for his product testing. His company is the one paying for the use."

"What?" I murmured, brows furrowing.

"You're too smart to act like you didn't hear me. Now, Nathaniel," she said, turning her attention toward the other party in the room, the one I had yet to make eye contact with and probably wouldn't be in the unforeseeable future. I hated being wrong, especially when it was none of my business to begin with. "Nash and I were discussing your request about personal property acreage. There is a plot along the far eastern field, very close to the creek that runs through the backwoods. It's a plot we haven't utilized since the girls were little. It would be a perfect place to build a home."

I interjected, "Hey, that's right next to my—"

"Yes, dear. The ten acres will butt up right next to your twenty. The twenty you don't live on or currently use. The twenty your father and I still own."

While Mom and Nate discussed the land in detail, I glanced around the office, trying to collect myself. What was it that set me off? I didn't normally fly off the handle like I just had. I was usually even-tempered, except with Aspen, but that's because my youngest sister knew how to press all my buttons. At most, I was blunt and told people exactly what I was thinking.

The more I pondered what triggered me, the more I realized my emotions stemmed from Nate's intention of staying. It was a mix of both elation and fear. What did it mean if he stayed? Was it possible that I played a part in his desire to remain here?

But as I watched his two daughters scurry into the office, I knew I had my answer. He wanted a life for his twins like I had growing up.

I'd never been to California, nor did I know which part of the state he previously lived in, but I could imagine the Smoky Mountains of Tennessee were a far cry from what they'd known up until this point.

"I'm sorry," I said out loud. All eyes fell on me, and I resisted the urge to squirm under their gawking. "Yes, I realize those aren't words you've often heard from me," I added, attempting to lighten the mood. "But I am sorry I jumped to conclusions. I think your girls will love it here, Nate."

I tried my best to avoid his stare, but I failed miserably. And when he smiled, I'm pretty certain I melted into a puddle on the floor of my father's office. My poor mom was going to have to clean up my mess later.

Chapter Ten

Nate

Alex didn't have to try hard to be sexy. She naturally exuded it, whether she wore a sheer black top like the other night or a pair of flannel pajamas. But watching her genuinely apologize for her outburst may have been the fucking sexiest thing I'd ever seen. I knew how much it took for someone to admit they were wrong, and for someone as strong as Alex, it must've killed her. But she'd done it in a way that left me aching to touch her. Unfortunately, my two hands were occupied as I walked with my daughters to the SUV.

Back at the house, Alex immediately ushered the girls up to their rooms for what she was calling a "pool party extravaganza" with her sister, Rory. I didn't quite understand what that meant, but it seemed like Molly and Eloise were going to have a great time.

I offered to cook dinner tonight, something that surprised even me. I was a novice in the kitchen, but I figured manning a grill was ingrained in the male DNA.

Alex eyed me speculatively when I told her I was going to run to the store to grab some steaks. I wasn't sure if she worried about my grilling prowess or the fact that I was leaving my daughters under her supervision for the first time.

It was probably a good bit of both. Luckily, her sister would be arriving shortly, so she wouldn't be overwhelmed. Sometimes, the twins had more energy than even the sanest person could tolerate, and even more so when they were excited.

The trio came down the stairs just as I finished locking my robot back up in the shed. Molly and Eloise wore matching unicorn one-pieces, which made them appear more identical than usual. Alex was still in her clothes from earlier, but something blue dangled from her arms, the strings swaying with each step.

As I double-checked that Molly removed her hearing aid, I overheard Alex beckoning the girls toward the kitchen to help her chop up some vegetables to cook on the grill. They bolted away eagerly. Uneasiness came over me, imagining my daughters with sharp knives in their hands, but I shouldn't have been worried. Peeking into the kitchen, Alex had already set up two stools for the girls to stand on. Behind Eloise, Alex cradled my daughter's tiny hand as they slowly sliced a carrot together. I had to chuckle at the way Eloise's little pink tongue snuck out around the corner of her mouth, and Molly watched on in fascination.

Together, they continued to slice the veggies before Alex stepped back with the knife and acknowledged me.

"Figured while I wait for Rory, I could set up some side dishes. Vegetable mix and potatoes okay?" she asked, as if she hadn't just described a perfect meal for grilling.

"Yeah, it sounds great. Thank you," I added, nodding toward my daughters, who were sneaking little bits of the carrots as they waited for Alex to continue her teaching. "I'll let you get to it, or we won't have anything left."

Her eyes shot down to the girls with their sticky bandit fingers before she returned them to me. "We'll see you in a bit."

As I pushed away from the entrance to the kitchen, I winked at Alex, knowing the ruddy shade I adored would climb up her neck to her cheeks. I wasn't disappointed.

There was an additional car in the driveway when I arrived home with the four steaks. I assumed the practical sedan belonged to Rory. Even as a young girl, I remembered her always being the overly cautious kind. Second-guessing every move we made when they'd join me and her brother to play in the fields. She was as goody-two-shoes as they came, which was what I supposed made her a great teacher.

Juggling both the case of beer, the bag of both red and white wines, and the package of steaks, I maneuvered my way into the vacant house. Someone pried open the downstairs window, letting in the warm late-spring breeze. The scent of grass and honeysuckle filled the room. Immediately, I closed my eyes as I took a deep breath. This was what I was after. This feeling of just being.

It didn't take long to realize the girls all made their way outside to the pool. Their screams of laughter were loud enough to make out the shenanigans even at this distance.

I seasoned the steaks and set them out to get up to room temperature. The quick internet search I made while at the store offered that as a piece of advice, along with the mix of spices I picked up.

The white wine now chilled in the fridge in the butler's pantry, along with my beer. I made sure to snag one before leaving the room.

Opening the screen door that led to an oversized porch, I made my way to the edge. Leaning over the railing, tasting the first sip of the wheaty fizz, I pondered if this was what I wanted in my new home.

The shock of Marisol and Nash offering to sell me a plot of their family land still lingered. And I knew they weren't charging me nearly what they could or should have.

I texted my parents to let them know the good news, hoping they'd find some sort of enjoyment for me and the girls, but my unread message squashed any chance of them celebrating my good fortune. Even a couple of hours later, they still hadn't read it. I considered messaging Sasha to let her know I found a place to settle down with our daughters, but I knew opening up that line of conversation wouldn't end well for any of us. Knowing her manipulative ways, she'd show up at our doorstep and demand a rekindling of something.

Sometimes I wanted to forgive her for everything she put me and the girls through. Her life was stressful, always seeking her family's approval within their lifestyle and business. She helped run her father's mass media corporation. They practically shunned her when she wound up pregnant. But even with our quicky wedding, that didn't stop her from gallivanting around town with whatever person tickled her fancy.

She also made sure I knew all about the affairs.

Off in the distance, Alex's voice rang out clearly. "Cannonball!" she shouted before a splash followed.

Taking another long pull of my beer, I took the steps down to the yard, making sure to stay on the path of stones as I went.

Alex was nothing like Sasha. Not just in age or appearance, but in her personality and heart. Alex was like an open book the way she wore her emotions all over her face. There were things in her past, like her ex, that had her shutting down, but I knew there was more to that prologue of her story, and it was clear it shaped who she was today.

As I got closer, her laughter rose above all the others, and I found myself laughing alongside her. It was infectious.

In my pocket, my phone buzzed with a message. A ridiculous hope speared through me that my parents actually responded. But as I tugged the device from my pocket, it was a message from Andrew. He demanded I join him tonight while he was still in Ashfield for a double date. I wasn't keen on going out tonight, or on a date at all, but I knew things with his sister couldn't go anywhere.

It wasn't only that she was Andrew's little sister, which was a big part of it, but she and I were complete opposites. Alex was wild and carefree, where I was as direct and straightlaced as they came. She was also fourteen years younger than me. At twenty-four, she didn't need to be saddled with a ready-made family. Hell, I was going to be forty in a couple of years. I had no business pursuing anything with her.

But all logic flew out the window when I stepped inside the gated pool area. There she stood, the vixen in all her glory dressed in the tiniest fucking bikini I'd ever seen, and my body and brain immediately stopped caring about all the reasons I couldn't want Alex Easterly.

Tiny scraps of material covered all the parts of Alex I wanted to get intimately familiar with. She stood at the side of the deep end, adjusting one of the ties at her waist, while my daughters looked on. They both wore life jackets, which gave me peace of mind because of the way Alex stole my attention. All the blood rushed from my head toward my cock.

My eyes were glued to Alex's trim waist, as Molly yelled out, "Daddy! Alex is going to do a cannonball! They are the biggest ever."

In fascination, I watched Alex's chest move as she sucked in a deep lungful of air and then launched her body into the air. I'm not sure how those flimsy scraps of material stayed together as she splashed into the water, soaking the twins in the process. Luckily, I was far enough away from the collision to not be an innocently soaked bystander.

"Hey, Nate," a voice said from my right.

My eyes widened when I realized I wasn't alone on the pool deck. I'd forgotten Rory was going to join us, my mind and body completely focused on the other Easterly sister currently climbing out of the pool again.

Rubbing my free hand along the back of my neck, I greeted Rory. "Uh… hey. How are you?"

"I'm good, thanks."

She wore a practical red one-piece, which suited what I remembered of Rory. Her hair was drying in the late-afternoon sun, leaving it in subtle waves as the ends dripped onto the towel resting at her waist.

The lounge chair beside her was free, so I settled in as we continued to watch Alex entertain my twins. Rory told me all about the end of the school year and how she was looking forward to the summer, especially a conference she was attending just before school started back up.

As I listened to her continue discussing the ins and outs of the conference, my eyes trained on the pool, where Alex shifted from cannonballs to launching the girls in the air one at a time, letting them splash down into the water. I smiled at the mixture of their laughs.

"You have it bad." Rory giggled beside me.

"Have what?"

"You have a thing for Alex. It's clear as day."

"Uh… I do not. I'm just enjoying watching my girls."

"Yeah, all three of them." Rory laughed again as I shifted uncomfortably on the seat.

"Funny," I murmured as I lost myself in the way Alex gently comforted Eloise when she got water in her eyes.

"My brother is looking for you. Apparently, you're not answering your phone." Rory rocked the cell in her hand. "He said he had to head back to Knoxville but could reschedule the double date."

"Oh… well… that's good," I replied.

"Hm… I see it now."

"See what?" I asked the sister who was becoming increasingly irritating. I told her so, and she smiled while shaking her head.

"Something, apparently, you're far too blind to see." She stood, tossing her phone and towel back on the lounger, then made her way to the edge of the pool. She was a bit closer than Alex had been standing.

Before I realized what was happening, Rory completed a perfect cannonball into the pool, surprising everyone. The splash soaked Alex and the twins. Droplets of water fell in my direction, coating me in the cool chlorinated water, and Rory surfaced with the biggest shit-eating grin. I guessed even the good ones could have a wild streak every now and then.

"I'm going to dry off and get the steaks started," I said to the group, who weren't listening. They were too busy playing mermaids in the water.

Before heading inside to grab the steaks, I checked over the grill in the oversized outdoor kitchen.

Colton had gas lines running to the grill, so with a quick click of the button, it came to life. I perused the cabinets and drawers, finding everything I'd need and setting them on the stone countertop.

Inside, I darted into the powder room, using the hand towel to dry my hair. It was shorter than I was used to, but that made it easier to maintain. Now that the purchase of my patent was complete, I considered growing it long again.

Within the vanity, I found a stack of clean hand towels, replacing the one I used. Unsure what to do with the one in hand, I opened the powder room door in hopes of finding the laundry room, only to collide with a she-devil in a blue bathing suit.

"Oomph!" she grunted as I reached out to grasp her bare arms just below the shoulders to steady her.

"Sorry," I murmured.

"No, no. It was my fault. I was coming to help with dinner. I just needed to use the restroom first."

"You don't need to help," I explained, my thumbs rubbing small circles on her arms of their own accord. At this point, I couldn't control a single part of my body when she was around.

"I know that."

It took a few seconds before recognition dawned. "You want to make sure I don't screw it up, don't you?"

Alex giggled, her eyes brightening like a freaking anime cartoon. "Can't say the thought didn't cross my mind."

"Thanks for the vote of confidence," I joked as I released her. The towel she wrapped around her chest slipped an inch, and she reached up to retuck the material. "I'll have you know that you can find just about anything on the internet."

"I'm well aware of that. I also needed to get the vegetables. So, you see, it wasn't all about you."

"Sure, it wasn't." I gestured for her to enter the powder room, letting her know I'd meet her outside.

Alex joined me just as I set the steaks on the grill. That was after I spent a solid five minutes making sure the temperature was exactly where the instructions specified. I'd always been a perfectionist, and it seemed that included grilling.

"Is everything exactly the way you wanted?" Alex asked as she slipped through the sliding glass doors with a plateful of aluminum foil pouches.

Startled, I spun toward her with the tongs pointed in her direction. Like they'd save me from an attack. "Sorry. And what do you mean?"

She lifted the grill cover and set the pouches on the upper rack of the grill before closing it and turning toward me. Even doing something as mundane as grilling, she looked effortless. Her damp hair clung to her upper body in a way I wished I could.

"I watched you from the kitchen window."

"Okay...?"

"You like everything a certain way," she stated, loosening her towel and flinging it onto the counter. "Everything has to be exact, or you feel out of control. That sound about right?"

She had no idea how right she was with her assessment. It was why my attraction to her left me so unsettled. She didn't fit in the box.

"Blame it on being an engineer. Things need to work exactly right, or they don't work at all."

Her lips pursed at my reply. I was positive she didn't like my answer by the way she remained silent until I lifted the grill cover and turned over the steaks.

"Those are only going to need about five more minutes."

"The instructions said seven on each side," I protested as I closed the lid, turning to face my adversary with her hands fisted on her hips.

"I'm telling you from experience, they only need five. But if you prefer yours well-overdone, then by all means, leave them on for seven."

"Alex, are you upset with me or something?"

Her voice was heavy and dark, and she kept her attention on the yard, avoiding making eye contact. I couldn't make it out completely, but I was pretty sure I made out the words, "Or something," under her breath.

"Look, Alex, I know things are weird right now. I've just got a lot riding on this project and getting the girls settled before they start kindergarten."

"And then there's Andrew." She turned her steely eyes on me, and I felt like I was under a microscope. She was taking in every heartbeat, every ripple of my pulse, every breath that left my lungs.

"He is a… complication."

"Sure. I don't want to upset my brother either. Thank goodness there's only two more weeks until Autumn returns, and I can go back to my apartment in town."

Fuck. Somewhere in the midst of everything, I'd forgotten Alex and I weren't exactly playing house. She was helping her sister with the B&B and would be leaving as soon as she got back. It was like she dropped an ice bucket of cold water on me, and the shock hadn't quite worn off.

"Yeah," I croaked.

"Until then, we should probably avoid moments where we're alone, unless you think you can control yourself." Her eyes twinkled. She was challenging me and my need for accuracy and preciseness. I might not have been able to control my surroundings where Alex was involved, but I could control my reaction to her. I hoped.

"I agree. It shouldn't be too hard."

Alex's gaze flicked down to my hips and back up. "Right. Not too hard."

Her hips swayed more than usual as she stepped back into the house, leaving me feeling far from confident about the gauntlet we just threw down.

Something was definitely growing hard, and I wasn't sure it was only my desire for control.

By the time night fell, I settled myself in one of the hanging benches on the porch with a glass of bourbon. The beer earlier wasn't cutting it for me. I didn't drink often, but I needed something to take away the itch to climb those stairs and knock on Alex's door.

She left me emotionally and physically spent before dinner without lifting a finger.

Rory left shortly after the meal, and I spent the better part of the evening cleaning up the girls before bed. They exclaimed the steaks were delicious—which I left the second half for only five minutes as Alex suggested—and I felt so proud of the fact that they enjoyed my meal. Even Rory complimented it.

I hadn't seen Alex when I finished getting the twins settled, which left me believing she was in her room.

Andrew's text about the double date postponement remained unanswered. I wasn't sure how I felt about dating again, especially with so much going on in my life.

Beside me, my phone rang, the chiming noise echoing across the porch.

Sasha was calling well after our daughters' bedtime, something I made her aware of time and time again. Over the last six months, she'd been much better about calling during the day, so to see her name on the screen now left me concerned.

"Hello?" I answered, instantly regretting my decision when my ex's voice came from the other end.

I zoned out during most of the call, so when Alex stepped out onto the porch, I was immediately caught off guard. Since darkness had fallen on the B&B, I assumed she'd gone to bed or started relaxing in her room. I hadn't expected her to join me that evening.

"The answer is no. Please only call during the times we've set." I ended the call before Sasha could argue.

"Everything okay?" Alex asked from the porch, her leg swaying back and forth on her bare toe.

I placed my phone in my pocket, then took a hearty sip of my bourbon before explaining that Sasha had been on the other end of the call. I didn't miss the slight wince from Alex.

"I'm sorry. That was rude of me."

"Naw. She's a lot to handle, that's for sure. If it wasn't for the girls, I wouldn't ever take a single call from her."

She nodded, then pushed off the doorjamb and sauntered toward me, a bottle of red wine in her hand. A single wine glass dangling from her fingertips. With a tilt of her head, she wordlessly asked if she could join me. I shuffled to the edge of the bench and used my feet to hold it in place as she sat down.

It was too dark out, only the dim light coming through the window just beyond us illuminating the porch to see. When she finally settled against the back of the bench, her glass was filled to the brim.

"Autumn was saying that Sasha signed away her parental rights?"

"Correct."

"That's so sad."

"Not really. Sasha never wanted to be a mother. The pregnancy and then the marriage weren't what she wanted."

"I mean, it's sad for you and the girls. They're so great."

"They are. But we're doing good, and hopefully we'll make a new life here."

Our eyes locked then, the pull too strong for either of us to turn away. Alex hitched one of her legs onto the bench as she turned to face me, her knee pressing up against my thigh. I was glad it was so dark out and she couldn't see the way her touch caused my lower body part to grow.

A breeze swirled, and her scent overwhelmed me. A mix of strawberries and the chlorine from the pool. Alex took a sip from her wine, and as she pulled the glass away, I noted a small, dark dot along her lower lip.

I couldn't control my reaction as I reached out and swiped the drop of wine away with my finger, then brought it to my mouth for a taste.

Her eyes flared at the gesture, and my name purred from her lips.

I needed to stop. I needed to quit taking a step forward and then two steps back. I was leading her on, and it wasn't fair to either of us. But I couldn't restrain myself when she was close by. It took only one night for my body to become addicted to her, a night I couldn't even remember.

"I don't like games, Nate. I feel like I'm in a constant game of ping-pong with you."

"I know, Alex. I just can't seem to help myself."

"Then don't. I want you too, Nate. I've never said this to anyone, but one night with you wasn't enough. I want more."

"I can't do that to Andrew. He'd kill us both, and I'd lose the closest thing to family I have."

"Hmm," she replied, and I wasn't quite sure what she meant, but as she gulped her glass of wine, it didn't take a rocket scientist to realize she was fed up. My palms started to sweat and my heart pounded. She was done with me, and the panic was overwhelming. Which was crazy in itself, because I was the one retreating at every interaction. I was the one who put up the barriers and drew the line in the sand.

Yet I was the one about to have a panic attack.

She stood, and the bench rocked with her exit. I didn't even use my foot to stop the motion. Because every sway brought me equally closer to Alex as it did farther away.

"Alex—"

"I'll see you tomorrow afternoon. I'll be at the market in the morning."

"Okay."

"Goodnight, Nate."

"Sleep well, Alexandra."

She ducked into the house, and I finished off my bourbon, immediately knowing one glass wasn't going to be enough. I felt twisted up inside, this never-ending magical maze of emotions that sealed up and reopened at their own will. It was the only explanation for why I was so wishy-washy with Alex. I should be strong enough to control my attraction to her. I should be able to walk around this bed-and-breakfast, not imagining she was here permanently with me and the twins. I should be able to tell my best friend I had a drunken one-night stand with his sister and desperately wanted a repeat.

I should be able to do all of that.

But here I was, pouring another two fingers of amber liquid into my glass, hiding away. I was a weak coward.

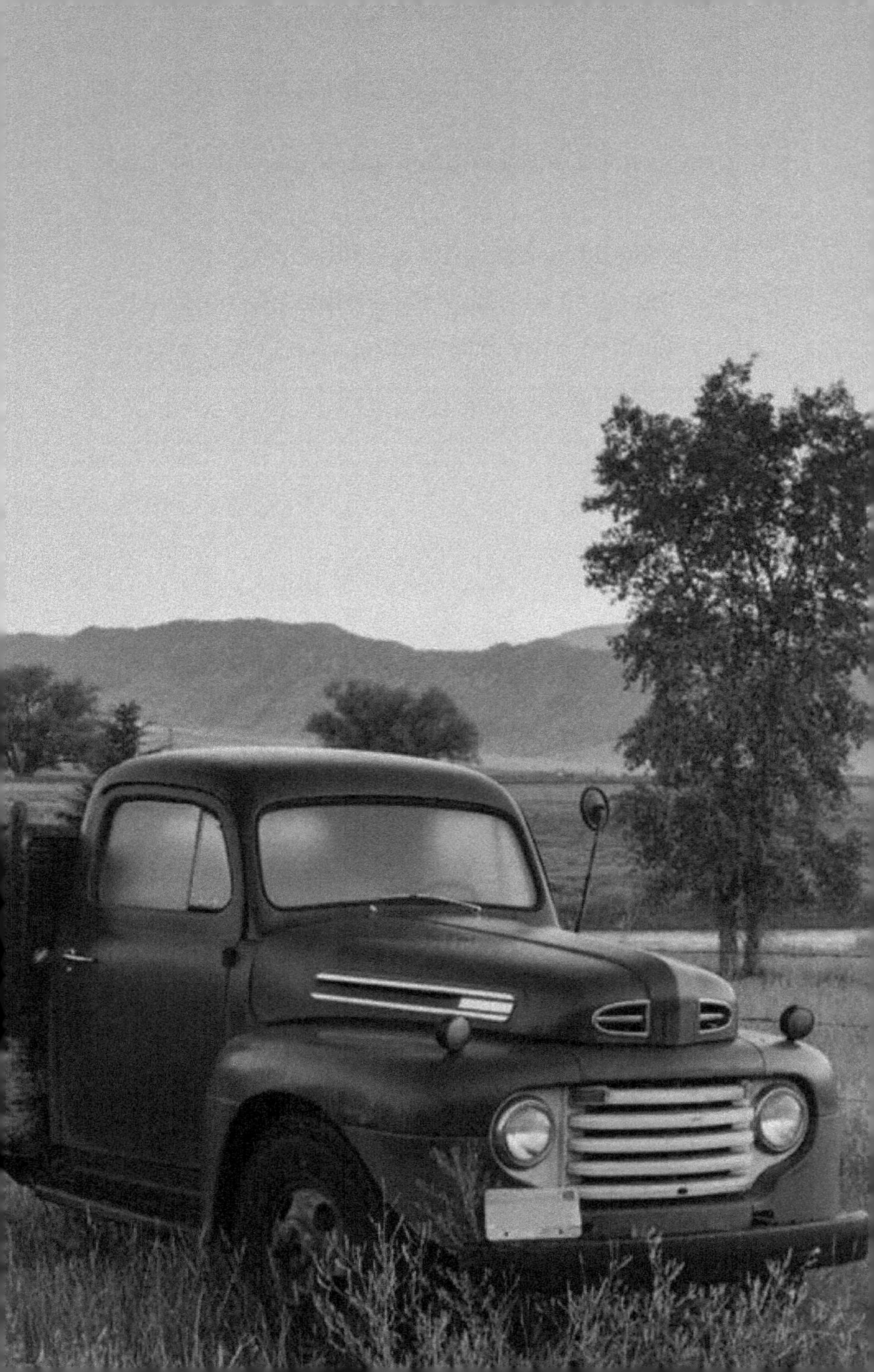

Chapter Eleven

Alex

The bed-and-breakfast was quiet when I slowly pried my bedroom door open. No one lurked in the hallway as I made my way down to the kitchen. I passed by an oversized antique mirror that hung in the hallway across from the formal living room. Squinting at my appearance, I took in my red eyes and dry skin—all a result of no sleep and too much wine. That red liquid had been my therapist late last night, and I was so lost in the one-sided conversation that I missed the sound of Nate coming back inside. Or maybe he didn't at all.

Glancing over my shoulder, I verified that the front door was locked. So he had at least gone to bed at some point.

With one last scan of my clothes, the Sunny Brook Farms T-shirt and cutoff denim shorts were going to have to do. My hair was haphazardly placed in a messy bun on my head, loose strands curling around my face. I was so out of it I didn't even apply any makeup this morning, just some sunscreen. There was no hiding the hangover that loomed over me like a dark cloud of remorse.

Today was going to be a struggle; that was for sure. Not to mention the weird conversation with Nate last night. I knew he treasured his friendship with my brother. I did as well. But I couldn't help that I wanted one more night with him, even though that wasn't my normal MO. But even that seemed like too much to ask from him. I was just going to have to wallow in my attraction to him from afar. Because it was clear, he would not do anything to mess up his friendship with Andrew.

My phone nestled in my back pocket rang, and I quickly pulled it out while I headed toward the kitchen so as to not wake anyone in the house.

My poor mood quickly reversed when I saw my best friend's name light up the screen.

"Tami!"

She and I had been inseparable since the age of three, when we met in dance class. We'd been together through the tragedy of her parents' divorce, boyfriends and breakups, and the gaslighting and emotional abuse at the hands of my ex.

Tami traveled the world as a flight attendant. It was the perfect job for her. She loved the drama club in high school, being on stage and all that entailed. Tami thought of every flight as a new audience. She also loved meeting new people and always brought back the best keepsakes from her journeys abroad.

"Hey, Lexi!" Tami was the only one I allowed to call me Lexi. Other close friends tried, but Tami shot them down.

"Are you home?" She just spent the last two weeks in South America after a few international flights she'd been assigned to.

"I got in last night. Jetlag is a killer, so I'm wide awake."

"Well, I'll be at the market this morning if you're looking for something to do."

"Oh, that's right. Sounds fun. Maybe Mrs. Hensen will do something off the wall."

Packing myself a small lunch to have while I was at the stand, I told Tami about last week's mischief with Mrs. Hensen and how she'd be expecting more bumpy cucumbers today. The twins picked some great ones yesterday.

I thought about telling her that Nate was the guy I slept with over a year ago. But that was the kind of reaction I wanted to see in person.

We ended the call, and I felt slightly better overall. Tami always had that effect on me, and I did for her as well.

Grabbing my bag and keys, I left in my truck. I usually drove her every day, but since I was covering for Autumn, she'd been holed up in the garage. I didn't care what anyone thought; your vehicle performed better when she was given special attention. A fresh wash and vacuum, some detailing, and a daily drive made my girl run like a dream.

This morning, she puttered and spat like I did when I hadn't had any coffee yet. But once she got on the main road leading to my parents' farm, she woke up a little more. With the window down, because there was no AC, I let the fresh mountain air sweep over me.

It smelled of dew and grass. At this early hour, farmers were out harvesting or planting, always working. I was 100 percent certain my father was already off in the far field getting ready for the day with the farmhands who lived on the property.

A smile graced my lips as I turned into the main drive of Sunny Brook Farms and headed toward the back of the farmhouse. Just as I approached the front of the house, I noticed a tiny figure sitting on the stairs. Alarmed, I shoved the truck into park and hopped out, my door hanging wide open in my escape.

It didn't take me long to figure out which twin sat hunched over with a tear-stained face.

"Eloise, sweetie? Are you okay? Are you hurt?" I asked as I dashed over and crouched in front of her. With shaking hands, I ran them over her head and body, checking for any cuts or blood.

The little girl sobbed again as she wrapped her arms around my neck, unable to answer my questions. I lifted her up and ran my hand over her back, doing my best to comfort her. It was obvious she was upset. Was her father and sister inside? I was so confused.

"Eloise, I need you to tell me what happened. Is your family inside?"

Sniffling, she wiped her nose on my shoulder, but I didn't care about the shirt. My concern was the four-year-old alone at my parents' house.

"They're still sleeping. I wanted to see the sun wake up, and no one was awake. Daddy says I'm a big girl."

"But how did you get here?"

"I don't know. I followed the trail and ended up here."

Shock rushed through me. This tiny little thing walked the ten-minute drive. I knew from experience as a child that it was about thirty minutes… and she did it in the dark.

"Eloise, you must've been so scared. Why didn't you knock on the door and get my mom?"

"Daddy said I'm not allowed to knock on doors."

"I think he'd have been okay with it, since it was an emergency."

Her small chin trembled. "I'm s-sorry."

"It's okay, sweet girl. Let me call your dad so he's not worried."

Her thin arms stayed wrapped around my neck, her legs around my waist. She reminded me of a spider monkey. Realizing I left my phone in the truck, I carried her over to turn the truck off and gather my things.

Opening my parents' door with my copy of the key, I called out to my mom. At that time of day, I knew she'd be in the kitchen, fixing up breakfast for everyone on the property.

"We have a guest."

"Oh, my word." My mother immediately dropped the whisk in her hand and rushed over to me and my cling-on.

As she stroked Eloise's back, I explained the situation as I pulled up the B&B's registration website. I never programmed Nate's phone number into my phone, but I knew it was listed in the registry for his stay.

As the phone rang, Eloise giggled and switched from my hold to my mother's. I immediately missed her warmth.

I triple-checked the number listed in Nate's contact information before pressing Call. With crossed fingers, I waited for him to pick up. Unfortunately, I was met with his voicemail greeting. At least I knew I dialed the correct number.

"Hey, Nate. This is… um, Alex. You know, from the bed-and-breakfast. I wanted to let you know I have

Eloise here with me. She wandered over to my parents' farm early this morning. Please don't worry."

The phone clicked off before I could finish my message, but Nate would get the gist of the call. I really hoped he and Molly didn't worry. Eloise was safe and unharmed.

After ending the call, I asked Mom if she could have Eloise help her with breakfast and change her into one of the extra outfits Nate kept on hand at the farm for when Mom watched them, while I loaded the crates for the market. She also pointed me in the direction of a new T-shirt, since mine now had a distinct snot stain on the shoulder.

Thirty minutes later, I had the back of my truck loaded to the brim with produce-carrying containers along with the market stand canopy. It was going to be a hot, sunny day, and I definitely wanted to stay as shaded as possible.

By the time I finished up, I entered my parents' kitchen to find the table and an extension filled with farm hands. Apparently, we were a few men short for the day, and Mom had been trying to get a hold of Andrew to help. Aspen, my youngest sister, was already seated at the table, ready to pitch in. We all spent our youth doing what needed to be done around the farm. Mid-season wasn't too bad, but the harvest time for corn in the fall could be brutal. This time of year, the hired crew were planting soybeans in the fields that were designated in the rotation. This allowed for better corn production in a couple of years in the same field.

"Dad, do you need me to stay? I can ask Tami to cover the stand for us."

As she was setting another platter of hash browns out on the table, Mom chimed in, "Oh, is she back?"

"Yes, arrived yesterday. Jetlag has her wide awake."

"Such a sweet girl."

I nodded at my mother as she continued her hosting duties and then turned back to my dad. We hadn't really spoken since my outburst over the land parcels going to Nate. This was sort of my way of apologizing to him again.

"Dad?" I prompted again.

"I think we have it covered. Plus, I believe you have a special helper today." My dad looked a bit rough around the edges after spending years in the sun. His skin was tan and wrinkled, but when he smiled, there was a definitive twinkle that no one could miss.

The entire table lit up as Eloise shouted, "That's me! I want to help!"

As happy as I was to have her join me, I wasn't quite in the right frame of mind to entertain a four-year-old and sell our produce. But I knew my parents were in a pickle, and the farm was their money maker.

"All right. Seems I have a helper with me today." I stroked the top of the girl's hair. Checking my phone, I noticed I still hadn't received a message or call from Nate. He was usually up long before me to take a run around the property. I hoped he was okay. It was the only reason I was hesitant to take her back to the bed-and-breakfast. If something was wrong, she would be safe with me.

The mix of worry over him, the waning adrenaline rush of finding his daughter on my parents' steps, and the hangover was giving me the worst kind of stomachache.

Before heading out, I made sure to grab one of the booster seats Mom purchased the weekend the twins arrived in town. This little girl was precious cargo, and I wanted to make sure she was safe. Some of these older trucks weren't equipped with seatbelts, but when Dad and I restored her, we made sure to have them added. Safety first.

After a bit of struggling and flipping through the manual, I had the seat installed on the passenger side and an ecstatic little girl buckled in. She was in awe of the truck and asked a million questions during our drive to the center of town. By the time I parked behind our stand, I knew I was going to have to purchase two booster seats for the truck. Molly would love it just as much as her sister did.

As I helped her jump down, I slid an oversized Sunny Brook Farm shirt over her head and onto her body. The material reached her knees, and we both ended up giggling. I twisted the ends of the material into a knot in the back and tucked it under, the way I had when I was little. At least now it looked more like a shirt and less like a dress.

We waved at the other stand owners as they began arriving. My family had a prime spot, smack-dab in the middle, across from the main entrance. My great-great grandmother had been one of the founders of Ashfield's farmer's market, so it only made sense.

After setting up the canopy and making sure I turned the ringer on my phone up as high as it could go, I tried to dial Nate one last time and even called the bed-and-breakfast's main line, but there was still no response.

"All right, buttercup, ready to help me set up and sell some stuff?"

"Yes, ma'am."

I cringed at the title. I was too young to be called ma'am. I mumbled to myself that it was just good manners as I pulled the canopy out of the back of the truck and set it up. Even at seven in the morning, the temperature was rising.

"Is Daddy going to be mad at me?"

Hefting the first crate out of the truck, I replied calmly, "Well, I know he's going to be a little crazy when he can't find you. But once he realizes you're safe, everything will be fine. But I'm sure he's spoken to you two before about wandering off. Something terrible could happen, and none of us want that."

She remained silent as I pulled out more crates and set up the stand a certain way. This was my favorite part—adding a bit of flare and design to something so simple. It's what drove me to want to open a cake shop. I had the same mentality about a simple cake flavor being spruced up by something intricate on the outside. Of course, I also liked to add a few unexpected things inside my cakes too, like jelly or pastry cream.

Just thinking about cakes gave me an idea for my afternoon. I needed to bake. That was the only thing I could think of to get out of my Nate fixation. I tended to hyper-focus when I was baking.

By the time the first customers started arriving, Eloise already helped herself to a few carrots and learned the art of pickling from the stand next to mine. She and Molly were going to have to try their hand at it later.

After the second customer Eloise charmed into a purchase, I decided I would bring the girls every weekend if that meant I didn't need to sweet talk anyone. Our farmer's market brought in people all over Eastern Tennessee.

As I was bagging another customer's selection, Eloise piped up. "What did you want to be when you growed up? Did you want to be a farmer?"

Chuckling, I replied, "No. I'm not a farmer. I just help out my family. I actually plan to open a cake shop in town."

"Oh, cake. I love cake." Eloise made sure to emphasize the word love as her eyes rolled toward the back of her head.

"So do I."

"Daddy doesn't like us to eat it. Lots of sugar."

"Well, he's probably right. But there are alternatives to using sugar."

"What's an alt… altnerative?"

"Alternative. It means substitute. Like switching one thing out for another."

"Oh."

I paused and waited for her to ask for examples, but as usual, Eloise surprised me and remained quiet.

"And to answer your first question. When I was little, I wanted to grow up and be a dancer."

Enthusiastically, she informed me she and Molly were dancers. I remembered that being mentioned when they arrived. I'd have to check in with my old dance teacher and see if she was still offering classes.

Opening the task tab on my phone, I made a reminder. There were still no missed calls, and my worry was elevating to new proportions.

Off in the distance, I heard my name shouted above all the sounds of the market. Tami fervently ran in my direction. Her curly hair bounced with each stride as her rainbow-colored crinoline skirt sashayed between her legs.

Tami always danced to the beat of her own drum, and her sense of fashion was no exception. I was still shocked that she took a job that required her to wear a uniform. I can't imagine what she would have said had she seen Nate in the market wearing his three-piece suit last Saturday.

I can't believe he's only been here a week.

Before she could catch her breath, Tami launched herself at me, arms and legs wrapping around me as if she hadn't seen me in years, not weeks. She gushed about missing me, while Eloise cackled next to me.

"Oh!" Tami exclaimed as she finally realized there was someone with me. Prying herself off my person, she kneeled down until she was eye-level with Eloise. "Who is this adorable creature?"

"This is my stowaway, Eloise. She and her twin sister, Molly, are staying at the bed-and-breakfast."

"Stowaway, huh?" she asked, looking up at me in question, and I gave her the condensed version. "Well, you both have had quite the morning. Tell me, though, did you get to see the sunrise like you planned?"

"I did!" Eloise shouted.

"Well, then we know it was all worth it. Plus, you get to spend the morning with my bestest friend."

"I like your tutu." Eloise's small hand reached out as she felt the crunchy material, smiling as she fisted a handful, then released it.

"Thank you. Do you think it clashes with my shirt?"

Eloise looked up at me with furrowed brows, so I explained, "Clashes means it doesn't go with it. Like they don't match."

Her pinched gaze traveled over Tami's outfit as my friend stood to her full height and twirled. "I like it," the little girl confirmed.

In fact, the top and skirt did clash to the naked eye. Tami wore a plaid red and navy tank top with the rainbow-colored skirt, but she could pull it off in only a way Tami could. She could make any off-the-wall combination work, because she oozed enough confidence to fill the Empire State Building.

Another hour passed where Tami and Eloise hung out with me at the stand. It was nice to have someone to talk to between customers. Even Mrs. Hensen was on her best behavior when she chatted. I was disappointed there was no more talk about bumpy cucumbers, but it was probably for the best. I didn't want to spend the time coming up with an excuse to tell Eloise why Tami and I couldn't stop giggling.

There was a lull in the crowd, and Tami offered to hang out at the booth while I walked Eloise around the market. I had a few things I needed to pick up if I planned on making cakes this afternoon. I could go to the store, but fresh was always preferred.

Our first stop was at the small library stand. Eloise's choice. I loved that she was fascinated by books. I'd never been a big reader as a kid. Not really one either as an adult except for romance novels, but that was more or less because I didn't have the time. She eyed a book about fairies the librarian said was a great starter book. Not passing up the opportunity, I bought it and another in the set for Molly. I made sure each could be read by themselves.

The girl's answering smile when I handed her the book was everything in that moment. I would do anything to keep her grinning like that. I could already hear everyone calling me an enabler and spoiling the twins, but I couldn't help it. I loved that rush of serotonin.

With the books hugged to her chest, Eloise and I made our way to a stand a few tables over. Mystic sold any and every spice you could imagine. I had no idea what some would be used for, but I wanted to try them all. Grabbing a few things from there, I moved onto

Farmer Chris's booth. His farm milled their own flour, and it was the absolute best for baking. I was determined to utilize local ingredients when I opened my cake shop, and using Chris's flour was number one on my checklist.

We chatted for a bit while Eloise stood at my side. Chris was only a few years older than me and had taken over the farm when his parents decided to retire and move south to Key West, Florida. Normally, his family would join him at the stand, but his wife was home with their newborn.

I asked if he would be interested in being one of my vendors for goods, and he heartily agreed. Locally sourced goods were what kept a lot of the farms in Ashfield afloat.

With one last stop at the jelly stand for some raspberry compote, Eloise and I made our way back to the Sunny Brook Farm booth. Tami had done a good job manning it in my absence, selling a few full crates of produce.

Just as I emptied the last crate onto the display, Tami tapped me on the shoulder.

"Don't look now, but Mr. Tall, Dark, and Handsome is headed this way."

Spinning around, I stared out at a frantic Nate with sweet Molly trailing behind him, going as fast as her little legs could carry her. This was going to be fun.

"Eloise!" he shouted, his voice hitching at the end in panic.

"Daddy!" she replied, dashing out from around the stand and running toward her father.

Everyone at the market stopped what they were doing and watched the tearful exchange. A few curious gazes flickered over to me but then returned to the reunion when I shrugged.

I couldn't hear what Nate was saying, but the way he held Eloise and pushed her hair back from her face told me everything I needed to know.

"So... want to fill me in?" Tami asked, nudging me with her hip.

"That's Nate Sullivan... and... he's the guy."

"What guy?"

I pulled my attention away from the family and focused on my friend.

"The guy... from last year. The one who left after I went to check on the bar's closing."

"What? No way."

I went on to explain the rest of the situation and the unfortunate part of Nate not remembering a single thing.

"And you believe him? I mean, no offense, but with the way you described that night after it happened and all the kinky shit you two did, it seemed pretty memorable."

"Believe me, when I opened the door to him, it was pretty damn obvious he had no idea who I was."

"Well, damn. That sucks."

"We made out… at my apartment on Wednesday… until my brother walked in."

"Oh, damn. What does Andrew think about all this? I mean, they've been best friends for like twenty years, right?"

"He doesn't know. He never saw anything."

"At least you get the memory, right?"

She was right, and I supposed I could live with that. Turning my attention back to the twins and their dad, I couldn't help but try to take a mental snapshot. Something else to add to the memory box. Was I going to see them around town? Sure, but it wouldn't be the same.

Nate must've felt my eyes on him, because as he stood, our eyes locked. It felt like time slowed as he gathered his daughters' hands and began walking toward our booth, right to me. It may have been hot outside, but nothing compared to the heat that coursed through me under his stare.

"Whew, I should go find myself some marshmallows, chocolate, and graham crackers, because this booth is about to catch fire with the way that man is looking at you."

"Shut it, Tami," I growled at her.

He stood before me, just on the other side of the table, a simple display of produce separating us. We stood silently; not even the girls spoke.

"Um… hi, I'm Tami. This one's best friend," she greeted, tilting her head in my direction as she held her hand out toward Nate.

The disruption was enough to rattle Nate free from our connection as he introduced himself to Tami. "I realize you already met Eloise. This here is her sister, Molly."

"Well, you're just as pretty as your sister," Tami announced, making both girls giggle. Tami's eyes ricocheted between me and Nate, then she added, "If it's okay with your dad, maybe I can take you to my favorite creamery's booth, where they may have something nice and cold for us."

It was a little early in the day for ice cream, at least for kids. I was a big believer in eating it any time of day. So it surprised me when Nate nodded. Tami stepped around the booth, her skirt in full display as she grabbed the girls' hands, and Molly eyed her in wonderment.

We watched them retreat, and Nate described my friend as "interesting."

"She is. And one of the best people I know."

Turning back toward me, Nate's lips were pinched into his mouth. They were almost nonexistent.

"Are you okay?" I asked.

"I… I want… no, need to apologize."

"There's no need."

He seemed torn up about the incident, and I could understand why.

"There is. I don't want to think about what would have happened had you not found her. God, what if she had been lost out there? These images keep running through my mind, and I can't turn them off. She's never done anything like this before. I just can't imagine—"

"Nate, you can't blame yourself or allow yourself to imagine what could have happened. She's a little girl who got herself into trouble. I'm sure my father could tell you all sorts of horror stories from me and my sisters when we were that age. But you had a stressful night, and she's okay."

I knew Nate had a monitor set up in each of the girl's rooms. Either he had been really out of it, or Eloise was very quiet when she made her escape. The girl was overly bright and spoke better than most of the older kids I knew. When I asked him about the monitor, he confessed he must've tripped over the charging cord, because it was unplugged. The monitors died sometime in the night.

"I also fell asleep without charging my phone. Seriously, anything that could have gone wrong... did."

"You're being too hard on yourself."

"There's never a day when I'm not. Definitely no Father of the Year over here."

"You're a great father, Nate. Was it a scary situation? Sure. But Ashfield is one of the safest towns."

"But what if—"

"Nate, stop. She's fine, and now she knows not to do it again. This was a valuable lesson for the three of you. And there is a bright side."

Scoffing, Nate looked at me like I'd grown two heads.

"She got to watch the sunrise. She said it was the most beautiful thing she'd ever seen, and I made her promise that, next time, she'd wake you up to join her."

His chin dropped to his chest, and his thumb and pointer finger covered his eyes. When he looked back up at me, the whites of his eyes were now red. "You know, I always thought it would be Molly who would give me my first heart attack."

Smiling, I added, "They've both got to keep you on your toes."

It wasn't long before Tami and the twins returned, all three with cups of homemade ice cream in hand. I was partial to the strawberry concoction myself and was glad to see both girls had chosen that flavor.

My heart swelled as they offered spoonful of the cold confection to their dad.

"And your heart grew three sizes that day," Tami quoted, earning herself an eye-roll as I stole her spoon and scooped out a dollop of ice cream from her cup. Mango. Delicious.

Just like the man worming his way under my skin.

Chapter Twelve

Nate

My heart still raced by the time the girls and I arrived back at the bed-and-breakfast. We stopped for lunch at Angelo's for pizza. They both claimed this would be our new tradition on Saturdays. I wasn't opposed in the slightest.

In the rearview mirror, I continuously checked on Eloise to make sure she was there and okay. There was no way to describe the fear and panic I felt when I woke to find she was missing.

I'd slept in. Something I never did. With my cell phone dead, I had no alarm to wake me before the girls reimburse Autumn for that. When I asked her if her sister was awake, she just shrugged.

I searched the house from top to bottom and even around the yard. So many thoughts intruded, like her drowning or an animal attacking her. Finally, my phone had enough charge to power on, and the relief I felt at hearing Alex's message was comparable to the twins' birth.

They'd been five weeks early, and we worried about their lungs and heart. It felt like I held my breath through the entire delivery. When they cried after taking their first breaths, I'd finally taken my own.

Sunny Brook Farms had been the first place I stopped. I had to track down one of the farm hands, since the house was empty. They told me Alex and Eloise were at the market.

I'd never be able to describe to someone what it felt like to hold my daughter in my arms again. She may have only been missing for a short time, but it felt like years to me.

"Daddy, we beat Miss Alex home."

"We sure did. Maybe we should do something nice for all her help today. What do you think?"

"Yes!"

I got the girls settled outside under the covered area of the porch with some paper and paint. Molly was most excited to try out the glitter glue we packed up before leaving California.

While the girls painted, I grabbed my laptop and began researching home designs. I wanted something similar to Nash and Marisol's home. It held the best memories for me, and I wanted my girls to have the same.

It wasn't long before I heard the crunching of gravel on the other side of the house. My fingers shook over the keys of my laptop. I was nervous to see Alex. After the meeting at the market, I felt exposed. Like she was a firsthand witness to my lack of parenting skills. As someone who was a perfectionist, it was a hard pill to swallow.

"Hey, everyone." Her head popped out of the opening of the sliding glass door. "I'm going to take a quick shower, then Eloise and Molly, you both can help me bake before I get dinner started. Is that okay?" She directed the question to the twins, but I sensed she was asking permission from me about the activity. I gave her a quick nod as the girls hovered over their artwork, not wanting to spoil their surprise for her.

Laptop aside, I got down on my knees at the table and helped my daughters cut out shapes. Twenty minutes later, Alex found us in the same position, only this time I had glitter glue stuck to my arms. I was pretty sure there was some in my hair as well.

Alex oo'd and ah'd at the self-made art, delighting the girls. Not that they were hard to please, seeing as Tami now took up the number-one friend spot after buying them ice cream this morning.

We followed our host inside, and Alex secured each of the pictures to the fridge with magnets. She told us that her mom said kids' artwork always made it to the front of the fridge. She and her sisters used to switch out their sibling's art for their own in a constant battle to see who had the most on the refrigerator. Alex made sure to point out, since there were two little girls at the B&B, and the fridge had two main doors, that they each had their own side.

She instructed the girls to wash their hands as she began unpacking the ingredients she purchased at the market from a bag on the kitchen island.

"You have a little something…." She pointed in the general area of my face.

"Yeah, they get a little crazy when glitter is involved," I joked, my stomach flipping over and over as the corners of her lips tilted upward.

"Don't we all?"

"I'm going to follow your lead and hop in the shower. Are you good here with both of them? I mean... I probably shouldn't even ask. You're not a babysitter or anyth—"

Her hand rested gently on my arm. "Nate. It's fine. I enjoy spending time with them. Go take a shower, then work on your project or something. We're good here."

I wanted to kiss her. Right then and there, I wanted to grab her face and press my lips against hers. My girls standing at the sink were the only thing holding me back. This woman was an angel sent down from heaven. I was certain of it.

"Thank you."

"No need to thank me," she spoke as she began pulling out measuring cups from the cupboard. "We probably should have conserved water." The words were mumbled under her breath, and I was sure she hadn't wanted me to hear them, but I did.

And as I stepped into the shower in my bathroom, with the hot water sluicing over my skin, I grabbed my cock and stroked it, because her words kept repeating in my head.

I spent much longer in the shower than I intended. After giving myself a handy while thinking about the woman currently watching my kids, I felt like a creep. She was downstairs in the kitchen, acting as Suzy Homemaker helping me out to get a quick shower, and there I was thinking about all the ways I wanted to strip her bare and leave her sore for days.

I was disgusted with myself, and it was only made worse when Andrew called me, asking if I wanted to join him tonight. I felt bad about ditching my friend, but I also didn't have anyone to watch the girls. Sure, I could ask his mom or Alex, but I couldn't keep relying on them.

Declining the invite, I pulled on a pair of boxer briefs, basketball shorts, and a black T-shirt. There was no reason for me to dress up, since I had zero desire to leave the house. Though, as I traveled down the stairs, I wondered if the girls would want to join me on a ride over to the property I was purchasing. All three of them. Nash emailed me the plot specs, so I should be able to find it easily enough.

With the adventure fresh in my mind, I practically hopped down the stairs two at a time. My greeting never made it past my lips as I stepped into the kitchen. Everyone's hair had been tied up into ballerina buns that sat on the top of their heads. Each girl rested a hand on the counter of the island as if it were a ballet barre and bobbed up and down.

"Now, this is called a plié."

Alex's movements were smooth and graceful, whereas my daughters were jerky as they mimicked her. Her arm swung up high in the air, a slight curve to the elbow, and her hand was turned inward.

She was beautiful as she moved. I was mesmerized, as were my kids, as they spent more time with mouths agape, watching Alex move than doing it themselves.

"One more move, then I need to get the cake into the oven so it's ready for decorating after dinner."

Releasing the counter, Alex positioned her body so that her right foot was in front, and with both arms level with her shoulders, her left arm reached out in front of her body. She bent slightly, then spun around twice before landing in the same position she started in.

Both Molly and Eloise stared up, slack-jawed. It was hard not to be amazed.

Clapping, I entered the room, making myself known. Alex quickly released her stance and began brushing off her clothes.

"That was amazing," I told her. This woman kept surprising me at every turn. "I didn't know you could dance like that. You should have done it professionally."

Her smile faded, and the sparkle left her eyes. I immediately felt terrible for whatever I said to take away her joy.

"Yes, well, we can't have everything we want."

I wanted to pry. I wanted to ask more questions about who told her she couldn't have everything. But I sensed now was not the time.

As she opened the oven and placed the cake pans inside, Molly asked her what that spin was called. I chuckled as both of them tried to repeat the word pirouette.

"Before dinner, I thought maybe we could explore the land where I am going to build our house. Would you like that?" I directed the question to the twins, but I hoped Alex knew I was including her in that adventure.

"Yeah! That's so fun. I can't wait. Can we go now? Is the house already there? Can I pick out my room?" Molly spewed questions out at the same rate my new program could read data. Which was alarmingly fast.

I heard Alex's chuckle from her stance by the stove.

"No, the house isn't there yet. You guys get to help me pick out the perfect house for our family. And we can go once the cake is out of the oven."

"But why?"

"So Alex can join us."

Piping in, Alex tried to decline the invite, but none of us Sullivans were hearing it. We shamelessly begged. I wasn't above it to get what I wanted, and having her sitting beside me on the UTV was it. She finally relented and agreed to join us.

To kill time, I opened my laptop to reveal the site with the house plans. Outside earlier, I narrowed it down to a few that reminded me of the Sunny Brook Farms house but on a smaller scale. There were only three of us, after all.

Molly and Eloise were sitting on the barstools, eating an apple with peanut butter. Carrying the device over to the island, I flipped the monitor around to show them my top four choices. Molly liked the one with the double porch, while Eloise picked the one with the gigantic fireplace.

"Which one is your favorite?" Alex asked as she came to stand beside me.

"I like them all."

Her eyes narrowed at me for a moment before turning back to look at the screen. She pressed the pad to flick through the images before returning to the third option.

"No. This is the one you like the best."

She was right.

"What makes you think that?"

"Because it suits you. It's both a farmhouse and craftsman style. A bit rustic and modern. Plus, it matches my parents' house."

"What makes you think I want something like your family home?"

She didn't respond. Alex shook her head and moved toward the sink, where she began running water to clean the dishes. I hated and loved that she knew she was right.

Acting put-out, I turned the laptop around again and asked the girls what they would think about living in the house of my choice, and after explaining we could add an oversized fireplace and a really big porch, they both seemed appeased.

Scrolling through the plan details, I called out the important things. "Three beds, three baths, full basement."

"Don't you think you need more than three bedrooms?" Alex asked.

I peered at her over my shoulder and smirked as her hips swayed with each swipe of the sponge against the bowl she held. "Naw, it's just us."

"But what about guests, or if your family ever expands?"

It was said innocently, but the image of Alex pregnant in my kitchen immediately popped up in my mind.

I had to cough to clear my throat before agreeing that it was a good idea. I probably did need an extra bedroom for my parents if they ever decided to visit. They still hadn't read the message I sent about the move now being permanent.

"Daddy, you and Miss Alex should dance. Like in that movie."

I glanced up at Molly in confusion. "What movie, sweetheart?"

She tapped her little chin with her index finger, leaving a smudge of peanut butter behind. "The one with the big dog and the girl who likes books. She has the big yellow dress."

"Beauty and the Beast?" Alex chimed in as she joined us at the island again.

"Yes!" Molly shouted, a piece of apple spewing from her mouth onto the counter, just missing my hand. Kids really were gross.

"Um...," I said, looking over at Alex for help but finding nothing but a smirk. "Maybe after dinner." I then silently prayed they'd forget. It wasn't that I didn't know how to dance or that I didn't want to with Alex. It was that having her in my arms was going to feel too good.

"Ugh. You always say 'after dinner,'" Molly lamented just as the buzzer for the oven went off.

Saved by the bell.

"Sorry, pipsqueak. Let's get the keys to the UTV, and we'll head on out."

It took only a few minutes to get everyone situated in the back of the vehicle. Alex triple-checked the girls' seat belts before she took her seat beside me. I found it endearing that she was being so cautious. It hadn't snuck past me that she even made sure there was a booster seat in her truck for Eloise this morning.

As I was pulling up the map on my phone, Alex pushed her body against me. At first, I thought she planned on getting cozy with me, but she continued to nudge and nudge until I stepped out of the UTV, and she took over the driver seat.

"I know this land like the back of my hand. I don't need a map to show you your property."

I tried to argue that I'd need to know how to get there on my own, since I started testing my prototype robot on Monday, but she didn't relent. Instead, she turned the ignition.

"Fine. You win." I crossed my arms against my chest as I sat in the passenger seat.

"I always win," she said as the UTV shot forward, and we were on our way.

Once we started going, I realized it wasn't going to be difficult to find the plot of land. When we reached Sunny Brook Farms, there were small paths leading in all different directions. The farther we got from the farm, the more forks in the road we came across. Alex continued to take the left paths until we reached the very end.

"Here we are. Home sweet home."

Once I extracted the girls from their seats, Eloise and Molly ran through the dirt plot. I had a sneaking suspicion Nash commissioned someone to trim down the yard just for me, because the other fields all had waist-high wheat and corn. Alex confirmed my inkling and pointed out that the testing plots were across the farm on the other side, closest to the event venue.

The hundred-acre spot was expansive. It went as far as the eye could see.

"Where is your plot of family land?" I inquired as we gathered the girls and got back into the UTV. Alex wanted to show them the creek at the back of the yard in the woods.

"Next door. Welcome, neighbor. But don't worry. I won't come over to borrow sugar or anything."

The field whipped past us, and in a few minutes, we were staring at large oaks and pines that were centuries old. They towered over us, and I bet they had some stories to tell.

The creek was serene, and the gentle patter of the water moving around the rocks was calming. I could sit there for hours and relax. I wanted to take it all in.

"So, girls. What do you think about building our new home here, maybe an acre away from the woods?"

"How big is that?" Eloise questioned. She was forever learning and investigating the world around her. Glancing beyond the forest, I pointed toward the top of a small hill and explained that was about an acre away. "Yes. I like it."

We didn't linger around long, as dusk would descend on the grounds soon. The days were getting longer, but I wanted to be back at the B&B before nightfall.

In the kitchen, Alex pulled out a wok, chicken breasts, and a slew of vegetables. I offered to run into town and pick up Chinese food, but Alex dismissed me.

"I can make some stir fry and fried rice. We don't need to order out."

I wasn't going to argue with her, because she seemed thrilled to get to cook the meal, and I was fascinated to watch.

As she continued to pull items from the pantry and fridge, I was growing overwhelmed for her. It seemed like a lot to take on for one meal. I asked her if she wanted me to assist in any way, but she just laughed in my face.

With my daughters up in their temporary bedrooms, I took the time to watch Alex. Really watch her. Even walking around the kitchen, her moves were lithe and fluid. It was amazing I hadn't noticed it before, because everything about Alex screamed dancer.

She was so patient with Molly and Eloise earlier. From the way she spoke about the moves and made sure the girls positioned their feet correctly, I could tell she was passionate about it. It left me wondering why she gave it up.

"Can I ask you about the dancing?"

Without missing a beat, she threw the vegetables and chicken in the wok. The instant sizzle was enough of an answer. It wasn't something up for discussion.

"Can I thank you again for coming to both my and Eloise's rescue this morning?"

"You can, but it's not necessary." She broke an egg into the pan with the rice and began stirring it all around. With her other hand, she tossed the wok back and forth over the gas stove a few times, setting down the spoon to pour in a few different sauces.

She wasn't kidding when she said she had it all handled.

Needing to do something, I walked over to the cabinet by the sink and began pulling out plates to set the table. I did the same with utensils and glasses. As I finished, she asked me to get the girls.

Dinner was fabulous, and it surpassed any Chinese takeout I'd ever had. Everyone cleaned their plate and had seconds. As I began cleaning up the dishes, the girls jumped over to the island and situated themselves on the stools as Alex began pulling out the icing for the cake. They informed me it was made from scratch earlier when they whipped up the cake.

I didn't need to taste it to know it was going to be delicious. But I was definitely going to have a piece or two.

Alex walked them through the art of the crumb coat and then applying a thicker layer on top. She explained normally you would chill it after the crumb coat, but since we were all going to devour the cake, it wasn't necessary.

The twins carefully stroked their spatulas across the cake, while Alex looked on carefully. When she thought no one was looking, her little devil came out, and she swiped her finger through a bit of icing. I stifled back a groan when she popped that finger in her mouth, sucking off the sugary mix. I was fucking envious of her finger and the icing.

Carefully, Alex covered the leftover icing and placed it back in the fridge. Bringing out a smaller container of green bags, Alex explained she was going to hand-pipe a few designs on the cake for decoration with a special tip she added to a bag.

She swirled her hand around a small section, squeezing the bag as she went. A perfect paisley pattern appeared on one side of the cake, then she repeated the same design in the opposite direction. Over the course of five minutes, she created something far too pretty to eat.

"That's a masterpiece," I murmured, while both Molly and Eloise claimed it was the prettiest cake they'd ever seen. "It's too nice to cut into now."

"Pssh, no, it's not. We're just messing around. But before we dive in, let me get a picture. Girls, smile." Whipping out her phone from her back pocket, she angled the device in a way to capture the sides and top. "Perfect." Stepping over to another drawer, she pulled out a large knife. "Now, let's dig in."

She waited to take her first bite until we'd taken ours. The flavors were indescribable.

"What is this?" I asked her as I took a hearty second bite. The cake had no chance of survival, because I planned to devour the entire thing.

"It's pistachio cake with a tart raspberry filling and sweet buttercream frosting. Do you like it?"

"Like it? I feel like I died and went to heaven."

Dropping her fork onto her plate, Molly cried out that I wasn't allowed to die. I had to pause my eating to explain that it was just an expression. A pretty morbid one, now that I thought about it.

"Alex, this is the best cake I've ever had. You are truly talented. I plan to visit your shop every day if you're making cakes like this."

"Really? You're not just saying that?" She peered at me from under her lashes. There was an insecurity about her question. With delicious cakes like this, I couldn't understand how she could doubt herself.

"I'm 100 percent honest. You have a gift."

"Thanks. I owe it all to my mom. She taught me everything I know."

Eloise chose that moment to innocently chime in. "My mommy doesn't want us. She said so."

I coughed and sputtered around my mouthful of cake. Thankfully, Alex took the reins on the response. "But you have your daddy and a ton of other people like myself and Andrew and my mom and dad who want you."

"You do?"

"Of course."

"Can you be my new mommy?"

Now it was Alex's turn to cough as she turned to look at me, her face a pasty shade of white.

"Alex and I are just friends, and she can be your friend, too."

My words sufficed, but with their pouts, I knew the answer wasn't the one they hoped for. They even turned down a second piece of cake, which I wasn't too upset about, because that meant more for me, but I hated seeing their forlorn faces.

Then I remembered my promise from earlier.

Setting my plate and fork onto the counter, I turned toward Alex. Gently, I took the plate and fork from her grasp and sat them beside mine.

"I believe I promised the girls I would dance with you after dinner."

She nodded in understanding. Pulling out her phone, her finger scrolled on the screen until a satisfied smile grew on her face. "Can you waltz?"

"I don't know." I wasn't a complete novice at dancing. When I was younger, my mother enrolled me in a senior's dance class to keep me entertained after school, since she wasn't home. That was ages ago, but I hoped it would be like riding a bike.

"Okay, I'll lead. The moves are slow-quick-quick. You'll start with your left foot, and I'll begin with my right. Basically, it's an elaborate box step. Does that make sense?"

"Yes?"

"Just follow me." She pressed a button on her phone, and a song began to play. As she stepped up to me, Alex moved one of my arms to her waist, my hand wrapping around her back, and the other she held up with her own. "Ready?"

I nodded, and then we were off. It took a few passes of me stepping on her toes to finally get the hang of the moves. And once that happened, Alex began moving us in circles around the kitchen. Thank goodness the space was oversized, because it felt like we were floating across the floor.

I finally pulled my gaze away from my feet and locked eyes with Alex. She smiled as we swirled around, but our stare never wavered. I was entranced by her.

My fingers rested on the hem of her T-shirt, the material dusting the top of her shorts. I slipped my fingers underneath the cotton to feel the softness of her back. My own grin swelled as I felt the hitch in her breath.

Being with her like this felt different. It felt like everything wrong in the world slipped away and it was just me and her. This nonsensical pair that somehow worked.

With each step of the dance, it was growing harder and harder to remember why I couldn't pursue her. Harder to remember why being with her was a bad thing.

"Daddy, the music stopped," Eloise said.

Embarrassed, Alex and I pulled apart. She ducked her head, her hair cascading around her face, most likely to hide her blush.

"Sorry."

"That was so pretty." Molly held her clasped hands in front of her with a dreamy gleam in her eyes.

"I don't think I did too bad. What do you think, Alex?"

"Um… yes. You did great. I… um, need to get something from my room."

As she brushed past me, I reached for her arm. "Are you okay?"

"I'm fine. I just forgot I needed to water the plants in my room."

Water the plants? Are there even any plants?

"Will we see you again tonight?"

"Maybe? I don't know."

Alex wandered off without a backward glance, and I wondered what prompted her retreat. Was my touch unwelcome? Did I take it too far? Maybe I had been lost in the moment, but I thought she had been as well.

The girls were confused about Alex's departure as they helped me wrap up the cake and place the dishes in the dishwasher. It was getting close to their bedtime, so I sent them on their way to get ready for their baths while I locked up downstairs.

When I reached the top of the stairs, instead of turning left to go to our end of the hall, I opted to go right. My hand hovered at her door, ready to knock, but then Molly called for me. With a heavy sigh, I dropped my hand and made my way to the girls' room.

But I made a decision, and I was done forgetting.

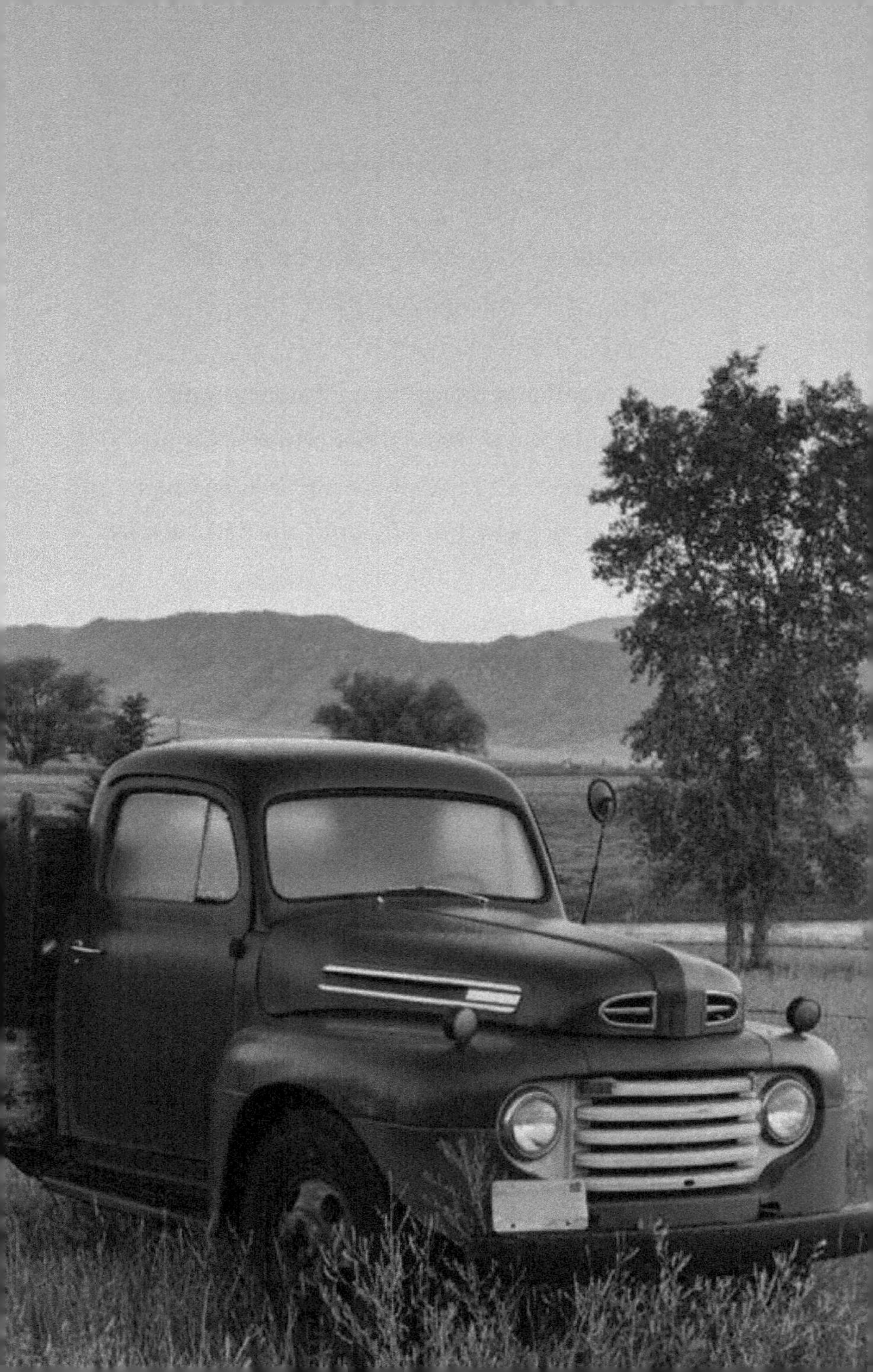

Chapter Thirteen

Alex

I was such a coward. I ran away at the first sign of being caught—by his daughters, no less. They were probably down in the kitchen, confused as hell. We'd all been having such a good time. Nate was a natural once he got the hang of the dance. And when he touched my bare skin, the world around us faded away into oblivion. For a few moments, I'd even forgotten there were two children seated at the island observing us.

Everything was turning into a muddled mess. With each day that passed, it got harder and harder to fight the pull I had toward Nate. I wasn't sure I could do it much longer. It had only been a week. One freaking week of agony trying to decide if pursuing a repeat with Nate was worth the anguish it could cost my brother.

The more I thought about it, though, I wasn't sure my brother would be so opposed to it. He loved hard, and Nate was like a brother to him. But if things didn't work out, would Andrew worry about choosing a side?

I was getting more and more worked up with each scenario that shot through my mind. Would Andrew get mad or not if he found out Nate and I slept together? Did it even matter? We were all adults, and if Andrew wanted to be upset, then he could. Everything was consensual. He may still see me as his little sister, but I was a grown-ass woman and could make my own decisions about who I wanted to sleep with.

It's not like we'd end up married. That wasn't in the cards for me. My therapist was dying to delve into the reasoning behind my anti-marriage stance, but it wasn't as serious as she suspected. I just never expected to find a love like my parents'. I thought I found my one true love in high school. He tricked me into thinking he was my be-all, end-all. And when I believed in him and his love, he destroyed everything.

Frustrated, I even considered messaging Andrew and telling him that he couldn't tell me what to do. It was petty, but I was so done playing this back-and-forth game with Nate. And we hadn't done anything more than make out since he returned to Ashfield.

I gripped my phone in my hand, debating whether it was worth whatever wrath Andrew would put upon us. Exasperated, I threw the phone on my bed and fell beside it, arms spread wide as I stared up at the ceiling.

I was so tired. My emotions were all over the place, and I needed to do something about this craving I had for the man down the hall.

Glancing over to the dresser across the room where I unpacked all my belongings, I considered grabbing my battery-operated boyfriend again to temporarily scratch the itch. But I knew it would be a poor substitute for the real thing.

"Get a grip," I mumbled. "In just two weeks, you'll only see him every once in a while. You'll be fine. And who knows, maybe when you go back to work, there will be a new passer-through." But who was I kidding? Ever since my night with Nate, I hadn't been able to bring myself to invite anyone back to my place for more than a quick make-out session or second-base touching. No one did it for me the way Nate did.

"Stupid good-looking fucker with a magic cock."

A knock on my bedroom door sounded, and I leaned up onto my elbows. God, I hoped whoever was on the other side of the door didn't hear the one-sided conversation with myself.

"Alexandra?"

My entire body shook as he called out my name. I'd never been turned on by my full name, but the way Nate said it was like my own personal aphrodisiac.

"Coming!" I hollered out in reply as I scurried off the bed.

I tried to look casual as I opened the door and blindly leaned against the jamb while also holding the doorknob with my other hand. Instead, I fumbled and missed the jamb, nearly falling over in the process.

Strong hands gripped my arms. "Are you okay?"

"Yeah. Fine. What's up?" I asked, gripping the knob with my hand to keep from reaching out and dragging him to my bed.

"Can we talk?"

"Oh. Um, sure. Where?"

Nate slipped by me into my room, wordlessly answering my question.

This was bad news. My attraction to him had grown exponentially with every day that passed. Having him here in my room, alone, was sending my body all kinds of mixed signals.

When I closed the door and turned to face him, he was standing about two feet away, hunger blazing in his eyes.

"What did you want to talk—"

The words died on my lips as Nate cupped my face with his hands and crashed his mouth down on mine.

He pushed me backward until my body slammed against the bedroom door.

"How dare you," he growled as he pulled his mouth away. I missed his tongue immediately. He nipped at the skin of my jaw, sending tiny sparks down to my lady bits with each punctuated word. "How dare you make me want you so desperately. I can't control myself anymore. Tell me why you want me to lose control like this. Tell me why I can't stop thinking about tearing all your clothes off and doing every damn dirty thing I've imagined with you."

I never believed in the spontaneous combustion of people, but with the way Nate spoke, I was certain my scorching body might just do it.

"Do it. Do everything, Nate."

Jaw held firmly in his hand, he tilted my face up toward his. "There's no going back. I may not remember last time, but I will remember this one."

"I want it. Give me everything."

In a flash, his hand was pulling my shirt over my head, leaving me in a simple cotton bra. I hadn't been expecting a visitor.

"So fucking hot," he mumbled as he flipped the cup down on one breast and latched his mouth onto the peak.

"Ah." I squirmed. His suction was strong enough I felt a twinge between my legs. Could I actually come from him playing with my breasts? It seemed like I was going to find out soon, as he dipped his hand into the other cup and ran his thumb around my nipple.

I raised on my tiptoes, using the door for support, as my core tingled with each suck and flick on my breasts. I'd never been overly sensitive there, but Nate had a magic mouth and generous hands.

The waves started to grow, and I chased that release. With zero refinement, I unbuttoned my shorts and shoved my hand between my legs. The touch of my fingers was enough to bring me one step closer to my climax. I ran two of my fingers in circles around my clit as I closed my eyes.

"That's so fucking hot," Nate muttered against my breast.

"Don't stop. Please, don't stop. I'm so close."

Nate quickly switched breasts and began sucking on the teased nipple. That feeling sent me over the edge. The convulsions rocked my body. I had to grip Nate's shoulder to stay upright as I fell apart.

My eyes opened as I felt weightless. Nate was carrying me over to the bed. As he sat me down, I realized my orgasm came so quickly I hadn't even removed my hand from my pants.

"I could watch you do that a million times," he said as he kneeled on the floor before me.

"Do what? Come?"

"No. Well, yes, but I meant touch yourself. I love that you know what makes you feel good."

"You make me feel good," I replied, a smirk growing on his lips.

"I want to watch you do it with nothing blocking my view."

Heat bloomed across my skin as he looked at me beneath heavy eyes. There was no point in cowering away. I wanted him to watch me just as badly. There was something so wanton in the power of bringing him to his knees.

His hands slid up my thighs as I nodded, stopping at the bottom of my shorts. Lifting my hips, I made it easier for him to tug the material down to my ankles. Swiftly, he removed my sandals and piled the shorts on top of them at the bottom of the bed.

Nate's hands followed the same path as before, this time snaking their way up to my hips. His fingers rested on the elastic waist of the simple panties. They were pale-pink and matched my bra, nothing overly feminine, but Nate's eyes flared as if he found me wearing leather and lace.

"Up," he growled.

The panties slid down my legs in the same fashion as my shorts, only Nate bunched them in his hand and brought them to his nose. He inhaled deeply, closing his eyes at the same time. The man looked like he was in ecstasy, and fuck if that didn't turn me on.

Opening his eyes, he latched his stare onto mine. "You smell so fucking good."

"Um… thanks?" I replied, sounding more like a question.

He tucked the small bundle in his back pocket, and I knew without asking that I wouldn't be getting those back anytime soon.

"Keepsake?"

That sexy smirk returned as he replied, "Something like that." His hands landed on my knees, and with a quick jerk, he spread my legs apart. "Now, let the show begin."

My movements were innocent and unsure at first as I trailed my fingers between my legs. I'd made myself come numerous times, but having an audience was a new experience. I dipped my fingers inside my sex to gather some of the wetness and spread it across the lips.

Nate praised me as I circled my fingers around my clit. I wanted to do whatever I could to please him. He encouraged me to move quicker, to forget he was there and take my own pleasure.

"Lie back, close your eyes, and pretend it's me."

I followed dutifully as I lay back on the bed. When I closed my eyes, I was brought back to my apartment. I remembered watching his fingers slide in and out of my pussy. He spread my folds, rubbed my clit, and glided back and forth until my legs quivered around his head. I mirrored those movements for him. He may not remember our night together, but I did. I could give him a glimpse of what we did.

Just as my knees began quaking, a soft, wet touch joined my fingers.

"Oh, God."

Nate's mouth was on me, licking me, tasting me. I wondered if the taste would be familiar to him, but I didn't linger too long on my thoughts, because one of his fingers slid toward my backside, spreading wetness around the tight hole.

"You like that," he said against my sex. "I can feel your pussy getting tighter."

With a quick brush of his nose, he pushed my hands aside, which was just as well, because they were worthless compared to his and took over. His tongue laved at my sensitive bundle of nerves at a pace that left me whimpering.

My legs began closing around his head, and I tried my best to keep them apart.

"Fuck my face, baby." Both his hands went to work as I squeezed my thighs around his head.

The pleasure was too much. It was too overwhelming as my release surged forward. I was going to come again, and it was going to be debilitating.

"Fuuuck!" I cried out. My hands gripped the blanket I laid on as I sought something to keep my body on earth. The tremors and quakes kept coming as I convulsed on the bed. Nate's fingers delicately rubbed circles on my thighs as I rode out the orgasm.

I wasn't sure how long my release lasted. It felt like eons by the time the shudders ceased.

"That was...," I started, but my words trailed off, because there was no vocabulary to describe how it felt.

"That was the hottest thing I've ever seen."

I was too exhausted to blush at his compliment. Doing my best to sit up, I propped myself on my elbows, my breasts still exposed from the rolled bra.

Nate's eyes were still glued to the apex of my thighs, and when I tried to close my legs, he playfully slapped my thigh to halt the movement.

"You have the prettiest pussy. Like... these lips right here," he said, stroking the sensitive skin, "I could suck on them all day."

"I feel weird with you staring at my... stuff." I waved a hand around, gesturing to the area in question.

"It's my pussy now. I can stare at it whenever I want."

"Um, no."

"Oh, yes." Nate chose that moment to stand. His large, burly frame towered over me. I tracked his movements to the head of the bed, where he lay down, arms open wide on either side of him. "And right now, I want you to bring that pussy over here. Sit on my face, and let me taste my other dessert."

Something about the way he demanded it, the way he insisted on me riding his face, left no question in my mind about my next move. I twisted around and slowly moved on all fours toward him.

"That's right, baby. Crawl to me."

As I reached the waistband of his shorts, a thought came to mind. I could give him pleasure at the same time.

With a devilish smirk in his direction, I dipped my fingers underneath the waistband and began tugging down his shorts.

Just as he lifted his hips in the air for me to remove his shorts, a cry came from his pocket.

What the hell?

"Fuck." His hand fumbled with the device as he pulled it out. I couldn't see the screen, but he pressed a few buttons.

"Daddy, my tummy hurts." I wasn't exactly sure which twin was crying, but it sounded like Molly.

"I need to go. Fuck. Baby, I'm so sorry."

"No, go. It's okay. I understand."

Like a switch flipped, he pressed his lips to my forehead as he tugged up his shorts. I covered myself with the edge of the blanket, using it as a shield of sorts. Just as Nate twisted the knob to the bedroom door, he turned to glance at me over his shoulder.

"I will make it up to you."

"I know."

He left the room, and I suddenly felt like he drained me of all my energy. My eyes grew heavy, and my limbs felt like massive weights. Reluctantly, I got out of the bed and got myself ready for the night. It was still early, too early to call it a night, but my body had other plans.

After a quick splash of cold water on my face, I felt slightly more alert. I pulled on a fresh pair of panties, shorts, and a camisole after brushing my teeth. I glanced out the window and noticed dusk was just settling beyond the tree line. The night was closing in.

There was a small television in the room, and I grabbed the remote. I considered lighting a candle to mask the smell of sex in the room, but I decided I didn't want to hide what Nate had done with me.

Slipping under the covers, I turned to rest on my side and scrolled through the guide menu for the cable network. At first, it seemed like I was going to have to settle on some reality television, but then a show from the 1990s came on. I wasn't around for the initial airing, but Andrew loved the reruns late at night, and I used to sneak downstairs to watch it with him. The Hey, Dude opener lit up the screen, and I hummed along to the theme song about killer cacti, smiling the entire time.

I wasn't sure how many episodes I watched. It seemed like there was a marathon or something with that and Salute Your Shorts. Darkness had fallen over the bed-and-breakfast. The shadows of the night settled in my room.

A quick glance at the clock on the nightstand displayed that a few hours passed. The day had been exhausting and long, so I decided to call it in early.

There was no sign of Nate returning, nor did I expect him to. I admired that he put his girls first before himself. There was a good chance he would settle in his daughter's bed until she fell asleep, most likely falling asleep himself.

Turning off the television, I hunkered down under the sheets and comforter until just my face was free of the confines. I thought sleep would come quickly, but I constantly checked the alarm, groaning at every hour that slipped by.

My frustration grew by the minute. I'd been about to fall asleep where I sat just after Nate left, but now I couldn't even count my way into slumber. I made it to two hundred and seventy-five sheep before I gave up. I chalked it up to my body reverting to my sleep schedule when I worked.

Since there was no hope of slumber anytime soon, I thought I could head down to the kitchen and get started meal prepping for the week.

But just as I stepped out into the hallway, another idea came to mind. I wanted to finish what I started.

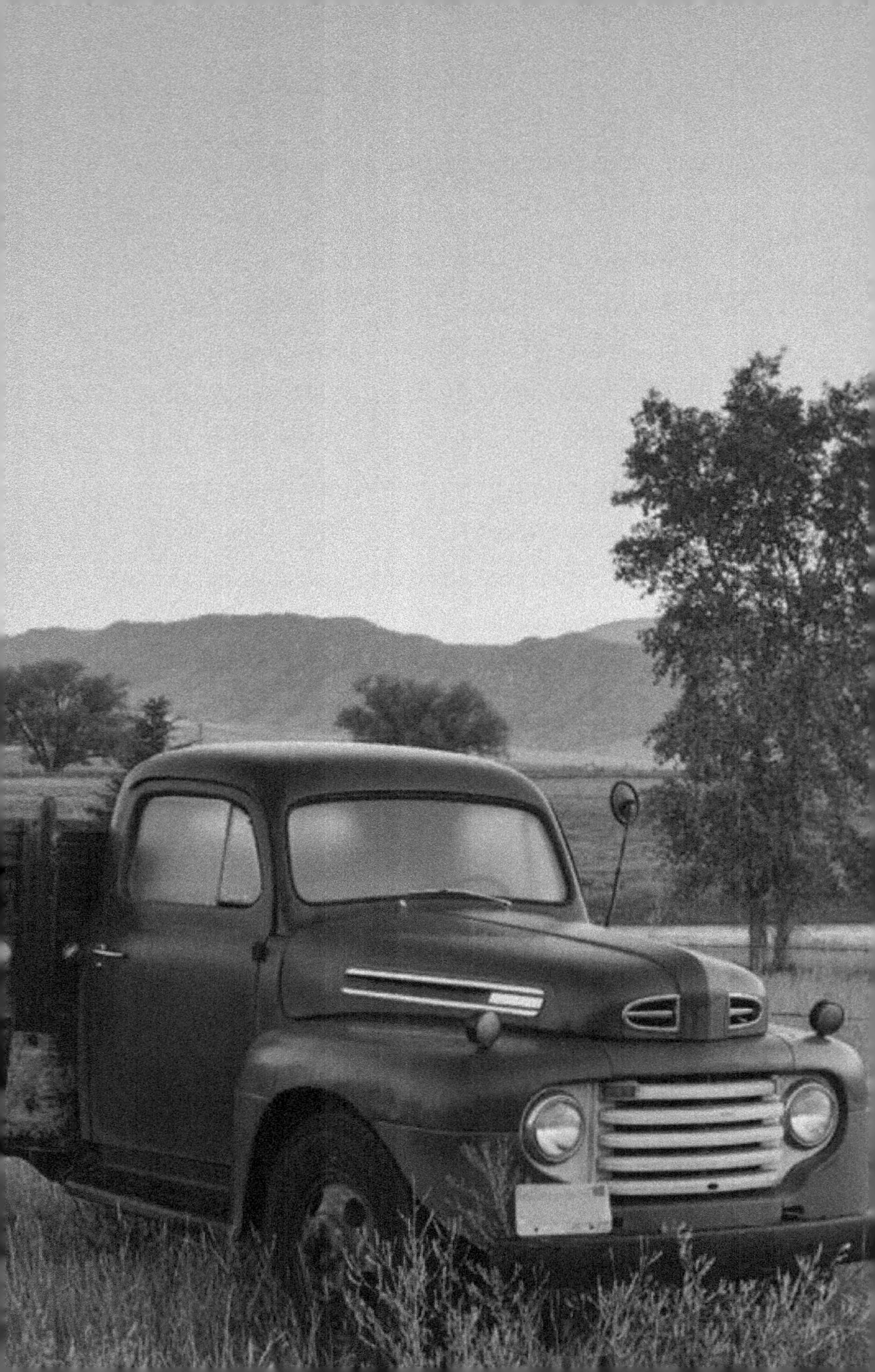

Chapter Fourteen

Nate

Molly had taken longer to go down than I expected. By the time I got her back to sleep after getting her a cup of water, it was almost midnight. As much as I wanted to return to Alex's room, I didn't want to chance waking her.

The day started off as one of my worst but ended with something wonderful I'd never forget. Alex had given me a gift tonight, and I planned on repaying her for it.

After getting Molly to bed, I tried to practice some of the tricks my therapist gave me to help with sleep. When the girls were left on my parents' doorstep, my anxiety constantly kept me awake at night. She offered multiple tools to see if they would help ease my mind. A few worked on occasion, but tonight was the exception. My mind kept darting back to Alex. The relief of hearing her voice on the phone this morning, the thrill of sharing the house plans, the seduction of our dance in the kitchen, and the lust I felt as she touched herself for me.

I was falling for this woman with each second that passed. And I needed to remind myself what happened with Sasha. Alex and I needed to keep whatever we had going on strictly to the bedroom. I was sure she'd understand I wasn't in the market for a relationship. Not now, not ever.

At some point during my mental talking to, I must've finally dozed off. The sound of my door clicking shut broke me from my slumber, and I jolted awake.

It wasn't uncommon for one of the twins to come into my room if they had a nightmare, but that was back in California. Since moving to Tennessee, there haven't been any incidents.

Searching for the lamp on the nightstand, I almost knocked it over in my haste to turn it on. My eyebrows climbed to new heights when I noticed it was Alex who entered my room.

"Alexandra, what are you doing here? Is everything okay?" I was ready to launch off the bed and wrap her in my arms, but she quickly told me to stay put.

"I want to finish what I started earlier. I want my turn."

It took my foggy brain a moment to realize what she was referring to, and my cock immediately jumped in my boxers.

"Lie back," she directed as she walked toward me. She'd covered up her body with a pair of flimsy shorts and a white tank with incredibly small straps I was pretty confident I could break with a single tug.

As she stepped into the light, my eyes flickered to her chest. Two bumps poked through the material. My mouth watered at the thought of tasting her nipples again.

"Do you think you can keep your hands to yourself?"

Tucking my hands behind my head, I nodded.

"Good. I'm pretty sure I remember what you liked last time."

Ah, fuck. She'd had her mouth on my cock before? It was a travesty I couldn't remember. My memory was a fucking disappointment.

Her small hands pulled down the top of the sheets and yanked them over to the opposite side of the bed. Before my daughters lived with me, I slept nude. But I made sure to cover up now in case there were any surprise visits.

Alex quickly made work of removing my boxers with a small assist from me lifting my hips. My cock throbbed with joy at her greedy smile. I was fucking thankful she didn't request that I turn off the light. I didn't want to miss a second of witnessing her lips around my dick.

Tentatively, she reached out and stroked a finger across the head. I shivered at the contact. I knew there was a wildness within Alex. I'd witnessed it just a few hours prior, but the innocent act completely entranced my body.

"If I remember correctly, you liked when I just barely touched you."

"Yep."

"And you really liked when I stroked the underside of your cock with my fingertips." She gave an example of the movement, and my hips jerked.

I held in my growl as I replied, "Yes."

"And most of all, you really liked when I swirled my tongue around the tip and dipped it just inside."

"Alex," I bit out. "I will like any fucking thing you do. There is absolutely nothing my dick won't like if you're the one doing it."

"Oh." She released my erection and tucked her hair behind one ear. I really hope she was going to touch my cock again sometime soon. Smiling temptingly, she leaned forward. "So, you and your cock would really like it if I used my mouth?"

Alex didn't wait for a response. She leaned forward and licked me from base to tip, then settled her mouth around the first inch. Her tongue swirled, and I knew I was a goner.

She released me from her mouth and placed her hand around the shaft. Stroke after stroke caused my erection to double in size. But when she spat where her hand met my stiffness, I about came right at that moment.

I knew the feral Alex was lurking nearby.

Slurping noises were the only sounds in the room as they mixed with my heavy breathing.

Christ, her mouth is like a vacuum.

My cock was in complete rapture as Alex wrapped both hands around the base, squeezing with each stroke. Her tongue swirled around the mushroom head just the way she described. The moment the tip of her tongue dipped the smallest amount into my sensitive hole, my eyes rolled back in my head.

I was so fucking gone for this girl. No other blowjob would ever compare. Alex knew exactly what she was doing.

It took me a moment to notice she was doing something familiar. Something that felt like it occurred before. I might not have regained the memory, but my body sure did remember this.

Slow… quick-quick. Her movements followed our waltz beat from earlier. Why was that so fucking hot?

The pressure began to build at the base of my spine. I hoped I could savor her a little while longer, but I was going to come sooner than I wanted.

Delving my hand in her hair at the base of her head, I held her in place as I pumped my hips up, my hard cock hitting the back of her throat with each thrust. The woman had zero gag reflex.

All too soon, my cum filled her mouth. A few drops spilled out of the corners, but Alex swallowed as much as she could take. Spent and utterly depleted, I relaxed my body against the bed.

Alex sat next to me, a satisfied grin on her lips. Those blue eyes twinkled as she took me in. "You used your hands."

I chuckled and then yanked her forward. She not so gracefully fell on my chest.

"It really couldn't be helped." As I settled down and allowed air to fill my lungs, Alex rested her head in the middle of my chest. I wondered if she could hear my heart pounding from the exertion. "That was... unexpected, to say the least."

Her hands came up on my chest, and she rested her chin on top of them, looking up at me in a way that made her look far more relaxed. "Did you enjoy it? Was it okay?"

I reached out and combed my hand through her hair, untangling the knots as I went. Sweat beaded along her hairline, leaving the roots around her face damp and wavy.

"It was the best fucking blowjob I've ever had."

"You said that last time," she joked, closing her eyes as I continued to stroke her hair.

"And I meant it then, too. Anytime your mouth is on my cock, it will be the best blowjob. Bar none. No others compare."

A tired chortle left her body as she rested her head back on my chest directly. Her arms laid on either side of my body, cradling my ribs.

"That feels so good," she fucking purred as I finger-combed her hair, and it sent a wave of lust straight to my cock.

"I'm glad."

"My sisters and I used to play with each other's hair when we were little. And at night, our mom would spend a few minutes with each of us to help us sleep. Autumn and Aspen always liked her to rub their back. Rory liked her to hum a lullaby. But I loved when my mom would run her fingers through my hair. I haven't had anyone do it in years."

"Well, my fingers are at your disposal."

It took a moment for the innuendo to sink in, and I felt a pinch at my waist. "Good to know."

We laid like this for another few minutes. Alex started running her fingers across the skin of my sides. Thank goodness I wasn't ticklish; otherwise, she'd have me squirming beneath her.

"I'm going to fall asleep. I should probably head back to my room."

"You could stay in here with me."

Alex popped up with wide, surprised eyes. "Really?"

"I mean, you don't have to. I get up before the girls most days. My alarm is set for six. You won't hurt my feelings if you want to sleep in your own bed though."

"Will you keep doing that thing with my hair?"

"Is that all you want me for now?"

"Yes," she said with a confident smile.

Wrapping an arm around her waist, I hefted her over my body and onto the other side of the bed.

Alex quickly snuggled her way down under the sheets, then turned to face me. She was too far away for my liking. My large hand centered on her back, and I pulled her toward me.

"That's better," I said, and she stayed facing me as I reached up and began sliding my fingers through her blonde strands.

Under the glow of the lamp, I could see the fatigue growing in her eyes until she closed them completely. A tired grin rested on her lips, just the corners of her mouth tilting upward in pleasure. When her purring noises faded, I slowly pulled my hand away. There was a small fear that I'd wake her and she'd put my hand back, but Alex remained curled up next to me.

Carefully, I twisted around and turned off the lamp before returning to face her.

There were things we needed to talk about. Lines had been crossed, and a friendship was going to be tested. But we could do that tomorrow.

I slipped an arm under her pillow and settled her head under my chin. I placed a soft peck on the top of her head before slipping my other arm around her waist.

Sleep was going to pull me under quicker than ever. My therapist and I needed to add blowjobs to my list of things to help me sleep. Or maybe it was Alex that gave my body the rest it needed.

No, it had to be the blowjob. Right?

Blackness filled the room with only the slightest glow from the moon coming through the window, when the next thing I knew, my alarm went off. It had only been a few hours of rest, but it was one of the best nights of sleep I'd ever had. I felt rejuvenated and alive. It had been years since I felt anything remotely close.

"Mmm," a soft moan sounded from beside me. "Is it time to get up already?" Her scratchy morning voice was intoxicating. Whatever morning wood I was sporting stiffened further.

"You don't have to get up. I'm just going to get a quick run and workout in."

Groggily, she sat up in the bed, the sheets pooling around her waist. Her lids only opened partly as she stretched her arms high above her head. My eyes shot to her breasts beneath the tank. I couldn't help they were in my line of sight.

"I should go back to my room."

"Okay. When I get back, we should probably talk."

"I know, but I need coffee first. I can't handle anything heavy without coffee."

Alex sat on the end of my bed as I put on a pair of athletic shorts and sneakers. I learned this past week that it was warm enough in the morning to go without a shirt.

Even in her drowsy state, Alex's eyes flared appreciatively. I may have flexed a muscle or two as I held out my hand for her. Together, we left the room, parting ways in front of the stairs. She continued down the hall to her room, and I quietly took the steps to the front door. I wore two armbands and each ear pod connected to a device. One was the monitor for the girls' room, which fit snugly in the holder, and the other was an old iPod I'd been storing music on for years.

The moment my feet hit the front porch, the early-morning air clung to me like a second skin. I spent a few minutes stretching before completing a round of pushups and sit-ups. I may have overperformed, hoping Alex was sneaking a view from her window, even though I was positive she'd gone back to sleep. Over the past week, I learned Alex was not a morning person. If she got her cake shop up and running, that was going to have to change. From what I knew about bakeries and dessert shops, which wasn't much, it was that they started early in the day to get everything ready.

Finished showing off, I strapped on a reflective band that wrapped around my chest and waist. It reminded me of the safety patrol sashes kids in school wore on the bus. I enjoyed running on the main road, and I didn't want to take any chances.

Today, I decided to take my run a bit farther than normal, telling myself I needed to make up for missing yesterday's run. I was a creature of habit, after all.

I learned in college that I enjoyed long-distance running, but never on a treadmill. I needed the sound of my feet pounding against the asphalt to push me farther. It was a way to clear my head of all the outside noise and focus on whatever project I was working on. My best ideas and codes came to me while running for miles.

Today was no different. A problem that had been plaguing me regarding my newest prototype finally worked itself out by the time I made it into town. I'd been struggling with how to maintain the moisture level of the soil during the AI testing within the robot. There would be an initial reading and then constant measuring against different portions of soil on the land. We'd considered creating a vacuum around the sample, but that tended to pull moisture from the soil.

But adding a small moisture detector specifically for a dispenser that the operator would have to fill prior to use would help resolve our issue. The technology was smart enough to know how to maintain the levels.

By the time I stopped, I realized I made my way to the far end of town. I'd get so lost in my head that I forgot where I was going.

Suddenly, the sound of a neon sign clicking brought my attention up to the window I was standing in front of. The bright red letters spelled OPEN below the Evergreen Florist sign. The sun was just beginning to rise, so it surprised me to see any businesses starting their day.

Taking a chance, I stepped inside with an idea in mind. I chatted with the owner, who said they only stayed open for a few hours on Sunday mornings. Her husband was a farmer, so the early hours suited them both.

I ordered a custom arrangement, and she promised it would be delivered this afternoon.

As I crossed the threshold back out into the open, I noticed a lot of the businesses were turning on lights and readying for the day. It was a far change from the town in California where we lived. Here in Ashfield, the day started before the sun. Inside the florist shop, her clock had read seven thirty, but it was clear she'd been working for a few hours already.

The morning sun beat down on my bare back as I ran home to the B&B. My lungs burned and muscles ached as I approached the house. As desperate as I was to go back inside and find Alex, I knew I needed to cool down, or I'd be paying for it later.

I stretched my hamstrings and quads, paying special attention to the slow stretch of the muscles.

Hands on my hips, I walked along the outskirts of the large farmhouse. I took in the beautiful brickwork, remembering how Andrew told me the house belonged to their ancestors. Autumn hoped to buy and restore the place, but Colton swooped in at the auction and bid way too much for it, sealing him as the new owner. Then he swooped in and stole her heart.

It was a cute story really, especially since I never expected to hear that Autumn returned to Ashfield. As a kid, she was always chattering about seeing the world. It made me wonder what called her back. I was also curious why Alex stayed. She should have gone to a dance or culinary school anywhere in the world. She was talented enough in both aspects, but here she was in this small town.

Finally, making my way toward the back of the house, I used the key to let myself in through the mudroom. Immediately, the smell of bacon assaulted my senses. My stomach growled at the smell of the salty goodness.

I grabbed a towel I placed on a hook earlier and wiped away any residual sweat before entering the kitchen.

"Alex?" I called out. "I'm surprised to see you up."

She stood at the stove, flipping strips of bacon, but my eyes were drawn to the tiny gray shorts that barely covered her ass. The bottom of her cheeks peeked out beneath the hem. She wore a cropped black T-shirt that showcased her toned stomach.

"Oh, good. You're back. Sit."

I knew when to listen to the boss, so I ambled my way over to the table and took a seat.

Alex set a bowl of sliced hash browns, plates of sausage and bacon, and a carafe of juice on the table.

"I wasn't sure how you took your eggs, so I made one sunny-side up, two scrambled, and two poached. Do you prefer white or wheat toast?"

My eyes were glued to the heaping plate she put in front of me. "Rye?"

"I think we have some. Let me check. I heard the girls stirring a few minutes ago, so they'll probably be down soon."

A couple of minutes later, Alex returned to the table with four slices of rye toast. I'd devoured the scrambled eggs and was currently enjoying my third piece of bacon. The girls hadn't made their appearance yet.

"Alex, you didn't have to do all this."

"Sure I did. It's sort of my job."

I wasn't even sure they paid her for all the meals she helped orchestrate. Not that it was any of my business. I knew from Andrew that the event venue on their family's farm was booked solid for years out. Each sister had a stake and a role, but each of them hired others to either take over or assist. Autumn was the event planner while Colton ran the B&B, but she had an assistant. Alex hired a local company to cater the meals. I wasn't sure about the other sisters.

"Join me?" I asked as she set the plate of toast beside me. I couldn't wait to sop up the runny egg yolk with the bread.

"I really shouldn't."

It reminded me of our first dinner, when she declined joining my family until the twins begged incessantly.

"Please."

"Fine. You and your girls have got to stop it with the puppy-dog eyes." Alex sauntered back to the kitchen, then returned with a plate of eggs. She had a smaller mix of what she served me.

As she took the seat next to me and began piling the sides onto her plate, I said, "I won't ever stop the eyes as long as it gets me what I want."

"And what's that exactly?"

Without missing a beat, I replied, "You."

The silence was so palpable we could have heard a pin drop.

"Nate," she whispered just as little feet pounded down the stairs.

My daughters joined us for breakfast and ruined our moment together. I preferred when we ate at the small table in the kitchen instead of the dining room. It felt too formal in there.

When we finished, the girls asked to go see more of the town. I didn't remember much from my time here almost twenty years ago, since my memories were tied up in Sunny Brook Farms, but Alex offered to show us some of her favorite spots. One being a watering hole at the far end of town.

Alex offered to help the girls pack up a bag with snacks and lunch after they got dressed, and I reminded them to bring their swimsuits before I hopped in the shower. I rarely lingered in my sweat for that length of time, but I wasn't about to turn down the meal she made for me.

When I rejoined the group, our host had a backpack filled with food and another bag with swimsuits and towels. I shoved my own rumpled trunks into it to join theirs, and that's when I noticed

Alex braided her hair so that it fell in two pigtails over her shoulders and repeated the design on the twins. They all looked adorable.

When we made it outside, there was an argument about riding in Alex's truck, but I overruled based on seating. Even though we weren't in the city, I wasn't taking a chance with the girls not being in booster seats.

Finally, we were off with Alex in the driver seat of my SUV as we headed toward town. The girls were excited about the adventure, but I was intrigued to learn more about the woman beside me.

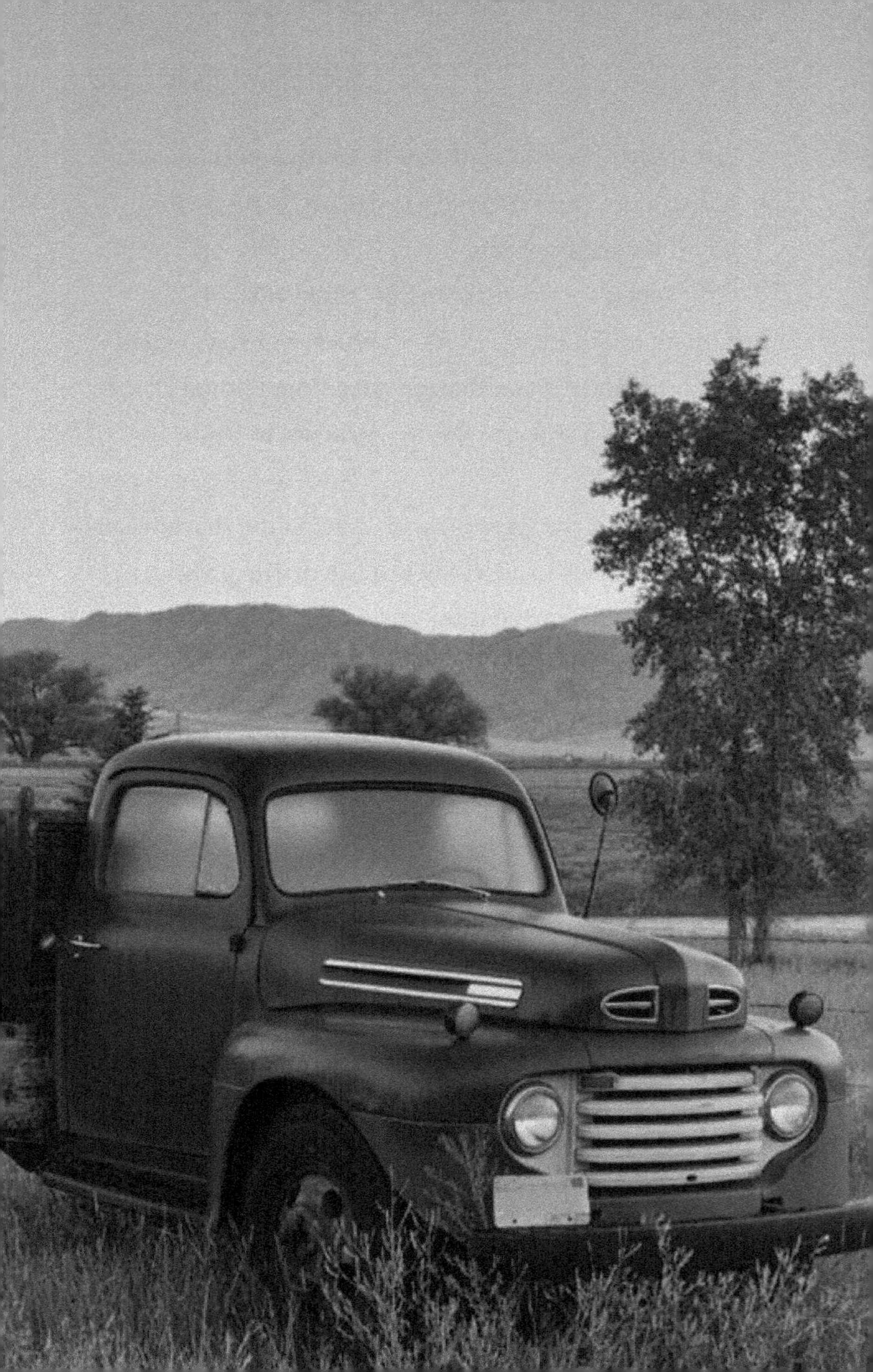

Chapter Fifteen

Alex

On the trek to the watering hole, which was nothing more than a small lake that had a natural spring supplying the water, I showed the girls all the places I liked in town. I pointed out the two-screen movie theater, the library, and the studio where I took dance classes. They were both very interested in the last one.

As we moved away from downtown, I showed them the new school that housed kindergarten through twelfth grade. It was built about five years ago, and students began attending a year later. Aspen had been one of the last classes in the old school.

Farther down the side road, I pointed out the first school ever built in Ashfield, which was nothing more than a single-room cabin, and then indicated the school I attended. They built the original part in 1902, and when I went there, there were two wings, one on either side, that separated elementary school ages from the middle and high school kids.

Someone recently converted it into apartments.

The road eventually changed from pavement to a rocky dirt path. I worried Nate was going to have a meltdown as the SUV rocked and swayed with each divot and pothole we crossed. I apologized at least six times, and he said it was fine through gritted teeth.

I wondered if he'd make me pay for it later. The anticipation of what might happen at bedtime was almost too much to bear. I did my best to hide the heat that bloomed across my chest and cheeks. I peeked at Nate, and he had an all-knowing grin on his face. It was clear I hadn't done a good enough job.

The path ended just before the tree line at the base of the mountain, and I pulled the SUV over to the side. Someone maintained the entrance and created a parking lot of sorts. Landscaping timbers lined a large rectangle on three sides, showing a place to park.

"Are you guys ready?" I asked as I turned off the vehicle with the push of a button. It was a change from the key-and-clutch combo I used for my truck.

Nate and I jumped out and moved to the back to let the girls out of their seats. Molly asked Nate a billion questions, while Eloise's eyes scanned around the area as she let me carry her.

"Where's the water?" the quieter twin asked me.

"Oh. We have to walk a little bit, but it's not too far."

"Hmm. Okay."

"When we get there, you'll find a really pretty willow tree with branches that just barely hang in the water. I used to hide underneath its cover when I was little. My grandma used to say that was where the fairies lived."

"Wow. I want to see the fairies," Eloise breathed with excitement. She scurried out of my arms and settled on the ground by my feet.

Nate and Molly joined us a second later. He carried both bags, and after settling the one with the swimsuits on my back, we started the short hike to the lake.

As expected, Molly and Eloise chattered the entire time, which meant Nate and I didn't need to add anything to the conversation. I was trying my hardest to keep my mind off the fact that he wanted to talk today.

"There it is," I said as we surfaced through the trees. Around the lake, there was a wide expanse of open field, almost as if Mother Nature placed the trees as a natural fence. A small waterfall from the mountain fed into the lake, keeping the water chillier than anywhere else in town. It felt great in the summer under the humid and hot blanket of the sun.

"Wow!" exclaimed Nate, his voice filled with astonishment.

Brushing past him, I headed toward the beach area. "Not what you expected, huh?"

"Not in the slightest," he commented, trailing after me.

"About fifteen years ago, Park Services took it under their wing and fixed it up when the town mayor petitioned for extra funding to increase the safety and preservation of the spring and lake. A park ranger ventures out here on a daily basis to do various things that I have no idea about, but I do know they make sure the cabanas are clean and nest-free."

"Nest?"

"You know, spiders, wasps, other wildlife. It gives us a place to change. In the midst of the summer when school lets out, this place is filled with people."

"What if you need to...?"

Laughing, I set my bag on a bench just outside the sandy area. "This is still the country, and those woods over there serve their purpose." I laughed again at the expression on his face.

Welcome to the country, city boy.

The twins rushed over to us, eager to get their swimsuits on and play in the water. I couldn't wait to see their expressions when they felt its temperature. We had some storms move up from the south recently, dumping some warmer rain onto the mountains, so it was going to be just above freezing. But I remembered as a kid not caring in the slightest and only being forced to leave the water when my lips turned blue.

I directed Nate and the twins over to the wooden cabana that resembled an outdoor shower but with multiple stalls. With the girls' bathing suits in hand, along with his trunks, Nate looked over at me wearily before opening the door.

Figuring they would take a while, I removed my clothing and pulled on my bikini out in the open. By the time they exited, I had my towel laid out and was catching up on the latest novel for our town book club. It was more like a gossip club, but I read the books anyway.

"That was surprisingly clean," he said as he laid his towel out beside mine. The girls were tiptoeing their way to the waterline.

"Told you."

"Should I be worried I didn't bring their life jackets?"

"It's only about three feet deep until you get closer to the falls. I have a feeling they won't go out too far."

"What makes you say that?"

His question fell away as both girls screamed, "It's freezing!"

"That's why."

He shook his head before standing and making his way to the water, mumbling that it couldn't be that cold.

He went about ankle deep before stepping back out. "Holy hell."

"We're in the middle of the mountains. Did you think it would be warm?"

Stomping over to his towel, Nate plopped back down. "I don't know what I thought. California water is cold enough. I should have known better."

"It warms up a bit by the end of summer."

The twins were still giggling about their dad squealing like a girl as they took small steps into the water. In a matter of minutes, they were waist-deep and splashing each other.

"Damn," Nate commented as both Molly and Eloise jumped out of the water, only to run back in. They were playing a game of some sort.

Setting my book on the towel beside me, I decided to watch the girls splash for a while. On my bent legs, I rested my chin and wrapped my arms around my shins.

"Should we talk about last night?" I murmured, not taking my eyes off the kids.

"Probably."

"Was it a one-time thing?" I asked, because I knew his answer was going to determine how we proceeded.

"I don't want it to be, but you need to know, Alex, it can only be sexual," he whispered. "Look at me, please." I turned my eyes toward him. "I need you to understand I can't do a relationship again. I won't do that to the girls or myself."

I didn't have to be a genius to know his ex, Sasha, did a number on him. My quick internet search of him last week disclosed little other than multiple affairs and her selling his ideas to outside companies without his permission. All over the course of just six months.

He didn't need to worry though. I had trust issues myself and was practically allergic to any sort of emotional relationship.

"I understand, Nate. You don't have to worry. I'm not looking for anything serious either."

Our attention fell back to the water. He asked about the sand, since it seemed out of place. I explained the park rangers brought in a dump truck of sand every spring to enhance the beach area. It was why the pathway was so wide.

One more question weighed heavily on my mind, and I took a deep breath before mentioning Andrew. "He doesn't need to know. It's just sex. No one will get hurt. I won't tell him, and you won't tell him."

"My lips are sealed."

I leaned back onto my elbows, tilting my face toward the sky. The sun was rising higher with each passing minute, and I savored its warmth. As I settled, I swore I heard Nate mumble something under his breath, but I couldn't make it out.

The next thing I was conscious of was something dripping on my face, and when I swatted it away, I felt the icy wetness under my finger. My eyes opened in distress before I remembered I was at the watering hole with Nate and the girls.

"Hi," Molly said, hovering above me. The tips of her hair dripped onto my face and bare shoulder.

"Um… hello." I sat up and saw Nate was setting up the picnic I packed us. "How long was I out?"

"About an hour," he called over.

"Sorry."

"It's no big deal," he replied, turning to face me with that sexy smirk on his face. "You had a very long night."

I pushed up off the towel and walked over to him, swaying my hips more than usual with each step. "That I did. Maybe we'll get a repeat tonight."

I really hoped so, at least.

"You were moaning in your sleep just now. What were you dreaming about?" he asked as he handed each girl a turkey sandwich.

I pried open a plastic bag that carried a few of my family's homemade pickles. Making sure to lock eyes with Nate, I took a hearty bite. "Wouldn't you like to know?"

In fact, I'd been dreaming of dancing again. That was something that hadn't crossed my memories during sleep in years. Sure, I continued to practice, but it was more for exercise than anything else. I blocked out all my recitals and times on stage after things ended with Stephen.

Eloise was most excited to try the pickles after I explained how pickling worked yesterday at the market. She ate two whole ones before we realized.

After a while, we packed up everything once we changed back into our dry clothes and headed back toward the bed-and-breakfast. Both girls fell asleep along the way, and with Nate driving us back, I almost did the same. It must've been something about sitting in a luxury leather seat with the warm breeze swirling through the window.

"If you want to stop in town on the way back, I want to show you something," I suggested, but Nate's eyes darted to the rearview mirror. "We won't need to get out of the car."

Instead of taking a right to go to the bed-and-breakfast, Nate turned left as I instructed, and we pulled onto the main road that took us downtown. At the first stop sign, I told him to take a right and then another left. Soon, we came upon the street with some of my favorite restaurants. Nestled between a Greek bistro and a coffee shop was a large space for sale. A sandwich shop had once occupied it, but they recently moved across the way, next to the ice cream parlor. It was a bigger space than this one.

"Stop here," I instructed. "I'll be right back."

I'd been tossing the idea around in my head for months, but as I finished up my last course, I thought this was the perfect opportunity to make the leap. I still needed to work out the business proposal, because I'd need a loan from the bank to fix up the shop the way I wanted it. I had some money saved, but it wasn't enough to cover everything. And I was stubborn enough to want to do it myself without my family's help.

"What's this place?"

My entire body launched into the air as Nate snuck up behind me, the pounding of my heart echoing in my ears.

Hand over my heart, I bellowed, "Oh my gosh, you scared me to death!"

He apologized with a chuckle that irked me more than it should've. Peering over my shoulder, I worried about the girls sitting alone in the car, but they stood just outside the open passenger door.

"They woke up when we parked. Happens every time."

Turning back to face the front facade, I stepped up to the door and used my phone to take a picture of the for-sale sign.

"This is where I'd like to put my cake shop."

Nate took a few steps back and eyed the street up and down and then did the same to the building. There were plenty of people milling about. It was Sunday, and church had let out, after all.

"I like it. It would be the perfect place. Your apartment isn't far from here either."

"Well, if I can get approved for the lease or sale, there's an apartment above the shop." I went on about wanting to perfect my business proposal before I did anything further. I could use my savings to lease the shop for a few months, but I'd need far more than that.

"Maybe we can do a walkthrough later? I'd love to see the inside."

"We?" I asked. It was the first time someone besides Tami took an interest in my plans. My parents and sisters had their own things going on, so I kept most of my intentions to myself. Though I knew they'd all be thrilled when it came to fruition, it was hard to pull their focus.

"You should tell your parents about it tonight at dinner. I think you're underestimating how much they'd want to be involved."

Maybe Nate was right. I told him so and that I'd talk it over with them at dinner. Maybe it would help keep my mind off the elephant in the room—Nate and our secret.

When we got back to the bed-and-breakfast, Nate went out to his workshop to fix something on his robot while the girls played with dolls in their room. I procrastinated dialing the leasing agency, even though it was Sunday and I doubted anyone would answer, instead emptying our bags from the trip and doing the laundry. But as the time clicked closer to dinner, I knew

I needed to bite the bullet and make the call to at least leave a message.

I was surprised when the call was answered. The woman was actually someone I'd gone to school with. She now lived one town over but maintained buildings all around the outskirts of Ashfield. We set up an appointment to view the space the next evening.

Excitement rushed through me as I ended the call. Things seemed to be finally moving in the right direction. Wanting to share the news with someone, I texted Nate and asked if he could come inside really quick. I knew he had the monitor with him, but I hoped he had his phone too.

I waited in the kitchen, and a few minutes later, I heard the screen door slam in the mudroom.

"Hey, Alex. Is everything okay?" Nate was covered in dirt and grime as he stepped inside the entrance to the kitchen, and I thought I'd never seen him look sexier. "Alex?" he prompted, pulling me from my trance.

"Oh. Sorry. I didn't want to leave the girls alone. I wanted to tell you the shop is still available, and I have a showing tomorrow evening. I'm so excited."

"That's great news. I'm so happy for you." And then he reached out and pulled me against him.

I didn't even care about the sweat and dirt that covered him from head to toe. There was nowhere else I'd rather be.

"Nate," I hummed as I felt the significant bulge in his shorts against my stomach. The monitor appeared in his hand, and after a few clicks, Nate set it on the counter.

His lips crashed against mine. This wasn't slow and sweet. This was an unquenchable hunger that we both sought to tame. My tongue begged for entrance into his mouth as Nate's hand snaked up my top and cupped my breast beneath my bra.

A breath whooshed from my lungs as he lifted me and set me on the kitchen counter. We were clumsy as my head bumped against an upper cabinet door and his knees slammed into a lower one.

His lips left my mouth and focused on my jawline and neck. "Fuck, I want you." He punctuated each word with a press of his mouth as he positioned my hips on the edge of the counter, aligning me with his erection. He rocked against me once, and my entire body trembled.

"Oh… my…," I whimpered as he repeated the motion again.

"I can feel your heat. Your greedy pussy wants my cock, doesn't it, baby?"

"God, yes," I replied, the world falling away from around us. It was just me and Nate and our starvation for each other. "I want you, Nate. Please." I didn't recognize my own voice. It was raspy and demanding.

Leaning my head against the cabinet, I savored each kiss he trailed down to my chest. His fingers skimmed across my thighs until he reached my cotton shorts. Slipping past the barrier, he pushed the material aside, exposing my sex, and ran his fingers across my soaked slit.

My body trembled at his touch, and I felt a rush of heat pulse in my center.

"I want you inside me, Nate. Please," I begged.

"I know you do, baby. Pull it out. I want to watch you."

Nate leaned back slightly, and my skin missed the feel of his lips. I struggled with the button on his shorts as he continued to run his fingers across my center. Finally, I dug my hand beneath the waistband of his briefs and wrapped my hand around the head of his cock.

We were being careless, but I didn't care.

I stroked him with one hand while the other moved his shorts and briefs down. Nate brushed his lips against mine once more as I aligned his cock with my entrance. He was mere inches away as the sound of feet thumping down the stairs froze us both.

"Oh my gosh!" I hissed. I pulled away from Nate, and he mirrored my wide eyes filled with horror.

Releasing his cock, I jumped down from the counter, realigning my shorts and top while Nate tucked himself back into his shorts. There was nothing I could do about my heaving breaths or pounding chest. I only hoped the twins didn't notice.

They came into the kitchen holding hands, asking if they could turn on a movie in the living room. It seemed like Nate was in pain as he hunched over the kitchen island, his voice sounding unfamiliar as he replied to the girls. Thankfully, they already figured out how to work the remote and streaming service.

When I heard the opening sequence to a movie, I walked over to Nate and gently placed my hand on his back. I didn't need to ask if he was all right. With the way his body angled over the island, he seemed to be in excruciating discomfort.

"Can I do something for you?"

Wordlessly, his arm jutted out and grasped my wrist, directing my hand over the tent in his shorts. It was harder than I've ever felt an erection be before. His entire body jerked at the contact.

"Oh, Nate," I cooed.

"I… need to go take care of this," he croaked as he stood to his full height.

"I understand. I'm so sorry."

"Definitely not your fault." Brushing past me, he pressed a kiss to the top of my head before hobbling toward the stairs.

Needing something to do to keep my mind off the man upstairs stroking his cock, something I wanted to watch terribly, I joined the girls in the living room.

But no matter how hard I tried to focus on the queen shooting ice from her hands, my thoughts kept returning to the kitchen and how desperate I was to have Nate. Thoughts about protection and consequences had flown out the window the second his lips touched mine. His cock had been so close to my center. Close enough I could feel the heat from the tip. I wanted it more than anything in the world.

It was probably good that the girls interrupted us before we made a drastic decision. Neither of us was ready to face those implications.

Too bad my pussy didn't get the memo, as she continued to throb in need.

When Nate made his way back down a while later, I swapped spots with him. If I was going to make it through dinner, I absolutely needed to pay myself some attention.

I didn't even need to use my vibrator. Just a few strokes of my own fingers did the job.

Now that we were both sated, there was a chance for us to make it through dinner without any complications.

I rejoined the group, and Nate rested his arm on the back of the couch, running small circles on the back of my neck with his fingers. I didn't know that spot would be a mainline of pleasure to my vag.

With every minute, the chance of making it through dinner grew smaller and smaller.

Thank goodness I wasn't a betting woman.

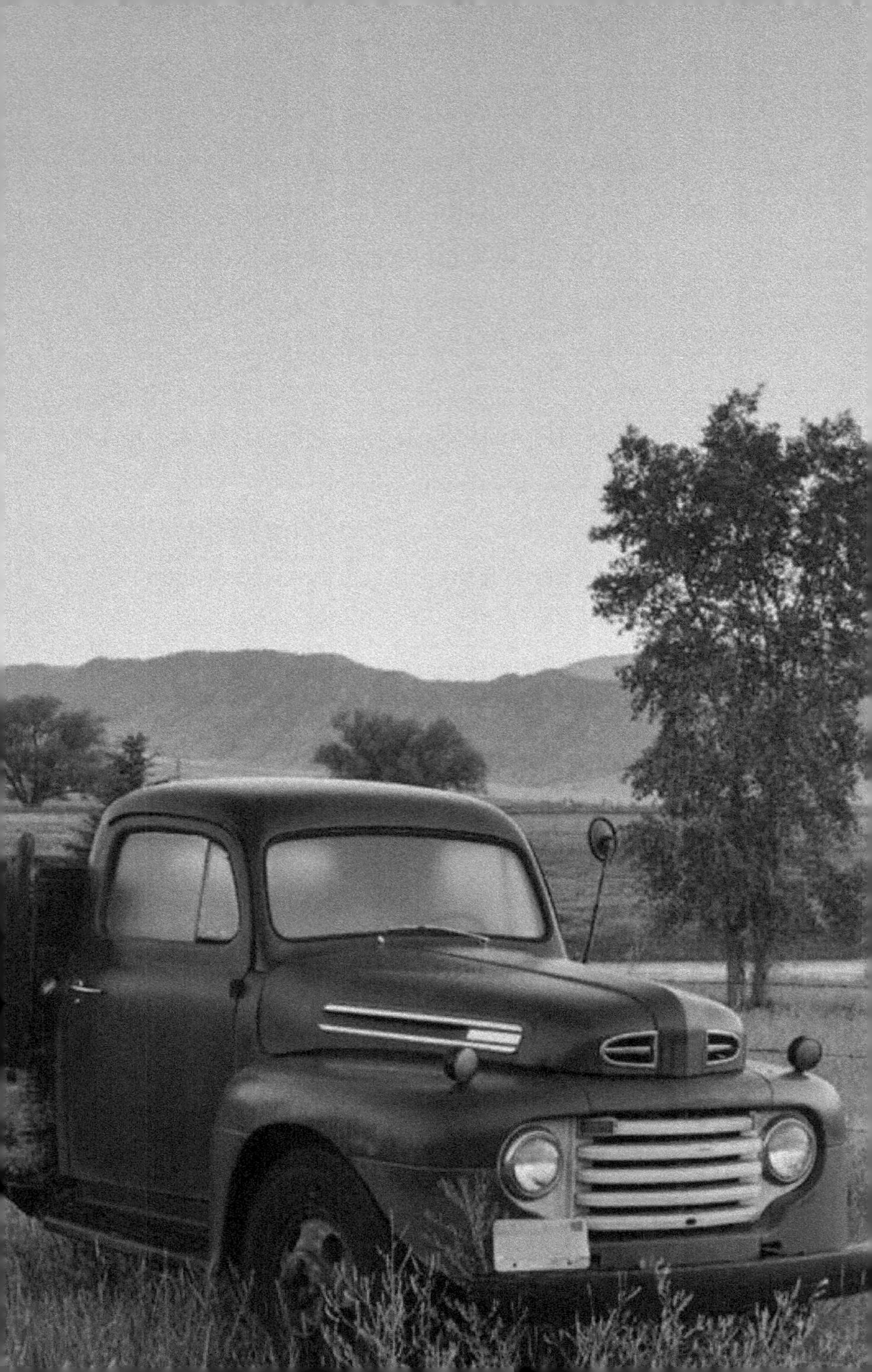

Chapter Sixteen

Nate

During the ride to Sunny Brook Farms, Alex continued to worry over someone figuring out we were hooking up. It was all a moot concern.

When we arrived, Alex was ushered into the kitchen with her mother, while Nash pulled me aside to go over some paperwork for the sale of the land as well as the leasing agreements. The latter I would need to forward to my legal department, but Nash already agreed I could begin testing onsite as soon as I wanted. The land was in its dormant period.

By the time Andrew arrived, the meal was ready, and chatter around the table filled the room. This time, the twins sat on either side of Marisol, which left Alex next to me. There was an instance where I intentionally dropped my napkin, a ruse to stroke my hand up her bare leg.

I thought it had gone unnoticed, but when I settled back in my chair, Rory smirked in the seat across from me. We were going to have to keep an eye on that one.

Alex was quiet during most of the meal. With how enthusiastic she was earlier regarding the cake shop prospect, it surprised me she wasn't jumping in to share the potential news.

I tried to catch her eye a few times, but she spent most of dinner pushing around the peas on her plate with her fork. No one was paying her any mind though, because to anyone who knew her, she wasn't herself, and they would've said something.

Not so quietly, I dropped my fork on my plate. The resulting clang halted all conversation. "Hey, so I think Alex has some news she wants to share."

Andrew's grip on his fork tightened. "You're not knocked up, are you?"

"Andrew!" their mother shouted. I was positive if Molly hadn't been sitting between Marisol and

Andrew, she would have smacked him on the back of the head.

"Sorry," he grunted.

"No, Andrew. I'm not. Thanks for thinking so highly of me."

An image of our rendezvous in the kitchen popped into my mind. Neither of us considered any protection.

Nash chimed in and gestured for his daughter to continue.

"So, now that I'm about to finish up my business degree, I've started exploring potential locations for a cake shop."

Collectively, the group started bombarding her with questions and shared in her excitement. I didn't miss the confused way Andrew asked if opening a cake shop was what she truly wanted to do. He must've had no clue how talented she was.

Under the table, I felt her hand land on my thigh. Reaching down, I grasped it in mine and intertwined our fingers. With a subtle squeeze of her hand, I pulled her attention for just a moment. Her smile was infectious, and I mirrored it immediately.

"Tell me more," Marisol asked.

Alex went into detail about the location being the old sandwich shop in town and how she envisioned the space. She was hoping for something bright and retro inspired. A place where people could order a piece of cake and sit down to enjoy it.

"Every day, I will have a specialty cake customers can order. Think, like, miniature versions of a larger cake."

Chiming in, I went into detail about the cake she made with the twins yesterday. "It was one of the best things I've ever tasted. Who knew pistachio and raspberry went together?"

"Well, hopefully the place is up to your liking." Leave it to Nash to be the voice of reason, but he was right. "Don't let the excitement overshadow the practicality."

"You're right," I said. "I'm joining her at the walkthrough tomorrow."

"Really?" everyone, including Alex, asked at the same time.

"Sure. I mean, I can at least make sure everything is in working order. The girls can stay in the shop's front."

"I can watch them." I expected Marisol to offer, but it was Rory instead. "Franny and I were just starting our lesson plans for next year, so we can cover it."

"Are you sure?" I asked after Alex explained Franny was Rory's lifelong friend and was a kindergarten teacher at the school.

"Yep. It's no problem." I didn't miss the cunning twinkle in Rory's eyes as she agreed. I felt like she had something up her sleeve.

Dinner gave way to dessert, a peach cobbler made by Marisol, and the conversation flowed toward my ongoing project. Nash hoped to venture out to the field to see my robot in action. If the changes I implemented this afternoon worked, I had a feeling the robot was ready for a larger scale model, and Nash would be the first one to get his hands on it.

While on dish duty, Andrew pulled me aside.

"Man, you missed out on that date last night."

"Sorry. We had an incident with Eloise, and I was just not up for it. Plus, I feel bad every time I ask your mom to watch the girls."

"Eh, she loves it."

"Probably, but they're my responsibility. And you know relationships aren't in the cards for me. I've got too much on my plate."

He nodded, but I sensed there was something else on his mind.

As he started walking toward the living room, I called out, "Andrew?"

"What if I asked Alex to watch the girls for me tonight and we went out?"

"Yeah? All right." Then he proceeded to call out Alex's full name to get her attention. When she joined us in the kitchen, he asked if she would watch the girls so I could have a night out with the boys.

Her brows furrowed as she looked back and forth between me and Andrew. There was a hesitancy in her agreement, and as she walked off, I knew I was going to regret my decision to go out with Andrew. My cock was going to be angry with me for the rest of the night.

As we were leaving, Andrew offered to let me ride with him and he'd bring me back to the B&B, but I needed another minute alone with Alex. It would also be the first night in a long time I wouldn't be there to tuck the girls into bed.

As I said goodnight to them in the family room, they seemed unaffected by my going out late. Alex queued up a bunch of shows that were popular when I was a kid, and they were going to have a marathon. She made no promises that any of them would end up in their bedrooms that night. This was a girl's night in.

While the twins hurried into their pajamas, I cornered Alex in the hallway. I thanked her for staying with the twins while I hung out with her brother.

"I know this isn't what either of us planned for the night."

"What exactly did you have planned, Nate?" she asked, stepping up against me.

"There was going to be a lot of finishing what we started in the kitchen earlier."

"Hmm... I like the sound of that."

I tucked a few strands of hair behind her ear. It was easy being with her like this instead of pussyfooting around every interaction. I could touch her, taste her any time we were alone. I craved it. "I really am sorry."

"It's okay. My brother misses his friend. I get it."

"I have a feeling he never liked to share."

We both chuckled as the girls came down the stairs, eyeing us suspiciously as we stepped apart.

"I won't be home too late."

"It's fine. We have everything we need."

I nodded toward the door as I held Alex's attention. She followed me outside while letting the girls know she'd be right back.

As she stepped onto the porch, I cradled her face and brushed my lips against hers. Alex's hands gripped my lower back as she stood up on her toes, and as my tongue swirled against hers, I felt her responding moan all the way to the tip of my cock.

Pulling away from her was agony.

From my rearview mirror, I watched as she stood on the porch until I turned onto the main road. I knew I'd have a good time with Andrew, but I was already wishing to be back at the B&B, watching cheesy shows with my girls. All three of them.

The bar was less chaotic than it had been last time. I assumed the day of the week made the difference. Monday was the start of the workweek for many, so they most likely wouldn't be out on a Sunday night.

I found Andrew seated at a high-top table with two other guys he introduced as Franklin and Simon. They'd all grown up in Ashfield together but scattered across Tennessee as they got older. Whenever one was in town, they tried to meet up. It was a coincidence all of them were here this weekend.

Andrew already explained a bit about me to them, so besides answering a few questions, we talked about the baseball game he pulled up on his phone. The televisions in this place only showed old movies, which I actually enjoyed. I didn't tell Andrew and his friends that though.

Conversation flowed to Autumn, specifically her husband, Colton. They couldn't believe Andrew now had a celebrity in his family. From there, they asked about his other sisters. He seemed bothered by Alex's passion to open a cake shop and was very vocal about her pursuing something that had a more substantial career path.

"She should be a chef and open a restaurant. That makes more sense than opening a place to buy desserts."

"Dude, her cakes are really good. Have you had one?"

"Why would someone eat cake unless it's a special occasion like a birthday? Why else would you need one?" The guys seemed to agree with Andrew.

"Maybe you can talk some sense into her, since she's like your maid right now."

I sneered in his direction at the insinuation of Alex filling in as host at the bed-and-breakfast.

"Can I ask you something?" I asked, and he took a pull of his beer and bowed his head once. The corners of the label had been torn away—a nervous habit of his. "Why does it matter to you so much? How does her career choice affect you?"

Cocking his head to the side, Andrew paused. "I just don't want to watch her make another mistake; that's all. I can't pick up the pieces again."

I wanted to know more, but I didn't ask him to elaborate. That was a story Alex could share, if or when she wanted to. "Who says you have to? Maybe have a little more faith in her."

One of the guys at the table, Franklin, inquired if we could move the subject to something less heavy. Something more like the Ashfield Summer Festival happening in a couple of weeks. The guys spilled the beans and joked that Andrew lost a bet and was going to be manning the dunk tank.

After my one beer, I settled in with a glass of water until the game ended. Franklin and Simon left first, and Andrew and I were close behind. He only had a couple of beers and was staying at the farm. Something about going over some financial contracts in the morning. I wasn't exactly sure what Andrew did for the farm, but he seemed to have his hands in everything.

My chest felt lighter with every passing mile back to the bed-and-breakfast, and I suspected it wasn't just because of my daughters.

A sigh escaped my lips as I pulled my SUV in front of the house. I looked up at the double porch, expecting to find Alex sitting on the upper swing overlooking the property. She confessed it was a favorite spot of hers and Autumn's.

I checked the time, and it wasn't too late, early compared to the normal hour I went to bed, but my kids would have been in bed a couple of hours prior.

They should have been, at least.

Opening the front door, the sound of the television resonated around the foyer. I didn't recognize the music, but as I turned the corner, I thought I remembered the show being called Wild and Crazy Kids. Alex was lying on the floor in a makeshift bed of couch cushions and blankets. Tucked in, wrapped in her arms, were Molly and Eloise. One on each side.

Pulling my phone from my pocket, I snapped a picture of the group, thankful for the light from the TV, so I didn't have to worry about the flash. That image was going to be a keepsake.

Slowly, I approached the group and kneeled beside them. I attempted to wedge my hands underneath Eloise's slight frame without waking Alex, but just as I lifted her in my arms, Alex's eyes blinked open.

"Nate?" she asked in that sleepy voice I was growing to love.

"Yeah. Sorry. I'm just going to carry them to bed."

"What time is it?"

"Not late. It's like ten."

"Oh." She gently slipped her arm from beneath Molly's head and rolled off their pallet. "Let me help you."

"No, no. I've got it. I'll be right back."

I made quick work of tucking Eloise into her bed. She barely squirmed as she settled in. I repeated the motions with Molly, who immediately tucked her stuffed bear under her chin before rolling onto her stomach.

Downstairs, I found Alex back on the now remade couch with a glass of water. She apologized for dozing off. I told her it was fine. That's what slumber parties were for anyway. Not that I was ever allowed to go to any growing up.

When I prompted her about what chaos they got into, she laughed, then plunged into the details of eating too much popcorn and painting each other's nails. I was warned that each girl had a different color on each finger, courtesy of Tami, who came stocked with an entire makeup and nail kit.

"We had a great time."

"I'm glad. I wish they had someone in their life like this long before now. I'm pretty sure their mother's idea of girl time was showing them her pageant crowns and sashes locked inside a glass cabinet."

Thinking of Sasha reminded me that I ignored her calls for the last two days. After everything that happened with Eloise, I wasn't in the right frame of mind to talk to her.

"That's really sad. But maybe look at the way she grew up. It may have been all she knew. Her mother may not have been very affectionate or loving."

I didn't like Alex speaking about my ex, but it was an interesting take I hadn't considered. I met her mother twice, and she was as cold as the tip of Mount Everest.

"I don't want to talk about my ex."

"I know. But you should," she said, and I felt my eyebrows reach my hairline as I sputtered. "Nate, she's still their mother, no matter what's on a piece of paper. Despite how awful she was to you and the terrible way she abandoned them, you should still try to talk kindly about her. Your words are going to be their only memory of her."

"I don't like this conversation."

Alex chuckled as she settled against me on the couch. I wrapped my arm around her shoulders and held her close.

"You don't have to like it. I'm just telling you what I think. You're their father, after all."

Closing my eyes, I rested my head against the back of the couch. "She wants to see them. She keeps sending me these messages, pleading with me. Saying that she's missing them growing up. Apparently, she bought a new condo with a pool and a view of the Hollywood Hills and wants them to visit before school starts."

"How do you feel about that?

"I feel like she's manipulating them. She knows the lies won't work on me, but she's showing them new and shiny things. We just got over the adjustment period of living with me when we moved here. We haven't even broken ground on a new house yet, and I feel like she's trying to pull them away."

Alex remained silent for a few beats. I brought my head up and turned to face her. She nibbled on her bottom lip as she stared at the television screen. "Can she contest the parental rights and guardianship?"

It was strange to hear my biggest fear vocalized by someone else. Despite all the legal work I'd done to ensure that it couldn't happen, the fear still simmered in the pit of my stomach.

"No. My lawyers made sure when all the paperwork was signed that she couldn't contest it. Ever. Those girls will always be mine."

"Then what are you really afraid of?"

I didn't have an answer. I wasn't sure what truly made me fearful of the girls spending time with their mom. Minus the fact that she was across the country, I didn't have any concrete reason to keep them from her.

"I think I'm just scared. Scared of her manipulating them. Scared of them wanting a life with her and then her rejecting them. Scared of her worming her toxic ways back into my life. There is still a mountain of lies she wove around her time with me that I'm still working my way through. I don't want that for them." Slouching over, I rested my elbows on my knees, my head hanging.

"You're a good dad, Nate," she said as her hand rubbed circles between my shoulder blades.

"I just want to protect them."

"I know."

Twisting my head, I gazed in her direction. "But you think I should entertain the idea of them spending some time with their mom?"

"It doesn't matter what I think or what anyone else wants. It's what you think will be best for them."

I wanted to tell her how sexy she was when she was being all maternal. It was the biggest fucking turn-on to listen to her caring about my kids and their well-being.

Before I could tell her that, she laughed and turned up the volume on the television.

"I'd forgotten about these episodes."

On the screen, a bunch of kids raced down waterslides holding ice cream cones. I remembered when they aired and wishing I could have been a part of those shows. It was the childhood I wished I had.

We settled back against the couch, the heavy conversation from earlier easily placed on the back burner.

We laughed through a couple of episodes, commenting back and forth about how we would have totally nailed that obstacle course.

After a while, I got up and poured us a glass of wine left over from the other night. The crisp White Zinfandel was refreshing.

I thought Alex was going to bounce off the couch when an episode of Double Dare came on the screen. She smacked my thigh in excitement so many times I was definitely going to have a bruise for the next few days.

We watched a few more installments until I felt Alex's full weight against my body. Grabbing the remote from her hand, I turned down the volume, her soft mewling snores filled the room.

This wasn't anywhere close to what I intended to happen tonight. But the more I thought about it, the more I knew it was even better.

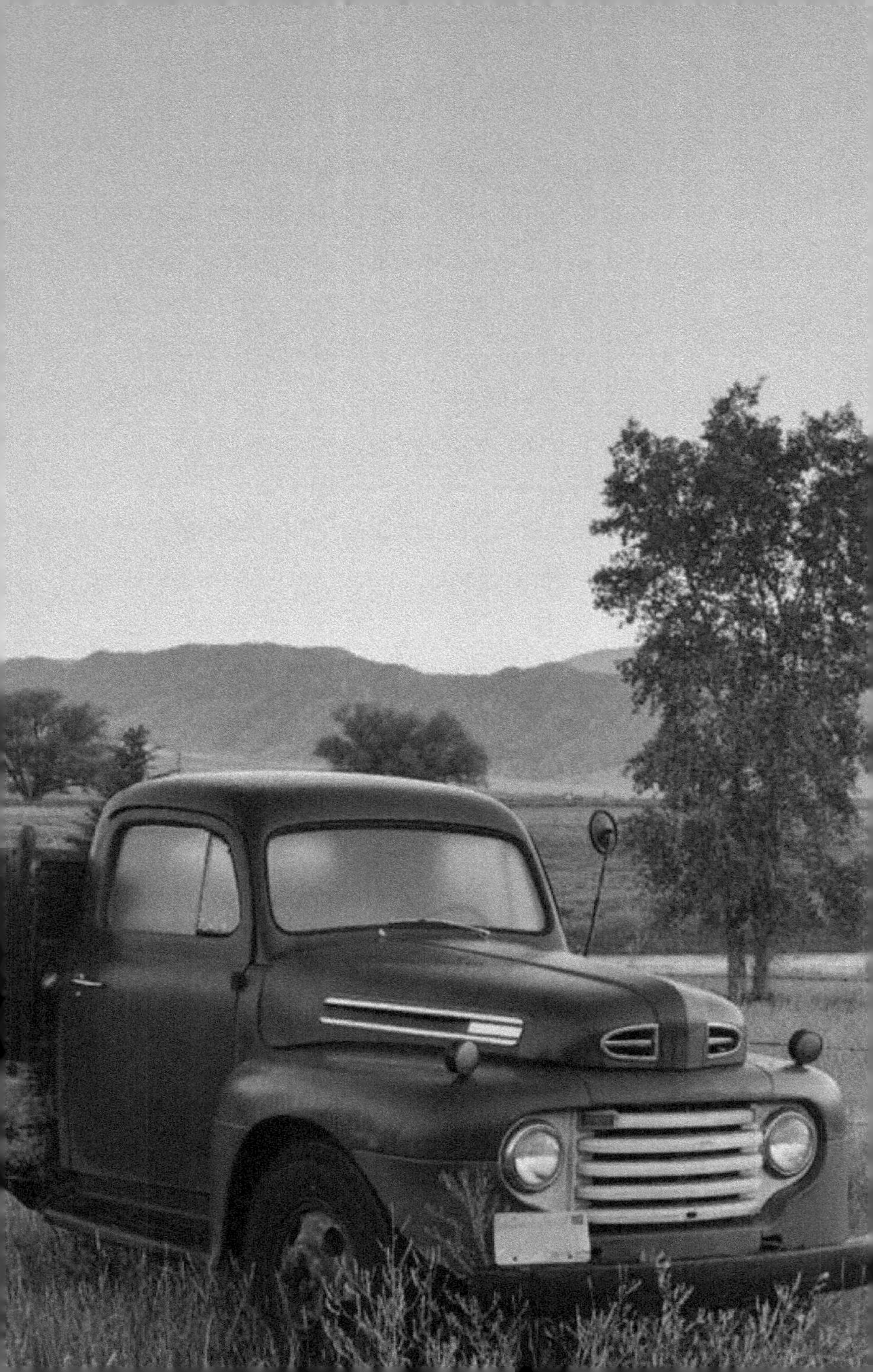

Chapter Seventeen

Alex

Sometime around two in the morning, Nate and I both woke up in fright. We'd fallen asleep on the couch, and the remote must've wedged itself between the cushions. The volume flared as an infomercial for a pressure cooker aired on the late-night network.

Once we threw all the cushions on the floor, we fumbled with the remote to turn down the volume and turn off the TV. After a moment passed, we both fell over in laughter. It seemed all our attempts to be alone were always interrupted. Even the innocent ones.

Instead of joining him, I headed to my room, despite his pleas. I didn't want to press our luck again. I watched from my doorway as he checked on each girl, making sure neither had woken from the sound. Both thumbs jutted in the air, so I took that to mean the girls stayed asleep.

I woke up the next morning cuddling the extra pillow. In my dream, it had been Nate beside me. One night with him in his bed ruined me.

The house was empty as I made my way downstairs. Nate planned to take the girls over to my mom's house so he could test his robot on my parents' land. I was still unsure of leasing the property, but I was coming around. My mom sat me aside and explained it was simply a way to make a little money for the farm. It was a business-to-business transaction, not Nate personally encroaching on the land.

The cleaning service was coming by the bed-and-breakfast around lunchtime, so I needed to find something to do. An idea popped into my mind, and I headed over to my mom's house. I might not have been able to use the B&B kitchen for the day, but I could surely use hers.

Surrounded by bowls of flour and sugar, I explained to my mom for the second time that I was testing recipes for the Summer Festival. I called the town council this morning and purchased a booth on a whim. If I planned to get my business going, then getting my name out there was the first step. I'd see if Rory or Aspen could help me come up with some business cards and maybe a website. Aspen was great at that stuff. She was a little tech whiz.

"I want to make small samples, like the ones I'll serve in the shop, for a one-bite eat."

"But you need six cakes?"

"Yes, Mom. Pay attention." Laughing, I told her she could just sit and watch with the girls. Molly and Eloise were fascinated as I ran my three mixers and two of my mom's. I wasn't sure what she was complaining about. She taught me everything I knew.

"Are you going to dance this time, too?" Eloise asked innocently from her perch on the counter. She was too young to feel the tension grow in the room.

It devastated my mom when I gave up dancing. Even after winning scholarships and being invited to audition for prestigious dance schools, I declined them all. Only my therapist knew the full reason why, though I was almost positive my mother could piece it all together.

With a gentle smile, I walked over to Eloise and dabbed a bit of flour on her nose, then repeated it on

Molly's. Both girls giggled in that sweet way they had. "We'll see."

I started with the same pistachio and raspberry cake from the other day that Nate loved. I swear he had hearts in his eyes after the first bite. Also on my list were a chocolate whiskey cake with caramel custard, a cookies and cream cake, chocolate and hazelnut spread, Champagne-flavored cake with strawberry compote, and orange creamsicle with vanilla pastry cream.

When I texted my mom the list of ingredients to see what she had on hand earlier, she replied with a wide-eyed emoji. Luckily, she had a bit of it stored in her pantry, but I had to make a stop by Chuck's Grocery Store to stock up on the rest. I made sure to stop by my favorite baker, Betsy, to check in. Mom may have taught me everything I knew, but Betsy knew how to add that extra umph to any dessert. She was the most excited about my venture into the baking world.

As I finished mixing all the doughs, I settled them inside the mothership of all double convection ovens. It really paid to have a farmer's wife who enjoyed cooking for all the hands working on the land. She always had the right kitchen tools on hand.

The girls asked all kinds of questions about the flavors and how I knew what they would taste like before making them. As requested, I spun around the kitchen with an ease that I hadn't felt in years. I remembered doing the same as a teenager, helping my mom in the kitchen.

I smiled at Eloise and Molly as I started stirring the batches of icing and checking on the compotes, jams, and creams on the stove.

"You should be on one of those baking shows. The one with all the crazy designs," Mom spoke as I tasted the chocolate ganache.

"The one Colton hosted last season?" I asked, whisking the chocolate a few more times.

"Yes, that one."

I huffed out a single chuckle as I made my way over to the girls, performing a pirouette along the way. "Taste," I demanded.

As expected, they both sighed in delight.

"Was that a pirwowet?" Molly asked as she tried to stick her finger in the bowl to grab another taste.

"A pirouette," I corrected. "Yes. Very good. You'll be professionals in no time."

Walking back to the opposite counter, I locked eyes with Mom. Her lower lids held pools of water. "Mom?" I whispered. "Are you okay?"

"It's really nice to see you dancing again. It's been too long."

"I dance every day," I argued, though she was right. I hadn't allowed myself to perform in front of anyone in years. Not since Stephen took everything from me. I'd had years of therapy to get to the point I was at now.

"Not like that. It's just really nice to see. I miss the girl who used to whirl around the house like a dancing tornado."

"I'm still that girl. Just less of a tornado and more like a strong wind."

Mom strode over and wrapped her arm around my shoulders. Her lips pressed against the side of my head before she pulled back and swiped her finger through the chocolate ganache.

"Be the tornado, Alexandra. Show everyone what you're made of." Rendering me speechless, she hollered for the girls to help her with a flower project outside. The twins never turned down the chance to get dirty.

Be the tornado.

I always felt like I was too much for everyone. Just a little too wild. Just a little too ambitious. When Autumn left in a hurry after her high school graduation,

I toned it down. The emotional downfall from Stephen decimated me to nothing more than a shell of myself.

Be the tornado.

Glancing around the kitchen, I decided that was exactly what I planned to do. I wanted everyone to know who I was. I was going to be the best cake baker in Eastern Tennessee. No, the country. I wanted people clamoring for my masterpieces.

Be the tornado.

I was going to take what I wanted. And right now, I wanted a night with Nate and no interruptions. I had a way to make that happen. Pulling out my phone, I typed out a quick message to Rory, asking if she'd stay the night with the girls. She immediately agreed, her text accompanied by a cucumber and cat emoji.

I was going to be the tornado, and I didn't care who got in my way.

Two dirt-covered masses came through the back door just as I finished setting the last cake out to cool. Mom followed closely behind them, steering them toward the first-floor bathroom.

"Think you can find something for each of them to wear while I wash their clothes?" Mom asked as she passed through the kitchen.

"Sure. Need any help?"

"No, I've got it. Whew, I forgot how dirty little girls could get."

"Worse than boys?"

"Always."

As the bathroom door shut, I ran up the stairs to my old bedroom. I was sure I still had a few shirts from high school stuffed in the dresser drawers. In the top one, my eyes landed on a few of my dance competition shirts. I knew they were small enough for the girls to wear as dresses. I got these before I hit puberty, after which none of my dancing outfits fit my developing body.

Downstairs, I knocked on the door and handed the shirts over to Mom. She eyed them, silently asking if I was sure. What the hell was I going to do with some ancient, child-size shirts?

Ten minutes later, both girls skidded into the kitchen, where I rested against the counter, scrolling through my phone. The shirts hit their knees, and it was the cutest thing I'd ever seen.

Once the cakes cooled, I let the girls help me with the crumb coat like they had the other day.

"Can I help?" my mother asked from behind me. I immediately handed her my spatula and watched the three of them work. "I've never done a special cake like this before. Most of my creations barely made it out of the pan before y'all devoured it."

"True. Sometimes it's nice to learn new things."

As she spread a thin layer of the buttercream around the two-tiered cake, she glanced over at me once, then asked, "So, how are things with you and Nathaniel?"

I stole a glimpse at the girls. They were far too interested in the task at hand to pay attention to the conversation. Did I want to disclose the details of my sort-of relationship with Nate to my mom? I wasn't even 100 percent sure what we were doing, other than exploring a sensual side of our attraction.

"Things are fine, Mom. He's a really nice guy."

"You know, he sent me those flowers on the table by the front door. Like I told you before, you should snatch that up before he's taken."

"Mom, please."

"Fine, don't listen to me. I just think it's interesting how invested he is in your cake shop."

"What do you mean?"

"It seems he jumped at the chance to tour the potential flagship with you. I would have thought maybe Tami or even me, your dad, or sisters would have been the ones you'd ask."

"I didn't ask. He invited himself."

She smiled in a way I'd swear the corners of her mouth curled up in mischief. "Exactly my point."

"Did you want to come?"

"Nope. I'll be there for the walkthrough when you buy the place."

"I'm confused," I confessed as I swapped out the girls' cakes and buttercream for different flavors.

"He invited himself, because he cares about you, Alex."

"Geez, Mom. I've known him for a little over a week."

"Pssh, time means nothing. When you know, you know. After the devastating death of my first husband, I never thought I'd love again. Then I met your father, and we were married six months later."

We all knew the story about Mom's high school sweetheart and how he died at war. Andrew was their only child. Mom moved to Ashfield to be closer to her grandmother when she met my dad. It was a whirlwind romance. A story for the ages.

"Just because it happened for you doesn't mean it happens for everyone else."

"It happened for Autumn."

As my irritation grew, I considered taking my personal spatula back from her. "Is there a point to all this?"

"If you can't see it, then no. I guess there isn't. All done," she said with a flourish as she handed my spatula back to me. Her cake was crumb coated to perfection. Just the thinnest layer of icing to keep the thicker layer from picking up any scraps.

"You're hired," I called out as she walked back down the hall toward the bathroom.

"Can't wait to start," she hollered back.

I cleaned up the kitchen and packed the cakes and icing to store in Mom's large fridge in the garage. It was next to the freezer where Dad stored meats in the winter. I was going to have to invest in some more fridge space for my apartment.

Back in the kitchen, Mom began prepping for her lasagna. I was almost jealous I wouldn't be here to eat it.

The girls were busy coloring at the kitchen table as my dad and Nate came through the mudroom, with Aspen trailing behind them. Her eyes were glued to Nate's ass like a bug drawn to a bright blue light. Not that I could blame her. He had a great ass, and when he turned around and leaned on the kitchen island, I saw how well the denim formed around the curves.

Normally, I'd call Aspen out for her perusal, but I let it slide. I got to see it up close and feel the muscles with my own hands.

Aspen and I had a weird relationship. We never really got along, though I tried. But I was the overly girly girl, while Aspen grew up as the tomboy who enjoyed farming with my dad.

I'd never told her, but I was always jealous of the time she got to spend with him. I used to think it was because she was the baby, but as I got older, I realized it was because she was the only one who showed any interest in what he was doing.

"Hey, Aspen," I called out, catching her off guard. When she turned around, her eyes were the size of saucers. "Would you want to help me teach Molly and Eloise how to play Go Fish?"

Her shock gave way to a beaming smile as she agreed and offered to grab the deck of cards. I helped the girls stow away their crayons and coloring books. By the time Aspen returned, the table was clear and ready for a match.

It took a bit of trial and error, but by the fourth round, the girls figured out the game. Thirty minutes later, they'd turned into card sharks before our very eyes. I'd never been prouder.

"I think they're sneaking cards under the table. Look, she has eight matches already. We just started this round!" Aspen exclaimed. The girls hadn't been sneaking cards under the table, but they'd been holding onto cards from previous games. I caught them doing it the last round.

"Just play the game, Aspen. They're four, almost five years old."

She harrumphed but went on playing.

"We turn five in August. Dad says we can have a big party," Molly informed us.

"Oh, that sounds fun. What kind of party would you like?" I asked.

"Tabitha had a petting zoo at her house when she turned five. I want a petting zoo like that. She even had horses."

Aspen and I stared at each other. I didn't realize birthday parties had become so elaborate. Were clowns not a thing anymore?

"Well, that certainly sounds like fun."

Nate joined us in the kitchen a few moments later and gathered the girls up to head back to the old farmhouse. I followed their lead.

I took a quick shower to get all the flour and icing out of my hair—an occupational hazard. I'd never gone to a showing, so I wasn't sure if there was a certain way I needed to dress. I opted for a seersucker knee-length skirt with a matching top. It exposed a band of my waist along the top of the skirt.

There was some time to kill while I waited for Nate, so I took the time to blow dry and curl the ends of my hair. After a few swipes of mascara, I stood in front of the full-length mirror in the room's corner.

I cleaned up nicely, though I did look like I was going on a yacht cruise. But I thought I looked pretty.

This is not a date, I had to keep reminding myself, but my mother's words were bouncing back and forth in my head.

I waited downstairs with the twins as they continued coloring their pictures they started at my parents' house. They asked to sit out on the deck, and I lounged on a chair, soaking in the late-afternoon sun.

Rory stepped out onto the deck a few minutes later with her best friend, Franny, in tow. I greeted them both and told the girls I'd be right back. Franny offered to sit with them while my sister and I went back into the house. As a kindergarten teacher, she was in her element amongst the crayons and sheets of paper.

"Thanks again for doing this."

"It's no sweat. We're going to have a fun time. Those girls are so sweet."

I went on to tell her all the things I learned they liked over the last week. She laughed when I told her all about our 1990s-themed slumber party the night before.

Nate came around the corner, and my breath caught in my throat. He was back in his suit, and God, he looked so fucking hot like that.

"You're drooling," Rory whispered, and I immediately reached up to wipe at my chin.

"You look nice," I told him, admiring the way he ran his hands over his head. It seemed he was still adjusting to having shorter hair. He stopped short with wide eyes when he looked up at me.

"Oh, I thought you were outside. Hi, Rory," he said, and she repeated his greeting. "Is the jacket too much? The only times I've walked through properties were for my home and business. Both times, I was dressed for work."

"Maybe a little?" I replied. He slid the blazer off and revealed a crisp-white shirt. I walked up to him and wrapped my fingers around the knot of his tie, loosening the material. "Maybe lose the tie too." My fingers made quick work of the silk and the top button of his shirt, revealing his powerful neck.

"Thanks," he said quietly with that sexy half-smirk.

Taking a small step back, I was mesmerized by the way he began rolling his sleeve up to his elbow, then repeated with the other.

"Dang, is it hot in here?" Rory claimed. We both turned to find her waving herself with her hand.

"I guess we should head out. The appointment is at four thirty."

Nate went out back to meet Franny and to say goodbye to the twins. Molly and Eloise couldn't have cared less that he was leaving. They were busy making paper boats with their new friend.

"Thanks again, Rory."

"Like I said, I'm happy to do it. Make sure you guys have a really *long* and *enjoyable* night."

As Nate and I settled in my truck, because I really wanted him to get the chance to ride in it, he turned to me. "I feel like Rory knows something I don't."

"She's always been full of secrets."

"You look really beautiful, by the way."

"Thanks."

"I particularly like those straps tied on your shoulder." He fingered the knot on one of them, and I shivered. "Makes me feel like I'm going to unwrap a present later."

"You just might, Nate. I'm full of surprises too."

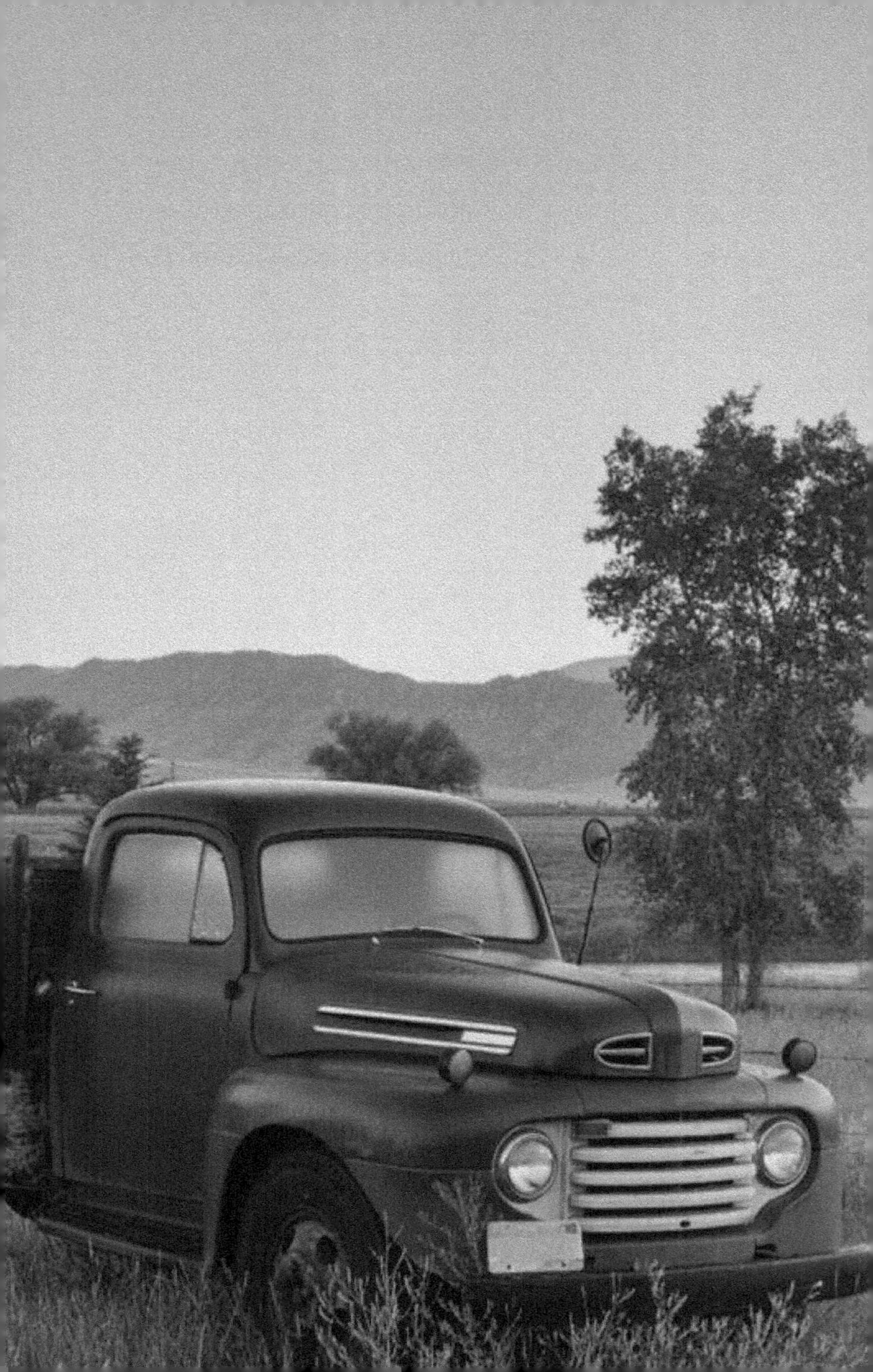

Chapter Eighteen

Nate

Despite the realtor's advances, walking through the space with Alex felt surreal. Alex asked her if we could explore on our own, and the woman hesitantly agreed. I wasn't going to tell her that I'd worried the agent was going to lock me in a closet for herself.

Despite the realtor, the location was perfect for Alex. With every step she took, she described what she'd put in that place. In the kitchen, she pointed to where she'd add the extra ovens and the flash freezer. Most of the kitchen equipment wasn't set up for what Alex needed. She was going to have to spend a pretty penny on the appliances, but we both knew the expense would be worth it.

There were stairs on the inside and outside of the building for the apartment, which gave me some relief. Upstairs, the apartment was bigger than I expected. Instead of a studio like she currently occupied, this one had a separate bedroom. It made the living area a bit smaller, but it opened up to the kitchen.

"This is really nice. What do you think?" she asked me as she peeked inside a few of the cabinets. Whoever lived here before took care of the space.

"I think that as long as you like it, then you should go for it."

"I really do. I could see myself here."

"Then let's get you those papers to sign."

She launched herself into my arms, and I'd never felt anything better. "Thank you for coming with me. I would've never noticed some of the piping needed to be replaced." She slid down my body, her skirt bunching at her waist along the way. It didn't take much for my dick to come alive.

"You're welcome."

I knew she felt the bulge growing behind my slacks. It was something I was going to have to ignore until later. I began running codes in my head to try to get my erection down.

"Kiss me, Nate."

Well, that definitely isn't going to help.

I planned on pressing a chaste kiss to her lips, but I was thwarted as her tongue softly swiped against my upper lip. All control flew out the window as I opened my mouth to her. Alex's arms wrapped around my neck, anchoring me to her as our kiss grew more intense.

Like the other day, the passionate moments with Alex caused the world to fall away. I could have been in the middle of the supermarket and not cared at all.

Reaching down, I gripped her ass and hoisted her onto the old dining table left behind by the previous owner. I needed to feel her hot center against my growing hard-on. I was desperate for it as her legs wrapped around my waist, bringing my hips in line with hers.

She mumbled against my lips, "I'm not wearing any panties," and my body jerked at her confession. I'd been staring at her preppy little outfit through the entire walkthrough, wondering if she wore those sweet cotton panties of hers again, like the ones I'd stolen from her the other night.

Only to find out she wasn't wearing any.

All the blood in my head rushed down to my cock. It ached behind the confines of my zipper.

"I want you to fuck me. I need you to fuck me."

There was no time to do anything else, consider any other options, besides unlatch my slacks and pull my cock out. It was so incredibly stiff that I felt a twinge when I wrapped my hand around the base.

On the counter, Alex spread her legs apart, feet resting on the tabletop. Her skirt bunched around her waist, and that fucking perfect pink pussy was on display.

I must've died and gone to heaven.

I stepped up to her, my cock straining in my hand as I smacked it against her mound just above the clit. She bit her lip in the way that left me wanting to suck on the plump skin.

"I don't have anything with me, Alex." I hadn't exactly planned on this happening. The condoms I bought at the store the other day were back in my room at the B&B. It was stupid of me not to put one or two in my wallet.

"I trust you." Later, when my brain received blood flow again, I would have to analyze those words.

"I'll pull out," I said through gritted teeth as I slipped my cock up and down her folds, coating my tip with her wetness.

"Nate. Please."

I put the tip in her entrance, just an inch, and it was the most exquisite feeling. I had to force myself to stop and take a breath before pushing further inside. She was so fucking tight. Her pussy squeezed my shaft with every centimeter I moved deeper.

I pulled back out after only going about halfway, then thrust forward until I could go no farther.

"Ah, fuck," I growled as I felt Alex's moan all the way down to my balls.

"Ms. Easterly, Mr. Sullivan, what do you think of the apartment?"

Alex's legs dropped off the table, and she pushed me backward, my angry, red cock slipping out of her pussy.

"Oh my God," she whisper-shouted as she jumped down off the table and adjusted her skirt. "Nate, put that away." Alex pointed to my dick, which only made him jerk at the attention.

Tucking my erection into my pants was pure agony. I could barely pull up the zipper the tent was so pronounced.

"We have the worst fucking luck," Alex murmured as she moved into the living area, leaving me and my pissed-off penis in the kitchen. Thank goodness I had a kitchen counter to hide behind as the realtor reached the top of the stairs.

She looked back and forth between the two of us but mentioned nothing as she asked what Alex thought of the place once more.

"I love it. It's exactly what I was looking for."

"Wonderful. I have the paperwork ready for the one-year lease. The building owner isn't interested in selling just the one space, unfortunately. But he did agree to any enhancements you need to make in the kitchen."

"That sounds good. Will the lease include the rent for the apartment, or will that be separate?" Alex and the agent began walking down the stairs, continuing their discussion, leaving me alone in the apartment.

It was probably best, so I could get my erection down. I didn't want to use my hand like I had the other day. It left me unsatisfied, and my craving for her only increased.

"How does it feel to be the proud owner of your very own cake shop?" I asked Alex as she dangled the keys in her hand. She couldn't occupy the space for a couple of weeks, as the plumbing for the building would be addressed.

"Surreal."

Instead of heading to the truck after signing the documents, Alex directed me down the street. I teased her fingers with mine as we strolled until she finally pressed her palm up to mine and interlocked our fingers.

"Where are we going, by the way?"

"I made some dinner reservations. I hope that's okay. I just… thought we could celebrate, if the place was everything I wanted, or commiserate if it wasn't. I lucked out that they had an opening. It's not a date or anything."

"I understand. It sounds nice, actually."

I wasn't going to complain about the mid-stiffness that refused to die down in my pants or the fact that she was going to sit across from me with my knowing she wasn't wearing any panties. It was going to be the worst kind of torture.

"There's a new restaurant I've been dying to try. One of the chefs on the food channel Colton works with came to visit for the engagement party. Story goes he fell in love with the town and decided to open a restaurant here. Apparently, it reminded him of where he grew up."

"Really? That's pretty cool."

"I mean, it's probably nothing compared to the places you've been wined and dined in California."

I didn't care for the way she sneered at the thought of me having money. She said it jokingly, but I could sense her annoyance. It made me think about the maid comment her brother said at the bar last night.

"You're right. I bet it's even better. I hate those stuffy places," I explained as she stopped in front of a nondescript brick building. It was separate from the rest of the block, as if it had been a home in a past life.

Inside, the space resembled the same as the outside. A lot of exposed brick and dark wood. Gas-style lamps hung from the ceilings. The place felt quaint and cozy. Once the hostess took Alex's name, she ushered us out of the foyer and through a hallway before turning into a room with three other tables. I could hear other guests chattering in the restaurant, but as we sat down, it felt like it was just the two of us under the dim light.

As the hostess set down our menus, I read the name of the restaurant within the embossment of gold filigree—Roland's. Recognition was immediate. He'd been a star on The Food Channel for decades.

"Holy shit. You didn't say this was Roland McEntire's restaurant."

For a moment, she worried her lip as she picked up the menu. "Is that okay? I should have asked. I'm sorry."

"No. It's…. Wow, Roland McEntire. I ate at his flagship in New York a few years back. I still dream about that elk he served."

Alex's eyes widened as she scanned the menu. I could already tell she was going to settle for a salad or soup. When there were no prices listed, it usually meant everything was expensive. Which surprised me that the restaurant was still in business and clearly packed, but I imagined people came from all over to eat here.

"Get whatever you want, Alex. I'm treating you."

"No. You absolutely are not. I invited you."

"You invited me to celebrate. And as my thank-you for showing me the new shop, I want to buy your meal."

She continued to argue until I told her that the salad was probably going to cost around fifty dollars and she had a new lease to pay for soon.

"This still isn't a date."

"Of course not," I told her as the server stepped up to our table, and I ordered a bottle of champagne, the real stuff, to toast to Alex.

She was reluctant to take the first sip, saying it cost too much, but she relented and complimented me on the selection. When the server returned, Alex surprised me again and allowed me to choose her meal.

It was something so simple. Only my daughters allowed me to pick out what they ate. Sasha would have scoffed if I ordered anything that wasn't a wedge of lettuce.

When the meal arrived, the tender filet mignon I ordered for Alex left her moaning in the chair across from me. The elk I ordered was even better than the restaurant's in New York. À la carte style, they brought out sautéed asparagus and scalloped potatoes along with a variety of sauces for our entrees.

We talked through the rest of the meal. Lighthearted conversations about the twins' birthday at the end of summer and if they were excited to start school. I'd gone online that morning and registered them for kindergarten, and I may have shed a tear.

I handed the server my black American Express card without even seeing the bill. Alex's pinched expression bothered me.

"Want to tell me what you're thinking?"

Her hair swung around her shoulders as she shook her head. "It's nothing. Just something I remember from a while ago."

Something about the way she spoke and straightened her back told me the topic was closed.

As the server returned with my card and the trio of sorbet I ordered, I slipped into the chair next to Alex instead of facing her.

"Easier to share," I explained as her brows furrowed.

With ease, I lifted the spoon and dipped it into the pineapple and mango sorbet, scooping out the smallest amount.

"Mmm, that's delicious," I murmured around the cold dessert. "Try some."

Alex plunged her spoon into the bright-pink dragon fruit sorbet as I rested my hand on her thigh. Her eyes darted around the room, but no one was paying us any attention. And if they did, it would look like we were having an intimate moment together.

With every millimeter the spoon approached her mouth, I hitched the material of her skirt up her leg until my palm met her bare skin. When her lips parted, I guided my hand between her legs.

"Spread," I demanded so only she could hear.

Her mouth closed around the spoon, and I slid my finger across her bare flesh before dipping inside her tight cunt. Alex moaned as she pulled the spoon free, and I wasn't positive if it was from the flavor of the dragon fruit or from my finger moving up to her clit.

Leaning over, I hovered my mouth close to her ear. To anyone looking on, we'd appear to be two lovesick fools cuddling close. It was a good thing they couldn't read lips at this angle.

"It drove me crazy through this entire fucking meal, knowing you were sitting across from me with no panties to cover my pussy. I want to make you come right here. So, you better eat that dessert nice and slow."

"O-Okay," she whimpered as I added a second digit and plunged it inside her channel.

"Now, feed me."

The spoon in her hand shook as she drove it into the lime sorbet, then held it out for me to taste.

"Mmm," I moaned. "It's delicious, but your pussy tastes better."

It went on like this for a while. She'd feed me and then herself. Every time her mouth closed around the spoon, I'd fuck her with my fingers. Sometimes, she let the spoon linger. Other times, she brought it out quickly, so I'd play with her clit.

Her eyelids grew heavy as she got close to finishing the three flavors. The spoon in her hand shook as she served me another bite of the dragon fruit. When she tried to pull the spoon away, I reached up with my other hand and held it in my mouth. I'd felt her walls tightening up around my fingers, and I knew she was close to the edge.

"Nate," she mewled, as I finally relented my hold on the spoon.

I leaned toward her again, pressing a kiss to her cheek before moving up to her ear. "Pineapple if you want me to finger-fuck you, or lime if you want me to play with your clit. Choose wisely which way you want me to make you come."

Her gaze skirted around the room again before she gripped her spoon so tightly that her knuckles turned white. Just when I thought I had the upper hand, Alex dipped the spoon in the last bit of pineapple and then scooped up a dollop of the lime.

So, she wanted to play that game.

Slowly, she brought the spoon to her mouth as the heel of my hand pressed to her clit. Her lips parted, and I smiled at one of the other couples in the room before returning my gaze to Alex.

Her eyes closed as she savored the flavors swirling in her mouth. My arm was growing sore from the awkward positioning, but as I thrust my fingers back into her tight channel, I knew we'd both get relief soon. Alex's legs shook under the table, and she reached down to grip my forearm with her free hand as the walls of her sheath tightened around my fingers.

Using my thumb, I flicked her clit as I plunged my fingers in and out of her slit.

"That's it. You like that, don't you?"

Alex clenched her eyes closed as she tightened her grip around the spoon. Suddenly, her body jerked, and she slammed her hand down on the table.

The people in the room looked over at us in alarm as Alex sat there with her face pinched, my fingers still moving inside her.

"Brain freeze," I said calmly to everyone, a few of the guests nodding in understanding.

It took a couple of seconds for her to open her eyes. She looked dazed and sated. I removed my hand from under her skirt, and while I held her gaze, I brought my fingers to my mouth and tasted her. Her blush deepened as I moaned around my fingers.

"Best flavor yet."

"That was... unexpected."

"I can't wait to get back to the B&B."

Smirking, Alex stood from her chair, the legs scraping as they slid across the hardwood floor. She held her hand out to me, and I latched onto it like it was my lifeline.

"Actually, I have a better idea."

Outside, the sky was growing dimmer, but sunlight still lingered around the tops of the buildings.

Once we stepped outside, Alex twirled around and pulled my head down for a kiss. It lasted only a second, and as she released me, a joyful smile graced those lips.

She practically ran across the street with me trailing after her, hollering at me twice to hurry up. I wasn't sure what had her so excited, but I was glad to be involved.

As we swerved around parked cars and down alleyways, I hadn't been paying attention to my surroundings. Before I knew it, we were climbing a set of stairs, the metal creaking around me. That only meant one thing. We were at the entrance to her apartment.

"I hate these stairs," I said as she ran up them, pulling me with her.

"I'll make it up to you."

At the top of the landing, Alex cursed a few times as the biometric lock failed reading her thumb.

"Finally," she said with a flourish as she pushed the door open and hauled me inside like I weighed nothing.

I started to ask what we were doing in her apartment, though I had a pretty good idea, but she placed her finger over my mouth.

"I get you for one full night, Nathaniel Sullivan, and this time, you're going to remember everything."

Chapter Nineteen

Alex

Nothing was going to stop us this time. Come hell or high water, I was going to fuck Nate without interruption. Our luck hasn't been the greatest so far. Three attempts made, zero completion.

With what little strength I could muster after the amazing orgasm at the restaurant, I pushed Nate up against the apartment door. His deep chuckle was like an aphrodisiac as it washed over me after I told him that Rory agreed to stay the night to watch the twins. My sex practically purred for his attention.

I yanked the bottom of his shirt from his suit pants and began slipping the buttons free. I had no tact. My fingers trembled as I undid the first three, then Nate's large hand fell on top of mine.

"Let's take it slow, baby. There's no reason to rush."

I stared up at him like an angry feline ready to pounce. "Nate, I am so fucking horny right now my pussy feels like it's going to explode."

"What do you need me to do to make it feel better?" he asked as he yanked at one of the straps on my shoulder, untying the bow.

"I need you to fuck me hard and fast. I'm begging you, Nate. I need it." I squirmed under his scrutiny as he trailed his fingertip across my collarbone and went to work loosening the other strap. "God, I'm so fucking wet right now."

"I'm going to take care of you, baby." He reached behind me and tugged down the zipper on my top. The material landed on the floor at our feet.

"I love your breasts," he said, cupping them. "They're the perfect size for my hands." I rubbed my thighs together as he flicked my nipples with his thumbs. This time when I started undoing his shirt buttons again, he didn't stop me.

My head rolled back as he released my breasts and bent forward to capture one nipple with his mouth.

"Nate," I whimpered. "Please."

When he pulled away, his shirt joined mine on the floor, and he toed off his dress shoes.

"Hard and fast, you say?" His fingers were working magic on his pants. They were unbuttoned and sliding down his legs in record time. His boxer briefs followed.

"I want to be sore tomorrow."

"I'll make sure you're sore for weeks," he assured, and I smiled, because he said the same thing the last time we fucked. And I felt him for days after. "Now take off your skirt."

The small hook that held the top of the skirt together came apart easily enough, but the damn tiny zipper wouldn't move. I was growing more impatient with every passing second as I yanked the tab over and over again.

I was so sexually frustrated that I was about to throw a temper tantrum and give up.

"Let me try." Nate gently took the tab from my fingers. With a slow, gentle movement, the zipper gave way with ease. "Sometimes, going slow can make all the difference." The skirt fluttered down to the floor like a parachute.

"How wet are you, Alexandra?"

Fucking soaked.

I loved the way he said my name. It shot sparks straight to my core.

"Why don't you find out?" I teased as I pressed my body up to his, my lips pressing a kiss to the top of his chest. I tightened my hold on his biceps as his fingers slipped through my folds.

"You're drenched, sweet girl." He slid back and forth again, the tip of one finger circling around my clit. "What has you so worked up?"

"You, Nate. I've been craving you for a year."

Using his free hand, his fingers shot into my hair and cradled the back of my head. He tugged at the strands to tilt my face up toward his. "No one else has had this cunt since me?"

I tried to shake my head, but he held me firm. "No."

"Ah, fuck. Hold on tight, baby."

In a flash, he gripped my ass and raised me in the air, flipping us around so my back pressed against the door.

The dull ache I'd been feeling since the orgasm at the restaurant quickly subsided as Nate's cock drove inside me until he could go no farther.

"Ah," I cried out as he stretched me.

I felt so full, but the moment lasted only a second before he slid out and pounded into me again. Slowly, he released one leg, and my toes barely reached the floor as he spread my other out wide.

"Yes." My entire body shook at the slight change. The tip of his cock ran over the spot again and again, the spot that only he seemed to be able to find.

"You're telling me no one else has been inside you since me?"

Nate was asking me a question, but I was so lost in my pleasure and the mounting release that it took me a while to figure out what he was saying.

"No one," I whimpered as he adjusted his angle again, filling me deeper than before.

"Fuck, yes. Only my cunt," he grunted.

The waves started building, and my body trembled in his arms. "I'm so close."

Before I could comprehend what was happening, he lifted me in the air, and my face was suddenly pressed against the couch cushions. Nate's cock plunged inside my core on my next breath, igniting the fire again.

My hands clamored for something, anything, to hold on to. The quilt that rested on the back of the couch made it into my hand, and I fisted the material. With his every plunge forward, I rocked back.

"That's it. Take what you want, Alexandra. Use my cock."

A shudder moved through me at his words. I loved his bedroom voice. The way it demanded and controlled. Just hearing him talk could probably get me off.

"There it is. I can feel you squeezing me. You're so close, baby. Tell me what you need."

I didn't know what I needed to get there. I hovered over the precipice, ready to jump, but something tethered me to the ground.

Releasing the quilt, I reached between my legs and rubbed myself, hoping that would get me closer. But I still couldn't fall over.

"I love when you touch yourself. My balls are so tight, sweet girl. This pussy feels so damn good."

"I need… I need…." My whimpers were almost full-blown cries at this point. The orgasm just out of reach was taunting me.

"Tell me," he demanded as another tremble shook through me.

"Spank me. Last time, you spanked me, and I came." I was begging for it now, the agony of a lost release growing.

His hand landed on my ass with a loud crack, and I cried out. The pain was nothing compared to the pleasurable step closer to my orgasm.

"Yes. Your greedy cunt likes that." He did it again on the other side, and my body took another small step closer to the edge. I was almost there. The tether frayed with each smack.

I felt something wet land between my cheeks, and with another smack, I felt his thumb swirl around my back hole.

And then I was falling into sweet oblivion.

"Ah, fuck."

I felt Nate's shaft slip from my body, and then a few seconds later, something hot and wet dripped onto my back. His grunts filled the room as he released. Thank goodness he remembered to pull out as we discussed, not that it was foolproof.

"Stay put. I need to clean you up."

My limbs were too heavy to move anyway. I had little plans to go anywhere for a while.

Nate returned with a washcloth and wiped away the cum on my back.

"You can just throw it away. I won't be back to do laundry for a while."

He seemed to think it over for a bit, but then he left my line of sight. I heard water running in the kitchen over my heavy breathing, then solid footsteps back to my bathroom.

"I went ahead and washed it with your dish soap and hung it on your shower rod to dry. No sense throwing it away."

I hummed in response.

"Can you move?"

"Nope. Pretty sure I'll die here."

He crouched beside me, that massive cock of his dangling between his legs. "That would be one awkward funeral, don't you think?"

"Probably."

"Up you go." Nate flipped my body on the couch and then hoisted my body into his arms, cradling me close.

"You like to move me around, don't you?"

"You're light as a feather. And I enjoy carrying you."

Together, we dropped down on the bed, and I scurried across the blankets and buried myself under the sheets. Nate yanked them away, a scowl marring his features, saying he wasn't done looking at me yet.

I tried to explain to him I didn't like being naked, but when he started asking more questions, I pressed my lips against his to silence his thoughts. That quickly led to me riding him until we both found another orgasm. That time, we made sure to snag one of the condoms I stashed in my nightstand. It wasn't slow and steady like he wanted. I took control that time.

We laid as a sweaty mess on my bed. Thankfully, darkness had fallen into the room and there was only the soft glow of the lamp on my living room end table, which I set on a timer. Fumbling around in the dark wasn't my favorite thing.

I laid my head on Nate's chest and listened to the pounding of his heartbeat. It slowed with each passing minute, and the constant pulse was lulling me to sleep. The only thing that kept me awake was his hand trailing up and down my spine. I could feel his finger touch every vertebra as he passed, and old thoughts started popping up.

"Your way too tense for someone who had three orgasms this evening. Want to talk about it?"

"Not really."

"Alex." Nate rolled out from underneath me and sat on the side of the bed, his arms resting on his strong thighs. "I wish you'd talk to me. I feel like there is this part about yourself you keep hidden away. I know this is just sex between us, but I hoped at least we were friends."

"We are. It's just… a lot."

"I'm going to get a glass of water. Would you like one?" he asked, glancing at me over his shoulder. I wrapped the blanket around my body again, and when he noticed, he shook his head in the slightest way.

As he stepped away, I closed my eyes and began telling him the sordid story.

"There is a reason why I gave up dancing, and it wasn't the right one. It started when I was in high school."

I went on to tell him I'd been a late bloomer, and until that point, I could still fit in children-sized clothing, which worked really well for a ballet dancer. Once the hormones surged, so did my breasts and ass. Not to mention the difficulty of keeping the ballerina-slim figure.

I'd work out for hours to maintain the figure I needed to fit in my leotard. It was around that time my dance teacher recommended me for more advanced classes that were offered in bigger cities like Knoxville.

Mom carted me back and forth every day after school and every morning and night during the summer, the days I wasn't at dance camp. I didn't notice the toll it took on her, but I loved it. My family supported me 100 percent.

Until Stephen St. James took note of me.

Once I started filling out, the boys of Ashfield started to notice me more. None more so than Stephen. He was relentless in his pursuit. And as the hottest and most popular boy in our school, I didn't take much convincing.

He immediately began resenting all the time I spent dancing and practicing. I didn't notice it at first, but he'd nitpick the way my chest looked in the leotard or how my thighs looked like sausages in the tights.

I grew more and more insecure every day. I'd skip practice or give my mom some excuse about why I didn't want to go.

Nate murmured, "Oh, the ways I want to kill Stephen and bury him in a field where no one can find him…."

I ignored him and continued. "The worst part wasn't just Stephen. It was that on the days he would drive me to practice in Knoxville when we were seniors in high school, he'd make the same comments in front of my dance teacher. She'd agree with him. She said if I wanted to make it in the dance world, I needed to stick to a strict diet, one she provided, and I needed to see a special kind of doctor to learn the ways I could fix myself.

"But I was happy with my body. I liked my curves and the fact that I filled out my jeans. It wasn't until someone I looked up to pointed out those parts of me that I became insecure."

"You didn't… you know…?"

"No. I told my mom what was going on, and she put a stop to it. We came back to the dance studio here. But Stephen and I were still a thing."

As Nate sneered at the fact that I didn't dump the asshole along with the big-city dance teacher, I went on to tell him that we planned to stay together while I danced for a professional company. I had scholarships for college if I wanted to go and auditions set up across the east coast. But he said he could never be with someone who thought dancing was an actual profession. He said I was no better than a stripper.

So I did the foolish, naïve thing and gave it all up. The auditions. The scholarships. All of it. For him. And then he left the day after graduation.

"I spent years in therapy learning he was a manipulator and fed off the abuse. He used to make me stand in front of the mirror with no clothes on, and he'd point out all my flaws. It's why I'm not a fan of being naked."

"I hate him. I didn't think I could hate someone as much as I hate Sasha. But I do."

"Nate, you don't need to hate him. I don't." When his head jerked toward me, I added, "He didn't force me to make any of those decisions. I did that all on my own. And I'm happy with where I am. Who knows if I would have ever made it as a professional dancer? I love what I do, and I'm so excited about starting this new chapter of my life. I worked so hard to get here. Just, sometimes I forget I'm not that young seventeen-year-old anymore."

His masculine hand cradled my face as he twisted toward me on the bed. I hadn't realized I was crying, but Nate gently brushed aside the tears with his thumbs. Reliving the story took its toll on me.

"You're the strongest woman I know. Thank you."

"I just… wanted you to understand. Your reasons for not being in a relationship aren't so different from mine. We've both been burned, and neither of us came out without scars. And that's okay."

"One day, I'm going to stand you in front of a mirror, and I'm going to lick and kiss every part of you that I find so fucking sexy," he said as he leaned forward and pressed his lips against my shoulder, repeating a trail up to my neck.

"Mmm. That sounds nice."

"I could do it now if you want."

"I think I'd rather just feel your cock inside me."

"Slow and steady this time."

"Whatever you say."

It was cathartic to tell him the part of myself I kept hidden away. Whenever someone asked why I quit dancing, I usually lied and told them I didn't love it any longer. Instead, I'd loved it too much.

He pushed me back on the bed and continued kissing down my body. With my soul exposed, his lips felt like tiny flames flickering over my body.

I murmured his name as he kissed me down to my toes and then worked his way back up to my mouth. Without pulling away, he reached into the pile of condoms we pulled out earlier and chose one. With a quick tear from his teeth, he ripped open the package and rolled it down his cock.

It felt different this time when he slid inside. Not just because I'd never been so wet in my life—his teasing me with kisses was enough to do that—but because I felt completely bared to him. There was no more shield protecting a part of me. I was wide open.

Last time, we never got around to the plain, missionary position. We ended up fucking on every available surface and found creative ways to use pillows, blankets, and even ice cubes. But now... there was something to be said about the way his cock stroked my inner walls and his hips aligned in the perfect position to rub my clit with every thrust.

"That's it, sweet girl. I can feel you gripping me," he said when a particular stroke left me gasping.

Nate reached for my hands and gently moved them up to my wrought-iron headboard.

"Leave them there," he demanded as he shifted up onto his knees and clung to mine. He spread my legs wide as he plunged himself back inside me.

"Holy fuck!" I cried out, my head thrashing. The new position brought him even deeper.

"Fuck, yes. God, I love how tight this cunt is. Fucking perfect."

The bedframe rattled against the wall as I clutched the thin posts, my knuckles already growing sore from my tight fists.

"Yes, right there!" I shouted as he lifted my hips in the air. "Don't stop. Please, don't stop."

"Come with me, baby. I want to feel it."

Nate's dexterous fingers reached my bundle of sensitive nerves, and I arched my back at the explosion of my climax. As I continued to jerk from the release, I felt Nate drive into me at a rapid pace, chasing his own explosion. I was going to have handprints on my hips from him gripping me as he spilled himself into the condom.

He hunched over me as he heaved in large gulps of air.

"That was amazing," I whispered, running my fingers over his sweat-soaked hair.

"You're amazing," he replied as he grabbed my other hand still wrapped around the iron and pressed a kiss to my palm.

"What made you cut your hair?" I wasn't one for post-sex conversations, but as I ran my hand over his head, it was all I could think about.

"Work. Thinking of letting it grow back out."

"I like it both ways."

"I like you all the ways," he said, resting his chin on my sternum as he looked up at me. It was a weird angle, and I was sure I had some weird double chin going on, along with the fact he could see right up my nostrils. But I was too tired to move or care. "Slow and steady, and hard and fast."

"Mmm. I like them, too."

Slowly, he moved off the bed, and my center immediately missed his warmth. With the condom disposed of, he moved back onto the bed, tugging my back against his chest. I wasn't much of a cuddler, but with Nate, I could make an exception.

"Get some sleep, Alexandra. It's going to be a long night."

I fell asleep with a smile on my face and a row of condoms within arm's reach.

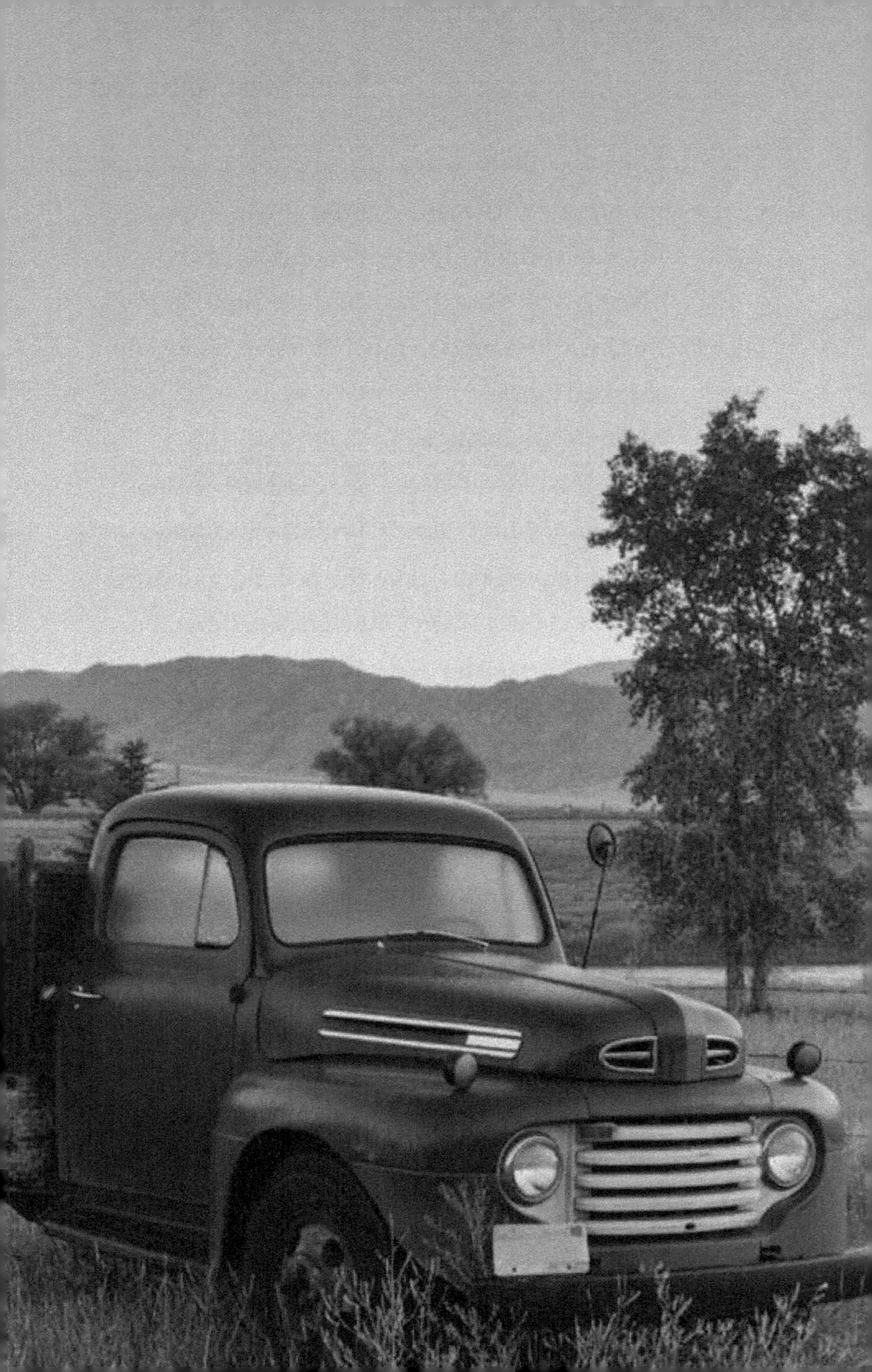

Chapter Twenty

Nate

I woke up that next morning with my cock still inside Alex as she rocked her ass against me. We were still in that spooning position as I came fully awake. I wasn't sure who slipped the condom on. We had sex three more times after we initially fell asleep. There was a good chance I put one back on subconsciously, because I just couldn't get enough of her and suddenly had the stamina of someone much younger than me.

Like her.

Slipping my arm around her, I teased her nipples between my thumb and forefinger. Her pussy clenched every time, and I craved it.

She moaned my name as she came apart, and I followed closely behind.

She was my new addiction, and I had no desire to seek an intervention for it.

Over the next two weeks, we were extremely careful. Only Rory knew anything. She became our occasional nighttime babysitter when Alex and I wanted some time alone without the fear of the twins walking in on us.

But we also got creative. There were times we snuck a quickie in the laundry room. Another was in the butler's pantry as the girls waited in the living room for their cakes to bake. Luckily, they were too involved in their competitive game of Go Fish to notice we were gone for longer than a few minutes.

I had bite and scratch marks on every part of my body. Alex was a screamer, and when she needed to remain quiet, my arm or back usually took the brunt of it, along with my palm over her mouth.

A few nights, we fell asleep in each other's room, the exhaustion from our projects and the mind-blowing sex taking its toll on us. We both ended up setting alarms on each other's phone to make sure we would wake up before the twins.

During most days, we focused on our own projects. We wouldn't get any work done otherwise, because we were insatiable for each other.

My robot was coming along. I had to tweak some of the coding, but the change in moisture control seemed to work. The last test on one of Nash's fields yielded almost perfect results.

Alex was spending her days trying new recipes to add to her collection. I really enjoyed being her taste-tester. She'd also been working with my assistant on her business plan. Alex was determined to get a small loan for the appliances and construction of the cake shop, and she wanted to do it without her family chipping in. She shut me down twice when I offered to invest. But I was determined to have the check ready with whatever dollar amount she needed if her plans fell through. I was proud of what she was doing, and I had the utmost faith in her skills and talent.

Neither of us had been looking forward to my third weekend in Ashfield. Alex walked around that Friday night in a completely sullen mood. Not even a trip to the ice cream shop with Molly and Eloise could cheer her up.

It wasn't hard to figure out why.

Autumn and Colton were to return in the morning. Which meant she would no longer be at the bed-and-breakfast on the regular.

Even though we both agreed to the friends-with-benefits label, what happened once she moved out had me questioning if it should continue. I could barely go a few hours without seeing her, touching her, tasting her. And there were many nights I'd woken up to Alex sneaking into my room and telling me what she wanted. Some nights, it was my cock in her mouth. Others, it was her riding me to her climax. And a couple of times, it was simply lying against me with her head resting on my chest and her leg twisted between mine.

I told her repeatedly that I'd see her almost every day. She hoped Autumn would let her continue using the kitchen for her cake experiments until she got her shop up and running, but she always had her parents' farmhouse as a backup.

It would work in my favor if she was able to keep using the B&B, but I spent enough time on Sunny Brook Farms that I wasn't too worried.

We could do this. We would do this.

"Come back to bed, baby." Alex had been pacing back and forth since midnight. She said when her anxiety was high, she would wake up with her heart racing. I told her there was a surefire way to calm her down, but she rolled her eyes and got out of bed.

It was her last full night at the B&B.

The girls pouted the entire day. They'd been absolutely distraught at the thought of Alex moving out of the house. When she set her suitcase and bag by the stairs, they'd gone so far as to hide them. Not well. We found them in the powder room.

Alex sat them down and explained she wasn't leaving them forever, and she was sure to see them almost every day. They thought she was leaving them like their mother had.

Which opened up an entirely different can of worms.

Sasha's calls had become even more frequent and frantic. She would dial my number for hours until I let her speak to the girls. It was the same time every day when I'd finally answer, so I could keep the girls on a schedule, but she was upsetting the twins with all her talk of them coming to visit. I hadn't agreed to anything, but when she mentioned it last, I told her I would think about it.

It wasn't me saying no, and that appeased her for a short time. Two days went by, then she started up again.

I tried to do some research on the internet about her, to see if she was in trouble, but nothing came up. There were a few images of her at charity events, but that was it. Most were too grainy to make out, but she looked thinner than I remembered. A dress I recalled her wearing once before hung off her already slight frame.

Alex suggested I take them to visit their mother as an early birthday present. That way, she could celebrate with them as well. The idea had merit, and I was still tossing it around.

But most of my time, my mind was preoccupied by the blonde currently wearing a hole in the rug.

"Alex, baby, everything will be fine. You're worrying over nothing."

"I just…."

"You just what?"

"I don't want to say it." She crossed her arms against her chest and pursed her lips.

"Now you have to tell me."

"No. You'll make fun of me."

"Doubtful," I replied, but when she still didn't respond, I reached out for her arm and hauled her back onto the bed. "Tell me, or I'll tickle that spot I discovered." I learned during a very thorough anatomy exam that Alex was extremely ticklish on the backs of her knees.

"No. Please, don't." She squirmed beneath me, waking up the part of me I just settled down.

"Then you know what to do."

"Fine." She pinched her lips together, then mumbled out something incoherent.

"What was that?" I asked, inching my fingers toward the back side of her thighs. Her hips bucked to try to get away.

"I'm going to miss you. Okay? There it is. I'm going to miss you."

"Now, was that so hard?"

"Yes," she hissed.

Leaning forward, I settled between her legs and pressed my lips to the tip of her nose. "I'm going to miss you, too."

She wrapped her arms around my neck.

Slow and steady that time.

When our alarms wailed the next morning, we made sure to fit in a round of hard and fast.

We'd been sneaking around Ashfield since Autumn and Colton returned. Autumn went the extra mile, as far as making sure we felt at home at the B&B. She was a great host and catered to our every need, but we all missed Alex. She stopped by on Sunday mornings to drop off some meals for the week, but it just wasn't the same. The girls missed her. *I* missed her.

Luckily, I found a house to rent for the rest of the summer and fall until my house was finished being built. We only had a couple more days at the B&B before we could move over to the rental.

Autumn argued with me when she tried to return the payment for unused weeks, but I told her to consider it a wedding gift. She and Colton deserved some alone time.

He and I hit it off immediately. I knew little about the ins and outs of hockey, but I knew enough to enjoy a game. I hadn't skated in years, but I promised Colton we could take a few laps on the ice when I got things settled in the rental.

My robot had been shipped back to my warehouse in California for transitioning into a full-scale model. I had hopes it would surpass my expectations and we could sell the patent. The more I stayed in Ashfield, the more I considered selling my business or becoming a silent partner. I wanted to raise my girls and spend more time with them. Focus less on the inner workings of the business and just create the robots and AI I thought would help the agricultural field.

They were growing more attached to me with every passing day since Alex left. Their fear of abandonment was unmistakable. Marisol and Rory tried to help. We even enlisted Franny, who we learned would be their kindergarten teacher in the fall. But so far, nothing was working. It didn't help that the day after Alex moved out, the calls from Sasha ceased.

I hadn't been surprised. That was typically what happened when she got bored. The twins acted like it was no big deal, but I knew otherwise. Having their mother cut ties with them, again, wasn't something they could easily brush aside. Even for four-year-olds.

To cheer them up, today we were headed toward Alex's new shop. She could finally begin her demolitions now that they fixed the piping in the building. Andrew and I helped move her belongings up to her new apartment the day before. He snuck away early, thinking he was getting out of hauling more items. He didn't know he opened the door for us to christen her new place.

I was hoping when I moved into the rental I could convince her to spend some of her nights there with me. The small brick ranch was just on the outskirts of town. A twenty-minute drive to Sunny Brook Farms and walking distance to Alex's apartment. I hadn't been picky. The girls and I just needed a place for a few months. It was furnished with new mattresses — something I hadn't even thought about. Autumn and Colton allowed me to keep my storage pod on their property until we could move into our new house.

"Does she have yummy cakes?" Molly asked from the backseat.

"No, sweetheart. It's not ready for food yet. But she's excited to show you the place and the designs she picked out. She even said you could help her choose some colors."

"That sounds fun! I'm really good at picking colors. Miss Franny said my purple horse was amazing."

"Daddy," Eloise said just above a whisper. "Does Alex miss us?" She had the hardest time with Alex leaving the B&B. After the incident earlier in the summer, she and Alex developed a special bond. Both girls were going to start dance classes next week once we got settled in the rental. I hoped that would cheer her up a bit.

"Of course, she does. You two are her favorite twins."

"I miss her." She sniffled, and my heart broke for my sweet little girl.

"I know you do. She misses you, too. She tells me all the time. Maybe we can set up a time when you guys can chat with her every day on video. Kind of like your mom did."

Sasha used to request video chats with the girls before we moved, but I put the kibosh on that when I heard her tell the girls she didn't like their haircuts. Like bangs were the end of the world.

I turned down the back road that led to the shop, thankful I eyed a few open parking spots on the street.

"Look, Daddy, there she is! She's waiting for us!" Eloise shouted as Molly squealed.

She stood waving on the sidewalk with the biggest grin, and my heart flip flopped. I told myself it was just the heavy lunch Autumn served us. I'd just take a few Tums before getting out of the car.

But as I stopped in front of her shop and she immediately pulled the door open to let the girls out, I knew it was something more than heartburn.

Strutting around the front of the car, I had the biggest fucking smile on my face. So bright it could light up all of Times Square. She was already a step away from the entrance, holding each girl's hand with one of her own. Alex peered over her shoulder at me, and her eyes sparkled like a firecracker. Her excitement was intoxicating.

The twins scooted under her arm as she held the door open while I made my way over to her.

"Hi," I said, brushing my hand over her arm on the way to capture the door. I needed to touch her more than I needed to breathe.

Her smile beamed as she responded the same way. I gestured for her to step inside, and then I followed her over the threshold. The girls were already running in circles in the main eating area.

Leaning over her shoulder, I whispered into her ear, "You should know, this is all they've talked about all morning. They didn't even want to watch Wild and Crazy Kids." The twins had taken up Alex's love of '90s shows in her absence.

"Well, I'll have to make the visit worth it then."

The girls weren't paying us any mind as I snuck my arm around Alex's waist. With a gentle pull, her back rested against my chest. "You're always worth it, Alex. Always."

Gracefully, she twisted out of my arm and faced me, then gently stroked my cheek before slipping away toward the girls.

In the corner under a window sat a portable table covered in papers. I followed them over to it and saw there were thirty or so pictures and design ideas Alex laid out. There were groupings based on colors and some based on the aesthetic. I noticed there was a common theme of pastels with gold accents. Anything she chose would be the perfect backdrop for her cakes.

We kneeled next to the girls at the table. Alex pointed out some of her favorites from each set. There was a bit of an eclectic flare in each of the items, the perfect embodiment of Alex.

"Hey, girls, I have a marker for each of you." She handed Eloise a blue marker and Molly a purple one. They immediately switched. "I'd love to see which items you like best out of the groups. Maybe you can even make a brand-new group. Just put a dot with your marker in the corners so I can find them. I want to talk to your dad about some of the appliances I was looking at. We'll be right over there in the kitchen, okay?"

The twins nodded, and with their tiny tongues poking out the sides of their mouths, they went to work.

"Come with me." Alex clasped my hand and tugged me toward the bigger kitchen in the back. It was where most of the baking would occur, separate from the one near the front. I wasn't sure what Alex planned for that one.

We turned a corner, and I commented on how impressed I was of how much work she accomplished in just a few days. The place was spotless.

She pushed through a set of swinging doors and ushered us into the kitchen.

"We don't have much time," she murmured, and she spun around and pushed my back up against a large stainless-steel refrigerator. My arms wrapped around her waist as she tugged my face down to meet hers. Our teeth clashed as we kissed passionately.

We hadn't seen each other since the evening before. I went back to the bed-and-breakfast after we christened the place, as she wanted to work on unpacking her things. Instead of a few hours, it felt like I hadn't seen her in years. I couldn't get enough of her mouth, her lips, her tongue. I wanted to sink myself into her with every passing second.

"God, I missed you," I whispered against her lips before diving back in.

I felt the cold stainless-steel touch my lower back as her hands pushed the cotton of my shirt up. Alex's hands roamed my abdomen. Her fingers dipped into each valley and trailed across each hill.

"Last night sucked," she whimpered as I nipped at her lip. Her fingers skimmed across the inside of my waistband, and my better judgment told me I needed her to stop.

"I know, baby."

Her lips brushed back and forth alongside my mouth, those miracle fingers scratching softly around my scalp. "Maybe we can sneak somewhere after dinner."

"Fuck, yes."

She teased me with her tongue, and I sucked it into my mouth, caressing it with my own.

"Eww!" two little voices cried out.

Alex and I jumped apart. I bumped into the fridge behind me and then rolled toward the counter. Alex knocked her hip on the corner of a stainless-steel counter and squawked.

"Why were you and Daddy kissing?" Molly asked Alex, her face scrunched up as if she'd eaten a sour lemon.

"Well, I… uh…." I could see all the white in Alex's eyes as she looked at me, hoping I'd answer the question.

Except I was in as much shock as she was. "Um… girls… you see…."

Molly looked at me expectantly, as if I could answer any and everything.

"Molly, that's what one-true-loves do, 'member?" Eloise replied, as if the answer was plain as day.

Huh?

"Oh! So, Miss Alex is Daddy's love, and that's why they were kissing?"

I spared a glance at Alex, but she was completely frozen in place. Her face turned a silky shade of white though.

"Yes." Eloise nodded.

Molly turned back to me, and I could sense there were more questions to come. Her tiny finger tapped a beat on her chin.

"Do you do it lots?"

"Um… yes? I mean, no? I mean…." Thankfully, she was already moving onto another question.

"Are you gonna get married and live happily ever after? I want a pwincess bed. I would be a pwincess, right? Do you have a castle? How do we get one?"

Molly prattled on with Eloise about the type of castle they thought I should move us all into. In two steps, I stood next to Alex and reached for her arm. She immediately flinched as if I startled her.

"You okay?"

She quickly nodded as she steadied herself on her feet. "Yeah. Sorry about that."

I shrugged. It had been a fright, but no big deal overall. My twins tended to move onto new topics in rapid-fire.

"Do you think they'll say anything?"

I was big on never asking my kids to keep secrets, but I had a feeling this was going to be a time where I broke my own rule.

Interrupting their discussion about canopy beds, I asked them to not tell anyone that Daddy and Miss Alex were kissing. When they asked me why, I tried to explain that a lot of people thought kissing was gross. Their bobbing heads seemed to agree.

Appeased, I took the girls back out to the front, and Alex followed. They yanked on her arms, excited to show her what items they liked. Surprisingly, all their choices worked well together.

"Girls, you did a really nice job. I love all of these. Thank you."

"You're welcome," they chimed together.

"You know what else I was thinking? What if I set up a little art station for any kids who come into the shop? Maybe I could even hang some of their drawings. Do you like that idea?"

"Yes."

"Uh huh."

"Great. Eloise, could you grab that bag under the table for me? I thought, since I had you both here, you could be my first artists."

The girls eagerly picked out the pictures they wanted to color. It was brave of Alex, since the twins struggled to color inside the lines, but the gesture was sweet regardless.

"I actually do want to talk to you about something. I got some of the loan documentation Friday, and I wondered if you could look it over with me."

"Ah, so your ruse to get me in the kitchen wasn't solely so you could kiss me?" I joked as I followed her to the smaller kitchen in the front. From here, the twins were in our line of sight.

"Keep it up, and it will be the last time," she countered with a smirk as she opened a binder resting on the counter.

Pressing a chaste kiss to her cheek, I replied, "I don't believe you for a second. Now, let's go over everything."

As Alex started flipping through the binder, it was obvious she spent a lot of time collecting data. She had average costs for appliances, cost of goods, average profit and revenue for a first-year shop, potential for online orders, software and bookkeeping fees. The list was endless and filled the majority of the binder.

The loan amount of fifteen thousand would cover most of the startup costs, but with the work needed on the shop to get it the way she wanted, it was going to be around three months until she could open the doors. Alex was lucky her family had the skills to pitch in and help when they had free time. I'd help, too, but Alex was going to have to tackle most of the manual labor unless she wanted to hire out.

The fifteen was going to cut it close.

I offered to loan her money before, full contract and everything, but she shot me down. Two attempts and no wins. I was about to ask her again, but she squashed that quickly.

"Before you even start, the answer is no."

"You're looking at this all wrong. You wouldn't even need the business loan. I could do a loan for you with no interest, Alex."

"I don't want you to waste your money on me."

With my thumb and forefinger, I lifted her chin so I could see her face. "Alex, you would never be a waste. But I understand wanting to do it yourself. I felt the same way when I started my business. I'll drop it, but I can't promise I won't bring it up again."

"Thank you. It is sweet of you to offer. You need to keep that money for your girls anyway."

I really think she underestimated how much I was worth. An internet search was a few digits short. My original robot had been one of a kind. The new prototype was going to be revolutionary. There were already insane bids on the patent flowing through the rumor mill. If a sale of that magnitude went through, I could buy all of Ashfield if I wanted and still have money to spare.

"In my professional opinion, I think you should ask the bank for twenty, just so you have a cushion in case any emergencies arise. You've done the math and can cover the initial payments for a year with your savings. And we both know your family would help you if you needed it. Not that you'd ever ask, because you're stubborn as a mule. If they won't extend to twenty, I think fifteen is still fine. You'll just have to shop around for some deals. Scratch and dents for appliances and such."

"Thank you. It feels nice to share this with someone and get their opinion, knowing they've run their own business. Makes it easier to trust myself."

"The pleasure is all mine."

I snuck a quick glance over my shoulder at the twins. They leaned over the table, coloring like their life depended on it.

Quickly, I sealed my lips over Alex's and waited until she melted against me before pulling away.

"*Your* pleasure is going to be all mine later."

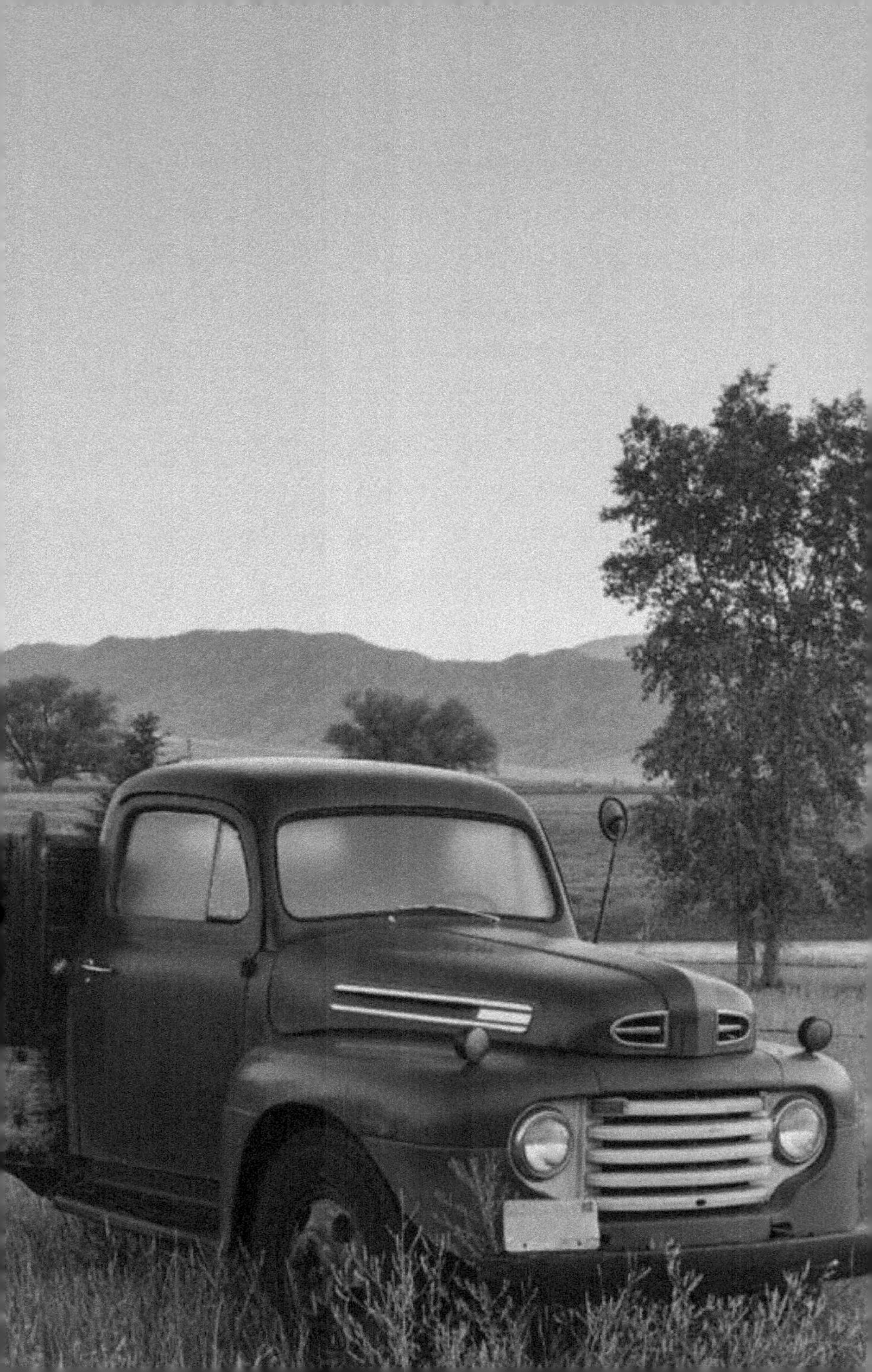

Chapter Twenty-One

Alex

There was something about watching my mother move around her kitchen fixing dinner that made me homesick. She took pride in every morsel she fed us, usually something from scratch she concocted. I hoped that in the time I hosted the Sullivans at the bed-and-breakfast, they felt that same sort of pride from my meals.

Every meal I made came from my heart, and I tried to find recipes that maybe Nate and his twins had never tried before. Not that we didn't have pizza or chicken nuggets on occasion, but I wanted to expand their palates. Not once did they complain. The majority of the time, Molly and Eloise finished every bite on their plates.

I had so much fun with them in the shop today. Watching their eyes light up when I showed them the pictures I wanted to use as inspiration made my heart melt. Nate had been helpful, too. I loved picking his brain regarding all the aspects of the business. There were a lot of things I hadn't considered and added to a new list in the back of my binder.

My last class for my business degree had been an entry-level ethics class I missed somehow. Since it was online, I was able to finish the workload in record time. I'd officially graduate at the end of summer. Earning my degree online meant I wouldn't get to participate in any of the pomp and circumstance regarding a graduation ceremony, but I didn't mind. Opening my shop was going to be all the pomp and circumstance I needed.

We talked about the opening date for the shop, and I circled the month of September. I really hoped to get it up and running by then, if not before, but July was already right around the corner.

Last week, Aspen and I sat down and worked on my website. It was still in preview mode, but she'd done a great job mocking something up. I didn't have any e-commerce available yet, but we left that as an option in the future.

The focus right now was to get the cakes ready for the Ashfield Summer Festival. It always took place over Fourth of July weekend. I had fifteen cakes ready to go, and I hoped to add a few more. I'd been experimenting with the circular single serving slicer I found online. I had hopes it would work the way I wanted.

"What's on your mind, Alexandra?"

I startled at my name. Looking down at my hands, I saw I'd torn today's newspaper into tiny shreds. "Nothing. Just wondering if Nate was able to find the battery for Molly. You know how the stores close early on Sunday."

Originally, the four of us planned to come here for dinner together, but halfway through their visit, Molly's hearing aid died. Nate tried to tell her she could hear without it, but she insisted on getting a replacement. Apparently, it comforted her to have it on, like a security blanket. I hoped she always felt that way as she got older and didn't let kids bully her for it.

Nate apologized and took the girls back to the B&B, but he couldn't find any of her spares. He'd been texting me since they left, and so far, three stores didn't have what they were looking for.

"Oh, no. I hope they find somewhere open. I know most of the pharmacies carry them, but like you said, they're usually closed on Sundays. Drats!" Mom exclaimed as the pot of water boiled over. Using her trusty dish towel she always kept on her shoulder while cooking, she grabbed the handles of the pot and took it off the burner.

Tonight's meal was homemade ravioli, and my crimping of the pasta was superb.

"You sure everything else is okay?" she asked as she stirred her sauce and placed the water pot back on the stove with the dial turned down.

"Yeah," I lied. "Tami is gone for another three weeks. I just miss her."

"I miss her, too. She's always fun to have around."

I did miss my best friend, but that wasn't what had me out of sorts. I was growing attached to Nate. No matter how hard I tried to convince myself it was just sex, the butterflies in my stomach erupted whenever he was near. When he walked around his SUV this morning, I thought I was going to throw up from how much they fluttered around.

Andrew was still a problem for us. He hadn't been around much, flying across the country recently to settle some contracts for Dad. Yesterday was the first time I'd seen him in a week.

We worried about the girls catching us, but they seemed fine. Today had been eye-opening when they saw us kissing.

It's what had me confused. I *wanted* people to know. I wanted to go to dinner with him at The Purple Goat where all the townspeople hung out. Or get a drink with him at the bar when the cake shop closed and not worry about the rumors swirling.

I wanted *him*.

Mom set a glass of red wine in front of me and then went about sweeping my scraps into her hand to throw away. If there was anyone I could confide in, it would be Mom.

"Hey, Mom. What do you think Andrew would say if—"

The rest of the question fell away as excited screams filled the kitchen.

"What would Andrew say about what?" Andrew asked as he sidled up next to me. "Hey, sis." He pressed his lips to the top of my head as Nate stepped into the kitchen, looking for his daughters.

"Oh, nothing. I was hoping maybe I could get you to read over some of the vendor contracts before I sign them." The lie came easily, but as I let it fester and grow, I realized it had merit.

"So, you're really doing it?"

"Yep."

"Then sure, I'll look them over. Thanks for asking. Hey, Mom." He stepped away from me and wrapped our mom in a hug, and Nate took my brother's place at the island.

Leaning over, he apologized for leaving earlier today. They ended up driving two towns over to find a big box store that had hearing aid batteries in stock.

I snuck a quick glance at Molly, and she was sitting on my dad's lap like nothing had been amiss. I studied her for a minute. It was the smallest of movements, one anyone else would brush aside. But as she tucked her hair behind her ear, she rubbed the aid. It really did put her at ease.

"What are you thinking about for later?" I whispered, trying my hardest not to move my mouth. Growing up, I swore these walls had eyes and ears. They told all our secrets to my mom. She knew everything.

"I'm not sure, but it will probably involve sneaking you into my room after everyone's gone to bed."

Disappointment stirred within me. I was going to have to wait until much later to be alone with him. Autumn and Colton had their own private quarters, but they usually hung around the first floor for a good portion of the night in case any of the guests needed anything.

Their hospitality was annoying.

"Not any sooner?"

"Not unless you know a place here where there is zero risk of someone walking in."

Nowhere in this house was safe. My sisters and Andrew knew all the good hiding spots. If they wanted to find me, they could.

"That stinks."

"Sorry. And I promised the girls they could call their mom." Nate turned away and looked off into the rest of the kitchen. "They… uh… want to tell her about your cake shop and how they've been helping you."

I blanched. Did she know about us? If she wanted to cause drama in Nate's life, would she figure out a way to use me against him?

"She only knows you're Andrew's younger sister. The girls talk about you all the time. I think it annoys her, so I haven't stopped them. I'm sorry if that upsets you." His apology was sincere, and I wished we were anywhere else so I could forgive him in our own special way.

"What are you two talking about over here? Nate? Want a beer?" Andrew leaned on the island across from us, blocking my view of Mom cooking.

"Just chatting about her shop. The girls got to pick their favorite ideas from Alex's stack. And, yeah, I'd love a beer. Thanks."

Andrew slipped out to the garage and grabbed a beer for Nate, calling out that I had one too many cakes in our parents' other fridge. I was testing new recipes any chance I could. Mom's was the easiest place to store all of them. I was starting to feel bad though, because other than a bite or two, most of them were going to waste. I'd been taking what I could to the coffee shop in town, and they agreed to let customers know when and where they could get one in the fall. The business cards I ordered were still in transit—another project Aspen knocked out of the park.

I'd been fumbling with a name ever since I started this journey. The restaurants and eateries in

Ashfield had such unique names. I wanted my shop to stand out with them. Names like Eat or Be Easterly, a tie into my last name, and For Cake's Sake were a couple of my favorites. Then, just before I began filing paperwork to solidify the business, the perfect name came to me. I wasn't even sure it made sense, but it was an ode to both things I loved: food and dance.

Show-Stopping Sweets.

Aspen took the name and ran with it, creating the most unique logo and website.

Things were moving along, and I couldn't have been more excited. I just needed to get started on replacing some of the appliances so I could store my own cakes there. And the kitchen desperately needed new ovens.

Autumn and Colton strolled into the house a few minutes later, hand in hand. They were so in love it was almost sickening. Not because they were gross, but because I never thought I'd have that for myself. I was so envious.

I stole a glance at Nate, who was seated in the living room with Andrew and my dad. He looked so relaxed with my family. It was a shame the small fissure in my heart cracked further every time we were together. I was too stubborn to be the one to break our agreement, no matter how much my heart broke. Because Nate was slinking his way into it every time he was in my bed.

Rory joined us next, and as Mom finished up with dinner, my sisters and I congregated in the kitchen while the men sat in the living room. It's what happened every family dinner. The only change was that perched on the knees of my father were Molly and Eloise. They invaded the men's zone and left us girls. Those little adorable traitors.

Rory and Autumn were asking me all sorts of questions about the shop and what ideas I had for it. Normally, I'd have my binder with me, but I decided to leave it at the shop today.

"The apartment is really nice. It's a lot bigger than the one over the bar. And… I finally gave my notice. Randy is no longer my boss."

"How did he take it?" Autumn asked, pulling off a chunk of freshly baked bread I brought over.

"He wasn't thrilled. I mean, I'd been there for like five years. But he did wish me well and said he knew I was going to be a success. It was nice."

"So, you still think you'll open in September?"

"That's the plan, but maybe even sooner. Some of the items that were on backorder either came in stock or I found at a scratch and dent warehouse. No one's going to see them but me and maybe another employee."

"Oh, you're going to hire someone?" Sadie, Colton's half-sister, asked around a mouthful of bread. Her cheeks were puffed out, reminding me of a chipmunk. A year ago, when Colton found out about her, we immediately adopted her as one of our own.

"I was thinking about it."

"I'd be interested, if you think you could work around my school schedule."

"Sure."

Mom called out for everyone to get to the table, and I told Sadie we could work out a time to discuss it more. It would be nice to have someone I knew and trusted working with me. And Sadie was sweet with a great work ethic. She was currently taking classes at the University of Tennessee and getting her master's degree, but she planned on taking the slow route like I did.

They extended the dining table with the center leaf. It was usually reserved for the meals when the farm hands joined the entire family. Since Autumn and Colton came home and the additional spots were needed for Sadie, Nate, Molly, and Eloise, it just made sense to leave it in place. Despite the extra piece of wood, the chairs still brushed against each other. It was a tight fit, but I knew my mother wouldn't have it any other way. I'd have to talk to my sisters about getting my parents a new, larger table for Christmas. I assumed Autumn and Colton planned on adding grandkids at some point.

Everyone shuffled around the table. Somehow, I lucked out with Nate on my left side. Rory was seated to my right. The twins were nestled on either side of Andrew. It was adorable how much they loved my big, grumpy brother. One of the pictures they drew at my shop was of them with Andrew under a big rainbow.

Mom sat out the dishes of pasta and sauce, and Dad carried my bread to the table. Once he sat down and took his helping, the bowls started their rotation around the table. As usual, there were no leftovers at an Easterly dinner. Not a morsel remained in the bowls. I don't know how my mom knew exactly how much to cook for everyone, but no one complained about having too little or too much.

"I have tiramisu for dessert. A Betsy special." Mom grabbed the empty bowls and carried them to the kitchen. The stack of dessert plates were passed out by the time she got back.

"Oh! I brought a new dessert wine. I want to offer it at the bed-and-breakfast. You guys can be my guinea pigs." Autumn scooted her chair back, and Colton did his best to help her slip by. When she was free from the wooden confines, she leaned down and kissed him on the cheek. "Thanks, babe."

Nate and I quickly glanced at each other and rolled our eyes.

"Daddy kisses Miss Alex, too. On the mouth," Molly said, scrunching her nose in the process.

"Yeah. He's her one true love, so it's okay." Eloise made it a point to add in that detail as she peered around Andrew and stared at her sister.

Silence.

It was the loudest fucking silence I'd ever heard.

I propped my elbows on the table and rested my head in my hands, rubbing small circles on my forehead to dull the ache I knew was going to form any second now.

"What? You've been... kissing my sister?" I couldn't look up at Andrew. When he was angry, those dark eyes grew wild, feral. When I was little, he used to remind me of an enormous bear ready to attack a little lamb.

I felt Nate's hand touch my leg, and I wasn't positive if it was to comfort me or himself. This was not a situation I wanted to be in, but we understood the risk when we gave in to our attraction.

"Are you touching her right now? Come on, man." I heard the sound of scraping and glanced up to find Andrew standing in front of his chair. Beside him, the twins' chins trembled from his outburst. They were not fans of yelling. I was about to tell him to calm down, but Nate spoke up instead.

"Dude, calm down. You're freaking out my kids. And it was just a couple of times, okay?"

Maybe it was the embarrassment, or perhaps it was the stress I'd been under, but as Nate threw in one more lie, I had enough.

"Really, Nate? A couple of times?"

"Alex, please," he said through clenched teeth. His grip on my leg tightened, but it wasn't painful. I turned to look at him and was surprised by how pale he was. He resembled more a teenager caught for stealing his dad's car than a billionaire CEO who demanded everyone's attention in a room.

He was scared. And that gutted me.

"Andrew," I said as calmly as I could muster. My voice shook to my own ears. The twins openly wept as my mom tried to hurry them from their seats. "I love you so much. But if you don't stop right now, you're going to say something you can't take back. So what if Nate and I kissed, or whatever? We're adults, and we're both on the same page about whatever this is. So, please, I'm begging you to just let it go."

Andrew seemed to mull this over for a moment, letting my words marinate and seep in. "But... he's going to hurt you. He doesn't do relationships, Alex."

"First off, he's right here," I said, blindly gesturing to Nate. "Secondly, I'm well aware that he doesn't want a relationship. Newsflash—neither do I. So, just let it go."

"You're what? Fu—," he started, but Nate slammed his fist on the table.

"Watch your language." It had been the hand on my leg, and I instantly missed the comfort of his touch.

"Friends with benefits then?"

"It doesn't matter what it is, Andrew." Nate pushed up from his chair and skirted around the table, heading toward the kitchen. "It's *ours*." He addressed my mother and thanked her for dinner, then rounded up the girls to leave.

Andrew stood frozen to his spot at the table while the rest of my family looked on as if they just witnessed their favorite soap opera play out in real life. Chins on fists, sneers directed at Andrew, heart-shaped cartoon eyes aimed at me and Nate's vacated spot. They were held captive.

The front door slammed, and I jumped up as if my chair were on fire. My heart definitely was.

"Nate!" I shouted and then repeated until he turned around. He'd been busy loading a crying Molly into her seat while Eloise whimpered at his leg.

"I need to get them home." He sounded so forlorn, so defeated.

"I know. Nate, I'm so sorry that happened."

Once he snapped Molly into place, he lifted Eloise and moved around the truck. I followed like a lovesick fool.

"Nate, he'll get over it. Andrew won't stay mad forever."

"I know he won't. I don't even know why he's mad. *He* doesn't even know why he's mad."

"He thinks he's protecting me."

"But it's *me*. I'm his best friend. He knows me better than anyone and should trust me. But by his reaction in there, he made it clear he doesn't trust me at all." He secured the belt for Eloise and then closed her door. I took a step back so he could open the driver door.

"He's going to realize he made a mistake, Nate."

"I know. Please tell your mom I said thank you again and that I'm sorry for the mess tonight. I'll make it up to her."

Something must have landed in my eye, because they burned, and it made my nose tingle. It had to be dust, because I could not cry in front of Nate right now.

"Okay," I whispered, afraid that if I spoke any louder, whatever was making my eyes burn would travel down to my throat.

"Look, I'll see you tonight. Yeah?"

I nodded as he pressed his lips to the top of my head. No real kiss. No peck on the cheek. Just a fucking head-topper.

Nate left in a whirl, his SUV kicking up dirt and dust as it traveled away from the farm.

I stood out there, watching the driveway for a while. The dust settled, and all remnants of their departure had fallen away.

An arm wrapped around my waist, and I knew who it was without looking. "Hey, sweetie. Want to come inside?"

"I think I'll just head back to my apartment, Mom."

"Hmm. But I saved a slice of tiramisu just for you. Snagged it before your father could get his hands on it. I know it's one of your favorites. Plus, I think your sisters want to chat with you, and you know how they can be."

I sure did. They'd do whatever they needed to keep me from leaving. Take the battery out of my truck. Hide my purse. Slip a piece of ex-lax into my dessert. I learned that last one the hard way when they wanted the details after my senior prom.

"Yeah, okay. Can I eat it out on the deck?"

"Of course. I may even join you girls." Mom tugged me in just a little before we turned and made our way back to the house. My sisters were all watching from the porch.

We settled out back on the L-shaped patio sofa that held all of us. Mom brought out a glass of wine and the largest piece of tiramisu, which was at least a quarter of the dessert.

"Thanks, Mom."

"Now, tell me—" She settled in beside me, tapping my thigh in that motherly way. "—do I get the credit for getting you two together?"

A giggle escaped. That seemed to cure my burning eyes and tingling nose. "I'm sorry, but no. Nate and I actually met by mistake over a year ago."

I left out the scandalous details but went on to tell them how much of a shock it had been when he arrived at the bed-and-breakfast. I spent another hour answering all my sisters' sordid questions. They were curious about how we made it work. He was a full-time dad and also way older than me. But somehow, we just made it happen, because we wanted it to. Autumn and Rory had known about my one-night stand mystery man, and to learn it was Nate made all the more sense as to why I couldn't stay away from him. That one night set a new trajectory for my future, it seemed.

While sitting on the back porch, I continued to look over my shoulder. Thankfully, Andrew didn't make himself known as my sisters, mom, and I sat outside. They all agreed with me that he would come around. Mom thought maybe he was upset we'd hidden it from him. Whatever the reason, I was angry at my brother for the way he pushed Nate away.

Whatever Nate and I were label-wise, I knew he needed a friend tonight. And I planned to be just that for him.

Now, I just needed to wait for his call.

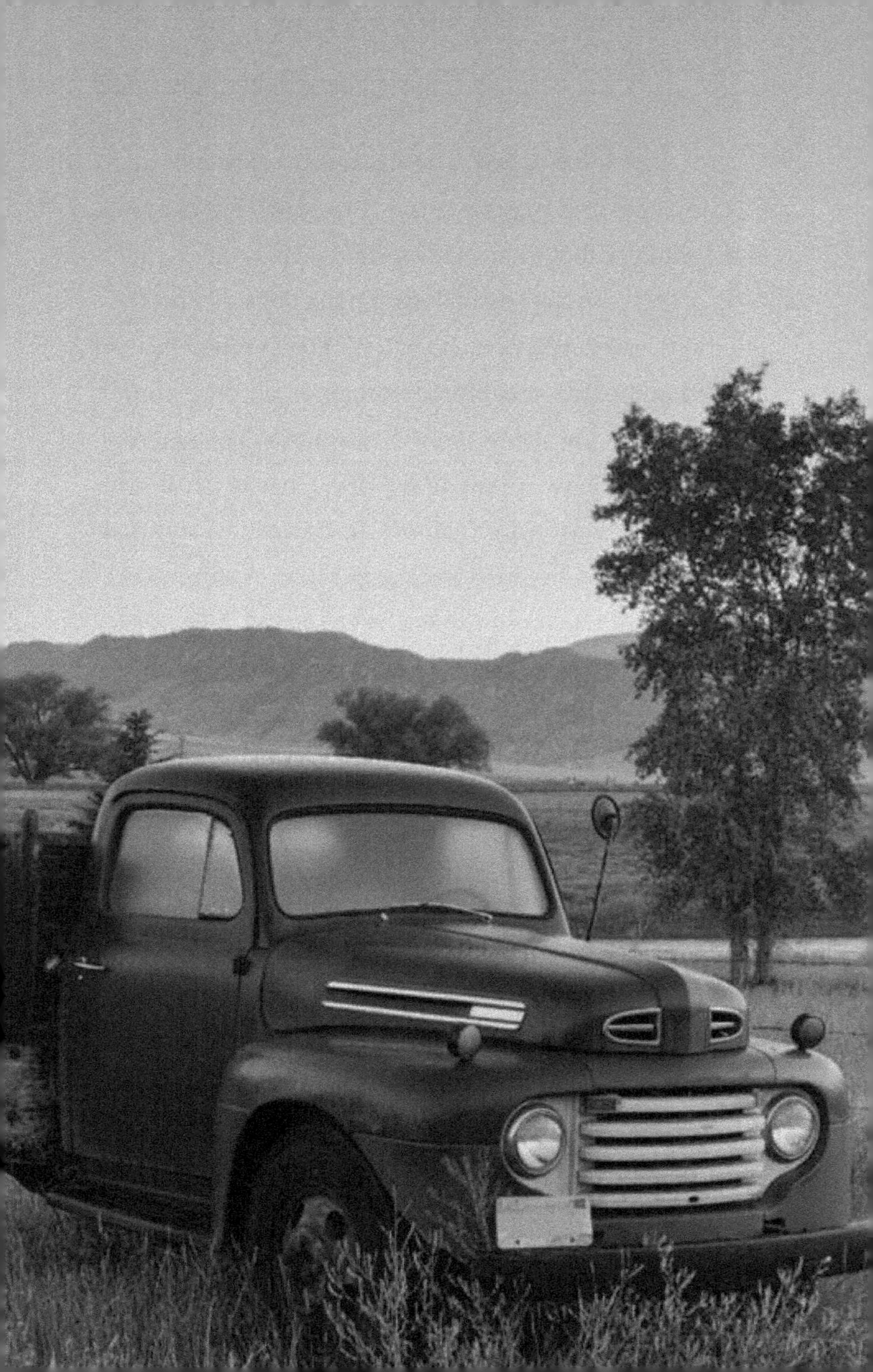

Chapter Twenty-Two

Nate

My finger hovered over the phone's Call button. I was torn up about what to do next. The twins were down in the family room watching *Bluey* while I stared at the package on my bed. The manilla envelope had been sitting at the bottom of the stack of mail Autumn had been collecting for me. My mail had been forwarded for weeks, but the postal service included it in the mail being held for Autumn and Colton while they were gone. The rest of my items had been junk. Anything else important was usually work related, and I was made aware of it by my assistant or legal department.

The date on the envelope was three days prior, so it was recent. And the contents changed everything.

I opened the legal-sized package thinking it was something related to the patent for my newest robot. The testing at our facility in California was going well and was surpassing our expectations. I had high hopes that it would get top dollar when the time to sell came. The industry heard rumblings of what the robot was capable of, but real-life data would seal the deal.

While on the road in search of the elusive hearing aid battery for Molly, I reached out to my assistant. I realized it was a Sunday, but I hadn't actually expected her to answer. I tossed in the idea of what it would take for me to step away and become a silent partner in the business. It would still be mine, but I'd need to move around the organizational structure. By the time we arrived at dinner, she emailed me three different organizational changes along with contract mockups.

But now, those thoughts hung in the air. I was going to have to reevaluate everything. The twins had been on the phone with their mom when I noticed the stack of mail. Autumn set it nicely on the dresser in my bedroom. Instead of sorting through it, I went back to Eloise's room and listened to the twins' conversation with Sasha. She was quieter than normal and seemed sad. I wondered if the girls' fifth birthday approaching put her out of sorts. It was a big milestone. In the background, I suggested they could do a video call, but Sasha declined, saying she didn't have her face on. She'd always been that way. She practically slept in her makeup, never wanting to be caught off guard without looking photo ready.

The girls were a little bummed out, but Sasha diverted the conversation to the petting zoo they wanted to have for their birthday. I still wasn't sure how I was going to make that happen.

With shaking hands, I dropped the phone back to my side and lifted the stack of paperwork again. MGMT changes, 1p/19p co-deletions, IDH mutations, X-rays, CAT scans, MRIs, and multiple biopsy results. It was all just gibberish to me, but the cover letter told me everything I needed to know. Sasha received a brain cancer diagnosis three years ago, and none of the treatments worked. The tumor was growing too fast. Her physician noted that nothing they'd done slowed it down. Due to its massive size, the number of headaches and seizures, and the level of drowsiness, her team didn't believe she had much longer.

It's why over the last few months she'd been so persistent about having the twins visit her. Sasha knew her life was coming to an end. I'd rarely ever spoken with her on the phone. She'd given up trying to speak to me and just forwarded copies of all the paperwork she received.

There was no question what I was going to do next. My time in Ashfield was going on hiatus. I just needed to break it to the twins and Alex.

I felt so lost and confused trying to meld together the version of Sasha who pretty much tried to destroy me and my business, and the Sasha who was dying in her home.

Leaning forward, I rested my arms on my knees and dipped my chin toward my chest. Blindly, I reached for my phone and brought up Alex's number again.

"Hey," she said hesitantly. I could hear the cackles from her sisters in the background.

"Hi." To my own ears, my voice was unfamiliar. It sounded defeated. Today felt like I lost both my best friend and the mother of my girls. It was too much.

There was a sound of rustling and then silence. "Are you okay?"

"Yeah, do you think you can come by?"

"Are the girls in bed already? It's still early."

"They're still up. I need to talk to you about something important."

"Oh... okay. Um... I'll be there in a bit."

Ending the call, I tucked all the loose papers into the manilla folder and carried it back to the dresser. Downstairs, I checked in on the girls and told them Miss Alex was coming over. When they asked about kissing, I couldn't hide my cringe. I wished that was the reason I needed her to stop by the B&B.

Thirty minutes later, Alex slipped into the house. Autumn and Colton trailed behind her, and neither made eye contact with me.

"Hey, Autumn. I know it's a big ask, but could you keep an eye on the girls for a few minutes? I need to speak to Alex about something."

"Yeah, no problem." She and Colton moved toward the family room, and she looked at me over her shoulder and sent me one of those pitied smiles.

"Can I talk to you in my room?" I asked Alex.

She looked toward the family room, then back at me before nodding. We hadn't had the best experience of keeping our hands to ourselves when we were alone in the room. Unfortunately, this time, I was pretty sure we wouldn't be getting sidetracked.

As we climbed the stairs, I didn't even stare at Alex's ass swaying in front of my face. That's how out of sorts I was. Nothing mattered except making sure my daughters had the chance to spend some time with their mother.

"What's going on, Nate? Is everything okay? You sounded weird on the phone." She turned to face me as she stepped into the room. Her eyes were brimming with tears, and it sounded like it was taking all her strength to hold it together. I hated I was about to send her over the edge.

"I'm going back to California. The girls and I leave on Tuesday," I said monotonously as I grabbed the envelope.

"What? Nate, Andrew is going to come around. You don't need to leave. Please. I...."

Turning around, I held out the envelope for her to take. She asked what was inside before reaching out to take it from me.

"Just read through it. It explains everything."

Slowly, I approached my bed and sat on the edge. Suddenly, my T-shirt felt like it was two sizes too small and was cinching my chest. I ripped it off over my head, hoping it would help the panic subside.

Beside me, the bed dipped.

"Nate, I don't know what to say."

"She's dying, and there is nothing I can do."

"I'm so sorry." Alex gently rested her head on my shoulder and wrapped her arm around mine.

My eyes blurred as I told her how I worried my girls would have no memory of their mother. It killed me inside. Like a boulder crushing me, my heart and lungs punctured by each individual rib.

"What can I do to help you and the girls?"

"I don't know. I'll have them pack up their things that aren't in storage. I guess I should ask Autumn about doing some laundry."

"How long do you think you'll be gone?"

I winced at the question. I didn't know exactly, but the doctor only expected her to last a few more weeks at the most. "Probably just until things settle."

I went ahead and gathered the girls' laundry while Alex joined her sister and the twins. I wasn't sure how I was going to break it to them. They didn't have a super-close relationship with their mother, but she was still theirs.

As they finished up the episode of *Bluey*, I settled them on the couch with Alex close by. I didn't force Autumn or Colton to leave, since they'd find out soon enough. I let the news out as slowly and gently as

I could. We'd be going back to California to see their mom before she went away to be with the angels. The girls seemed confused and asked when she'd be coming back. And I hated telling them that she wouldn't be. Beside them, Alex sniffled, and it broke my heart to see her taking my ex's prognosis just as hard as I was.

They seemed unfazed by the news, but I had a feeling once they saw their mother, things would start to make more sense. Just from the lab work, I could tell she'd lost a considerable amount of weight. Weight she didn't have to lose in the first place.

The girls went to bed easily enough, and when I joined the group back downstairs, Autumn rushed over to gather me in her arms. She said she'd take care of whatever I needed and that we could keep the storage container on her property. There were so many things I needed to do before I left, but I felt overwhelmed and so extremely tired.

Colton offered me a drink, but I declined. Alex stood in the kitchen's corner worrying her lip.

"I think I'm going to head up. I'm… so fucking tired."

Acknowledging no one, I made my way back to my room. Alex restored Sasha's labs back into the envelope and returned it to the dresser. Since my shirt was still discarded somewhere on the floor, I slipped out of my shorts and settled into bed. With a quick switch of the lamp, I bathed the room in darkness. A little glow from the rising moon shone through the window, but I was too drained to get up and shut the curtains.

As tired as I was, my mind wouldn't turn off. I kept replaying different moments from today. It started off so well, and then it all went to shit.

Just as I was reliving the last twelve hours for the fifth time, there was a light knock on the door and then the squeak of the door opening. I knew without looking that it was Alex. My body instantly responded to her.

"Hey," she whispered. "I just want to lie with you, if that's okay."

Wordlessly, I rolled onto my back and threw the covers open on her side. I was thankful for the faint moonlight, as I got to watch her shrug out of her clothes and slip in beside me. She snuggled close, resting her head on my chest. It was one of my favorite positions.

"Go to sleep. I'll be here when you wake up," she murmured.

My eyelids grew heavier with each passing second, and then the sweetness of slumber took over me.

The twins refused to pack their things the next day. I'd been up early setting up flights and finding a rental property close to Sasha's condo. She refused to go back to the hospital. After booking the flights, I'd taken the time to call her, and we spoke for a good hour. Alex sat by me the entire time—not out of jealousy, but she was there to comfort me. A few times, I felt her lips on my shoulder as I teared up. She was my life vest in this unforgiving ocean of chaos.

Somehow, Alex convinced the girls to clean up and put their clothes in their suitcases. A reference to *Mary Poppins* seemed to do the trick.

By the time dinner came around, we were all just one step away from falling asleep at the table.

The Easterlys sat around the table in the formal dining room with us. It felt surreal to be back in this room. We hadn't eaten a meal in here since those first couple of days when the girls and I arrived. I recalled how hesitant Alex had been to sit at the table with us that night. Only after some serious puppy-dog eyes had she caved. And now her entire family was here supporting me and my daughters.

Even Andrew had shown up, though he hadn't uttered a word to me or Alex. It still meant everything to me that he came.

Marisol tried to argue the kitchen duty away from Alex, but I knew my girl needed this. She wanted to take care of me and the twins. But I also knew Marisol wanted to take care of *her*. Because Alex was hurting despite how many false smiles she gave. I could see right through them.

The chicken fajitas were delicious, not that I expected anything less. When he finished, Andrew even thanked Alex. It was the first time I heard him speak since he arrived.

"So, what time is your flight in the morning?" Nash asked as he took a hearty pull from his beer.

"It leaves at 7:00 a.m. It was the earliest one I could get."

"And you have a place to stay?" Marisol added as she scooped the dirty plates up from the table.

"We do. I was able to secure a short-term rental close to Sasha's place. They originally said I couldn't move in for another two weeks, but, you know, money talks," I tried to joke, but it fell flat.

That awful awkward silence took over the room. It was something I'd never witnessed around the

Easterlys. I had no idea what to say around them. With each small smile or pat on the shoulder, I could feel their hurt on my behalf.

Standing from the table, I thanked them all for joining us for dinner. I joked that I still had a house to build, so we wouldn't be gone too long, but their chuckles weren't genuine. The problem was we had no idea how long Sasha had, and I wanted the girls to be with her as long as they could.

Gradually, everyone started to leave the B&B. Even Colton and Autumn retreated to their private space. Marisol made me promise to keep in touch before she wrapped me up in her arms. Why hadn't I been granted a mother like this from birth? The Easterly kids had no idea how good they had it. Maybe if I did, I could've saved my kids from the heartbreak they were about to experience. Because maybe then I wouldn't have made any of the decisions that led to meeting and marrying Sasha to begin with.

But then I wouldn't have them. And I wouldn't have traded Molly and Eloise for any kind of perfect childhood of my own.

"We love you, Nathaniel. All of us. Don't forget that." Gingerly, she patted my cheek and walked out with Nash. He was a man of few words, but he choked up expressing his condolences.

"We never want to see our children hurting," he said, and though he didn't say it specifically, it felt like he was referring to me.

I stood on the front porch, watching the trailing brake lights of cars. Alex was still inside helping the girls clean up after dinner. One person still hadn't left, and I felt his presence on the front porch before he said a word.

"Hey."

"Hey," I replied, my hands tucked deep in my pockets.

"I… er… I'm sorry to hear about Sasha. She wasn't always my favorite person, but I hate that she's sick."

And dying.

I let those unspoken words hang in the air.

"Thanks," I mumbled.

"Can I do anything for you? For Molly and Eloise?" he asked as he stepped up beside me. Andrew's large frame leaned against the railing of the porch as he turned to face me.

"Can you look after her, please? I need to make sure she's okay." I didn't need to say her name for him to figure out who I was referring to. I hated that I was leaving just as she was getting her business started. I wanted to be around for all of that, to help her. And now I was being called back to my ex. Even if it was for reasons out of my control, I knew my retreat was going to hurt her.

"Um… yeah. Of course I can."

"Thanks."

His gaze turned back toward the landscape ahead of us. The light summer breeze brushed along the top of the tall grass just beyond the yard, forcing it to sway. "Can I ask you something, Nate?"

His voice turned more serious than before, and as he dropped his head forward, I braced myself for his words. But in true fashion, he surprised me when I grunted my agreement.

"What would have happened had this thing with Sasha not popped up?"

"What do you mean?"

"With Alex. What was your plan with her?"

"I don't know. Your sister is amazing, and she understands me. I never feel like I need to be someone else when I'm with her. And we both know she couldn't give two shits about my money. She probably wishes I didn't have it. But neither of us wanted to share whatever it was we were doing. And I won't lie to you, Andrew. I have every intention of starting it up again when I get back. I'm hoping that's sooner rather than later. I... I can't stay away."

Andrew's demeanor changed as he straightened and faced me.

"You're in love with her," he said matter-of-factly.

Quickly, I turned my head to make sure there was no one lurking around. "I am not. Don't kill me, but it's just sex, man. We enjoy each other."

"Keep telling yourself that. And yeah, I'll keep an eye on her. I may stay close for the rest of the summer. Dad needs me to work on a few things."

"Thanks, Andrew."

"Travel safe and check in, yeah?" He stepped around me and headed toward his truck.

"Hey!" I called out. "Am I forgiven?"

"Don't hurt my sister, and we'll see," he shouted as he hopped into his seat.

He honked as he reached the end of the driveway. At the same time, Alex walked out onto the porch. She asked if I worked things out with her brother, and I shrugged. Things weren't back to normal yet, but I hoped they would be soon.

Together, we tucked the twins into their beds. They both lamented the fact they were leaving the bedrooms Autumn decorated for them. Even now, the rooms reflect them with artwork and toys we added since arriving.

Alex leaned over each one of them and whispered in their ears. I couldn't hear what was said, but both Molly and Eloise threw their arms around her neck and hugged her close. Whatever she said transformed the twins' scowls and left them grinning as they fell asleep.

The night felt like a finality. She joined me in the shower, and I proceeded to push her up against the cold tile wall as I slid into her pussy. I was ravenous for her, afraid to miss one single second of coming apart with her.

After she flew off the ledge, I washed her hair with the special shampoo and conditioner she left in the other guest bathroom. I snagged it before Autumn could give it back to her sister. Alex now used it anytime she stayed the night.

We fell into bed completely naked. I didn't even bother with the briefs this time, because I knew Alex would have them off within minutes. I should have been a fortune teller, because my prediction came true the second her wet hair hit the pillow and her small hand wrapped around my cock.

There was no sleeping that night as we frantically fucked all over the room. Hard and fast. Slow and steady. We made our own personal mixtape of sexual positions and speeds as the night wore on.

As an early glimpse of the summer day peeked over the tops of the trees, I hovered above Alex's writhing body, plunging my cock into her core where she needed me most. My lips muted her cries of pleasure. With our time running out and the light chasing after us, our coming together felt different from before. It was still as desperate, but there was a sense of something more that was exchanged with each kiss and thrust. Something that left me reeling as I spilled myself into the last condom I had.

We were making love and saying goodbye at the same time.

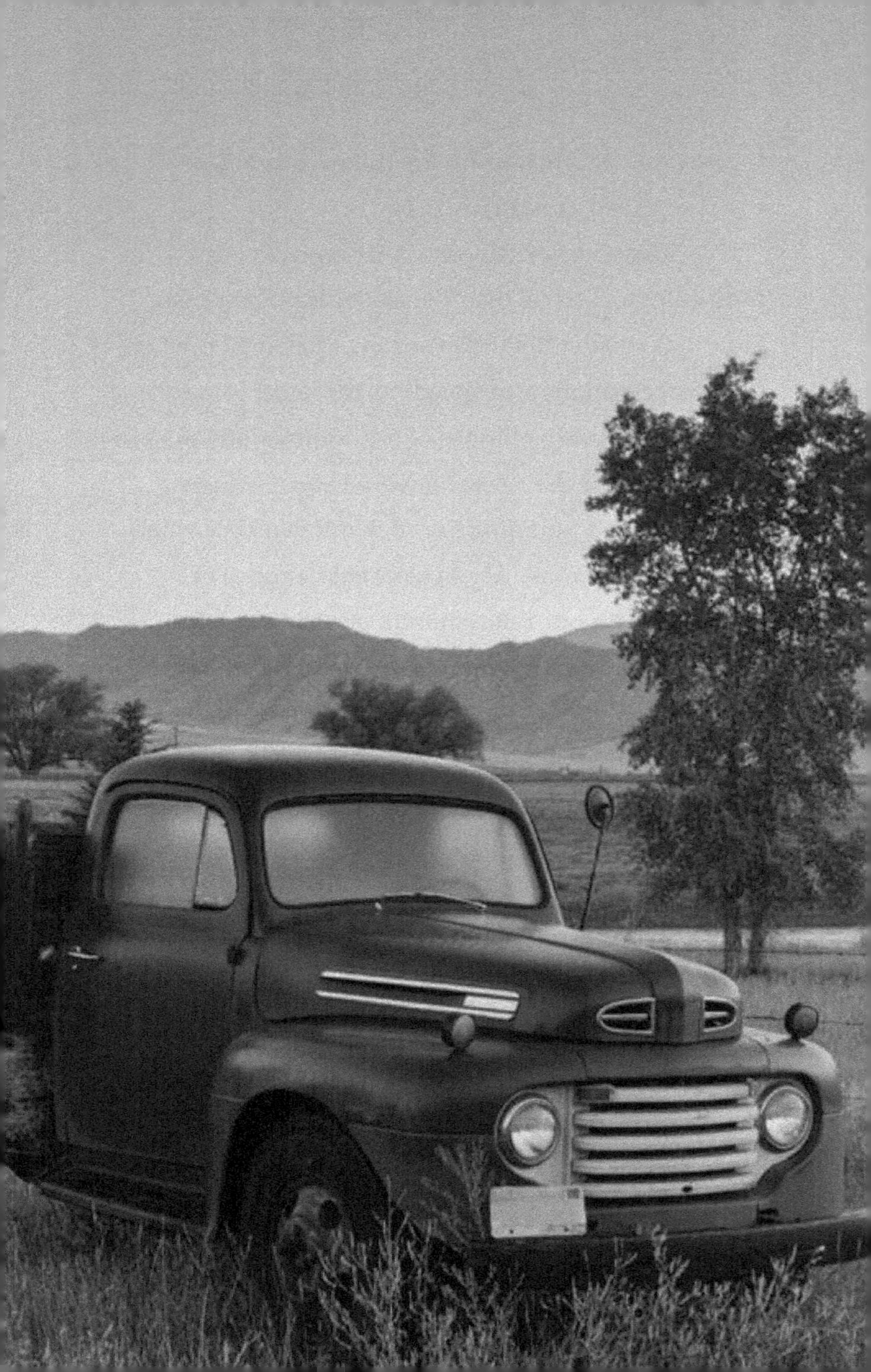

Chapter Twenty-Three

Alex

"Is this the last of them?" Andrew asked as he set the last container on the table. Today, the stations at the farmer's market were converted into stands for the Ashfield Summer Festival. Across the way, in the large open field, they set up a small carnival. A Ferris wheel and carousel spun as the mayor anticipated everyone's arrival.

Yesterday, I sold out of my one-bite cakes and had to spend most of the night baking all new batches. I didn't mind, because I hadn't slept a full night in the weeks since Nate left. It seemed my body could only pass out when I was in his arms.

"That's it. Thank you for your help, Andrew. I know this is the last place you want to be."

Since the blow-up three weeks ago, Andrew started coming around to me owning a cake shop. I wasn't sure if I had Nate or my mom to thank for that. He and Nate were on better terms and texting regularly. Well, whenever Andrew remembered. He was terrible about checking his messages.

"It's the least I could do."

I had been struggling since the Sullivans left. And it wasn't just Nate who I missed. Those two little girls took a part of me when they went back to California. We talked almost every day, and I loved chatting to them about the shop and showing them my latest cake experiments. The days their mother was struggling with her health were the hardest on all of us. They were too young to understand what was happening, and Nate worried he made the wrong choice. I did my best to assure them they needed this time with her, at least when she was feeling up to it.

We tried not to video chat when they were at Sasha's place. I wanted to respect their time together, but the girls slipped a few times. Luckily, it was usually in a room away from her bedroom. I spoke to Nate when he could, but he seemed to spend a lot of time at Sasha's bedside. My sisters thought that was strange, but I understood. He was making amends with her.

Nate was too kind to stay angry at someone who was losing their life.

Not even Andrew was upset with Nate's choices, and he despised Sasha up until recently.

"Here she is," Andrew said from behind me. I whirled around to find him holding up his phone, and there were two little faces in the foreground. Beyond them was a smiling Nate. I couldn't help my lips curling up to match theirs.

"Hi, girls! How are you this morning?" It was early here in Tennessee, so I knew it was even earlier in California. But Nate explained Sasha did better in the morning than the afternoon, so they all woke early.

"Good. We got to have ice cream for breakfast this morning!"

"Oh, did you? That sounds fun. What flavor?" I asked them as Andrew handed me his phone and went about unloading the rest of the containers.

"Vanilla. The others hurt Mommy Sasha's belly."

"Vanilla is always yummy, if you ask me. Are you all doing anything fun today?"

As the girls chatted about the video games and movies they planned to watch, I tried to lock eyes with Nate. At first glance, I could see how tired he was.

Those bright brown eyes I loved so much of his were dull and faded. His face was a bit gaunt, and he had scruff growing on his chin. God, I just wanted to wrap my arms around him and take on all his troubles.

As the girls finished up, I turned the phone around and showed them all the cakes I brought with me to the festival. I kept the carnival out of the background, since I knew the girls well enough to know they'd be sad they missed it.

Off in the background, I heard a kind voice beckon for Nate and the girls. I could sense Nate's waning smile as he apologized for ending the call early.

"Can you call me tonight? Maybe we can do that thing we did the other day?" I asked, holding the phone close to my lips to whisper into. Nate and I tried to find creative ways to have phone sex. Usually, he snuck into the bathroom if he was at Sasha's place. If he was at the rental, it was hit or miss. The girls were usually glued to his side and had taken up sleeping in his bed.

"I will do my best, baby." Nate looked over his shoulder and huffed out a heavy breath as he apologized again and then ended the call.

"Everything okay?" Andrew asked as I set his phone on the table. His hands were busy sorting out the cakes I packaged up.

"Yeah," I said, faking some enthusiasm. I hated how tired Nate seemed, and I told Andrew so.

"He's got a lot going on. I'm sure that's all."

"Yeah, I know. I can't imagine what he's going through. Oh, I got a message from the delivery service this morning, and they're going to deliver the appliances on Monday morning. Do you think you can help me out?"

"Sure. I'll let Dad know what's up so he isn't expecting me."

"He's really enjoyed having you close by. We all have."

"Yeah, yeah."

We'd all been pressuring Andrew to move back to Ashfield, but he was adamant about staying in Knoxville. Something about more single women.

The second day of the festival went off without a hitch. So many people I didn't recognize stopped by and grabbed the free samples along with my business card. I had three different sample flavors available, and by far, Nate's favorite—the pistachio and raspberry—was also the crowd favorite. I had large individual slices available for sale, and I sold out by lunchtime. An hour later, I was out of everything.

I was beaming when the last slice was sold to Mrs. Hensen. She'd come back around three times and claimed she was going to let everyone on her knitting blog know about my cakes. I hadn't known Mrs. Hensen even knew how to knit or run a blog. I was learning new things every day.

Not sure what else to do, I started packing up my empty containers and folding up my custom table runners with my new logo created by Aspen.

"Should I just leave the business cards and a table runner with maybe a note that I sold out of everything?"

"I think that's a good idea. That way they won't think you were a no-show."

Unfolding the runner, I wearily replaced it on the stand. I didn't think anyone would steal it, but the chance was still there, since there were so many people from out of town in Ashfield today. It wasn't a big deal, but I learned I was a penny-pincher when it came to business expenses.

"What do you want to do now?" Andrew asked me as he leaned against the bed of my truck. He'd allocated the day to help me.

"How are you with a paintbrush?"

Five hours later, Andrew and I hopped up on the counter in the main area of the shop and took hearty bites of the pizza I ordered. A company had come in and painted the walls a soft cream color. I hired a local artist to come paint a mural on the longest wall. It was a dessert smorgasbord.

I added some wainscotting along the other walls that would serve as a place for the small bistro tables, and I wanted them to pop and mirror the pastels the mural artist used. With Andrew's help, we painted the boarded trim and the front of the counter. The spot where the display case would sit was currently vacant. I was in search of a new one, but I hadn't found one that called out to me yet.

I wasn't giving up though. The days I wasn't working on recipes or updating the interior of the shop, I was off at the antique markets, trying to find what I was looking for. Molly, Eloise, and I all agreed on the same inspiration, and I was determined to find it.

"Think you can help me hang a few pictures while you're here?"

"Sure. Let me get some sustenance first." He grabbed another slice of the New York style pie.

As we ate, Andrew kept sneaking glances at me. It was something that all my family did whenever I was around. Like they were waiting for me to break down and fall apart.

When we finished the pizza, I cleaned up the counter and tossed the trash away. The coffee shop owners stopped by and chatted with us for a bit. They were so excited to have me moving into their building. Their customers had been enjoying the samples I left with them.

When they left, I darted back to what would be my office. Right now, it was filled with tons of boxes of baking and office supplies. I really needed to unpack them, but instead, I grabbed the stack of gold frames and carried them back into the main room.

"I was thinking we could scatter these around the room."

Andrew lifted the first one off the top of the stack and smiled. It was one of the pictures Eloise colored. I didn't even have to label them to know which pictures belonged to which twin. Molly's colors were warm and bright. She filled the dessert images until I almost couldn't make out what they were. Eloise was very precise in her coloring. At almost five, she was pretty good at staying within the lines, but she usually stuck with one or two colors.

"You miss them, don't you?"

Without skipping a beat, I replied, "Yes. So much."

"They'll be back soon."

I really hoped he was right.

Together, we worked to hang the twelve pictures around the shop. Andrew even made me use a level, which I thought was ridiculous, but he was obstinate. When we finished, he wrapped his arm around my shoulders and pulled me in close.

"This looks really great, sis. I'm sorry I ever doubted you." It was the first time he apologized for his outburst and the way he questioned my decision to open a cake shop. Andrew rarely apologized for anything, so I was going to let those words soak in.

"Thanks, Andrew. That means a lot. Here's to hoping I can pull it off."

"You will. We all believe in you. And there is a certain person in Cali who isn't going to let you fail."

***

Every week seemed to blend into the next until a month had passed. The cake shop, the book club, the meals for the B&B. My time was spent everywhere but at my apartment as much as possible. That was when I was alone with my thoughts, and years of therapy did nothing to quell those feelings.

I'd only spoken to Nate and the twins a few times since Sasha's death. By accident, I was able to speak with her for a few minutes a couple of days before her health took a turn for the worst. I'd been speaking with the twins—a call initiated by them. They said their dad was on his work phone in the living room.

They were busy showing me around Sasha's condo, which was one of the nicest places I'd ever seen. A lot of marble and glass. I couldn't help but notice it wasn't very kid-friendly. They skipped into a bedroom and introduced me to their mom. She was propped up against her headboard, reading a fashion magazine. Even with her pale and sickly complexion, I could tell she was a stunner before her disease took over. I'd seen pictures before, but they didn't do Sasha justice.

The twins held the phone as they started a conversation, but then they thrust the phone at their mother and scurried away to find a piece of paper. I was at a loss for what to say other than a greeting again that she parroted.

"Sorry about this," I said with a chuckle. I knew how those girls could be when they had their mind set on something.

"It's okay. I'm not really surprised. They've been wanting me to talk with you since they got here." Her voice held the kind of scratchiness I could tell meant each spoken word was painful. My heart ached for her.

"Your girls are little spitfires," I told her, unable to fight back the smile as I recalled all their shenanigans.

"They are. They must get that from me. Ha, listen to me being all maternal. I didn't know I had it in me." Sasha glanced away toward the bright light of her window that overlooked the city. A few beats passed before she turned back to me. Her eyes had lost their luster.

"Thank you. I don't think I've ever said those words before, which is why my nurses hate me. But thank you, Alexandra, for loving them. For being there and taking care of them when I couldn't and was too stubborn to be the mom they needed." She struggled to take a breath, and I took that moment to swipe at the tears I knew were pouring down my face.

"I *do* love them, Sasha. I would do anything for your girls." *And for him*, I silently added.

"I know you do. And I know you're the one who convinced Nate to bring them out to me, even before he knew about the cancer. He told me everything. I can't ever thank you enough for that. For letting me have my girls for one more day."

"I...." I choked on a sob and had to reach around in my kitchen for a paper towel, because something needed to sop up my tears. "You're welcome."

Even on the other end of the line, I could hear the twins' not-so-subtle cries of joy as they bounded back toward the room.

"I'm glad they have you. All three of them. They deserve it. I wasn't the mom or wife they needed."

"Mommy Sasha, why are you crying?" Eloise asked, her voice so serious.

"Oh, these are just happy tears. Miss Alex was telling me how she's going to name her Champagne-flavored cake after me, since it's my favorite kind. I can't wait to try hers."

***

July 23rd changed the lives of my sweet Sullivan clan. I sent flowers, cards, games... anything to help them take their mind off the hell they were going through. Not even Andrew could get Nate on the phone for more than a few minutes at a time.

He was pulling away from us.

When we did talk, he was always apologetic. He finally started to look more alive than he had prior to Sasha's death, but he was always distracted. Even during the video calls where I'd do everything he begged of me, he always seemed... preoccupied.

I considered flying out to California to see him and the girls. Maybe I could cheer them up? Maybe I could be some form of family connection they were lacking? I didn't know, but watching them suffer was killing me.

The longer we were apart, the more I wondered if they ever planned on coming back.

I found a different antique store two hours away, and I was busy walking down the makeshift aisles when my phone buzzed with a video chat.

"Hey!" I exclaimed when I saw Nate's name flash on the screen.

"Hi, baby." He was sitting at a desk in what I assumed was his business office. The skyline of a city shone behind him. His eyes were rimmed in red, like he hadn't slept in days.

They pretty much matched my own.

"I'm so glad you called. I found an online posting of a display case from a bakery that was around in the 1950s. I'm checking to see if it's still here."

"Really?" he asked, his gaze beaming at me.

"Yeah. I'm searching now. Tell me about your day. How are the girls? I miss them."

"Good, we're... managing. I've had some issues with Sasha's parents, but it's all resolved now."

"Oh?" That was the first I heard about any issues with her family. "Was it about the girls?"

"No, about her will. But it's all good now."

I wasn't about to pry and ask more. I could tell by his tone that the conversation regarding her was over. I still wondered why he hadn't returned home though. Maybe the will had been the reason.

"Any news on when you think you'll be returning? I wanted to ask you about the gift for the twins."

A chipper voice called out Nate's name from the background and said he was needed for an organizational change meeting. I had no idea what that meant, but it sounded important.

"Hey, I need to go. I'll call you tonight, okay? Wear that tank top I like."

He loved when I wore just a white camisole with no bra underneath. The man was obsessed with my breasts.

"Sure. Just text me a time. Oh!" I cried out as I locked eyes with my pièce de résistance. "Nate, look." Quickly, I turned around the phone and showed him the curved display with gold trim and etched glass. It was one of the most beautiful things I'd ever seen. It was the cake display of my dreams.

"That's perfect for your shop, Alex. I'm so happy for you. I'll talk to you tonight."

Nate ended the call shortly after, and I flagged down one of the workers. The shop was one step closer to opening, and all I needed was the confidence to flip the switch on the Open sign.

My truck purred as I drove her down the main street of Ashfield with my new display case strapped into the bed. I texted my dad and Andrew when I left the antique shop, hoping they could lend a hand and help me carry it into the shop. I made sure it worked while I was still in the store, and they'd been extremely helpful in getting it loaded into the back of my truck.

Sitting on the bench outside my store, Andrew and my dad sat with ice cream cones in their hands. They waved as I pulled up and parked in front of the shop.

"Wow, she's a beaut, Alex," Dad said as he came around the truck to greet me, ice cream melting down his fingers.

"Thanks. I can't wait to plug her in. I'm so excited."

I was beyond glad to share this moment with my dad. My mom and sisters were going to stop by later to check on the progress. But Andrew surprised me the most. He made time every day to come help with whatever I needed.

It was all coming together.

Now, all I needed was Nate, Molly, and Eloise to come back.

Chapter Twenty-Four

Alex

It was about ten degrees too warm in my apartment. The gorgeous windows let in so much sunlight that the air conditioner couldn't compete. That's what happened in mid-August in Tennessee.

I knew it would only be a matter of time before one of my sisters came by to check in on me. The twins' birthday had come and gone, and with each day that passed, I pushed farther and farther away from my family. My calls with the girls only happened occasionally now, and the ones with Nate were even rarer. They missed the first day of school in Ashfield, but Nate enrolled them in a private school while they were still in California. He seemed happy with the choice, but I could tell the girls were less than thrilled. They spoke about how Miss Franny would have been the best and most fun teacher.

In the local paper, there was an article about Nate and his AI agriculture robot. Apparently, I wasn't the only one who noticed his absence. It said his newest patent sold for far more than he and his company anticipated.

The overseas purchase required him to travel all over the world to sign contracts and meet with the companies. The twins were staying with their old nanny. I'd spoken to her a few times. She was nice but a bit stricter than I had ever been. But they all seemed happy. With every day that fell off the calendar, any hope of their return diminished.

I learned yesterday that Nate's company ended the agreement for the land they leased from my father. They still paid my parents handsomely, but that commitment was over. Nate kept the land he purchased for a home. I'd taken one of the B&B's UTVs over that way when I was missing the Sullivans. It sat in the same condition it had before, which only made my heart miss them more.

Whenever I asked Nate what was going on, he'd steer the conversation back to my shop, or the girls would interrupt. It was growing harder to remain optimistic.

The only thing that kept me going was that my shop's grand opening was happening soon.

After deliberation with my family, and some serious talks with my therapist about taking the leap, I chose the third Saturday in August as my grand opening. Quite a few weeks earlier than I had originally planned.

On August 19th, the doors to Show-Stopping Sweets would open to the public. Aspen set me up with some ads on social media and the local newspapers within a hundred-mile radius of the shop. Colton also plugged the shop on his social media accounts, posting pictures of my cakes and their flavors. So many people commented they were hoping to check it out. I was still trying to come to terms with it all.

In one week, I was going to live my dream. I thought Nate would have been a part of the grand opening with me. He'd done so much to help when I was getting it off the ground that I thought he deserved to see the final product. I sent him pictures of all the new appliances and the redone eating area. He and the girls loved it all. They especially loved all their artwork on the walls.

It was bittersweet sitting here in my apartment, staring at the birthday gifts I wrapped for each of the girls. Could I have mailed them to them? Probably. But I was hesitant. It felt like a final goodbye if I did. This was like a part of them I was able to hang on to.

A knock sounded on my door, just like I expected. I wondered which sister was sent to check on me this time. Rory was in school, so I doubted it was her. Aspen was probably helping Dad on the farm. Corn harvest started in September, so they were busy prepping for that.

That left Autumn. Probably the one I least wanted to check up on me. I was envious of her. Envious for so many reasons. For her chance to fly the coop, her chance to do exactly what she'd always dreamed of and make a name for herself, and she married the most perfect man for her. She had it all, and it killed me. But I didn't want to be jealous of my sister. I was so happy she got everything she worked for.

"Are you going to let me in?" a voice called out after the second round of knocks, and I jumped up from my couch.

"Tami? I thought you were in Paris!" I exclaimed as I began undoing the newly installed locks and opening the door for my best friend. She wasn't alone.

"Mom?"

"Yes, sweetie. We've called an intervention."

"A what?" I asked as they strolled into my apartment. It was the first time Tami stepped foot inside. She'd taken back-to-back jobs all summer, and I hadn't expected her home for another two weeks. For her to come here was huge.

"An intervention. I'm tired of seeing my girl like this. We all are. So, I'm stepping in. Tami is here to help me. Now, take a shower and get dressed. I have somewhere I want to take you."

"Where?" I asked as Tami dragged me toward the small hallway, her nose scrunching as if she smelled something rotten. It was probably my T-shirt I'd been wearing the past three days.

"Like I'm going to tell you."

"Fine. But I don't like it."

"That's why it's called an intervention and not a girls' day. Now, hurry. We're on a time crunch."

One very hot shower later and in an outfit chosen by my best friend, I sat in the back of my mom's sedan while she and Tami sang together to some 1980s pop song. Tami really was born in the wrong decade.

With her style and music choices, she definitely fit the '80s aesthetic better than today's.

It was the middle of the day, so traffic was sparse as we hopped on the interstate. I still had no clue where we were headed, but my eyelids began drooping about five minutes into the highway portion of our trip.

I wasn't sure how much time lapsed when I came to, but the car was parked in front of a strip mall. I wiped at my eyes, the dryness making me want to scratch them out. Then my grogginess subsided, and I realized where we were.

"Mom?" Fear clawed like nasty spikes all over me. How could I not recognize the place? It was where my dreams fell apart.

She turned around in her seat. It was like I was seeing her for the first time. Mom was… tired. Those wrinkles around her eyes deepened, and there was a misery there I'd never noticed.

"I should have said something back when I noticed you changing. I spoke to other dance moms, and they said you were just being hormonal. It was a girl thing. But then I watched you step back from dancing, and it killed me. You *loved* it. I'd never seen anyone light up the way you did when you danced.

And then I saw that again when you danced for Molly and Eloise.

"This was the place that took that joy away from you, and I want to give you a chance to take it back. Own it. I can't do much to that no-good ex of yours, who I am certain convinced you to give it all up, but we can all rest assured that he will get what's coming to him. Rumor is his daddy recently lost their fortune gambling.

"Regardless. We're going to go in there, and we're going to dance our hearts out."

"You're coming?"

"You're damn right I am. Right now, they have a class open to the public."

I wasn't sure I could go in there and face the teacher who wore me down with Stephen, but the temptation to go inside was overwhelming. I hadn't stepped foot into a dance studio in years.

"Is it ballet?"

"I think it's a mix. Either way, it will be fun," Tami chimed in as she unlatched her seat belt. Now, the choice of spandex shorts and an oversized shirt made sense. Mom and Tami wore something similar. I don't know why I didn't catch on to that before.

For the first time, I was excited about something that wasn't the cake shop. I needed this, and I told Mom and Tami that as we strolled into the studio. Then I stopped dead in my tracks. Along with some regular students, Autumn, Rory, Aspen, Colton, Sadie, and Andrew stood inside, anticipating my arrival.

"What are you guys doing here?" My smile was stretched so wide my cheeks hurt. God, when was the last time I smiled?

"You didn't think we'd let Mom and Tami have *all* the fun, did you?" Andrew prompted as he adjusted his basketball shorts over a pair of spandex shorts. Colton was dressed the same.

"I can't believe this." I rushed over to my family, squeezing them with all I had. "Rory, how did you get out of school?"

"I took a sick day and called in a substitute. No big deal."

"Wow, you guys. This is… too much." In the corner, I found my mom's purse and tossed my phone inside.

"Who's the teacher?"

Just as I asked the question, in strolled one of the most famous faces in the dance world. I'd been a fan since I was a little girl and watched her dance as Clara in *The Nutcracker* and then again as Odette in *Swan Lake*. Tatiana Kropotova was a world-wide ballet legend. And here she was in Knoxville, Tennessee, teaching a public dance class.

Who convinced her to make the trek and leave her retirement?

I glanced around at my siblings, but my eyes kept falling onto Colton. He had the money to pay her for sure, probably at the hands of Autumn. Andrew had money in stocks, so it could have been him, too. I didn't miss the way they were all glancing back and forth at each other like it was musical chairs with their stares. Whose gaze would be the last one standing?

Dammit.

Someone was going to come clean by the end of this session.

"Someone pinch me," I murmured as she stepped over to an ancient stereo system in the corner. "Ow!" I jerked my arm back and sneered at Tami. "What was that for?"

"You asked for someone to pinch you. Here I am, at your service."

"I hate you, you know."

"I know. With all your heart. Now, let's get down and boogie."

I was still in awe of the fact that Tatiana Kropotova was standing at the front of the classroom where I'd once been so beaten down I'd thrown in the towel and hung up my pointe shoes. But here I was, watching my idol call a class to session as an '80s playlist pounded in the background. My mom and Tami definitely had something to do with this. And that left me even more confused.

Tatiana clapped her hands in a way that brought us all to attention and fall in line. My sisters pushed me forward until I was standing front and center along with some people here for the public class, while my family hung out along the back line.

I wasn't going to let that last too long.

Tatiana directed our class in numerous moves that even the most talented dancer struggled with, but my smile never faded. In the mirror, I watched my family move their hips and spin on their feet, all while they laughed and poked fun at each other. We were all having a blast, and whatever fears I had about being back in this dance studio faded away.

She choreographed three different routines for us to dance out. A particular scene from *Center Stage* flashed through my mind with each step. She even had us perform leaps round-robin style. I couldn't get enough of my siblings jumping and twirling across the hardwood. Colton was surprisingly flexible with his leap. His hockey background definitely helped. I stole a look at Tatiana and smirked at her surprised face when he performed an almost perfect grand jeté. Andrew was the last of my family to take the leap.

He missed his cue, and Tatiana clapped her hands in his direction. And then he missed it again, which only ignited the Russian beauty's anger. Her clap echoed around the room, and the entire class stood at attention.

"Andrew, please," I heard Sadie say as she nudged him. None of us wanted to witness Tatiana's wrath after she snapped at one attendee at the beginning when they answered their phone.

A few expletives flew from his lips before Andrew took his stance. In the blink of an eye, Andrew launched in the air, his legs twisting underneath his frame as he spun at his highest peak and then landing in perfect position for a tour jeté. It was a small move compared to Colton's, but to watch Andrew complete it flawlessly was remarkable.

He stood to the side with my siblings as the rest of the class went about completing their jumps and twists. Before I knew it, my turn had come, and all eyes landed on me.

Moving gracefully in my socks, I positioned myself in the middle of the floor and waited for the crescendo of the song. Setting my feet into place, I launched one leg into the air and performed four Italian fouettes followed by a grand jeté before joining my family. They all stared at me in awe. Mom reached out and tugged me closer as she wrapped her arms around me.

Tatiana slowed the music for a cooldown, and then the class was brought to a close. I hunkered in the corner with my mom, too afraid to push my way through the crowd to meet one of dancing's elite artists. I had no doubt my family was going to do it for me.

As the pack started to dissipate, I felt another hand on my arm. My older brother was there to push me, or catch me, whichever I needed. And while I loved their support and having them here, I still felt the absence of Nate. Not only would he have been the first one to drag me to meet Tatiana, but he would have looked so damn sexy in spandex.

"What has you smiling like that?" Mom asked as she unraveled herself from around me.

"I was just thinking Nate would look really hot wearing spandex."

"You know he would have been here if he could," she replied, repositioning her ponytail. Mom kept her blonde locks just below her shoulders so she could pull it back when she was cooking or working on the farm. She looked so much younger with it pulled off her face.

"I know."

Beside me, Andrew adjusted the hem of his shorts with his free hand. He was miserable in those biker shorts he wore, but I appreciated it. "Have you heard from him recently? I haven't in like three days besides a couple of text messages."

"I just know he's in Tokyo. Or was. Last he told me they were having some issues with contracts, and legal was moving at a snail's pace."

I nodded. It seemed Nate hadn't been keeping in touch with Andrew as much either. I heard the same story four days ago.

"I miss the girls. They would have loved this."

"Yeah, they would. Now, off you go," he said with a quick shove at my back, launching me forward. With just socks on my feet, I practically slid into Tatiana as I tried to regain my balance. I sneered at Andrew over my shoulder as he and my sisters all cackled like freaking hyenas.

Be the tornado.

I ran the mantra through my head twice before taking a deep breath and positioning myself in front of one of my childhood idols.

"Tatiana, I'm Alex. I am so honored to get the chance to watch you dance."

"Alexandra, you dance beautifully. Just as I was told. It's a pleasure to meet you." Her strong accent sounded like music to my ears. I could listen to her speak for hours. "Would you care to dance with me for a time? This studio is rented out for another two hours."

"Oh… er… I'm a little rusty. It's been years."

With a gentle wave of her hand, she effortlessly glided over to the stereo and pulled up a mix of classical songs. "Pssh, it's like riding a bicycle. And besides, we have an audience."

My gaze darted across the reflection in the mirror. I almost expected Nate to be standing there, but instead, it was the enthusiastic smiles of my family eagerly waiting to see me perform.

"Sure. Yes. I'd love to dance with you," I told one of the women I practically worshipped. That fear of being in this studio washed away like a summer chalk drawing after a storm, and I was ready to take my control back.

"Wonderful. Let's begin." Tatiana swirled around the dance floor, looking no more retired than a current member of a ballet company.

I memorized her steps and followed them as best as I could. My arms and legs ached. My back bent in ways it hadn't in years. But all the while, the smile never left my face.

When we finished, my family erupted in applause. There was no hiding the tears that streamed down my face. I'd never been so emotionally overwhelmed in my life.

My thanks to Tatiana was brushed aside as if *I* were the one doing *her* a favor. And maybe I was somehow. But I was filled with so much elation I didn't care either way.

Someone had given me a piece of myself back, and I had a sneaking suspicion of who that might've been.

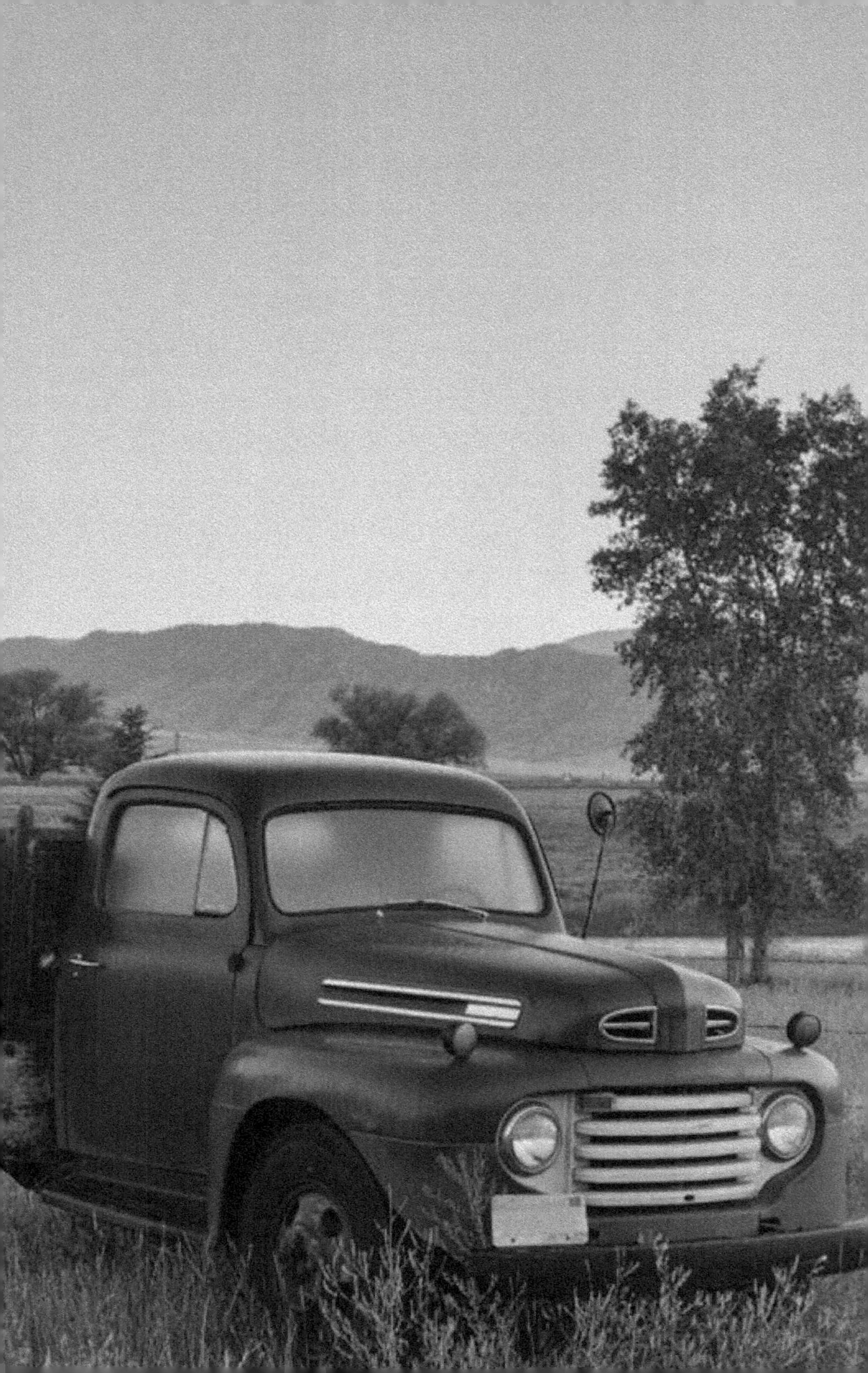

Chapter Twenty-Five

Nate

Five hours and three canceled flights later, Molly, Eloise, and I finally landed in Charlotte, North Carolina. Every flight I booked anywhere remotely close to Tennessee had been postponed or called off. At the last minute, I was able to get three first-class tickets from Los Angeles to Charlotte, and I hurried the girls to the terminal. They were tired of eating airport food, and so was I.

The car rental agency took pity on me and upgraded us to the largest SUV they had. There was a five-and-a-half-hour drive ahead of us, and I prayed I could keep my exhaustion at bay. I just kept reminding myself where we were headed—back home.

I planned to be back in Ashfield early this morning, but those plans were crushed when none of our flights made it. Only Andrew knew about the lengths I'd gone to get back to Alex. I crammed months and years' worth of contracts and paperwork into a couple of weeks. I spent so many days and nights on an airplane I wasn't sure my stomach was ever going to recover. It was hard to live off peanuts and airport food.

But soon, it was all going to be worth it.

Overnight, my old assistant was able to secure another rental property very close to the one I booked earlier this summer. It was waiting for our arrival today, but I was hopeful we weren't going to have to rush over. We had people we needed to see.

My phone pinged with another text from Andrew as I crossed the North Carolina border into Tennessee. He'd been snapping pictures of Alex dancing with Tatiana Kropotova. I hated that I wasn't there to see the surprise on her face, but the dance studio owner assured me she would record the class for me. Thankfully, it wasn't the same woman who had verbally beaten down Alex back in the day.

It took some begging and charitable donations to get Tatiana to even speak to me about my proposition, but after hearing *some* of Alex's story—I wasn't about to divulge all of her secrets—Tatiana readily agreed to surprise her in a class. I told Andrew my plan, and he worked with his family to make it all happen. I just hoped they would keep my upcoming arrival a secret.

I planned on being there to see Alex dance. Our phone conversations were few and far between. It wasn't only because I was busy, though that was the excuse I gave her on the phone, but I was so afraid I would spill the beans. Not only about Tatiana, but about returning to Ashfield. If I hinted at anything, it would only disappoint her, because I had no idea when I'd get everything finalized.

We hired a new CEO to fill my position at the company, but he backed out the day before the onboarding meeting, and we had to start the process all over again. I thought we were in the clear at that point, but then legal denied the purchase contracts with the company that was going to buy the patent and prototype model of the AI agriculture robot. They'd left some sections unsigned and wrote in loopholes to change the product.

I spent almost a month sorting everything out until both parties were happy with the final product. For legal reasons, I could only disclose so much to Alex.

She knew I was tying up loose ends on the patent, but that was it. She said she understood, but I could feel her pulling away with each call I missed.

I was exhausted.

The nanny I'd used while in California stepped in when I started traveling. I was so grateful for her, though she reminded me a bit of an old, crotchety headmaster. Either way, I trusted her with Molly and Eloise. They were devastated when I had to enroll them in kindergarten at a local private school. Their only appeasement was that I told them we were going to be heading back to Ashfield soon, and the school was only temporary. I kept them registered at the Ashfield Elementary School, calling and explaining the situation. They were more than accommodating.

A few more miles passed on the interstate before we had to make a pit stop. I needed a coffee, and the girls needed the restroom. I didn't want to add more time away from Alex, but it was necessary. While waiting for my coffee, I showed the twins the images of Alex dancing in the studio with one of the women Sasha said was one of the best ballet dancers of their time.

My chest still ached when I thought about her passing. We made amends in the way two people who never should have been together could. It had been her idea to have Alex meet one of the ballet greats. And though Sasha wasn't the most maternal person, I was surprised she had baby books for the twins. All their hospital garb was taped inside and all of their milestones listed in chronological order. Most of their firsts happened before they came to live with me, so there weren't many blanks, but there were still things to fill in. Lost their first tooth. Learned to ride a bike with no training wheels. First day of school. Tied their shoes.

They actually just mastered that one before we left Ashfield. Marisol taught them some song that helped them remember. Sasha asked me to take the books back with me to make sure Alex continued to fill them out. When I scoffed at her, she just pushed the books closer to me on the bed. It seemed both Sasha and Andrew believed I was in love with Alex.

It took Sasha's death to realize that maybe I was. Adding to my desire to get back to Ashfield, I was 100 percent certain I was head-over-heels for my best friend's little sister.

I sure hoped he didn't kill me.

"Daddy, she's so pretty when she spins." Molly acted out the move, nearly knocking into the barista as she stepped around the corner to hand me my beverage. I quickly apologized and wrangled the girls back to the rental.

"How much longer 'til we see Miss Alex?"

"Just a little while longer. Do you guys want to drop your stuff off first or head straight on to see her?"

"We want to see her!" they shouted in unison. Same volume and tone. I was convinced it was a twin thing.

"Then that's what we'll do."

With all the time I spent away from them and having them spend their birthday in California, they knew there wasn't much I wouldn't do for them. Even seeing Alex while wearing our clothes covered in airport germs.

I had one more surprise for her that was being delivered soon, and I really hoped I'd get to be there to see her face when it arrived. Sometimes, it was hard to tell how Alex's emotions would veer. I had a sinking feeling she was going to be angry at whatever I did, because I'd been gone for so long.

The girls were practically bouncing in their seats as we got closer to Ashfield. The moment we took the exit ramp off the highway, they immediately knew we were only about an hour away. Pop radio did little to drown out their excited rambling.

We'd only been gone for two months, but it felt like years as we approached the entrance to the town. We passed the plot of land owned by the Easterlys that would have housed my custom warehouse. Which was really just an oversized workshop.

The small movie theater was playing one of the latest movies and an oldie as well. The best kind of double feature.

People were milling about as the end of the business day approached. There were curious looks our way, but most smiled or waved. I was thankful for the tinted windows. I wasn't ready to give away our arrival just yet.

"I can smell her cakes already, Daddy."

"You sure about that?"

The only smell around us was of the leather seats.

"Yes. It's cake."

"Okay, sweetie."

A quick glance in the rearview mirror and I saw Molly sniffing the air curiously.

"Two more turns and we're there. But we have to be quiet, okay? Only Uncle Andrew knows we're coming."

"What if she's not there?" Eloise asked as I maneuvered the SUV into a parking spot on the street in front of the coffee shop. It worked in my favor that the rental wasn't the same as what I had before.

Alex's truck was parked out in front of her shop, but if my plan went how I hoped, she was still traveling back from Knoxville with her mom and Tami.

I worked on getting the girls out of the car, grabbing their bookbags on the way. There was no telling how much longer they'd be, so I wanted to make sure the girls had something to entertain themselves with.

Using the key Andrew mailed to me, I opened the front of the shop and hurried the twins inside, locking the door behind me. I took a moment to take in the place in person. The pictures hadn't done it justice. The pastel colors and gold fixtures gave the shop a classic and whimsical look. The mural was a work of art on its own. I was beyond impressed. This was exactly what Alex described and spent months agonizing over. She did this all on her own, and I was so fucking proud.

"Daddy, look, it's our pictures."

Taking a step closer to the gold-framed artwork, I noticed the crayon-colored artwork that I was so familiar with. The frames lined the walls, and I vaguely remembered her showing me a glimpse of this when I was so stressed at Sasha's and running on zero sleep.

She put a part of my family in her shop, even when we weren't here.

"God, I love her," I mumbled to myself.

Eloise had already set out her coloring supplies on one of the bistro tables, while Molly was darting back and forth, taking in everything she could of the space. After a couple of minutes, Molly joined her sister, and I decided to take a look at the kitchen. The top-of-the-line appliances sat next to some glass-door freezers and refrigerators. They were already filled with cakes and icings. With her opening a week away, I wasn't surprised.

From within my back pocket, I felt my phone buzz with an alert.

Andrew
5min

Me: 👍 <thumbs up>

"Girls, we need to pack up. Alex is on her way."

I thought they'd put up more of a fight, but they eagerly shoved their things back into their bags and ran over to me on their little legs. Early this morning, I dressed them in matching outfits. The rompers were both covered in cupcakes, but Eloise wore yellow, and Molly wore green. They allowed me to braid their hair, something I'd been trying to master alone on every flight back and forth from Tokyo. I'd been practicing with some electronic charging cables, but a flight attendant took some pity on me and brought me three long strips of cloth he cut up and tied together on one end. He was a dad of three and helped me with the basics. I was getting better at it every day.

The girls and I ducked into Alex's office, which was still more of a storage closet than it was a space for a business owner. I was definitely going to have to tackle this space for her before the grand opening. If she'd let me.

The bell above the shop's door jingled, and the girls and I exchanged glances. Their eyes brimmed with excitement I was certain mine mirrored.

Her voice carried across the mostly empty space, and my heart launched into my throat at the sound. It was sweet and feminine and everything I'd been missing. Hearing it on the phone was nowhere close to listening to the sweet melody in person.

"I have the best idea for the cake I could make Tatiana. I cannot believe she wants me to design something for her charity event. And I got to dance with her. Oh my gosh, it's just all so surreal. Hey, why are those chairs pulled out?"

The twins reached up and gripped my hands.

Whoops.

In our excitement, we must have forgotten to put those chairs back under the table.

"Mom, why are you looking at me like that? Is Dad here? I know he was going to help with the vendor deliveries today."

"He did say he was on his way."

Thank you, Marisol.

Andrew must have clued her in on my scheme to surprise her daughter.

"Okay, let me go grab the vendor order sheet so I can check it off when they arrive. I think they said they'd be here around four."

With each step that sounded on the vinyl planks, the louder my heart pounded in my chest. The girls were already giggling when Alex stepped through the office entrance.

"What the—"

"Surprise!" they shouted as they sprung toward Alex, who stared at them wide-eyed.

"Nate?" Alex's eyes glued to me as if she were seeing a ghost. I guess to her I sort of was.

"Miss Alex, we missed you." Eloise tugged on Alex's oversized peach-colored shirt to get her attention.

She kneeled down and held out her arms for both of them. "I missed you both so much."

I looked on as the woman I loved wrapped her arms around my daughters' shoulders, squeezing them tightly and pressing her lips to the top of their heads. Her arms flexed, and I knew she didn't want to let them go.

"Nathaniel," Marisol greeted from the door as if she'd been expecting me.

"Andrew tell you?"

"Pssh," she said, her eyes rolling with the sound. "I keep telling y'all that my children can't hide anything from me. That includes you, dear."

"I should have known."

"Well, you'll know for next time. Now, come give Grandma Marisol a big hug. I've missed you."

The twins moved out of Alex's embrace, though the forlorn expression Alex wore left me thinking it was the last thing she wanted them to do. Marisol enfolded them the same way Alex had, then ushered them off for a piece of cake from the kitchen.

"I... I can't believe you're really back." The last word died on her lips as she choked back a sob.

"Come here, baby. I've fucking missed you."

Alex threw herself into my arms, and I knew in that very instant that this was exactly where I needed to be. All the hard work I'd done these last few weeks would keep me from ever having to leave her again.

"I'm sorry I'm crying. I can't help it." She sniffled again and tucked her head closer to my neck.

"That's okay. I'm just glad you're not angry at me for being gone so long."

"I am, but the tears are winning right now."

"I'll take those over your punches any day," I joked, trying my damnedest to get a laugh out of her.

It took a few minutes for her tears to subside, and when she pulled back, I missed her immediately. I finally had time to take her in. From every freckle on her nose to the dirty sneakers on her feet, she was the most beautiful woman I'd ever seen.

"I still can't believe you're here," she whispered as her gaze traveled over me. I felt it scorching my skin.

I really hoped Marisol would want to watch the twins for me tonight.

"I do have a house to build, you know." I reached out for her hand, unable to keep from touching her. I needed that physical connection.

"I almost believed the town rumors of you not returning, when Dad said you ended your lease on those properties. And then the girls missing the first day of school.... I just didn't know what would make you come back."

Yanking her arm, I tugged her close and pressed my nose into her hair that smelled like a mix of honeysuckle, vanilla icing, and sweat. "The same thing that brought me here in May is the same reason why there was never any doubt I wouldn't make it back. This is where my family is. It's where *you* are."

"Yeah?" she asked, tilting her face up to mine.

"Yeah. I love you, Alexandra. I was always going to find my way back to you."

"That's good, because I love you too, Nate. So freaking much."

Alex pushed up onto her toes and pressed her lips against mine. It had been too long since I savored her, and I was like a junkie needing his next fix once I tasted her sweet lips. Reaching my arm out blindly, I searched for the edge of the office door. Feeling the wood in my hand, I began closing it, only for Marisol to call out that a delivery driver was here.

"My God, why are we always interrupted?"

"I promise I'll make it up to you tonight." Alex pressed a chaste peck to my cheek and skipped out of the office, leaving me in a thunderous, horny mood.

One minute and some adjustments later, I made my way to the front of the shop, where Alex was signing the invoice and ushering the vendor order into the pantry area.

"This place is amazing, Alex. I knew it was going to be something special, but this is… so you."

"Thanks," she said, eyeing the interior. The girls were busy playing with two dolls they packed into their bags, and Marisol was looking on.

"How many days until the opening?"

"Five, and I feel like I'm going to vomit every time I think about it."

Chuckling, I told her she'd be fine, as I wrapped my arm around her waist, unable to keep my hands off her.

"When they're done, do you want to grab some dinner with your mom and dad after he gets here? Maybe we can convince them to take the twins later?"

"I like what you're thinking."

It took another ten minutes of grunting and groaning before the delivery was complete, and Alex was satisfied with everything on her inventory list. Many were from local farms instead of outsourcing.

Once the men left, Marisol called out that Nash was outside waiting for her and the girls. She was taking them for the night and wanted no arguments about it. Not that she'd get any from me.

We both said goodnight to the twins and watched the sedan and truck pull away. "We're just going upstairs and getting something delivered later, right?"

"Fucking read my mind," I told her as I hefted her up and over my shoulder fireman-style. I headed toward the back of the shop after locking the front door and made my way up the steps.

"I'm so glad these aren't those metal stairs."

"Stop talking and take me to bed," she demanded as she swatted my ass.

"Don't have to tell me twice."

We left a trail of clothes from the front door to her bedroom. I wasn't even positive we shut the interior apartment door. But I didn't give a fuck, because I was buried deep inside the woman I loved.

"God, yes!" she cried out as I pounded into her from behind. There was a blush-colored handprint on her ass that I freaking adored.

I chased after my climax when I felt her walls tighten around my shaft. And when we both exploded, I twisted our bodies so that I cradled her on top of the sheets. She didn't try to cover up.

"That was... so good." There was no choice but hard and fast. We had time to make up for.

"I fucking love your pussy."

"Just my pussy?" she asked, turning over to face me, a mischievous grin curving her lips.

"No. I love *you*, Alexandra. All of you."

"Well, now." Alex lifted her body and swung one leg over my hips. I settled onto my back as she reached down and gripped my hardening cock in her hand, aligning it with her entrance. "I think that earns you some slow and steady."

She slid down, inch by glorious inch. "Yes. I love slow and steady," I bit out as she swirled her hips.

"And I love you." Alex leaned forward, her hands braced on my chest, and pressed her lips against mine. Then she showed me how much she loved slow and steady too.

***

The grand opening had been the only reason Alex and I left the bedroom over the next five days. Marisol and the Easterly sisters all understood our need to spend some time catching up and offered to babysit the twins while we worked, or made love, sometimes both.

When the custom sign I ordered with the help of Aspen and Andrew arrived, I thought Alex was going to have a fit. They installed it the evening I arrived back in Ashfield, and when I showed Alex the next morning, she punched me in the bicep, which was harder than I expected, but then she cried into my shoulder. She said it was the most beautiful sign she'd ever seen.

Her plan had been to use the window decals until the shop was financially in the black and could set some money aside for an outside sign that lit up. It was my gift to her, since I knew she would never let me pay off her loan.

Yet, at least.

On the day of the grand opening, we woke before dawn to get things ready to start baking. She had the recipes down to a science and knew exactly how long everything would take. The single servings were a great idea, because it made the cakes go a lot further. She described them like cake pops, but rectangular and not on a stick.

The entire family chipped in that morning, and when the doors opened, no one was surprised to find a line curving around the building, eagerly anticipating a piece of heaven.

Tatiana even made an appearance, to Alex's shock. And she loved the rose cake Alex concocted after their session together the week before. She simply called it the ballet cake.

After just a month, Show-Stopping Sweets was already a major success. The local restaurants were eager to serve her cakes on their menu. Roland McEntire was so impressed with the desserts that he mentioned them to one of his cohorts at The Food Channel. Alex wasn't keen on being on television, but she appreciated the gesture all the same.

I came up behind her as she was wiping down the counter after the noon rush. The shop closed at 3:00 p.m. unless someone requested a later pick-up for a custom cake.

"You amaze me."

"Aw, thanks, babe. I still can't believe the shop is doing so well. And with the custom orders coming in,

I'm really going to have to consider hiring another baker."

I began untying her apron and slipped my hands under her shirt to feel the warmth of her skin. "It's a good problem to have," I murmured. "Now, come with me. I have something to show you."

I never tired of seeing her smile, and as she spun around, I knew I'd do whatever I could to keep that look on her face. I hoped where I was taking her would do just that. Alex removed her custom apron and hung it on a hook next to Molly and Eloise's matching ones. The mini aprons had been gifts for their birthday along with their own baking utensils. The girls loved coming into the shop and helping.

I hurried Alex to my SUV and allowed her to mess with the dial that adjusted the radio. I was too nervous to listen to whatever was playing.

The sun was shining brightly, and soon the chill of fall would cascade over the town. You could almost smell it in the air.

The bed-and-breakfast came into view, and I took the new gravel drive just past it that had been cut through and laid a week ago.

"Oh, are we going to the property?"

"Yep," I replied as the gravel ended. "Come on. We have to do the rest by foot." We weren't exactly where Alex assumed. We were actually closer to her plot of family land. She'd been so busy she rarely had the time to venture out this way and spoil her surprise.

"Nate, what's going on?" She trailed behind me, the sound of her skirt swooshing between her legs. We were just to the crest of the hill, where she'd figure it all out—I hoped.

"Didn't you choose a spot closer to the B&B—Oh!"

The construction crew laid the foundation for the house earlier in the week, and framing started going up. I didn't throw my money around much, but I enlisted a crew that would work night and day for a pretty penny. It was worth it.

I adjusted the plans I originally chose and added a couple more bedrooms. I hoped one day that my family would grow.

"Nate, is that...?" she asked, turning around to face me.

"That's our house. Me, Molly, Eloise, and... I hope... you."

"What?" she whispered.

"We want you to move in with us more than anything, Alex. I love you. *We* love you. Please say you will."

"I…. Can I design the kitchen?"

"Of course. Anything you—"

She stopped my words as she sealed her lips to mine.

"Is that a yes?"

"Duh."

"Would you have changed your mind if I said no to the kitchen?"

"You'll never know."

Epilogue

Nate

"I need more of those Sasha Delights!" Alex called out from the front counter as I stacked containers. I was in the kitchen, restocking the inventory for the display and the front fridge.

Alex named her champagne-flavored cake with strawberry compote the Sasha Delight as an ode to Molly and Eloise's mother. I knew one day the twins would grow to appreciate the gesture. At six, they were still too young to understand the significance. Even I had a hard time grasping it after the tumultuous relationship I had with my ex. But Alex insisted on having something nice for my daughters to remember their mother.

Almost a year later and Show-Stopping Sweets was doing more business than Alex had ever imagined. She had three full-time bakers and spent most of her time experimenting with new flavors and mixes.

The twins were in the kitchen with me, wearing their matching aprons. At the new house, they had a set as well and baked with Alex every chance they got. And danced. And watched the old 1990s shows. We all did. Those were some of my favorite nights together.

The three of us shared a secret smile. The Sullivans were up to no good.

Out front, I carried the container and pressed my lips to Alex's cheek before heading back toward the kitchen. Andrew corralled the girls into the office, where the rest of the Easterlys were hiding.

Suddenly, over the shop's speakers, a song started playing. It was the same song Alex and I had been tricked into dancing to a year ago. I scoured her playlist until I found it.

"What the—?" Alex asked as she looked around the ceiling. The customers in line looked confused until I walked out wearing one of my suits I knew she secretly loved. I didn't get to wear them often, since I was only a silent partner in my business now, but I broke them out every once in a while. Alex commented she liked the way the ends of my regrown hair brushed against the collar.

"May I have this dance?" I asked, holding out my hand to her in the middle of the dining area. If I were still a teen, I'd probably have a face the color of beets. But I was comfortable enough in my love for Alex to ignore everyone in the room.

She hesitantly removed her apron and rested it on the counter before ducking around the corner to join me. One of the other employees took her spot at the register. Not that it mattered, since everyone was frozen with dreamy cartoon-heart eyes.

Her hand rested gently in mine as I wrapped my other around her waist. It was just pure luck she was wearing that seersucker top and skirt she'd worn our many times to Roland's. It was a tradition now. She didn't know we were headed there after this.

"Now, the last time we danced like this, you led, but I think this time I'll take the lead. If that's okay?"

"By all means."

Effortlessly, I took a step forward, and she followed with her right, and then we glided across the floor. I'm sure it looked a bit stiff, but I felt like Fred Astaire. I'd been practicing enough with online tutorials, so I wasn't a complete klutz.

As the music began to crescendo, I spun Alex out with my arm, but instead of twirling her back in fully, I stopped us with her back against my chest, my lips brushing against her ear.

"Alexandra, you're the only dance partner I want in my life. The only woman I want to remember spending my nights with. The only woman I want to mother my children. We love you. *I* love you."

"Nate?" she whispered as I turned her around. I kneeled down on one knee and held out an open black box with a marquise-cut diamond glistening in the light.

"I want you to be my wife, my partner. I want us to be a family. I want ours to grow. I want everything with you. Please, say you'll marry me."

Her shaking hands slipped away from her mouth as she reached for the sides of my face.

"Nathaniel, there is no one else in the world for me. I would love nothing more than to be your wife and a mother to Molly and Eloise. I love all of you so much."

The crowd around us erupted, and I slipped the ring onto her waiting finger before crashing my mouth onto hers. The Easterly clan dashed out of the office to congratulate us, my best friend being the first to reach us and welcome me to the family, officially.

Molly and Eloise held out the pictures they'd been drawing in the kitchen for Alex. They were of four stick figures with happy smiles on their faces and a flurry of backgrounds in true six-year-old artistry.

"Can we hang these up?"

"Of course, I know right where they'll go."

I watched Alex crouch down and hug each twin as they cried with excitement that she would be their mom.

Andrew and Nash joined me first. Both extended their congratulations with a hearty handshake. I'd spoken to Nash a month ago about asking for his daughter's hand in marriage, choosing a time when Marisol wasn't at the farm. Just in case Nash denied my request. I had nothing to be worried about, though. The man that was more like a father to me than my own readily agreed.

Earlier in the week, Andrew had helped me concoct the plan on how to propose to Alex. It has been his idea to incorporate Alex's love of dancing.

"Can't believe she actually agreed to marry your ugly ass," Andrew said beside me. Our friendship took a while to rebuild after the dramatic way he learned that I had been sleeping with his sister. But Andrew had finally come around after I proved to him I planned to move heaven and earth to be with Alex and make her happy.

"Neither can I," I joked in return.

"Any word from your parents?" Andrew had encouraged me to reach out to them. It had been surprising since he didn't care for them or their treatment of me. Neither of us had to worry, though. My calls and messages to them went unanswered. Just like the news of Sasha's death and my move to Ashfield.

"No." I decided to no longer waste any energy on establishing a relationship with them. My girls could now call the Easterlys family and that meant more to me than anything.

Marisol left the gathering around Alex and joined us with a smile brighter than the sun. She quickly wrapped her arms around me in the loving way I'd never received growing up.

"Welcome to the family, my boy."

"Thanks. We still have to make it to the altar."

"Oh, I have no doubt your engagement will be a short one," she added as she tucked her arm through

Nash's while glancing over at her daughters huddled around Alex, Molly, and Eloise.

"What makes you say that?"

"A mother just knows things."

Alex slowly made her way over to me, while her sisters stood with the twins. One of her arms wrapped around my waist and she tilted her chin up. Without a second thought, I bent down and pressed my lips against my fiancée's.

"Ew. Get a room," Andrew said as he pretended to gag and walk off to join his sisters. Nash and Marisol followed closely behind.

"Any reservations on becoming Mrs. Alexandra Sullivan?"

Her answering grin was all the answer I needed. But she added, "None at all," then rested her head on my chest. I gazed at the group that surrounded my girls.

I had no idea before college that Ashfield was going to be the place where I'd spend summers with my best friend. I couldn't have imagined it would be where I'd meet the love of my life and start the family I always dreamed of having.

I couldn't have imagined that everything I ever needed was right where I wanted to be.

Stay in Touch

Newsletter: http://bit.ly/2WokAjS
Author Page: www.facebook.com/authorreneeharless
Reader Group: http://bit.ly/31AGa3B
Instagram: www.instagram.com/renee_harless
Bookbub: www.bookbub.com/authors/renee-harless
Goodreads: http://bit.ly/2TDagOn
Amazon: http://bit.ly/2WsHhPq
Website: www.reneeharless.com

Acknowledgements

I can't begin to tell you all how much I loved writing this book. Every second was utter bliss. There are so many people to thank for helping me bring Alex and Nate to life.

Patricia Rohrs, for alpha reading this book and holding my hand whenever I questioned where the story was headed and wondering if this book should even see the light of day.

Crystal Burnette, for believing in me and loving this story as much as I did (after convincing me over and over that it did, indeed, *not* suck).

Kayla Robichaux, for your keen eye and working on a ridiculous timeline. Your work was invaluable.

Lisa Hemming, Sally Sutherland, Kelli Harper, for being some of the sweetest and brightest beta team I've ever had.

Carolina Leon, for being the absolute best PA and for all your advice.

And to all the readers that read this book and loved it. Thank you for taking a chance on Alex and Nate.

About the Author

Renee Harless is a *USA TODAY* bestselling romance writer with an affinity for wine and a passion for telling a good story.

Renee Harless, her husband, and children live in Blue Ridge Mountains of Virginia. She studied Communication, specifically Public Relations, at Radford University.

Growing up, Renee always found a way to pursue her creativity. It began by watching endless runs of White Christmas- yes even in the summer – and learning every word and dance from the movie. She could still sing "Sister Sister" if requested. In high school, she joined the show choir and a community theatre group, The Troubadours. After marrying the man of her dreams and moving from her hometown she sought out a different artistic outlet – writing.

To say that Renee is a romance addict would be an understatement. When she isn't chasing her kids around the house, working her day job, or writing, she jumps head first into a romance novel.

Milton Keynes UK
Ingram Content Group UK Ltd.
UKHW010811081123
432193UK00001B/48